Enola Gray Mysteries

Volume 1

A. S. French

Neonoir Books

Enala

Amy

Ginger

Bruce

Kronos

Becky

Parker

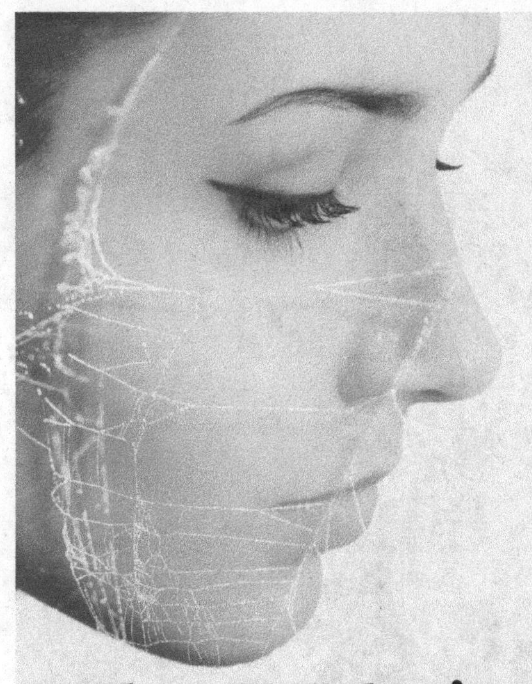

The Spider's Kiss

AN ENOLA GRAY MYSTERY

A. S. FRENCH

Chapter 1

Ten Years Ago

On the night my parents were murdered, the spiders came to me.

I focused on their glistening skin as they protected the nest. I made myself as small as possible in the wardrobe, holding my breath so the intruders wouldn't hear me on the other side. Light shimmered through the gap in the door as I hid from the bad men. My mother's screams echoed inside my head as I gazed at the spiders to blot out the noise.

My heart tried to crawl out of my chest, and my hands shook so much I thought they'd fall apart as the nest burst open. They swarmed out, tiny prickly legs skittering over me and into my clothes. They crawled up my arms, over my neck and onto my face. I wanted to scream, but I couldn't. If I did, the spiders would scamper over my lips and swarm down my throat.

But if I didn't stay quiet, the bad men would know where I was.

With tears running down my cheeks, I peered through the gap in the wardrobe as the eight-legged creatures scuttled over my forehead. They stole into my hair, my eyes meeting my mother's as their tiny legs crept over my skin. I shut my mouth, hoping they wouldn't crawl up my nose.

It was impossible to stop breathing for too long, pushing my face into my mother's clothes and inhaling the sweet jasmine clinging to her dresses in that cramped space. I held out my hands as the spiders scurried into my palms. My fingers trembled as the tiny babies fell into my lap.

That's when the smoke crawled under the door.

Chapter 2

Computer Love

The one-eyed dog spat at my feet. A night spent killing aliens on my computer had left a crick in my neck that throbbed like a bastard. I peered at the offending item nestled on my shoe and sighed at the mangled plastic head of a politician whose name I refused to utter; the bloke kicked out of his bank because his opinions were so vile. Imagine that, a financial institution with principles.

I needed a purpose in life, and this wasn't it.

'What have you been feeding your mutt, Larry?'

Lawrence Hart was the last customer in the Bits & Bytes computer shop, and as the manager, I had the pleasure of dealing with him. The rest of the staff cowered in the corner, terrified of Larry's reputation as an angry little man.

He patted the dog's head. 'He's been sniffing around the homeless people stinking up the park. The council should dump them all on a barge in the ocean.'

Did I mention Larry was also a twat?

I stuck my tongue into the side of my mouth, tasting toothpaste and blood. 'What's the problem this time?'

Larry was a regular customer, with a fresh complaint once a week. My work colleagues said it was because he had a crush on me. The only thing I wanted to crush was his head.

'It takes forever to start,' he replied.

I gripped the screwdriver and imagined shoving it into his eye in search of brain cells. A recent article in *Psychology Monthly* claimed that most violent thoughts were never acted upon, but that didn't apply to me. The same report called them violent intrusive thoughts and said they were widespread. I'd had them for at least ten years, but this was the wrong time to release the tension building inside me.

'I told you before, Larry, you need to delete some of the porn clogging up your hard drive.'

He narrowed his eyes at me. 'Did you go through my files?'

I took a deep breath, picturing my fingers pushing through his eye socket. 'Not me personally, no.'

He grinned at me. 'Do you still have that pet tarantula?'

'Dirty Harry? Yeah.'

'Why do you call him that?'

He'd asked me the same question dozens of times before. 'It's after the Clint Eastwood flick of the same name.'

'Yeah, I know that, but why that film?'

'It's the first movie I remember seeing. My dad had a DVD copy, and I watched it one night when the babysitter fell asleep.'

That was a lie. My father had been dead a year when I saw *Dirty Harry*. During one of my numerous prohibited departures from the children's home, I'd snuck into a late-night showing of a Clint Eastwood double bill at the local flea pit.

He nodded. 'I thought about getting a spider, but the girlfriend said no.'

I assumed she said no to him a lot. 'You still haven't told me what the problem is, Larry.'

His dog farted, and I nearly spewed all over the counter. As I touched my throat, somebody out back turned the music up, and I recognised the first bars of The Stranglers' "Strange Little Girl" coming through the speakers.

Larry grabbed his tiny mutt and held its gurning mug to my face. 'Daisy, you naughty pumpa lumpa.' He smirked at me. 'I got the name from *Willy Wonka*, you know, the umpa lumpas.'

My lips cracked as I smiled. 'How original. Now, about this laptop of yours. Do you want us to fix it or not?'

As he approached, I caught another whiff of the dog's arse. 'A little bird told me a new computer shop is opening on the High Street, near that fancy boutique. That'll be competition for you, won't it?'

I glanced at the clock on the wall, seeing it was five minutes until we closed. All I could think about was getting home, putting my running clothes on, and escaping into the fresh air. It was already dark out; the darker it was, the better I liked it. I needed to run, to pound my feet, until the agony swept through me.

With my trauma on repeat, I turned the music up loud inside my head, rushing through my internal jukebox for the loudest, most screeching guitars. Dozens of tortured singers screamed their lyrics at me until they soothed my aching mind.

I pushed the laptop towards him. 'You're more than welcome to take it there, Larry.'

He scratched at the spot on his chin until it bled. 'No, I like it better here. You have the best customer service, Enola.'

My name on his lips was like a slug between my teeth. 'So what do you want us to do?'

The mutt slathered all over Larry's fingers as he drummed on the counter to the music. 'Make it work faster. Can you do that?'

I grabbed a notepad from my pocket and scribbled the details into it. 'It'll take a few days. Is that okay?'

He nodded. 'Will you add some of those new AI tools to it?'

'Which AI tools?'

'You know, the ones that will write a book in a day for you. I've always fancied writing a novel.'

Yeah, I could see somebody with a limited intellect using something that wasn't really artificial intelligence to produce a novel nobody would likely read. Still, it probably couldn't be worse than some of the recent bestsellers I'd endured. The one where a killer got away with murder and then hired a private detective to investigate the same murder still hurt my head.

'Let me guess, Larry – you're a *Game of Thrones* man?'

He continued scratching his broken spot. 'Absolutely. Who doesn't like a bit of dragons and naked women, eh?'

Most normal people, I didn't say.

'I can't wait to read it.'

He winked at me, his blood dripping onto the counter as he left. I watched him go and pictured a crimson river flowing from his head.

Now, that was a purpose.

Chapter 3

Run For Your Life

A hot wire was in my blood and an unlit cigarette in my trembling fingers. A bitter chill that slithered out of the dark gnawed at my skin. I gazed at the fag, resisting the temptation to thrust it between my weary lips. I crushed the ciggie in my scarred palm, picturing the last time I tasted tobacco four years ago, the night I broke a copper's nose. That was a hell of a way to spend my sixteenth birthday.

With my headphones in place, I prepared for my run, a desperate attempt to escape the suffocating idiocy of the day. I sorted out the playlist while feeding Dirty Harry. I popped the laptop near his enclosure, so he had something to enjoy while I ran a five-mile circuit around the former council estate I called home. For some reason, Harry was fascinated with old British sitcoms, so I left a loop running of *Rising Damp* and *Fawlty Towers*. When I returned, we'd watch *Whatever Happened to the Likely Lads?* together as I fed him pizza.

I stepped out of the flat, and the night embraced me. A faint drizzle settled on my face, giving me new energy. The

Lou Reed album everyone hates had its way with my fragile mind. Some music had this uncanny ability to scramble my thoughts, as if the lyrics and melodies conspired to trigger a switch in my brain, transforming me into a swirling vortex of seething rage. It was a hate tornado unleashed within me, tearing through my soul with reckless abandon.

However, I couldn't blame poor Lou for my anger issues. They started ten years ago when masked thugs ripped away my childhood and murdered my parents. In the aftermath, the government, in their infinite wisdom, poured ample amounts of money into psychiatrists and therapists, hoping to piece together the fragments of my shattered psyche. However, as if that weren't enough, they also subjected me to the whirlwind of foster homes and care facilities, bouncing me around like a lost shoe searching for the right sock.

Yet, amidst the chaos and instability, there was one place where I found comfort, a haven that provided respite from the storm. In my dear friend Seraphina's company, I discovered a treasure trove of music that would forever shape my existence. She introduced me to a world of sound, curating a collection of songs that resonated with my wounded soul. Music was the only thing that allowed me to forget who I was and who I had been.

I sprinted past the disused gasworks as the playlist flicked to the first record I ever bought, Blue Oyster Cult's "Don't Fear the Reaper." I'd saved up all the meagre pocket money the children's home gave its inmates, hoarding it for something more than what the other girls blew their cash on, searching for a connection to the world I'd lost.

I found it at a car boot sale one windy Sunday afternoon. I was drawn to the shiny black vinyl nestled amongst the old books, rusted coins, broken tools, and dirty cutlery. I knew an antique record player was at the children's home because Seraphina had shown it to me.

'What is it?' I asked her.

She smiled at me in reply. 'It's the thing that dreams are made of, Enola.'

The other girls laughed at me when I brought the record back, clutching it to my chest.

'What the fuck do you want that shite for when you have all the fucking songs you need online?' a girl called Angie said. She had a terrible use of language for an eight-year-old.

I remembered the first time I dropped the needle onto the vinyl after Seraphina had set the turntable up and how all the hairs on my arms lifted as the music started.

'Why this song?' she asked me.

'It had to be.' I replied. 'As soon as I saw it on that stall, it was fate.'

The Reaper had visited me earlier than he should have, so I knew the record was calling to me that day. So my life, like an ancient mysterious pyramid, was based around three significant points: music, running, and Dirty Harry.

Plus one other thing: revenge.

Vengeance. It consumed my every thought in my dreams and nightmares, there when I turned the shower to scorching hot, there when I looked in the mirror, there as I picked at the scars on my skin, and there each second I had to deal with idiot customers in the computer shop.

But that was during the day; the night I used to let off steam and run. I changed the playlist into something more cathartic. Death metal released the pent-up rage within me with its thunderous guitars and guttural screams. Then, the Jesus and Mary Chain and My Bloody Valentine added layers of distorted beauty, like ointment for my damaged flesh. It was an unconventional mix but became my sanctuary, pulsating through my blood as I ran.

Blood. The one constant seemed to follow me everywhere, from my parents' bedroom a decade ago to now with the cut on my cheek from where the stapler fell on me at work. How the fuck does an IT manager get attacked by a shitty stapler? Then again, how did I get to be an IT manager? Still, Bits & Bytes wouldn't worry Microsoft or Amazon any time soon. There was no fear of artificial intelligence strolling into the shop to take all our jobs.

As I ran, my fingers brushed against my new scar. The sky transformed into a vast canvas, painted in hues of deep navy, adorned with twinkling stars and a slender crescent moon. As a kid in the care home, I'd imagined living in another world and was foolish enough to tell that to one of the other internees. My dream didn't take long to spread like wildfire, burning through childish brains to create a daily inferno fired in my direction.

'Space girl,' they called me, that or 'Alien,' like the creature from the movie with the same name. That was when I started collecting spiders and dropping them into various shoes, socks, and underwear. I stopped after a few weeks when I realised it was cruel to the spiders.

The first time I combined my love of music and arachnids was when I nicked Bowie's *Ziggy Stardust and the Spiders of Mars* from the local record shop. All the psychiatrists and therapists I'd spoken to over the years could never understand how my duration in the wardrobe - with those hairy legs crawling over me while my parents were murdered a few feet away - hadn't given me arachnophobia. It had done the opposite instead, and the day I got my flat and acquired Dirty Harry was the happiest of my life.

I kept on running, pounding against the pavement and

grass. The neon lights fizzing through the metropolis danced in the mist's embrace, their vibrant hues reflecting off the ground like a shimmering mirage. Each step I took echoed with hushed anticipation, as if the buildings held their breath, waiting for the mysteries of the night to unfold.

And experience had taught me that darkness contained many secrets.

The temperature dipped, kissing me with a newfound chill. I passed the neon-lit pizza shops, their tantalising aromas drifting around me, enticing nocturnal wanderers with promises of cheesy delight. The shadows grew deeper as I ran, casting an eerie mask over the landscape. I avoided the crack house, a notorious den of despair and desperation, a place the police conveniently overlooked, where the misplaced and broken sought refuge from a world that had long forgotten them. With Seraphina's help, I'd escaped my addictions four years ago. Well, most of them.

Abandoned homes and factories loomed ahead. I sensed the figures lurking in the shadows. Some moved like zombies, lost souls caught in the clutches of addiction and hopelessness, and their spirits diminished to mere echoes of their former selves. Others observed with predatory eyes, their gaze sharp and calculating, hunting for their next fix or victim. They scrutinised me and knew better.

The wind rushed past my ears, whipping my hair behind me. The sweat beaded on my forehead, the clothes sticking to my skin. I pushed myself harder, my legs matching the beat of the music, Nine Inch Nails telling me my head was like a hole.

My muscles burned, but I pressed through it. The pain was nothing compared to the rush the exercise gave me. As I reached the end of my route, I stopped, panting heavily. I closed my eyes and let out a deep sigh, with the adrenaline coursing through my veins. I'd be sore tomorrow, but for now, I was invincible.

Yet, I was also unsatisfied.

It was as if time had frozen and consumed most of my life. The sense of forever was overwhelming, unproductive, vast, shallow, and filled with obstacles.

Then, the shapes stepped out of the shadows.

'Fucking hell, Mick, look at this; it's the midnight skank Olympics.'

There were three of them, the dimness behind their eyes matching the gloom surrounding me. One of them, a tall, muscular man with a shaved skull, pulled out a switchblade and began flicking it open and closed, the glint of the blade catching the moonlight. Another heavy, a skinny goon with a bandana tied around his head, chuckled.

'Looks like we've got the place to ourselves, boys. Time for some fun.'

The third one, a burly thug with a thick beard, pulled up a baseball bat and swung it menacingly. 'Yeah, let's get down with the skank Olympics.'

The smell of damp concrete and stale urine hit me, mixed with a strong scent of marijuana. It brought back vivid memories of my teenage years, wild, dangerous times that had taught me a lot about life. But they were behind me now.

Then I punched the baseball thug in the face. My hand ached as his nose exploded in an eruption of blood and snot as he wailed like a strangled cow. I kicked the skinny bloke in the balls, and he crumpled like paper. The goon with the knife stood there, open-mouthed and wide-eyed. Then he lunged with the blade, aiming for my throat. I stepped aside and jabbed my fingers into his side. He threw up over the other two and collapsed on top of them. They wriggled on the floor, worms desperate to be hooked and dangled in the river. I stared at them and considered what to do. I hadn't gone looking for violence, yet here it was. It had found me once again, that shadow of the Reaper.

'Something terrible happened to me ten years ago,' I said. I retrieved the discarded baseball bat. 'And ever since, I've had to take my frustration out on others, so I'm glad you morons volunteered tonight.'

It wasn't the same as jogging, but it was exercise.

I wiped my fingerprints away when I finished.

Dirty Harry was missing me, or I might have stayed longer.

Plus, I had to be up early.

And I hated wearing black.

Chapter 4

Let It Be

'She picked a bloody scorching day for it,' my neighbour Ginger drawled. Shielding her eyes from the searing morning sun, she extended a cigarette towards me, a thin wisp of smoke trailing lazily from its tip.

I shook my head. The memories of my past dalliances with booze, drugs, and cigarettes flooded my mind, a cacophony of reckless nights and hazy mornings. The taste of poison had lingered on my lips for two years, seeping into my senses and staining what remained of my heart.

But it was behind me now.

The sun beat down, intensifying the sweltering heat. The air was a stifling blanket that clung to me, suffocating and relentless in that hated black dress. Beads of sweat formed on my brow, trickling down my temple in a slow, deliberate descent. The acrid scent of smoke intertwined with the intense flavour of summer, creating a paradoxical cocktail of temptation and repulsion.

Ginger's hands spared her eyes from the blinding glare, her fingers casting elongated shadows against her face. A hint of wistfulness danced in her gaze, mingling with the weariness of her features. I saw the echoes of a thousand stories stamped in the lines and crevices that mapped her skin. Her weekly visits to her mother in the care home were taking their toll.

I took a deep breath. 'You know Seraphina died from lung cancer, right?'

Ginger's slender hand grazed through her cascading locks of Pre-Raphaelite flame-red hair, the vibrant strands catching the sunlight and setting the world ablaze. She scrunched up her face so it looked older than her thirty years.

'She'd want me to enjoy myself, Enola, especially today.'

I had Seraphina to thank for putting me on the straight and narrow. Sometimes, the path could turn crooked, like with those thugs, but things were much better in my life for knowing her. Her influence had not only transformed my existence, but had touched the lives of countless people.

'Sixty-three is no age to die.' Ginger's flatmate Bruce joined us. He bore an uncanny resemblance to Lurch from the Addams Family and had a face that looked lived in by a bunch of squatters. He gazed at me. 'You're wearing a dress. I've never seen you wear a dress before.'

I pulled at the fabric as it clung to my hips. 'I own nothing black.' Too many unsettling encounters with goths and emos in my teenage years had left me with an aversion to black outfits. Dark blue was about as close as I got. 'So I had to rent this monstrosity.'

Bruce dragged on a vape and blew strawberry smoke at me. 'Rent?'

I cringed at the sweet aroma invading my senses. 'There's a shop in town where you can hire clothes or costumes. When I was there, a drunken Spider-Man wrestled in the street with a Roman centurion.' I tugged on the dress again, the material sticking to my frame like a second skin.

'It suits you,' Ginger said.

I was preparing an appropriate insult when our ride arrived. The Bits & Bytes car had a cartoonish plastic computer with a comedy face, arms, and legs wobbling on top of it. The shop owner stepped out of it with holes in his jeans and a t-shirt proclaiming, "All Tories Are C#nts."

'You're not taking us in that,' Ginger said.

Bruce frowned. 'He can't go dressed like that.'

I didn't reveal that our driver, Sid Storm, had borrowed the offending clobber from me. It still had the tomato sauce stain on the front from my last cooking disaster. Sid held out his arms and grinned.

'Come on; you know Seraphina would have loved this.' He scrutinised me as if I'd stepped out of a spaceship. 'Did somebody replace Enola with a pod person?'

I pushed him to the side and got into the passenger seat. The others finished their terrible smoking habits and followed me into the car. At my feet were a toy dinosaur and a plastic Hulk who'd seen too much sun as his green skin had turned pink. I stood on Hulk's head, and he squeezed out a few words.

'Don't make me angry.'

'Good advice,' I said.

Sid started the engine. 'Sorry for the mess. It was my weekend with the kids.'

I kicked Hulk away from my uncomfortable shoes. 'It's Saturday.'

He drove off. 'I know, I know. I didn't think they'd appreciate attending a funeral, so I left them with Bill for the morning.' Bill was Sid's new husband.

'There's a blow-up Donald Trump doll back here,' Bruce said.

Sid laughed. 'Don't you be interfering with it. I have to deliver that to a hen night later.'

As he drove to the cemetery, laughter surrounded us. Happy recollections of our friend flowed, their echoes dancing within the confines of the car. Seraphina had entered our lives for the better, but amidst the light-hearted banter, my mind wandered, tethered to memories of that fateful day when I first met her in the home.

It was the fourth anniversary of me becoming an orphan. The revolving door of children's homes had become my reality, each a temporary refuge. Prospective foster parents had come and gone, their fleeting presence a glimmer of possibility soon extinguished. It seemed my soul bore an invisible mark, a stain that repelled the well-intentioned and shattered my illusions of a perfect match.

Perhaps my unfiltered tongue deterred them, the stream of obscenities that flowed from my lips like a torrential downpour. Or maybe it was the relentless gnashing of my teeth, a manifestation of the pent-up anger and frustration that coursed through my veins. Whatever the reasons behind those rejections, I reached a point where I no longer cared. Resignation had settled upon my shoulders, a cloak of indifference that shielded me from further disappointment.

Then, like a flicker of light in the encroaching darkness, Seraphina appeared. I remembered the precise moment our paths crossed, as if the universe conspired to weave our destinies together. I was watching a documentary about UFOs in the TV room when she approached me.

'That's an interesting shirt you're wearing.' It was a Sex

Pistols "Anarchy in the UK" t-shirt I'd nicked from a local shop. 'I used to hang around with them as a teenager.'

I scrunched up my eyes and peered at her. 'You don't look old enough.'

She sat near me. 'That's because I spend my nights drinking the blood of virgins.' She offered me her hand. 'I'm Seraphina.'

I refused the offer. 'Is this a trick to see if I'm having sex?'

She shook her head. 'I'm only being friendly.'

I'd constructed invisible barriers around me long before, which were still strong. 'How old were you when you met the Pistols?'

'Sixteen. I walked into a boutique on King's Road in the summer of 1976, and they were trying on clothes. A few older girls worked in the shop, and they took me under their wing. Soon after that, I was wearing racoon makeup and PVC skirts.'

She had warm eyes and a broad smile to melt my usual untrusting manner.

'What did your parents think?'

Seraphina glanced at the kids, who switched the TV to a music channel.

'My mother died when I was little, and my father was too busy working to notice what I did.' She showed me her phone. 'How many of these have you listened to?'

I took it from her and scrolled down the albums. 'Shit! There must be thousands.'

'I can copy them all onto your mobile if you want.'

'What are you after?' I said.

She got up and shrugged. 'Let me know if you change your mind.'

Three days later, I had a thousand punk and new wave tunes for the latest playlist on my phone.

I'd changed my phone since, but I still had all those songs.

'We're here,' Sid announced, the engine purring to a halt outside the cemetery gates. I opened the door and stepped onto the gravel, the surface pressing against the soles of my shoes. He followed, and we led the others through the wrought-iron entrance, the gate creaking in protest, as it swung open.

A hush fell over us as we entered. The scent of damp earth mingled with the faint aroma of decaying leaves, carried on a gentle breeze that whispered through the towering trees. I stared across the graveyard at the endless rows of headstones stretching before me. Each marker held a story, a life frozen in time, immortalised in stone. The sky was an ashen canvas, its palette devoid of warmth as if the sun had retreated behind a shroud of melancholy. Soft tendrils of mist descended, veiling the scene in an ethereal haze.

As I strode between the graves, sorrow and longing embraced me, wrapping around my heart. As I pressed forward, the gravestones became more than mere markers of the departed. Instead, they were a chorus of whispers, a mosaic of lives lived and lost. Each name etched into the stone bore witness to the echoes of love, laughter, and tears that once resonated through those who rested beneath our feet.

I thought of my parents, resting together near where I walked. Did they rest? I hoped so, though I knew such a thing was beyond me. I hadn't visited their graves since the joint funerals, unable to face the reality of their deaths. Something always lingered in the back of my head that they would turn up one day, telling me it had all been faked for some mysterious, terrible reason.

As we approached the gravesite, a small group had already gathered. As a general rule of thumb, the younger you die, the better the turnout for a funeral. For me, the dream was to shuffle off this mortal coil when I reached a century, with no one at the crematorium apart from a couple of stragglers who had turned up for the wrong person.

The mourners huddled together, their faces engraved with sadness. I recognised some of them as Seraphina's friends and family, a distant cousin and the niece she never got along with. Some cast disapproving glances at Sid, but nobody said anything as we followed them into the small chapel. We sat at the back, and I dug my fingers into my palms. Then, as the priest started the service, I gazed at my hands, peering deep into the scars from the fire a decade ago. My parents were already dead when I tried to drag them out of our burning home, but there was only one thing on my mind then. Eventually, somebody hauled me outside before the blaze could damage any more of me.

I stared at the casket. Flowers surrounded it, including those I'd commissioned in the shape of a raven to represent Seraphina's favourite album from her favourite band.

Then the impossible happened, and a tear rolled down my cheek. It was the first time I'd cried since my parents' joint funeral. I wiped it away as the music burst out of the chapel speakers, and Johnny Rotten sang about us all being so pretty and vacant. Everybody shuffled out when it finished, but I hung around to control my emotions. Then, I followed them to the grave. I stood behind the others as they lowered the coffin to the ground, not noticing the woman as she sidled up to me.

'Seraphina talked about you a lot,' she whispered. 'She said you reminded her of her youth.'

I turned to her. 'Are you a relation?'

She shook her head. 'An old friend from our wild days.' She removed something from her bag and offered it to me.

'Who are you?'

She didn't answer. Instead, she reached out and handed me an envelope. 'It's for you.'

I took it and examined the paper. It was plain and white, with no writing on it. I opened it and pulled out a single sheet, a letter written in neat handwriting. Handwriting I recognised: Seraphina's.

There was never the right time to tell you this, Enola, but if you're reading this, I assume something has happened to me. I'm sorry, but there's been a secret I've kept from you all these years. I knew your parents, and I know why they were murdered.

The words swirled before me like letters in a hurricane, and I dropped the paper.

Then, my legs gave way.

Chapter 5

Happy Hour

Her grip tightened around my arm, but I didn't resist, peering at the crumpled letter nestled in the mud, its ink smudged and barely legible. I clenched my teeth, finding toothpaste in the corner of my mouth.

'Who are you?' I demanded.

For a moment, the woman hesitated, her emotions flickering across her face like shadows dancing in the twilight. 'I'm Gemma Mead. I knew your parents, as Seraphina did.'

My heart pounded against my ribs, its rhythm matching the intensity of my thoughts. A surge of conflicting feelings rushed through me, a shattering mix of hope and apprehension.

'That can't be true,' I uttered. Seraphina, my friend for six years, would have told me.

Wouldn't she?

Gemma blinked, her eyelashes flickering like lights on a slot machine. Then, with a swift tug, she guided me beyond the prying eyes of the others towards the bushes near the church.

She released me when we reached the shadows. 'I advised her to stay away from you. I warned her she was jeopardising your life, but she wouldn't listen. So, I distanced myself from her.'

Confusion gnawed at my thoughts as I tried to understand her revelation. The rain grew heavier, each droplet crashing against my skin like icy claws tearing secret layers from me.

'You're not making any sense,' I muttered.

She looked cautiously around us, guarding our conversation from unseen ears. Then the words tumbled out of her. 'Your parents were placed in a witness protection program. Seraphina and I were officers in that operation. She carried the weight of responsibility for what happened to you. She longed to help you after your tragedy, but circumstances and time conspired against her.'

I locked eyes with her, desperate to see the lies in her expression. The tremors in my legs intensified, and I found support in the rough embrace of a nearby tree, its bark digging into my palm, grounding me during a sudden downpour. The raindrops bounced off my skull, adding to the pain throbbing through my brain.

'Why didn't she tell me?' I choked out, my voice strained with anguish and betrayal.

Gemma's eyes glistened as she replied. 'She was waiting for the right time.' She cast a wary glance over her shoulder, a sense of urgency engraved on her features. 'And then this happened. Somebody got to her.'

As the ceremony finished, my focus shifted towards my approaching friends, their solemn expressions mirroring my sorrow. The air hung heavy with freshly turned earth, mingling with the faint fragrance of funeral flowers, their vibrant hues muted by the sombre atmosphere.

'Seraphina died of cancer,' I murmured.

Gemma's tone wavered as she spoke, her words seeping into the rain. 'She was in remission,' she said, her voice barely above a whisper, drowned out by the patter of raindrops upon the umbrellas that dotted the cemetery. 'They made it look like cancer.'

Water trickled down my face, merging with the tears that settled on my lips. I blinked against the deluge, struggling to comprehend her words. 'They?' I croaked, my voice laced with disbelief and a newfound surge of anger.

'The same people who took your parents from you, Enola.' The revelation reverberated in the space between us, punctuated by the rhythmic drumming of rain.

At that moment, Ginger hurried over, her presence a temporary respite from the weight of the revelations that engulfed me. Her voice cut through the atmosphere, eager and oblivious to the storm brewing inside me.

'Are we going to the pub?'

The Pig and the Poke ranked as only the second-worst drinking establishment I'd ever visited. The dubious distinction of first place belonged to a dive bar nestled within a secluded Prague side street, where toothless patrons roamed, and the stench hung heavy, reminiscent of an unwashed abattoir.

I glanced across the room, taking in the ramshackle state of the boozer. The wallpaper clung to the walls in tattered fragments, its faded patterns a reminder of the 1970s. The carpet bore the battle scars of spilt beer, a sticky testament to countless brawls, stinking of sweat and desperation.

The punters formed a peculiar assembly of characters. They looked straight out of a Bukowski novel, a mix of wannabee writers, part-time gangsters, and jaded media hacks nursing their own secrets. Half of them were familiar faces, old acquaintances I'd crossed paths with before, while the rest bore weary expressions and jaded eyes.

Sid delivered our drinks. Gemma, however, distanced herself from us, looking guarded and wary. Likewise, Ginger and Bruce exchanged cautious glances, their unspoken questions hanging in the air. I'd shared the contents of the letter during our drive to the pub, and from their expressions, it seemed none dared to voice the obvious question lingering in their minds.

So I did.

'Why were my parents in a witness protection program?'

Sid laughed. 'The clue's in the title, Enola.'

I resisted the urge to stick my fingers in his eyes and placed the letter on the table.

'You and Seraphina were officers working for the program, Gemma?'

She nodded. 'That's where we met.' She glanced around the pub as she spoke. 'We became more than colleagues, but it was frowned upon in the force. So she left, and I stayed. That put a huge strain on our relationship, and we broke up.' She smiled at me. 'But we kept in touch, so I knew she got a job in social services. Seraphina did it because she believed it would help her find you. And it worked.'

Sid wiped the beer from his chin. 'Seraphina was a copper. That's hard to believe. She hated the police.'

Ginger laughed. 'That was the band she disliked. She always thought Sting was a twat.'

Bruce shook his head. 'She claimed most people were twats, including me.'

'You are a twat,' Ginger and Sid said in stereo.

They seemed to be having a good time, but I wasn't. 'Do you know why my parents were in the witness protection program, Gemma?'

She sipped at her glass of water. 'We helped all kinds of folks, from victims of domestic violence to those who witnessed gang-related crimes, but our superiors never told us why individuals were in the program. There had been incidents where officers had revealed people's whereabouts to those looking to do them harm.'

'What did you do for those people?' Ginger said.

Gemma sank into her chair. 'We gave them fresh identities and helped them settle into new communities. We also supported them with several things, like therapy or job training, to help them rebuild their lives.'

I dug my nails into my palms. 'So, my parents weren't Amelia and Tony Gray?'

She shook her head. 'No. I knew nothing about them, only that they had you after entering the program. Seraphina discovered more, but wouldn't tell me what it was.'

'Wow!' Sid said. 'Just when you thought your life couldn't get any weirder, eh, Enola?'

I grabbed the letter and stuffed it in my pocket before finishing my drink. Then I stared at Gemma. 'Come on. You're taking me to Seraphina's flat.'

She got up without protesting. 'I don't have a key.'

'That won't be a problem.'

Sid reached for his jacket. 'I'll drive you there.'

I didn't argue, telling Ginger and Bruce not to wait for me. Then I followed Gemma outside, with one thought crushing my brain.

Who were my parents?

Chapter 6

Heart and Soul

Seraphina's flat lay within one of the less prosperous corners of town, where security measures were non-existent, and the building's entrance was a revolving door for stray dogs and the walking dread. The shabby surroundings were an excuse for her to avoid inviting me over, always meeting somewhere else or at my place.

'It's too grungy for somebody with your high standards, Enola,' she'd joke.

Leaving Sid in the car, Gemma and I strode the creaking stairs of the rundown apartment building, our footsteps echoing in the empty hallway. Everywhere smelt of hairspray and cheap deodorant, an attempt to mask the underlying odour of decay and neglect. I reached into my pocket, retrieved a hair clip, and picked the lock in less time than it took to get pregnant.

We entered the cramped confines of the flat. Dampness clung to every surface, and a terrible aroma originated from the kitchen. The room seemed to shrink under the weight of the poky space, the furniture dog-eared and bearing the scars of entropy. A washed-out tapestry adorned one wall, its colours muted, reflecting a past that had faded away. The worn carpet appeared to exhale as we stepped across it.

The sense of Seraphina's absence loomed larger than ever. Her spirit was woven into the fabric of the flat as I peered at her record collection and the hundreds of books stacked on overflowing shelves. I closed my eyes, surrounded by the echoes of her existence, and a mix of emotions washed over me, a blend of sorrow, determination, and a glimmer of hope I'd find answers to all my questions.

Gemma's voice forced me to look at her. 'Why are we here?'

I stowed the hair clip back in my pocket. 'Are you certain Seraphina didn't die of cancer?'

Gemma nodded. 'Positive. Just a fortnight ago, she assured me the doctors had granted her a clean bill of health. And have you noticed how swiftly they arranged her funeral? Almost as if they were eager to sweep it under the rug.'

She was right about the funeral. After all, it had been a mere three days since Seraphina's passing, and the absence of an official death certificate only added to the growing list of uncertainties. 'Search for anything unusual.'

Seraphina murdered. A speeding train spat steam into my veins as I wondered what might have happened to her.

I entered the bedroom, drawn to the movie posters garnishing the walls, an iconic *Blade Runner* and the haunting image of the original *Nosferatu*. The room carried an air of nostalgia, a testament to Seraphina's eclectic tastes. I turned to the dresser drawers. As I rummaged through them, the weight of the past bore down on me, flooding my thoughts with memories of her unwavering support during my time in the children's home. She'd been a guiding light, imparting knowledge and wisdom. Yet, amidst her guidance, she'd concealed the truth, her connection to my parents and the tragedy that had unfolded before my eyes, leaving scars that still haunted me.

A screaming tornado thundered through my chest, and I sank against the edge of the bed, noticing a copy of *Jude the Obscure* pressed against the carpet. My trembling fingers reached out, turning the book over to reveal an inscription, a gift from Seraphina on my fifteenth birthday.

'It's this or Harry Potter,' she'd teasingly remarked.

'What's it about?' I'd asked.

Her response marked the beginning of a transformative journey for me. 'The novel delves into the struggles of a young man as he endeavours to rise above societal constraints and carve his path in a world resistant to change.'

Seraphina was serious and playful as I snatched the book from her, retreating to my room to read and listen to my playlist. She hadn't been wrong with the description.

I'd forgotten she'd borrowed it from me last month.

Her smiling face was imprinted on my brain as I caressed the pages, feeling the texture beneath my fingertips. It was as if each word and crease held fragments of Seraphina's presence, sparking vivid memories within me. Her stories of rebellious youth flooded my mind, tales of her encounters with punk bands in 1970s London.

Her anecdotes touched a nerve with me, threading a bond between us that transcended the generational gap. She understood the attraction of rebellion, the allure that had captivated me during those wild years. And in her own way, she sought to safeguard me from the dangers she'd witnessed first-hand, a delicate balance of support and freedom.

'What was it like?' I asked her.

'It was a different time,' Seraphina replied, a hint of nostalgia in her voice. 'The world was changing, and we were right in the middle. We were part of a movement shaking things up, which was exciting.'

I was fifteen, and I didn't want to shake things up. I wanted to tear it all down, to destroy and revel in the destruction.

And I still did.

'I needed to belong to something greater than myself,' Seraphina had said.

She possessed a captivating beauty that transcended mere physicality. Her radiance emanated from within, a beacon of compassion that had illuminated my darkest days. She'd been the first to see beyond my troubled past, treating me as an equal rather than a broken child to be pitied or commanded. I discovered a sense of worth and belonging in her presence, an oasis of solace amidst the desolation.

Now all of that was tainted.

As I stood in her flat, doubt and turmoil churned within me. Gemma's words floated from the other room, eating away at my memories. I couldn't deny the scepticism tugging at my heart. Unresolved questions swirled in my mind, twisting with conflicting emotions. Anguish, rage, and a profound sense of loss threatened to overwhelm me. Seraphina had been my anchor, my guardian, amidst the chaos of existence. The mere notion of her life being cut short, like my parents' murder, sent shivers through me. What would be left of me if another pillar of stability crumbled to ashes?

I didn't know what I'd do if it were true.

That was a lie. I knew exactly what I'd do when I found the people responsible.

I clung to the book and put my other hand on the

carpet, finding a lump underneath it. Gemma walked in as I stood.

'There's nothing through there apart from out-of-date food and milk.'

'Milk?' I said. 'Seraphina was allergic to milk.'

She nodded. 'I know.'

I kicked at the lump and heard a crack. I dropped the novel onto the bed and knelt, lifting the fabric and pulling it back. The wood had come away from the floorboards, and I dug my fingers into the hole.

'There's something in here.'

I pulled at the wood, and it broke with a snap. I threw the bits to the side and reached inside to pull out a small notebook. A dark spider clung to the cover, peering at me through yellow eyes. I offered it my palm, and it skittered over my scars. Gemma grimaced. I gently placed the spider in the hole in the floorboards. Then I opened the notebook. I scanned the pages filled with names, addresses, and phone numbers before handing it to her.

'Do you recognise any of these because I don't?'

She shook her head. 'No, sorry.'

She returned it to me. 'I suppose I'll have to go through each one.'

'We can do it together,' Gemma replied.

I studied her for the first time since her unexpected appearance at the funeral: a pocket-sized woman in her late forties, her expression projecting an air of weariness and longing. It was as if an invisible sign was on her forehead that said she wanted nothing more than to be at home watching *The Crown*.

The gentle curve of her lips held a trace of melancholy, while her weary eyes contained a glimmer of untold stories. I observed the slight slump of her shoulders and gazed at the lines imprinted upon her face. The faint scent of lavender clung to her, reminding me of the flowers at the cemetery.

I tucked the notebook into my pocket. 'Wasn't there a noticeable age disparity between you and Seraphina?'

She shrugged. 'It bothered others more than it did us,' she confided, her voice shaded with a hint of reminiscence. 'Especially my husband.'

I nodded, an understanding smile dancing upon my lips. 'Ah, let me guess – another copper?'

'In the same unit as us,' she revealed.

I grabbed the Thomas Hardy book from the bed. 'That must have made things interesting.'

A wry grin tugged at the corners of her mouth. 'That's one way of putting it.'

Inspiration ignited within me, a flicker of an idea dancing to life. 'Is he still a police officer?'

'Yes, a chief constable.'

I whistled. 'You certainly know how to pick them.'

She glanced across the room. 'So, what do we do next?'

I stared at the vampire poster on the wall. 'Are we to be partners now?'

A gentle smile graced Gemma's lips. 'That's up to you, Enola.'

I placed *Jude the Obscure* alongside the notebook, their juxtaposition symbolising the intersection of past and present. 'Did you divorce your husband?'

A flicker of darkness shadowed her features, a brief glimpse into the depths of her unspoken turmoil. 'No.'

My eyes met hers. 'What's his name, the chief constable?'

'Robert. Robert Mead.'

I nodded. 'Great. Let's you and I pay him a visit.'

I loved having a purpose.

Chapter 7

Back to the Old House

Sid kept the chatter to a minimum during the journey towards the fancy country house of the chief constable. His voice mingled with Gemma's, but the words drifted past me, lost amidst the chaos in my mind, a thousand tiny assassins kicking the insides of my head to death.

I rolled down the car window, hoping the scent of the countryside would kick-start my tired brain. Instead, an unexpected onslaught of memories flooded in and carried on the breeze. I gazed upon the towering trees, their branches reaching towards the sky, as a whirlwind of emotions consumed me. The idea somebody had murdered my parents because of their involvement in a witness protection program festered inside me, each implication like a thunderclap in my mind. The weight of this knowledge and the realisation that my closest friend had concealed this truth from me for six years gnawed at my sanity.

'We're here,' Sid announced as he pulled into the driveway of a very expensive house.

'I hope the chief constable pays you alimony,' I said.

Gemma didn't reply as she got out of the car.

'I'll wait for you,' Sid said as I followed Gemma.

'Why are we here?' she asked me.

'To get some answers.' I didn't knock, pulling down the handle and pushing on the door. It opened without any trouble. I stepped inside as she protested.

'You can't just burst in, Enola.'

I took a moment to absorb my surroundings, immersing myself in the grandeur of framed paintings and fancy ornaments. Pine-scented air filled the room, and the floor shone with ambient light. A magnificent chandelier hung in the centre of the ceiling, its countless crystal facets catching the sunlight and scattering colourful patterns everywhere.

'Did you live here?' I said.

Gemma pulled at the top of her shirt as if we were in a sauna. 'For five years before I left.'

She guided me into a sprawling living room. Crafted from dark, polished wood, the furniture exuded an air of timeless elegance, inviting me to sink into its embrace. Bookshelves, brimming with expensive-looking hardbacks and glittering trinkets, decorated the walls while a majestic grand piano stood in one corner.

A large window with flowing curtains offered a glimpse into the world beyond. The garden, a tapestry of vibrant colours and lush foliage, beckoned with a silent invitation. Sunlight filtered through the glass, casting warm hues upon the room and caressing my face. Everywhere was sunny, apart from inside my heart.

'Does he come from a rich family?'

Gemma nodded. 'They've owned land around here for centuries.' She ran her fingers over the piano keys. 'John must be in his study. Follow me.'

'For a chief constable, he's not very good with security,' I said.

The study had more books, an unlit fireplace, and a large desk with a man sitting behind it. He looked up from his paperwork, a surprised expression on his face. He didn't acknowledge me.

'Gemma, what are you doing here?'

I answered for her. 'We need to talk about Seraphina.'

He twisted his head towards me, giving me a look I felt in my throat. 'Who are you?'

I moved closer to him. 'I remember you now. You were there when the social workers and your detectives investigated me.'

'I have no idea what you are referring to, young lady.'

He fidgeted in his chair, glancing between his estranged wife and me.

'Seraphina was my friend. Somebody murdered her and then covered it up, chief constable. Gemma admitted it to me.'

His expression hardened. 'I don't know what you're talking about.'

Gemma stepped forward, her cheeks flushed like red balloons. 'Please don't lie to us, John. I know you're part of this. Seraphina told me years ago you were corrupt, and I wouldn't believe her.' She glanced at me. 'Things would have turned out differently if I had.'

'Really, Gemma, I knew you were unhinged, but this is ridiculous. What am I supposed to be part of?'

'Seraphina said she had evidence of the organised crime gang who paid you, John.'

He shook his head and laughed. 'Does this young woman know where you've been for the last five years, Gemma?'

Her lips trembled. 'That's got nothing to do with this. I have the emails from ten years ago, proving how you revealed the new identities and the address of Enola's parents. It's all over for you now. You might as well tell us who you're working for because it's not the police.'

The chief constable looked at me. 'You're the kid in the wardrobe, Enola?' He didn't wait for an answer. 'They wanted to kill you once they discovered you'd seen everything and survived the fire. However, of course, I convinced them you wouldn't be any trouble. You were only a mewling brat, after all.' He smiled at me. 'There's no need to thank me.'

'You're responsible for my parents' deaths?'

'Well, I didn't slit their throats or start that blaze, but I guess you could say I bear some responsibility since the killers were only there because I gave them the address.' He stared at my hands. 'It must have hurt trying to drag their dead bodies from the house while that inferno raged around you.'

I took a deep breath. 'You need to tell me who did it.'

He laughed at me. 'I don't need to do anything for you, child.' Then he reached into his desk and removed a gun. He pointed it at Gemma. 'You never were too bright, were you, love? Fancy coming here and admitting you have evidence against me. How did you get to be a copper in the first place?' Then he aimed the weapon at me. 'I should have let them kill you ten years ago. Now I'll have to wash the blood stains from the expensive carpet.'

'You don't have to do this, John.'

He sighed. 'But I do, Gemma. The lines between good and evil have blurred in this terrible modern world. Corrupt law enforcement agents are exploiting their power for personal gain. Meanwhile, criminals have infiltrated the government, using their influence to control the masses. The leaders who should work to improve society focus on their interests and authority. The economy is in shambles, with those in power hoarding resources and opportunities for themselves. The environment is collapsing around us, and we ignore the warnings. The ordinary people are left to struggle, with no one to trust and no hope for a better future. Even the most basic necessities, like toilet paper, are in short supply due to rampant inflation and the behaviour of idiots. It's a dark and dishonest culture where the strong prey on the weak, and the truth is constantly manipulated to suit the needs of those in power. So what can I do but go along with it?'

I was about to call him a fucking twat when he pulled the trigger.

Chapter 8

Kiss With a Fist

Gemma flung herself before me. The roar of the gunshot shattered the stillness, rumbling in my ears like a nuclear explosion. Time seemed to slow as I lunged forward, grasping Gemma's trembling form as she crumpled against my chest. We staggered sideways, crashing into a bookshelf.

The sound of splintering wood was a thunderclap, blending with the intense smell of old books and the taste of blood in the air. Sharp, jagged pieces of broken literature rained on me, creating a wild symphony of paper and ink. The shelf dug into my shoulder, sending searing pain through my arm. With a jarring thud, we collided with the floor, my arms clinging to Gemma's quivering frame. An onslaught of paperbacks bombarded us, their frenzied descent amplifying the chaos. A tattered copy of *Fight Club* whizzed past my eye.

'I'm sorry,' Gemma gasped.

Blood oozed from her chest, staining my clothes in a macabre tapestry of scarlet. The metallic aroma of burning copper flooded the air, mingling with the scent of fear and desperation in the room. A kaleidoscope of discarded novels lay haphazardly around us, their pages fluttering like wounded birds in the aftermath of the violence.

I eased Gemma's limp body away from mine, the weight of her diminishing strength palpable against me. I propped her against the wall, staring at the wound between her ribs.

'You'll be okay,' I said, knowing she wouldn't be.

'I should have done that years ago,' the chief inspector said behind me. 'Especially after she left me for that cow.'

I gripped the dying woman's hand. 'How many have you killed?'

John Mead lifted the weapon to his face. 'Who keeps count of these things?' He stepped away from the desk. 'It wasn't me who murdered your parents, though I know who did, and you'd be surprised by the number of crooked medical staff in the nation's hospitals. As for your friend, all it took was a little syringe of something deadly and a willing coroner to fake a death certificate.' He rubbed the pistol against his chin. 'There's nothing people won't do for money. Even if they're already rich beyond most people's understanding of the term, they still want more. And they'll kill for it.' He touched the side of his head with the gun. 'Humanity is evil; it really is.'

Adrenaline thrust me forward like a wild animal into the corridor. The ominous click of the trigger echoed through the air, a symphony of impending doom that spurred me to greater speed. His angry shouts reverberated behind me and bounced off the walls, joining the sound of drums thumping in my head. I struggled to move in that fucking dress, stumbling through the dimly lit place as I staggered into a room full of furniture and junk.

My chest heaved in harmony with the frantic rhythm of my pounding heart, each breath a jagged gasp that mirrored the anxiety coursing through my veins. I scoured my surroundings, seeking an escape from the house and the lunatic chasing me. That's when I spotted a window and made a beeline for it.

However, fate had other plans for me as Mead reached the room and fired again. A bullet pierced the wooden table, sending shards of shattered fragments into a chaotic frenzy and catching my arm.

I spun around to see him aiming the gun at me, grinning like the Mad Hatter.

'You think you can just run away from this?' he mocked. 'I won't let you ruin everything I've worked so hard to build.'

I glanced to the side, searching for a weapon and grabbing an ornamental dagger from the wall. The handle chilled my skin as I waved it at him. The blade caught the ambient light, casting a glimmering glow over his ghoulish grin. In that moment, the world distilled to a singular focus, a clash between my will to survive and his desire to murder me.

'Now, what are you going to do with that, Enola? Didn't your parents tell you not to play with sharp things?'

I bit my tongue and tasted blood. 'You did all this for money, killed for personal gain.'

He narrowed his eyes at me. 'Isn't that why most people kill?'

I gripped the blade. 'No, some do it for revenge.'

I threw myself at him as the volcano exploded in my veins.

He fired again.

The searing heat of the bullet kissed my cheek as it missed me and burst into the wall. The room shook with the echoes of the gunshot, mixing with the obscenities he screamed at me. I crashed into his chest with bone-jarring force, digging my nails into his ribs. The impact echoed off the walls as we collided with a table full of porcelain figures. A cacophony of shattered pottery erupted around us, the brittle fragments embedded into his flesh, their sharp edges tearing into his back.

Yet, his fury continued. Defiance clung to his heart like a viper's grip. Another gunshot punctuated the chaos, the air crackling with the discharge near my head. This time, his aim discovered a new target in the chandelier. An explosive eruption of glass and metal shattered into a shower of deadly pieces that rained down. In the storm of destruction, a rogue shard found its way to my cheek, drawing forth a crimson ribbon of pain.

He grabbed me, and we plunged onto the plush carpet, our bodies entwined in a desperate struggle for dominance, my legs fuelled by an unyielding determination, pressed against his chest.

Desperation gripped his face as he attempted to raise the pistol, his fingers clawing at the weapon in a frantic bid for control. I thrust the blade through his wrist, severing the connection between his grasp and the gun. The air thundered with his anguished screams, a chorus of pain that echoed through the room.

As his agonised cries clawed at my ears, I covered his mouth with my free hand. His house was in the middle of nowhere, with the nearest neighbours two miles away. I was unsure why the noise hadn't attracted Sid's attention, but it was better if I could keep him from coming inside.

Mead tried to bite my fingers, but I pushed them further between his lips, forcing him to breathe through his nose. He dropped the gun as tears formed in his eyes. With my weight pressed into him, I controlled my breathing. Then, I gathered my thoughts and spoke.

'Who do you work for?'

I removed my hand for his reply. 'Fuck you, girl.'

I reached down with my free hand and squeezed his balls. 'You won't be fucking anybody ever again if you don't answer my questions.'

Pain seeped out of his face. 'What do you think they'll do when they discover I've spoken to you?'

'They're not the ones with your cock in their fingers, are they? Now talk.'

He squirmed beneath me, but there was no escape for him. 'Do your worst, girl.'

That was already a given, but I needed information from him first. 'At least tell me why somebody murdered my parents.'

Drool slithered over his lips. 'They betrayed the wrong people, those prepared to wait ten years for revenge.'

I knew how they felt. Revenge was all I wanted.

I pushed my knee deeper into his ribs. 'What are their names?'

His face lost colour as he struggled to breathe, and I twisted the knife further.

'What are you doing, Enola?'

Sid's voice startled me, and I turned towards him. It was enough to loosen my leverage on the chief constable and move me off his arm. He brought it around and punched me in the hip. I flew off him, letting go of the blade, and hit Sid in the legs. He went down like a domino and banged his head on a table. Mead jumped up with the knife still in his palm. He used his free hand to pull it out, his blood dripping all over the carpet.

Then he leapt on me.

Chapter 9

Bad Blood

I got my leg up in time to knock him off me, sending the chief constable rolling over the shattered bits of porcelain. Tiny Victorian figures were prostrate around me, their little heads peering in my direction. A pained groan escaped Sid's lips as he lay sprawled on the floor, his body intertwined with broken pieces of chinaware. Meanwhile, Mead sprang to his feet, focused on the knife that had fallen within his reach.

He grabbed the blade and lunged for me. My hand shot out, grasping his wrist in a vice-like grip. We danced violently around the room, our bodies entwined in a fierce struggle, our movements a wild ballet of desperation. Everywhere became an obstacle course of overturned furniture, causing us to stumble and collide with the unforgiving walls. A searing pain jolted through my side as the knife glanced against my hip, and I howled.

Summoning every ounce of strength, I twisted my body to shove him backwards. His balance wavered, his steps faltering, about to topple over. Exploiting the gap in his defence, I jerked forward. My knee, driven by an automatic survival instinct, collided with his gut with a thunderous blow. Mead grunted like a pig, paralysed by the unexpected assault.

Time seemed to slow. Then I hit him in the belly again.

He bent in half, wheezing for air, hunched over like a wilted flower. It was the perfect opportunity. I kicked the knife from his grasp, its metallic glint vanishing amidst the shattered remnants of porcelain figurines scattered on the carpet.

Nevertheless, he refused to stop. His anger exploded out of him, with a howl reverberating through the room. He launched himself at me again. I braced myself as he charged at me in a blind rage. I stepped aside, thrusting my elbow into the back of his neck. The impact caused him to stagger and lose his balance.

Years of frustration and fury surged within me, driving my fists to rain down upon him. Each blow was a visceral release, pain surging through my hands and arms, but I couldn't stop.

As I overpowered him, we gasped for air, our bodies drenched in sweat. He lay sprawled on the floor, wheezing while I stood over him, clutching the knife in my trembling hand. Adrenaline coursed through me, intensifying the rapid thumping of my heart.

He grinned at me. 'I guess you better call the cops.'

I glanced at Sid, unconscious nearby. 'Your mates will look after you, won't they?'

Mead wiped the blood from his lips. 'What do you think, Enola?' He pushed his back into the wall and nodded at Sid. 'What do you think will happen to him and your other friends when the police release me?'

My breath came in rapid, suffocating bursts, with a

thousand explosions erupting in my head. 'You murdered your wife. You'll go down for that.'

His laugh irritated the hairs on my neck. 'Don't be so naïve, girl. You and your little friend broke in here, shot Gemma, and attacked me. That's how this will all play out. You know it.'

He was right. I knew that.

'You might as well tell me who killed my parents and Seraphina, then.'

Mead couldn't stop laughing, even as he spoke. 'Nope, there's no chance of that. It shall be an extra little thing to torment you with. Someday, perhaps a few years in the future, when your mate there is getting fucked in a prison cell, somebody might pay you a visit in yours and tell you what happened that night, just before they slit your throat.'

I looked at him and knew he was right again. All he said would come true. I didn't care about myself, but I couldn't let that happen to Sid. I couldn't protect my parents or Seraphina, but I wouldn't let bad things happen to any more of my friends.

So I walked over and stamped on his balls.

Mead jerked up and screamed. Then I punched him in the face. He went out like a light, folding like a shit poker hand. My hand throbbed as I stood over him briefly to ensure he was out before turning to Sid. I checked his bruise and made sure he was okay. Then I got my hands under his shoulders and dragged him outside. The sun had turned the heat into overdrive and scorched my cheeks. A flock of birds hovered above, and a curious fox peered at me from the extravagant garden. Perhaps it hoped I was bringing Sid out as its meal. I propped him against the car and shooed the animal away.

I returned to the house, finding Mead still unconscious.

I retrieved the knife and searched for the gun but couldn't find it. Then I moved into the other room to see Gemma. My heart shrank when I saw her lying in a pool of her blood. I stood on trembling legs, gripping the blade so hard I wasn't sure what would snap first, me or it.

'I'm sorry,' I said as I went to her. I closed Gemma's eyes and checked her pockets, but they were empty. If she had a mobile phone, she hadn't brought it with her.

I heard moaning from the other room as I returned to see Mead crawling on the floor like a slug. His face burnt a bright red as he struggled to speak.

'I'm going to fucking torture you before I kill you, girl.'

My throat was dry as I stood over him. 'So, will you tell me who is behind all this?'

He lay on his side next to the porcelain head of Queen Victoria. 'Go fuck yourself.'

I sighed and went to him, reaching down for the Empress of India's tiny face.

'We are not amused, chief constable.' I scanned the room and found the booze cabinet. I strolled over, opened it, removed some expensive rum, and took the top off. I hadn't had a drink in four years, but if any occasion demanded me to fall off the wagon, that was surely it.

Instead, I poured the entire bottle over him.

He snarled at me. 'What the fuck?'

I left him muttering obscenities and emptied the drinks cabinet over him and around the room. Then I reached into my pocket and removed the lighter I'd taken from Sid's jacket.

'This is what you call poetic justice.'

He watched me flick the lighter into action. 'You wouldn't.'

I grabbed a copy of the *Daily Mail* from the table and lit it.

'Don't be stupid, chief constable. Of course I fucking would.'

The headline demonising child immigrants went up in flames, and I threw the rag at his feet. The fire leapt into the alcohol-stained carpet with unbridled glee and rushed towards him. I could have put my hands over my ears to drown out his screams, but I didn't.

I watched him shrivel and burn for three minutes before leaving. Sid was rubbing his head with a blank look on his face.

'What?' he said.

I helped him up. 'Give me your keys. I'll tell you everything on the way home.'

He didn't protest and got into the car. I took one last glance as the flames raced through the house, with a mixture of sadness and satisfaction inside me. I'd waited a long time for some answer, but there was something more important I desired.

Revenge.

Now I knew I was going to get it.

Chapter 10

Barbarism Begins at Home

The first night in a children's home, I couldn't sleep. A woman with leather skin for her face brought me a baby doll.

'That should help you,' she said before scuttling off.

I peered at the pale plastic, wondering if she thought it would replace my dead parents in my heart. Was it a substitute for my mother or an indicator of what the future might hold for me?

My life was a mess, surrounded by cold institutional walls that offered no solace, a lost soul amongst kids who had endured the system's trials and tribulations way longer than I had. They were tough and street-smart, a stark contrast to my vulnerability. It didn't take long for them to view me as an outsider.

Yet, the adults entrusted with my care only deepened my sense of displacement. Overworked and underpaid, they wore their exhaustion like a heavy cloak, their patience and understanding worn thin. They failed to see beyond their duties in their weariness, dismissing me as an inconvenience rather than a person deserving of kindness and attention.

I tried to make friends with the other kids, but it was impossible. Each of them carried their own burdens, their haunted eyes betraying the battles they fought within. I sensed the weight of their struggles, an unspoken barrier that kept us at arm's length. They regarded me cautiously, the offspring of parents stolen by violence, an enigma they couldn't decipher.

The corridors buzzed with whispers, spreading like wildfire, each word more twisted than the last. They painted me as the villain, the mastermind behind my parents' deaths, with rumours swirling that I'd set the fire to hide my murderous secrets.

I tried to clear my name, showing them the scars on my hands from the blaze, hoping they'd see the truth. But their response was anything but sympathetic. They laughed callously, mocking my vulnerability like heartless villains in a drama.

Their cruel taunts stung deep into my wounded soul. The rejection, tinged with malicious intent, hurt me further, leaving me isolated and misunderstood. I yearned for acceptance, for someone to see beyond the surface and grasp the truth that lingered inside me. Instead, I found myself cast aside, a pariah in their midst, and my attempts at connection met with scorn and ridicule.

Faced with their indifference, I clung to the flicker of resilience that remained within me, but I was an outsider no matter how many homes they transferred me to. Yet I didn't let the difficulties break me; determined to make the best of the situation and survive. I observed and learned from the other kids, watching how they interacted with each other and the adults and mimicking the survival skills they developed. As a result, I grew a thicker skin, learning to stand up for myself and not take crap from anyone.

That's when the fights started. Six months after my parents' deaths, one kid punched me hard in the back of the head. Then others did the same, sometimes on their own, but also in groups. It continued for weeks until I lashed out and broke an older girl's fingers. The kids left me alone after that, but my reputation as troublesome grew.

That reputation followed me everywhere they sent me, no matter their distance. Then, after four years, everything changed when I arrived at Castle Dean Children's Home.

It was a privately owned place with a live-in "mother" for actual orphans in the system instead of those whose parents were alive and working towards getting their children back. And it was for girls only. The lowest number of kids in the home was ten, and the highest while I was there was forty. Most of the time, it was just a holding spot until a foster home opened up. I was there from fourteen until sixteen.

The place was spotlessly clean, at least on the ground floor, where guests or outsiders would go. Upstairs, where they kept us, was a nightmare. We each had a bed, and what fit in our suitcases. When I arrived, all I had left were my clothes. What little possessions I'd taken from home after my parents died had long vanished into the system of previous children's homes.

At Castle Dean, we kept our bags under our beds, and several girls slept underneath their beds because of past trauma. The first floor smelled of urine since a few kids wet the bed, and the only time the staff washed the sheets was when a new girl arrived. The dirt caked the floors, and nobody took off their shoes if they could help it. Sometimes, I'd sleep curled up on top of my suitcase. I'm pretty sure the floor was rotting through, and they nailed the windows shut, so no fresh air ever entered the "living quarters". It was freezing during winter and sweltering hot in the summer. We ate upstairs, bathed upstairs, and the only reason we left there was to be paraded around for the guests or moved to a new home or school.

When the guests came, we'd put on our "nice clothes" which "mother" would choose from our suitcases. They didn't permit us to wear that outfit on any other occasion. We'd line up and be judged by the "guests". I'm sure a few of them were paedophiles looking for a fresh plaything. As "mother" spoke, we would keep our mouths shut unless spoken to, unless we wanted to be beaten or go without food. If somebody asked about our treatment at the home, we'd say it was amazing. Some girls had learned how to fake happiness long before ending up there. We'd smile and happily answer how "mother" would make us the most delicious meals when, in reality, they were TV dinners, and we'd be taken somewhere for a field trip every Saturday, and we all played together. In truth, we rarely talked to one another, had any toys to play with, or had anything else to occupy our time.

The other children were there, but not with you. Even if there were many girls near you, you were alone. We were like prisoners, separated and afraid to make friends because nobody hung around forever. If you heard crying at night, you covered your ears with your pillow and slept. We mostly stayed in our beds when we were there. Each of us found a small thing to fill our time. One girl I remember would fold and refold her clothes. Another counted the cracks in the walls. I cared for the spiders. And there were plenty of them. There were no mobile phones or the internet. It amazed me when I saw kids with their phones at school.

And you never spoke about your life at Castle Dean

with the normies in the outside world. That would only get you into trouble. Some school kids would torment me for where I lived and for being an orphan, as if it was all my fault. But my reputation followed me to most places. They hurled plenty of insults at me, but I ignored them.

I found one friend my age during my time there, Amy. At first, it was great how we rebelled against the world, but there's only so much crime a teenage girl can do before it consumes her.

That's when I met Seraphina.

Chapter 11

In My Life

S id dropped me outside my flat. 'We're not going to the police?'

I'd told him about Mead killing Gemma, but not what I'd done to the chief constable. I explained the fire away as the copper starting it as part of his suicide and murder plan.

'Do you remember the last time they dragged you down to the station, Sid?'

His eyes, marked with darkness, revealed the haunting memories still lingering within him. A peaceful protest encountered an eruption of violence as the police charged in, their batons shattering bones and banners. They'd singled Sid out in that chaos, his outlandish hair attracting the unwelcome attention of those in uniform. The weight of their blows and the clutches of their grip had torn him away from our ranks; his defiance met with brute force. The van doors slammed shut, imprisoning him in a metal cage reeking of oppression and injustice. They charged him with obstruction, meaning he now had a police record. And it wasn't "Message in a Bottle."

In addition, it had left him with a simmering distrust of any authority.

'Yeah, I guess so, but still, Enola, what happened in that house is pretty fucked up.'

I stretched my arms and yawned. 'I'm knackered, Sid. Thanks for the lift, but you can do what you want.'

I entered the building, shuffling along the gloomy corridor. Getting closer to the flat, the voices of my neighbours seeped through the walls, their murmurs carrying an air of secrecy. I strained my ears, trying to decipher the snippets of conversation, the words dancing like shadows beyond my grasp. The faint scent of fried food lingered around me. It mingled with the musty aroma of age, a fragrance that clung to everything like a memory etched in the stone. Dust particles floated in the golden shafts of light streaming through the cracks in the ceiling.

As I stood outside the door, the voices became more distinct, the emotions within them palpable. I sensed the tension, the undercurrents of joy, sorrow, and whispered secrets that intertwined in the air. I pressed my fingers into the wall, seeking a momentary respite from my turmoil. Ginger and Bruce's words clashed, their debate revolving around their dog, Kronos. Their heated exchange passed through the wall, a mixture of frustration, affection, and the complexity of human relationships.

As I listened, the scent of stale air mingled with traces of dog food and the distinct aroma of a wet mutt. It must have been bath night. It intermingled with the subtle notes of disinfectant that lingered in the hallway. Kronos barked, and I thought of Dirty Harry, my only constant companion, waiting for me. In the children's home, pets were a distant dream, a longing that could never be fulfilled. Even a simple goldfish was beyond our reach.

Ginger's tirade abruptly ceased, replaced by a burst of laughter that filled the air like a contagious melody. The sound cascaded through the walls, merging with the harmonious clinking of glasses, their jovial chorus a stark contrast to the grimness of my existence. I lowered my gaze, fixating on my hands, which bore the lingering scent of alcohol. The pungent stench of smoke clung to my clothes, a reminder of the day's events.

Hearing their carefree and bohemian lifestyle, envy washed over me. It coursed through my veins, igniting a longing for the freedom they seemed to embody. They lived in the present, unburdened by the weight of their pasts, their laughter serving as a testament to the joy that eluded me. For a fleeting moment, I yearned to shed the layers of restraint that confined me, to let go and embrace the untamed essence of my being.

However, the shackles of my past gripped me, constricting my every move. The ghosts of my losses and the insatiable thirst for revenge held me captive, leaving little room for spontaneity or uninhibited self-expression. My path had been defined by sorrow and a burning desire for retribution, rendering me perpetually bent out of shape, my true self obscured by the shadows of my trauma. Yet, amid their laughter, a whirlwind of emotions surged within me, a sense of longing intertwined with resentment, a bitter cocktail that stirred restlessly, searching for only one thing.

Revenge.

It had started with John Mead's death. Previously, I'd relieved my violent urges by aiming them at other deserving candidates, like those three thugs the other night. But now, I could direct them to more justifiable targets. Once I discovered who they were.

I entered my flat, locked the door, and threw my jacket

over a chair. My toes tingled as I kicked off my shoes, the faded beige carpet soft and comforting under my feet. I went to the kitchen, peering at the two-burner stove and miniature fridge. The counters contained unwashed dishes from last night's curry, and a half-full coffee mug sat next to the sink.

Across the room was my cosy sofa, covered in a fluffy blue blanket. A small table with a lamp stood in front of it, surrounded by piles of books and magazines. To the left of the sofa, a narrow bookshelf held my collection of mystery novels and CDs. Two photos were on the shelf, one of Seraphina, the other of my parents and me at the beach, taken a week before they died.

A sudden pain shot through my hip, and I limped into the bathroom big enough to fit a toilet, sink, and shower. The tiles were a dingy white, and the grout was yellowed from years of neglect. I was still wearing the dress from the funeral. I'd forgotten about it in the struggle with Mead.

My body ached as I slipped out of it, discovering tears along the back and what looked like blood. Not my blood.

'Fuck!' I couldn't return it to the rental shop in that state. And with possible incriminating evidence on it.

I dumped it on the floor and peered into the mirror, seeing several blue and purple bruises forming on my flesh. There may even have been finger marks from where Mead had grabbed me. The stink of smoke drifted off me and lingered in the bathroom. My reflection disappeared in the mirror, and I saw the chief constable clutching his broken balls on the floor of his expensive house. Then he went up in flames, and a rainbow of yellow and red was everywhere.

I should have felt guilt or remorse.

Yet I didn't.

There were no feelings inside me.

I guess I was a monster, after all.

I stripped the rest of my clothes off and climbed into the shower, turning the water as hot as possible. It sizzled against my flesh, creating a cloud of steam in the bathroom. Inside the haze, I saw various scenes from that house, including Gemma dying near me and the chief constable screaming in agony. The memory of his howls calmed my nerves.

The vapour dissipated as I turned the shower off and got out. I went to the bedroom, the water clinging to my naked skin, and crawled onto the bed. I pressed play on the CD next to me, and Mick Jagger warbled about not always getting what he wanted.

Then, I closed my eyes and revisited my past.

I saw it all again, as clear as day. The sound of the door kicked in, my mother's screams, and the cold and calculating gaze behind the masks of those who took my parents as I hid from them. My legs trembled as I ran away from the screaming, not towards it. Shouldn't I have gone to help? Instead, I lay curled up in the small space of the wardrobe, the smell of my mother's perfume still lingering on the clothes as the spiders appeared.

Tears pricked my eyes as I experienced again the utter terror and helplessness that consumed me that night, the feeling of being completely alone. My heart punched against my ribs, the familiar sense of panic creeping over me. I gripped the sheets as anxiety sped through me, struggling to breathe as smoke invaded my lungs. Then, the fire covered my hands, and I jerked up and screamed.

I sat there naked and shivering, trying to hear the music but only getting white noise filling my skull.

Then, there was a knock on the wall. 'Are you okay, Enola?'

I bit into my bottom lip and tasted blood. 'I'm fine, Ginger. It was only a nightmare.'

'All right, but let us know if you need anything.'

'I will. Goodnight.'

'Goodnight, Enola.'

I lay back and stared at the cobwebs on the ceiling.

And I wondered how much sleep I'd get.

<h1 style="text-align:center">Chapter 12</h1>

<h1 style="text-align:center">Search and Destroy</h1>

I was dressed and out of the house an hour after slipping into bed, unable to sleep. Finding Gemma's address was easy online, and I stood outside the building, waiting for somebody to enter or leave. A group of teenagers peered at me from the other side of the street. A stray dog howled in the distance, or perhaps it was a werewolf feeling nervous on the estate. Considering where John Mead had lived, it was a bit of a comedown for Gemma.

I zipped my jacket up against the cold, sniffing teenage angst with an aroma of dope hovering over everything. A tall bloke stumbled up the steps and scrutinised me.

'What you waiting for, love?'

He had a face to sink a thousand ships and smelt like a wet weekend in Grimsby.

I put my hand on his dirty coat. 'I forgot my key, so I need some handsome fella to let me in.'

He gave me a look I could feel in my underwear. 'Well, that's just fine and dandy, darling.'

He opened the door and led me inside. The corridor

was as dark as his personality, smelling like somebody had eaten a rat and then puked it all over the walls.

I wriggled out of his grasp. 'Best if you go home, mate.'

His eyes were piss yellow as he glared at me. 'You can't do that to me now.'

I removed the knife from my pocket and showed him the shiny side. 'Run along, bozo.'

I heard the hamster on the wheel inside his head, moving slower than a slug but leaving a similar trail on his brain. Eventually, he thought better of it and slunk into the shadows.

When he disappeared, I found Gemma's place and picked the lock. I took a deep breath and pushed open the door. The flat was small, with a cramped living room and kitchenette. I scrutinised everything, drawn to a photo of Gemma and John on their wedding day. Considering what she'd said about him, it surprised me to see that. I wondered if there were photos of her and Seraphina somewhere.

I went to the desk tucked in the corner, my fingers grazing the worn surface as I sifted through the scattered papers. The stack included bills, a handful of letters, and a weathered notebook. My heart quickened as I flipped through the notebook's pages, discovering a diary of sorts but nothing about Seraphina or my parents.

Then I noticed something. Nestled at the back of the book was a small piece of paper. My fingers trembled as I read the text. 'Woods - family connections to the NCA?'

The NCA – what was that?

Setting aside the paper and notebook, I reached for my phone. With a few taps on the screen, I started an internet search for those cryptic letters. Among the staggering ninety-two million results, one caught my attention: the National Crime Agency. Intrigued, I tapped on the link, discovering that the NCA was the government's primary weapon in combating serious and organised crime.

Organised crime. The notion lingered in my mind, intertwining with the fragments of information I'd gathered. Were my parents in the witness protection program because of their testimony against an organised crime syndicate? John Mead's vague mutterings had hinted at his association with shadowy figures from the criminal underworld.

With this thought, I explored every spot in the flat, driven by a desperate need for answers. Gemma had told her husband she possessed evidence of his corruption and messages from Seraphina. So where were they? I searched for a computer or mobile phone.

I scoured everywhere, peering through each cupboard and drawer. I even lifted the carpets, examining the hidden depths beneath the floorboards as I had at Seraphina's. However, besides the cryptic note concerning the NCA and "Woods," there was nothing of value. Frustration tinged my emotions as I typed that name into an online search on my phone. The screen flooded with countless results, overwhelming my senses. I refined the query to include the NCA, but only discovered more junk.

My head throbbed as I surveyed the room. The sparseness of the surroundings surprised me. Gemma Mead was about forty, yet this was the sum total of her life, which wasn't much.

Was this what was waiting for me as I got older?

My brain ached as I crossed to the window and peered out of it. The authorities must have learned of John and Gemma's deaths by now. The longer I waited in the flat, the likelier they'd catch me.

Outside, the piercing sound of a barking dog cut through the night, adding to my anxiety. I glanced at my phone again, my fingers scrolling through news websites in search of any mention of the events at the Mead house. Disappointingly, there was no information online. Perhaps it was too early for the media to know.

Stuffing everything into my pockets, I cast a final sweeping gaze across the room and wiped away any lingering fingerprints from the surfaces. There was no need to tempt fate and give the coppers something to connect to me. My juvenile record was sealed, but I wouldn't put anything past the police. Though I noticed a few strands of fabric from my clothes stuck to the chair, I dismissed the concern. Forensics were unlikely to scrutinise such minute details.

The floor creaked in the shadows as I closed the door behind me. Half-expecting the creeper from earlier to ambush me, I braced myself for an attack. However, the corridor was empty, missing any lurking presence. Stepping into the chilly embrace of the night, a shroud of gloom enveloped me.

Then, a searing pain erupted at the back of my head, reverberating through my skull. I staggered forward, my vision blurred and hazy as I fought against the encroaching darkness, clinging to consciousness. Grasping a railing for support, I strained to make sense of everything, blinking through the agony as muffled voices approached.

The pavement hit me like a falling star.

Chapter 13

Hit Me With Your Best Shot

'**W**ell, well, well,' somebody said. 'It looks like we've got ourselves a little rat here.'

My elbow ached as I stood, gazing at a veritable rogues' gallery of room temperature IQs. I assessed my options as my pulse raced. Three against one wasn't too bad odds.

'You boys should run along home while you still can.'

The ginger-haired kid pointed at me. 'She looks like one of those birds out of *Sex and the City*.'

His mates laughed at him, and the goon built like a bodybuilder spoke.

'*Sex and the City*? That's the show about three hookers and their mother, right?'

They snorted like hyenas. So I tried my luck.

'Now boys, I'm only here for some gear from my usual dealer, but she's not home. So perhaps one of you handsome chaps could help me out with some cookies.'

'See,' the ginger lad said, 'I told you she was a skank.'

I pretended to be upset and touched my chest, feeling the knife inside my jacket. Then I reached into

68

my trouser pocket and removed five twenty-pound notes.

'I've got the money.'

The bodybuilder stepped forward. 'Who were you seeing in there?'

I returned his stare. 'Gemma Mead.'

He sneered at me. 'The copper?'

Was she still a police officer? She gave me the impression she'd left the force.

'Yeah, she was bent. Didn't you know? Both she and that husband of hers are in the pockets of the Woods.'

'Who?' he asked.

I winked at him. 'Yeah, of course, we've never heard of them, right?' I laughed. 'I'm not wearing a wire.'

The third thug, the one with a skull tattooed on his throat, finally spoke.

'You should take your top off so we can see.'

'Yeah, yeah,' Ginger Hair said. 'Take that fucking top off, skank.'

'Boys, boys, it's far too cold for anything like that. Three shrivelled worms don't make a snake.'

The bodybuilder grabbed my arm. 'How about we go into the copper's flat and find out?'

His fingers pressed into my skin, and I saw the situation rapidly getting out of hand.

'A fish gets caught by opening its mouth,' I said.

He glared at me. 'What?'

I smiled at him. 'It means think before you speak, as there's no taking it back. So the next thing you say to me will determine how this ends.'

He dug his big, thick, sausage-like fingers further into me. The pain soothed my nerves. 'You'll be opening your mouth for the rest of the night, skank, don't worry.'

My smile twisted into a wide grin. 'I never worry.'

Then I stamped on his foot.

'Fuck!' he said before letting go of my arm. Then I kicked him in the balls, and he howled even more as he crumpled to the ground. I kneed him in the jaw and enjoyed the sound of his bone cracking.

I turned to the others. 'You blokes love your cocks and balls so much, yet they're the weakest part of you. Are you two next?'

Their eyes locked in a silent exchange, and excitement poured through my veins. My chest throbbed, echoing the anticipation of what was to come. Then, with lightning speed, Ginger Hair jumped at me. He was quick but clumsy, making it easy to shove my palm into his jaw. The impact sent him reeling backwards, his equilibrium disrupted by the unexpected blow, while a sharp pain seared through my hand.

Meanwhile, the tattooed brute snarled, his bulky frame poised to strike back. His thick fist hurtled towards me, but I evaded him with nimble footwork, like dodging an unwanted suitor on the dance floor. Two years of martial arts classes had served me well.

I had my former friend, Amy, to thank for that. I wondered what she was doing as I waited for the idiots to make their next move. The second thug surged forward, snarling at me. I ducked under his outstretched arm, jabbing my elbow into his abdomen. A guttural howl escaped his lips as he swung wildly at me. I avoided his attempts with dexterity and precision, kicking him in the knee. He collapsed, gasping for air.

Ginger Hair, screaming obscenities at me, rose to his feet, his features contorted with unabated fury. Charging forward with a feral roar, he sought to overpower me with his colossal fists. He looked powerful but was nothing more than a lumbering brute used to dealing with people even stupider than he appeared to be. I evaded his lunging attack, nimbly moving to the side. Then I shoved my fingers into his throat. A final cry erupted from his lips as his body dissolved into a simpering wreck.

The three thugs lay writhing and moaning at my feet, diminished to wriggling worms. My hands throbbed with a mixture of exhaustion and triumph. Cracking my knuckles, I relished the satisfaction of unleashing some pent-up frustration.

'Who sent you?' I said. None of them spoke. 'Come on, boys. It wasn't a coincidence I found you waiting for me when I left the copper's flat. So who told you to harass me?'

They scuttled backwards like crabs, desperate to escape but only finding the entrance to the flats. I removed the knife from my jacket and held it up, so the moonlight reflected off the surface. Somewhere in the dark, a dog or a werewolf was howling.

Ginger's lips trembled as he spoke. 'Are you going to hurt us?'

I pointed the blade at him. 'You probably deserve it, don't you? I'm guessing this isn't the first time you've attacked somebody.'

'Please,' Ginger Hair whimpered. 'I've got a baby daughter.'

'Well,' I said. 'I'm not one to separate children from their parents, but I'm assuming your kid will be better off not having you as a father. So I'll be doing her a favour.'

As I spoke, a montage of haunting memories slithered through my head. The touch of the spiders' skittering legs sent shivers down my spine as I saw my mother and father die for the thousandth time. The image plagued my conscience. Could I subject another innocent child to the same fate, rendering them an orphan with my own hands?

He sobbed in the dark. 'I'll tell you.'

'Shut the fuck up, you cunting twat,' the bodybuilder said.

I waved the knife at him. 'Now, I enjoy a good obscenity as much as the next person does, but that's a tad excessive, isn't it?'

I didn't wait for a reply and stamped on his shin. Outside of my collection of punk and new wave songs, the crack of bones was my second favourite sound.

He screamed, sobbing as I returned to the ginger lad, suddenly feeling like I'd stumbled into an alternate universe with a twisted version of the Spice Girls.

He wiped the tears from his cheeks. 'One of Beck's men paid us to hurt you.'

'Beck?' All I could think of was the American musician.

'Nathan Beck,' Ginger Hair said. 'He's a record producer. He owns the Deviant nightclub. Do you know it?'

I put the knife in my jacket and stepped away from them. 'I don't, but I soon will.'

It rained as I left, the water cooling the fire in my veins as a smile crept from my lips.

I hadn't visited a club in such a long time.

Chapter 14

Manic Monday

The Bits & Bytes office was a hive of activity for a Monday morning. Joe, the primary sales assistant because he was the only staff member who could count without using an electronic device, happily shared the local newspaper with the rest of the grunts. First, we had Ted, the tech man, who was great with his fingers if it was plastic or metal and not anything living, according to his long-suffering girlfriend, Tina. Next was Caroline, the accounts manager, a woman who owned leather love seats, lampshades of Mickey Mouse masturbating, and who named her cat Dogshit. Dave, our delivery driver and customer service expert, was at her side. Dave couldn't come to work one day because he had a frog in his throat. He and his mates had been doing magic mushrooms in the forest when some bright spark challenged him to swallow a frog. The result was Dave spending two days in the hospital. He was lucky Sid didn't sack him on the spot. And of course, there was Sid, who hadn't said a word to me when I walked through the door at eight o'clock.

Now, they were all too busy staring at the front page of the local newspaper. I guess you could never have too much murder in the news.

'First, somebody attacked those blokes near the viaduct Friday night.' That was my doing. 'And now these two coppers killed on Saturday. It's getting like *Midsomer Murders* around here,' Ted said.

'I know those three who were mutilated on Friday,' Dave replied. 'They deserved it.'

Ted waved the paper at him. 'It doesn't say they were mutilated here.'

Dave shook his head. 'It's all over Facebook. Stewie Barnes lost an eye and the tops of two fingers. Fred Weller's missing half an ear and most of his nose, but Paul Stone got it worse.' He moved closer to the rest of them. 'Apparently, whoever they messed with stamped on his cock and balls so hard the doctors had to remove them.'

Caroline grinned as Sid and Ted grimaced.

'What do you mean, they deserved it?' I said.

Dave grabbed the paper and showed me the photos of the three blokes I'd encountered the other night, pictures that looked like they'd been taken in a police station.

'They've been mugging little old ladies and stealing from single mothers and others for years, but the coppers never had enough to put them away. Sometimes there'd be witnesses, but Stone and his gang always scared them off.' He returned the paper to Ted. 'So whoever did that deserves a medal. Everybody on Facebook is singing their praises.'

'We can't have vigilante justice,' Sid said.

Dave laughed. 'You call the police, and most of the time, they don't arrive. Even when they do, the coppers are sometimes worse than the criminals. Look how many of them have been caught doing terrible shit in the last few years, and I bet there are loads more who get away with more atrocious stuff. That's why vigilante justice is necessary. People need to take matters into their own hands.'

Sid glanced at me. 'Is that what you think happened to Mr and Mrs Mead, Dave? Somebody killed them because of some criminal activity?'

Dave frowned. 'Nobody's speaking about that on Facebook. So your guess is as good as mine.'

'We're too soft on criminals,' Caroline said.

As office manager, I should have ended the conversation because nobody would get any work done, but I was curious to hear their thoughts on the subject. I didn't doubt myself or my actions, but some validation would have been an excellent way to start the day.

Ted shook his head. 'Bring back hanging, eh?'

Caroline thought about it. 'No, there are too many miscarriages of justice for that. But I believe certain offenders should never be released where there is irrefutable evidence of guilt. You can't reform child abusers or rapists. It's in their DNA.'

'Criminals are born, not made?' I said.

She looked at me with deep sadness in her eyes. I'd worked with these people for a year but knew nothing about them. We'd had office parties and nights at the pub, but it had all been the usual superficial stuff. I enjoyed working with them, but we were not much more than strangers when I thought about it. Even with Sid, I knew very little of who he really was. Now, I was trusting him to keep my secret.

'I think it's a bit of both,' Caroline said.

I nodded. 'Nature and nurture.'

Ted scratched his head. 'What's that?'

'The biological and genetic factors that affect somebody's behaviour are referred to as nature,' I explained. 'The environment and experiences that shape a person's conduct are known as nurture.'

I paused for a moment, gathering my thoughts. 'With criminal behaviour, there are different beliefs. Some people think a person's inclination for crime is determined by their biology and genes, and criminality is inherent in their nature. However, others argue that the environment and experiences push individuals towards criminal acts.'

Leaning forward, I continued, 'Take, for instance, someone growing up in poverty, surrounded by violence, and lacking proper guidance and support. Under such circumstances, they may resort to crime to survive or out of sheer desperation.'

Sid peered at me, and I wondered what he thought of me after yesterday's events. 'What do you think, Enola?'

I shrugged. 'Biology and genetics can make someone more likely to exhibit certain behaviours. However, the environment they grow up in and their experiences truly shape whether or not they resort to criminal behaviour. It's never just about nature or nurture alone. It's always a tangled blend of both factors working together.'

It was probably the only serious conversation I'd had with any of them in my year at the job. The bell ringing in the shop dragged our focus away from criminals to the day's first customer. Dave scuttled off to deal with it, and everybody else shuffled away, all apart from Sid and me.

'Can we have a word in your office, Enola?'

Since Bits & Bytes was his business, what choice did I have?

I led him inside and closed the door. 'Coffee?'

'What happened in that house, Enola?'

I poured myself a drink. 'It's probably best if you don't know the details, Sid.'

He slammed his hand on my desk. 'And what happens when the coppers come knocking on our doors?'

'Why would they do that?'

He slumped in the seat opposite me. 'Because we were there the day someone murdered the Meads.' I waited for the next bit. 'And I saw you trying to kill him.'

The veiled accusation hung in the air between us. As much as he hated the police, I doubted his conscience would let him harbour somebody he believed was a murderer.

'No, you didn't, Sid.'

'I didn't?'

I sipped the coffee, enjoying the taste in my mouth and the smell drifting over my skin. 'I wanted answers from him about Seraphina's murder.'

He screwed up his face. 'Seraphina died of cancer.'

I shook my head. 'Not according to Gemma Mead.' I removed the letter from my pocket and handed it to him. 'And Seraphina claimed she knew who killed my parents.'

He read the note, his face turning white as he did. 'Fuck!' He gave it back to me. 'Is this true?'

I shrugged. 'I don't know. That's why we went to see Mead.' I stared into his eyes. 'He threatened to kill you.'

Sid rubbed at his head. 'Was that when I blacked out?'

'It was.'

'So, you saved me?'

'I did.'

He puffed out his cheeks. 'I guess I should leave it well alone, right?'

I nodded. 'Absolutely.'

He turned to go. 'I'm organising a work night out for the pub. What do you think?'

I lifted the coffee to toast him. 'Count me in.'

When he closed the door behind him, I opened the search engine on the computer.

Then I looked for Nathan Beck.

Chapter 15

Queen of Clubs

I elbowed my way through the dense crowd at the Deviant nightclub. The thumping bass reverberated through my chest, resonating in sync with the pounding beat. The club seemed to vibrate beneath me, amplifying the intensity of the music. A haze of dim lights and swirling smoke filled the air, casting an ethereal glow over everything.

The dance floor was a mass of sweaty bodies, moving and gyrating in perfect synchrony with the pulsating rhythm. The atmosphere was electric, charged with an undercurrent of excitement and desire. As I navigated the sea of dancers, I saw flushed faces and glistening skin immersed in the intoxicating melodies.

Stopping to catch my breath, I surveyed the surroundings, absorbing every detail. Thoughts of Nathan Beck swirled in my mind as I tried to piece together the puzzle of the place and why he would send a bunch of thugs to intimidate me outside Gemma's flat.

The air smelt of alcohol, perfume, and the pungent smoke of a frenzied dry ice machine, churning out clouds that engulfed the room like a scene from a low-budget horror movie. Amidst the swirling mist, the patrons revealed themselves, an eclectic mix of characters. Men festooned with metal piercings, proudly displaying nails through various parts of their faces, their attire comprising little more than studded leather jockstraps. Equally audacious women paraded around in outfits that left nothing to the imagination, as if their lingerie demanded admiration from all who looked at it. Clad in a simple jacket and jeans, I felt underdressed in comparison.

Raucous laughter pierced the pounding music, competing with the clinking of glasses raised in wild cele-bration. The walls pulsated with a kaleidoscope of neon lights, casting an eerie glow that bathed the crowd in an otherworldly aura. Faces were illuminated in a mesmerising dance of vivid hues, creating an ethereal and disorienting spectacle.

I weaved through the multitude, avoiding elbows or feet that might trip me up. Some of those high heels would puncture a lung if you fell underneath them. And that was only what the blokes were wearing. I finally reached the bar and leaned against it, trying to catch my breath.

The bartender approached, shouting over the din. 'What can I get you?'

I shook my head; my attention focused on the VIP area in the back. Nathan Beck was supposedly there, surrounded by his entourage of yes-men and women. Before leaving for the club, I'd checked Beck's bio online: fifty-five years old, renowned music producer and club owner celebrated for his work in the entertainment world. With over three decades of experience, he'd built a reputation as one of the business's most influential and creative figures.

A decade ago, he opened the Deviant nightclub, which

quickly became a hotspot for the glitterati of the entertainment industry, attracting people from across the country and all over Europe. However, standing at the bar and scanning the surroundings, I noticed the place was only half-full. And there was no sign of Beck. I looked at his photo on my phone, seeing a tall man, over six feet, with broad shoulders and a muscular build. His hair was speckled with grey and styled in a sleek, short cut, and deep wrinkles framed his sharp blue eyes. His chiselled jaw seemed sculptured from the finest granite.

His music studio and luxury home were nearby, so perhaps it was too early for him to be in the club. A bloke who looked like he spent most of his time polishing his head sidled up to me and winked in my direction. I sighed and walked away, heading into the ladies toilets.

As I pushed open the heavy door, the strong scent of floral air freshener and cheap perfume hit me. The place was shrouded in flickering fluorescent lights, casting a pale glow on the dingy, green-tiled walls. Chipped and stained sink basins lined one wall, and rusting stall doors the other. The tiles were dirty and slippery, the stickiness of the floor attacking my shoes.

Chatter and laughter bounced off the ceiling as young women gathered in front of the mirrors, touching up their makeup and dressed in daring and provocative clobber. They sported tight leather corsets, fishnet stockings, and stiletto heels. Their hair was styled in gaudy bright colours, from neon pink to electric blue, in high spikes and festooned with studded ties. In addition, they were decorated with heavy jewellery and piercings.

One wore a short PVC skirt barely covering her arse and a tight corset showcasing her ample curves. Another sported thigh-high boots and a miniskirt made entirely of chains. They all had bold red lipstick, emphasising their full lips and eyes lined with thick black kohl. They complained loudly about the men in the club.

'Ugh, these guys are so fucking clueless,' the Dua Lipa lookalike announced. 'Do you know what that guy in the cheap suit said to me?' Her friends shook their heads in unison. 'He slides up to me on the dance floor, his grin nothing but a mouthful of white teeth, and goes, "Is it hot in here, or is it just you?"' Their laughter lit up the room. 'I told him to fuck off and take a cold shower.'

Another chimed in, 'And don't even get me started on their dancing. It's like watching a baby giraffe trying to walk for the first time.'

They laughed as the woman in the PVC skirt spoke to me. 'You had any luck, love?'

'I'm hoping to meet Nathan Beck,' I said.

She dropped her lipstick into the sink, where it rattled and rolled, leaving a red mark in the centre. 'Oh Christ, you're not another of his wannabees, are you?'

They all stared at me, crestfallen. 'What do you mean?'

PVC grabbed my arm. 'You know he hasn't produced any decent music for years, right?'

I caught my reflection in the mirror and wondered if I looked young and naïve to them. 'I've been writing songs since I was twelve.' That was true. I had a drawer full of terrible punk tunes scribbled on dirty bits of paper. 'I want to show them to him.'

Electric Blue hair smiled at me like a mother beaming at a kid who couldn't tie her shoelaces. 'He's not interested in what other people want. Beck has his own project he's been trying to get off the ground for years.' She looked at PVC. 'What is it again?'

'He wants to create a female Bowie,' PVC said. 'And

keep her under his control. He's had loads of young girls at his studio, none of which have been the right one.'

Electric Blue snorted. 'Yeah, well, not for the music, at least. I'm sure they've been right for lots of other things.'

Their combined laughter hurt my head. 'There was nothing about that online.'

They all stared at me as if I'd just got off the boat.

'He has a terrible reputation,' PVC warned. 'So you stay away from him.'

'I can look after myself.'

Electric Blue nodded. 'Me too. I took a self-defence class last year.'

'You need more than that,' I replied. They looked at me with curious eyes. 'You must go on the attack, not just defend yourself.'

PVC turned up her top lip. 'What do you mean?'

'Never be passive around men,' I said. 'The predators pick up on that and see it as a weakness. If you're in a dangerous situation, you should strike first.'

'How?' Electric Blue asked.

I flexed my fingers and showed them. 'If you can, always aim for the balls. A kick is better than a punch unless you have a heavy weapon on you, like a lead pipe or a baseball bat. And make sure you put all your weight behind it. If you can't reach the balls, aim for the throat, particularly if you can jab your fingers in there. One good stab, and they'll struggle to breathe. But whether it's the throat or the balls, they should bend over or go down. Once that happens, you hit them again, preferably on the back of the head. More than once, if necessary. Avoid using your fists, as you might break your bones that way. Instead, use your elbow, as that bone is quite sturdy and packs a thump. The nose is an excellent attack point. Don't punch, but use the flat part of your hand near the wrist. Another option is to keep something weighty in your handbag, like a small brick. Then you swing that at them and do some damage, especially if you go for the face.'

They gazed at me wide-eyed and open-mouthed.

Then they burst out laughing and patted me on the back.

'Remind me never to upset you,' PVC said.

They shuffled out of the bathroom, leaving me to gaze into the mirror. I applied lipstick and pictured what it would be like as a female Bowie.

It was time to meet Nathan Beck.

Chapter 16

Poker Face

Taking a deep breath, I headed to the VIP area. As I approached, I sensed the gaze of the bouncers on me, sizing me up. They stopped me when I reached the entrance.

'What do you want?' the biggest said.

I smiled at him. 'I'm going to sing for Mr Beck.'

The bouncer looked at his colleague, two apes with ten brain cells between them. The other one slipped into the VIP room and left me with Bozo. He glared at me as if I was shit on his shoe, and Seraphina's voice came floating back into my head.

'Don't underestimate how much the stupid hate the clever and how much the mean hate the decent.'

The music got louder as I waited, some God-awful techno rubbish that made my bones wobble. I love dance music, but this wasn't something you'd dance to; it was more like a tune serial killers listened to when torturing people.

Thoughts of Seraphina consumed me once more, stirring a mix of emotions within me. How could she have kept such a secret from me for six years? The weight of her silence during my time in the children's home bore down on me. If she'd revealed her connection to my parents, perhaps it would have altered how I viewed her. Now, knowing she played a part in the witness protection program that ultimately led to the death of my mother and father, I couldn't help but feel like an unwanted orphan, rejected by everyone.

Gorilla Number One returned and grunted at me. 'You can go in.'

I entered the room, wrapped in a refreshing gust of cool air. The change in atmosphere was palpable as the music shifted to a more soothing melody, providing a respite from the previous frenzy. The surroundings radiated opulence, boasting plush velvet couches and a soft ambient glow emanating from the dim lighting.

At the heart of it all sat Beck, the master of his domain, wearing a self-assured grin, broadcasting an aura of power and authority. Clad in a meticulously tailored suit that stressed his imposing figure, he completed the ensemble with a pair of gleaming black dress shoes. Surrounded by a flock of young women, he held court, captivating them with every word. His impeccably styled hair slicked back, and his piercing blue eyes had a magnetic allure. With a glass of fine brandy in hand, he swirled the amber liquid, embodying sophistication and control.

'Ladies, let me tell you, this is the life. The good life. And it's all thanks to my talent and my connections.' He took a sip of his drink and stared at me. 'You can't achieve anything without family and friends to support you.' Beck lifted his hand and beckoned me over. 'You've come to sing for me?'

I scrutinised them all, him included, seeing a river of

booze and drugs swimming behind their eyes. I nodded. 'I'm your next superstar, your female Bowie.'

He twisted his head away from me. 'I don't need a singer.'

The music seeped out of the walls as I reached into my jacket and removed bits of paper. I scrunched them between my fingers and threw them onto the table near his drink.

'That's what you need.'

He peered at them as if they were used nappies. 'What's that shit?'

'My lyrics. I've written dozens of songs.'

One of the women draped her legs over his. He pushed her off him and glared at me. 'I don't need a songwriter. I've got fucking machines to do that for me.'

The stink of the alcohol lifted off the table in a great wave. It drifted over me, sinking into my skin, mouth and nose. It was intoxicating, playing havoc with my senses as the pounding bass made my skull vibrate. Four years of sobriety teetered on the brink of me falling off that wagon. Not so much because of what I inhaled, but more to do with the fire churning inside my guts that screamed for a release, one that would burn everything around me.

Heat covered my cheeks as I puffed them out. 'What do you want?'

His shoulders cracked as he stood, flexing his full frame like King Kong before he beat on his chest and strangled a dinosaur.

'It's not about what I want, but what I need.' His eyes blazed red as they moved up and down on me.

'What do you need?'

Beck put a meaty hand on my shoulder and squeezed. I

didn't move, knowing he was testing me, trying to intimidate me, or both.

'What I need, girl, what I desire, is somebody to mould into the next global superstar. Someone who will listen to me and do everything I say without question, regardless of what I ask them to.' He pressed a bit more. 'Do you think you can do that?'

I considered punching him in the balls as he dug his nails deeper into my flesh, but that wouldn't get me anywhere. 'We won't know unless we try.'

We stood like that for an eternity, with the volume rising all the time, not only of the music but also of the sound of my heart throbbing inside my head.

Then he let go and flexed his fingers. 'Follow me.'

He pushed past the table, knocking bottles and glasses over in his wake. Two beefy blokes stuck to his shadow, and I followed them out through the back.

Beck led us into a gloomy corridor with windowed rooms on either side. I glanced in a few as we went, seeing thrashing bodies rolling around on beds, not knowing where one person started and another ended. A cacophony of moaning and groaning floated out of open doors, and everywhere smelt of sweat and sex.

I covered my face with my hand to shield myself from the unpleasant stench as I stepped outside; a noxious combination of industrial waste and contaminated water assaulted my senses, causing my nose to wrinkle.

Beck slid into the backseat of a car, and I hopped in beside him. I didn't bother waiting for introductions, gripping the plush leather as one of the bouncers took the driver's seat. Then, the engine roared to life, propelling us away from that wretched place.

'What's your name?' he said.

I put the seatbelt on while he ignored his. 'Enola.'

He laughed. 'That's alone backwards. Did you know that?'

'Yeah, I saw it in a movie.'

He moved his head up and down like a nodding dog. 'So you're a wannabe singer?'

I watched the city pass by outside the window. 'No. I want to be a superstar.'

Beck grabbed my leg and grinned. 'Well, let's see what we can do about that.'

Chapter 17

The Whole of the Moon

Beck lit a cigarette as we entered the music studio. The bouncers had retreated to the house to look after his dogs. I heard them barking even though there was a courtyard separating the two buildings.

Vintage posters and gold records lined the walls. I went to a large mixing console, footsteps echoing against the wooden floor. Beck loomed over the far end of the desk, blowing smoke over the equipment. The hum of electricity and the soft glow of screens filled the room. He narrowed his eyes and scrutinised me.

'Why do you want to be a singer?'

I hesitated for a moment. 'Music has always been a huge part of my life.' I had Seraphina to thank for that. 'It's a way to express myself and connect with others. And singing, well, it feels natural to me.' I didn't really care about the singing; it was my words I wanted to get out into the world. He must have seen that in my expression.

'You're more of a writer than a singer, right?'

'I suppose so.'

'Yet you left your lyrics at the club.'

I shrugged. 'There's more where they came from.' I didn't tell him it was Ginger's shopping list I'd tossed onto that table.

I felt him undressing me with his eyes. 'So, you want to be the next Taylor Swift or Lorde?'

'Fuck that shit. I'm gonna be Johnny Rotten and Bowie mixed with Ian Curtis. And maybe a pinch of Iggy Pop.'

Beck continued to scrutinise me. 'You can't shock anybody anymore. So that doesn't sell anything. Today's youth don't care about revolution or improving the planet.' I resisted the urge to tell him he was full of shit. 'All they want is the comfort blanket of their digital world, where everything is safe, and nothing can hurt them. That's what we need to break through.' He got up. 'Follow me.'

We moved into another room, the only light source coming from a glowing fish tank. He went to it and opened a small cage on a table, removing a wriggling rodent. Then he threw it into the tank.

The water bubbled in a frenzy of activity as the frightened creature sank to the bottom, and a flash of fins and teeth swarmed on it. The container turned red, and the room smelt of blood. I moved to the aquarium, seeing huge eyes glowing in the water as they tore the mouse apart.

'You have piranhas?'

He blew more smoke at me. 'It's illegal, but what the coppers don't know won't hurt them, eh?' Was that a hint? 'You're the only potential who hasn't run out of here screaming when I show them my pets.' A slug crawled over his mouth, trying to impersonate a smile. 'You must be tougher than you look.'

'You don't know the half of it, mate.'

Beck went to a wooden table cluttered with boards and sketches. He beckoned me over. I glanced at the information, seeing ideas for a young female singer dressed like a woman from the far future.

'Mysta Moon?' I said.

His eyes lit up like gigantic candles. 'She was a comic book character in the 1940s. She's in the public domain now, so I'm looking for somebody to be my Mysta, to transfer her from page to reality, in the studio, on the stage, and on the screen. I'm going to remould her for the twenty-first century, make her the voice that speaks to everyone who wants to do something more with their life. And it will be an interactive adventure, where the consumers can mould Mysta to their needs in a digital world personal to them.'

'Great,' I said. 'And who'll be paying for this nonsense?'

The cigarette slipped from his mouth and hung over his bottom lip. 'What?'

I peered at the red drifting through the fish tank. 'I did some digging on you, Nathan, before going to the club. And I don't just mean the stuff anybody can find online. I'm talking about the things only the dodgiest people know, like how you can't afford to run this studio and the nightclub and how your debts are growing daily. And that includes a couple of million quid you owe the tax woman. So, how are you paying for anything?'

He spat the fag onto the floor. 'Who are you?'

I shook my head. 'Didn't you send your thugs to attack me outside Gemma Mead's flat?'

'The copper? She's dead. What's she got to do with you being here?'

'You knew her then?'

Beck moved forward to grab me, but I dodged his grasp. He stumbled into the table, knocking sketches of Mysta Moon all over the place.

'Fuck! You're going to pay for this.' I kicked the back of his leg. He tumbled onto the floor and banged his head. 'Fucking hell!' He got up and glared at me. 'You fucking cow!' He took a mobile phone from his pocket, and I knocked it from his hand. It joined Mysta on the floor.

'There's no need to call anyone, Nathan. We can sort this out between the two of us.'

'You're not a singer.'

I shrugged. 'I do a mean Poly Styrene on the karaoke, and people have marvelled at my Lydia Lunch.' I glanced at the sketches at my feet. 'Though I guess I'll never be Mysta Moon.'

'What do you want?'

'Good, straight to business. I like that. So, I'll ask again. Why did you send those thugs to attack me outside Gemma Mead's flat?'

'That was you who hurt them?'

'Possibly. Why were they there?'

'I was instructed to monitor any strangers entering and leaving the building. That's why those three idiots were there. It's all I know.'

I shook my head. 'I'm trained to spot a liar from fifty paces, Nathan, and you're nowhere near that far away. So, try again.'

He shrugged. 'I know nothing else. I swear.'

The sigh crept out of me. 'Oh, you'll do more than swear very soon.' I glanced at the walls. 'I'm assuming this is all soundproofed since it's a recording studio?'

'Of course it is.'

'Excellent.' I removed the knife from my jacket. 'Turn around.'

'And if I don't?'

I lunged forward and stabbed him in the leg, plunging

the blade as far as it would go before removing it. He hit the wooden floor and swore like a trooper.

'Fucking hell!'

I wiped the knife on his cheek. 'Now, are you going to behave? You're a big man, but you're out of shape, and I've had lots of practice at this. So what do you say?'

He placed a hand on the wound to stop the bleeding. 'What do you want?'

'Do I have to repeat the question?'

'I don't know anything else.'

I sighed. 'You're lying. So where do we go from here?'

Beck spat at my feet. 'Do your worst.'

What was it with these people? Things would be so much smoother if they just told the truth. I blamed the modern world. All those times we see our leaders, politicians and others blatantly lying in the media and getting away with it had given the public the excuse to do the same.

I glanced at the fish tank. 'Now tell me, Nathan, do your pets only eat defenceless mice?'

'You wouldn't,' he said.

Sid Vicious was singing inside my head as I thrust the knife into Beck's other leg. He rolled on the floor and screamed, blood seeping out of him.

'Last chance, Mr Beck.'

He tried to crawl away. 'Fuck you.'

I placed my foot on his hip and shoved him towards the aquarium. 'You know, I might have made a good Mysta Moon.'

I pushed Beck against the stand and wiped the blade on his shirt. He swore at me again as I stood and got behind the tank. Then, I leveraged my hands against the side and tipped the contents over him. The water stopped him from screaming too much, and the fish found his blood quickly. It was impressive how the little buggers could go through him like kids in a candy store.

I watched him squirm for a few minutes before leaving, seeing the crimson liquid soak the unfortunate Mysta Moon as I went.

I guess I wasn't going to be a singer after all.

Chapter 18

Dirty Deeds Done Dirt Cheap

I was preparing to leave for work when there was a knock on the door. A sense of apprehension washed over me, as I suspected who might be on the other side. I opened up, seeing two police officers. One was a bloke in a crisp blue uniform, and the other was a woman clad in plain clothes. The stern expression etched across her face hinted at the seriousness of the situation, while her partner projected an air of readiness, poised to spring into action if needed. His hands looked like they were used to strangling things.

'Miss Gray?' she said, looking at me critically.

I yawned. 'Yes.'

She showed me her warrant card. 'I'm Detective Inspector Jenkins, and this is Constable Davis. We're here to ask you some questions about Gemma Mead.'

I took a deep breath, trying to steady my nerves. I had a feeling this wouldn't be a pleasant conversation. 'Okay, come in.' I stepped aside so they could enter.

'Were you just leaving?' DI Jenkins asked.

I rubbed the sleep from my eyes. 'I should have been at

work ten minutes ago.' Bits & Bytes was a twenty-minute walk away.

She nodded. 'Hopefully, we won't keep you long.'

I took the single-seater, and they sat on the sofa opposite. Davis had a pen and notebook in his hands.

'I thought you'd record everything digitally,' I said.

Jenkins smiled at me. 'This is only an informal chat, Ms Gray.'

My phone vibrated with a new text, but I ignored it. 'Fire away.'

'When was the last time you saw Gemma Mead?' the inspector asked.

I'd been thinking about this since the other night. 'It was at Seraphina's flat on Saturday afternoon.'

Jenkins looked at her phone. 'This would be Seraphina Shaw?'

I nodded. 'That's right. I met Gemma at Seraphina's funeral. I didn't know she existed before then.'

'Why did you go to Ms Shaw's flat?'

This was another thing I'd considered since the Mead fire.

'There were still a few of my things at Seraphina's, CDs mainly, and Gemma asked if she could come along. She said they'd been a couple once, but that was news to me. Seraphina never spoke to me about her private life.'

'How did you know Ms Shaw?'

'She was employed at the children's home where I lived from fourteen to sixteen.'

'Were you aware they'd worked together as police officers?'

I shook my head. 'It was news to me that Seraphina had been a copper.' I leaned forward. 'Did she work with you?'

DI Jenkins smiled. 'So tell me, how did you get to Ms Shaw's flat?'

This was another thing I'd been contemplating for the last two days.

'I borrowed my friend Sid's car and drove there.'

'How did you get into the flat?'

'I had a spare key.'

'Had?'

'I pushed it through the letterbox when I left.'

She peered at me, seemingly trying to unpick my thoughts with the power of staring.

'We'll need the contact details for Sid.'

'Sure,' I said. 'Have I done something wrong?'

Her smile reminded me of a squashed insect. 'No, Ms Gray, but are you aware of what happened to Gemma Mead?'

'I saw it in the news, yes. Just terrible. Those poor people.'

'Do you know why somebody might have wanted to kill Gemma or her husband?'

I shrugged. 'I only met her once and didn't know him.'

Constable Davis finally spoke. 'What did the two of you talk about?'

My phone buzzed again. 'I asked her about Seraphina, their time together, but she wouldn't tell me much. I think she was a very private person.'

'Where did you go after you left Ms Shaw's flat?'

'I returned the car to Sid and walked back here. The funeral and everything finally took its toll on me.'

'Did Ms Shaw ever talk to you about her job as a police officer?'

'No. As I said, I only discovered that when Mrs Mead informed me at the funeral.'

'Didn't you find that strange?' Jenkins asked. 'You were friends for six years, and she kept that secret from you.'

'Perhaps she was embarrassed.'

Davis lifted his eyebrows and looked like he wanted to slap the handcuffs on me.

'There was a bit of an age gap between you, wasn't there?' Jenkins said.

She was fishing for something, but I wasn't biting. 'We had a lot in common.'

Jenkins placed her phone on the arm of the sofa and studied my flat. 'Such as?'

'Music, movies, books, new technology, and other stuff.'

The inspector glanced at my hands. 'Did she know about your past?'

'Do you?'

'It's not a secret, Ms Gray.'

'Obviously not.'

'The two of you didn't talk about what happened ten years ago?'

'Have you caught my parents' killers yet?'

Silence sat between us like the iceberg that sank the *Titanic*.

DI Jenkins stood, and Davis followed. 'Do you have those details for your friend?'

'Of course.' I grabbed my phone.

'Perhaps we can drop you off at work. Then we'll speak to Mr Storm as well.'

I hadn't told them Sid's surname, meaning they already knew things they'd asked me. Had they spoken to him? I hoped not, as I hadn't told him what lies to tell. Not that lying to the coppers would bother him as he deeply distrusted the police. Not just for what they did to him at the protest, but also for the time they beat up his grandfather during the miner's strike.

Davis wrote down the information I gave him as I glanced at my phone, seeing two messages from Caroline. Then Jenkins's mobile rang, and she answered it.

'What? This isn't a wind-up?' She stared at Davis. 'We're at her flat. Okay, okay. I'll see you there.' She ended the call with a thunderous expression.

'Problems?' I said.

DI Jenkins gripped her phone. 'You work at the Bits & Bytes computer shop?'

'Yep. Why?'

Dark shadows covered her face. 'It's on fire.'

Chapter 19

Firestarter

I jumped from the police car, my heart racing at what I saw. Thick, black smoke spiralled into the sky, engulfing my workplace. The computer shop, which had become my second home, was now a raging firestorm. Flames danced hungrily at the windows, devouring everything in their path and tearing through the roof with destructive fury.

'Stay here,' DI Jenkins ordered, but I ignored her and sprinted towards the inferno. A wave of scorching heat crashed against my skin, searing my senses, and the acrid stench of smoke invaded my lungs, making it difficult to breathe. The deafening roar of the raging fire assaulted my ears, its relentless fury like a charging freight train. Amidst the chaos, I could distinguish between the urgent shouts of the firefighters and the sharp hiss of the hoses as they battled against the fire, desperately struggling to rein in the uncontrollable blaze.

I staggered closer to the blazing building despite the protests of the officers trailing behind. They grabbed at me, attempting to restrain me, but I shook them off, driven by an overwhelming desire to help my colleagues.

Approaching the flames, I saw the outlines of three figures trapped inside, their desperate pleas echoing through the smoke-laden windows. Their frantic pounding against the glass resonated in my chest, igniting a surge of anguish within me. My heart implored me to charge into the raging fire, but a paralysing fear rooted me to the ground.

The searing heat engulfed me, causing rivulets of sweat to cascade down my forehead. My eyes burned, blurred by tears, yet I refused to look away. The weight of past loss hung heavily upon me, spurring a deep resolve not to let my colleagues meet the same tragic fate.

I needed to take action.

Just as my determination wavered, someone pulled me back and hugged me.

'Thank God you're all right. I thought the worst when you didn't reply to my texts.'

Caroline let me go and wiped a tear from her cheek.

'Where are the others?' I asked.

Her tears came again, sobbing and unable to speak. She glanced at the blaze, and I knew who the three silhouettes were. My legs trembled, and I sank to the floor, sitting there as heat and smoke drifted over my face.

'You need to move back,' a firefighter ordered.

DI Jenkins dragged me up and led me from the chaos, stopping next to Caroline, who was comforted by Constable Davis. I peered into the heart of the fire, seeing two other blazes from my past, one recent and the other not. The stink of the smoke lingered on me, and I pictured the chief constable writhing in torture because of what I'd done.

Then he went up in flames, and I was inside that wardrobe again, crawling out of it as our home turned yellow and red. I rushed to my parents and ignored the blood weeping from their throats, touching their shoulders as sparks jumped from the floor and ran up their petrol-soaked clothes. It was as if the blaze was alive, a living, breathing thing that sprinted towards me. My hands burned as I fled the house, throwing myself to the ground, lying there and crying, the whole of me in agony. Burning spiders clung to me as I watched the inferno consume the building.

'Are you okay, Enola?' DI Jenkins said.

I pushed the past from my head and stared at her. 'What happened?'

'I don't know,' she replied. She turned to Caroline. 'Were you here when it started?'

Caroline's hands shook as she raised them to her face. 'I'd only gone out for a few minutes to get the morning doughnuts. Sid was desperate for a sugar rush and loved the toffee special with his coffee. A bit of toff and coff, he called it. And Dave, young Dave, he....'

She cradled her head in trembling fingers, her shoulders heaving with unrestrained sobs. I lifted my gaze, fixating on the valiant firefighters in their battle against the relentless blaze. The crackling and popping of the inferno filled the air, overwhelming any other sound, drowning out the wailing sirens of the fire trucks and the urgent shouts of those trying to quench the flames. Through the dense veil of smoke, their figures flickered like shadows, darting tirelessly amidst the chaos, wielding hoses as lifelines, desperately attempting to subdue the raging hellhole. The pungent stench of melting plastic and seared metal invaded my senses, attacking my nostrils, causing tears in my eyes and my throat to constrict with a suffocating tightness. I observed the firefighters' unwavering determination etched upon their faces, their every movement deliberate and synchronised. Yet, deep down, I acknowledged the grim reality: there was no hope for those trapped in the building.

'We should move you away from here,' DI Jenkins said.

Caroline reached over and squeezed my hand. 'I was returning to the shop when I heard the explosion. I thought it was a car backfiring, and then I saw the flames at the windows. Sid was at the door trying to escape, but it wouldn't open, and the others were behind him. I don't understand why they didn't leave. The door was unlocked when I left, but even if it was locked, it was easy to unlock it from their side.' She gazed at me. 'Why couldn't they get out, Enola?'

'I don't know, Caroline.'

'Why weren't you here?' she said. 'You've never been late, not once, all the time you've worked for Bits & Bytes.'

'Something came up at home, so I was late leaving.'

I looked at DI Jenkins. I would have been in that blaze if she and Davis hadn't knocked on my door.

Jenkins left us to speak to a firefighter; I knew it wasn't an accident. Instead, somebody had locked my colleagues inside and set the shop alight.

They were after me.

Sid, Dave, and Ted died because of me.

I let go of Caroline and dug my nails into my palms until the blood came. It trickled down my hands and stained the pavement. She placed her head on my shoulder and sobbed. The fire increased, with great flames reaching into the sky like fiery fingers grasping for the sun. Smoke lingered on me, creeping into my mouth and nose so I couldn't smell anything else.

Somebody slaughtered my parents.

Somebody killed Seraphina.

Now, those same people had murdered my colleagues.

I slowed down my breathing and steadied my heart.

There was nothing left to do but to find those responsible and kill every motherfucking one of them.

Chapter 20

Smoke and Mirrors

DI Jenkins took Caroline and me to the hospital. I coughed most of the way there because of the smoke still in my lungs, but I was okay apart from that. Then she drove me home.

'Should I organise a counsellor to visit you?'

I shook my head. 'This isn't the first time I've had to watch people die, remember?'

'Do you have any idea why somebody would set fire to your workplace?'

'So, it was arson?' I inquired, seeking confirmation.

'That's right. The chief fire officer confirmed it while the paramedics were checking you over. Someone hurled petrol bombs into the building and deliberately blocked all the exits. It seems there were multiple individuals involved. Unfortunately, the CCTV cameras in the vicinity were not working.'

'If you hadn't been at my flat, I would have been inside the shop when the fire started.'

'Do you believe it was meant for you?'

I shrugged, a mixture of uncertainty and resignation in my response. 'Death seems to have a way of following me.'

'Why would anyone want to harm you?'

'Perhaps it's connected to the unresolved murders of my parents,' I suggested, my voice tinged with sadness and a lingering sense of unease.

'It appears to be more than a coincidence,' she said.

'The police haven't got very far in discovering who killed my mother and father ten years ago.'

DI Jenkins sighed. 'It's not my investigation, but I'll need to look at the original case files.'

'Are you in charge of investigating the Meads?'

'I'm part of that team, but it looks like we'll have to expand our searches because of what happened today.'

'You were the lucky one who got to talk to me?'

'I guess so.' She removed a card from her pocket and gave it to me. 'That's my number if you need to speak about anything.'

I glanced at her number. 'How long have you been a copper?'

'Twenty years. Why?'

'So, you were around when my parents died?'

'I was, but it wasn't my case.'

'Did you work with Seraphina or Gemma?'

'No, they were in a different unit.'

'The witness protection program?'

'Yes. Did Seraphina tell you that?'

'No, Gemma did at the funeral.' I opened the door and stepped out. 'Do you have contacts at the NCA?'

'The National Crime Agency? Sure, why?'

'No reason,' I said. 'There's one other thing that struck me as I gazed into that fire.'

'What?'

'Well, what if this whole business has been about me all along? What if somebody wanted me dead a decade ago, the skinny ten-year-old me, and now they're trying to finish what they started?'

'Why would anyone want to kill a child?'

I shrugged. 'I don't know. That's your job to find out.'

Leaving DI Jenkins to ponder my words, I returned to the flat. I kicked off my shoes and slumped into a chair, the weight of the recent events crashing down on me. I sat there, numb, the echoes of the blaze replaying in my mind. The haunting images of my colleagues consumed by flames, the acrid scent of smoke, and the blaring sirens pierced my addled brain.

For as long as I could remember, I had considered myself resilient and unbreakable, like a fortress. Nothing could penetrate my defences. Now I knew I was wrong.

Tears streamed down my face, a torrent of emotions surging within me. The injustice of it all weighed on my heart. My parents and colleagues, innocent people lost in a senseless crossfire, their existence abruptly extinguished. The burden of guilt pressed down on me, engulfing me in its suffocating grip. If I hadn't taken the lives of Mead and Beck, would Sid, Ted, and Dave still be alive?

Was it all my fault?

Wiping away my tears, I took a deep breath, gathering my strength. It was time to take action. But where to begin? Neither John Mead nor Nathan Beck had provided me with any leads.

Fatigue swept through me. It would have been easy to close my eyes and fall asleep, but my anger wouldn't let me. I needed somewhere to start, but where?

I glanced across the room and saw something useful: the notebook Seraphina had hidden in her flat and the paper from Gemma's place. I ignored the ache in my legs, got up, and grabbed them both. I flicked through the book first, staring at the names and addresses, desperate to recognise anything. But I didn't. Then, there was the paper and the mention of the Woods and the NCA.

The Woods. They had to be an organised crime family or people connected to criminal activity.

Perhaps I should have told DI Jenkins about it. I removed her card from my pocket, staring at the number as if it was a lottery ticket and I was about to win the jackpot.

Then, another idea struck me. If the killers had started the fire in the shop to get to me, what would stop them from attacking me in the flat? I wasn't safe. And my neighbours weren't either, not when the murderers could firebomb the building.

As that thought crushed my spirit, there was a knock at the door.

'Enola, are you okay?' It was Ginger's voice. Then her dog barked. 'Bruce and I were about to take Kronos for a walk and wondered if you wanted anything?'

'I've brought your Stooges CD back,' Bruce said.

I needed to get away from the building to keep them and the other residents safe, but I couldn't leave Dirty Harry alone.

'The door's unlocked. Come on in.'

The door was hardly open before Kronos bounded in and ran for me, slobbering all over my face before I could stop him.

'Don't you feed this mutt?' I said as I struggled with him on the sofa.

Bruce dragged the whippet off me. 'Leave her be, boy.'

Ginger sat next to me and put her arm around my

shoulders. 'We heard what happened at the shop, Enola. How are you feeling?'

They'd been my neighbours for a year – both of them ten years my senior – and they were my only friends apart from Harry now Seraphina was gone: my only human friends.

'I'm fine.' I glanced at Bruce with his dark eyes and nervous twitch. 'Do you need to vape?' I asked him.

He shook his head. 'It's about time I gave up. I've been a nicotine fiend since I smoked my first cigarette on my fifteenth birthday, perched on some steps during my school lunch break. Everybody else was doing it, so I thought, why not? It tasted disgusting, like I was sucking on bonfire fumes while eating a hot potato.' Bruce was a natural storyteller, and I assumed he wanted to say something to distract me from the day's events. 'But I persevered, and soon I was hooked. I must have looked like some Dickensian urchin, trailing around town in my school uniform, puffing on a ciggie and pretending to be cool.'

Ginger laughed. 'You should have seen him when we first met. As well as smoking over a hundred cigarettes a week, he was sharing a flat with two mates and ten cats.'

This was news to me. 'Ten cats? Why so many?'

He shrugged. 'My parents had many animals around the house when I was growing up.' He glanced at Dirty Harry chewing on insects in his habitat. 'Proper pets they were, so I've always loved having something cute and fury in the house. They just seemed to flock to me when I was at university, strays and orphans. And you can't turn them away, can you?'

Ginger grinned at him, and he returned the warmth of her smile. When I first moved into the flat, I assumed they were a couple, but she soon put me right about that.

'We met at university, but it's never been like that between us. We're much better as mates.'

I'd warmed to them both immediately. And they were the only people I could trust now.

'I need you to do me a favour,' I said.

'Anything,' they replied together.

I walked over to Dirty Harry's enclosure and dropped more food inside. 'I have to leave for a few days and hoped you could look after Harry for me.'

Bruce grimaced, but Ginger beamed. 'Of course. You know I've always loved the little fella.'

Kronos went to the container and peered through the glass at the tarantula. 'Great, just don't feed him to the mutt.'

'Are you sure you're okay, Enola?' Bruce said.

I nodded. 'I'm fine, but with the funeral and now today, I need a break from here to reset my brain, you know?'

Ginger agreed. 'Yeah, sure we do.' She glanced at Bruce. 'Would you like me to give you something to heal your aura?'

She was a practitioner in healing energies and all things mystical. She might even have been a Wiccan, but I refused her generous offer.

'I'll be all right.'

Bruce approached me. 'I've just made a killing online if you need money.'

'Fucking hell, Bruce!' Ginger shouted.

'What?' he said. 'Enola knows we'd give her anything we have.'

Outside of Seraphina, they were generally the nicest people I'd ever met. And now I didn't know about Seraphina.

Ginger dragged him to the side and whispered in his ear.

'It's okay, guys. I don't need anything, but thanks for the offer.'

He pulled away from her and looked sheepish. 'Ah, Enola, I'm sorry for my poor choice of words. I shouldn't have said I made a killing.' His cheeks turned pink. 'You know how useless us computer people are with the real world.'

Ginger punched him in the arm, and he scowled. 'Enola's an IT manager.'

'I was,' I replied.

It suddenly struck me that I was out of a job and had no money apart from a few hundred quid, not even any savings. And the rent was due next week.

'Well,' Bruce said. 'The offer is always there.'

I grabbed both of their hands. 'You're such good friends to me, but I'll be fine after a few days away from here.'

I let go of them and filled a bag with clothes, a few other essentials, plus the notebook and paper.

'Where will you go?' Ginger asked. 'To see Amy?'

I laughed. 'Amy? I haven't seen her for four years, and we hardly separated on the best terms.' She'd tried to stab me with a knife she'd given me as a birthday present. 'No, I'll go somewhere where nobody knows me.' Which wouldn't be too difficult.

I moved to the window and peered outside. There appeared to be more shadows than normal.

Or was it my paranoia?

It didn't matter. I couldn't stay in the flat.

But where to go?

Chapter 21

Death and Night and Blood

I stepped into the darkness, inhaling the aromas of wet dogs and stale pizzas. Moonlight danced in the puddles, reflecting a shimmering mosaic at my feet. Contemplating my next move, I weighed my options. A hotel seemed too predictable, where my pursuers could easily track me down. Seeking refuge at a shelter carried its own risks; trust was a luxury I couldn't afford. Rain dropped on me, its touch dampening the card clutched in my hand. I glanced at DI Jenkins's contact details, but doubts swirled within me. How could I trust her when even the chief constable had proven corrupt?

A sudden recollection stirred, reminding me of something I'd saved in my phone four years ago when I left the children's home. It was a minor miracle I'd transferred it to every new mobile since. I navigated through my contacts, searching for the details of the Network, a lifeline of safe houses for children and women in need. I dialled the number, the sound of each ring resonating through the silence, but my expectations remained low, doubting if anyone would answer on the other end after all this time.

That was until a woman answered. 'Do you require help?'

'I need somewhere safe to stay.'

'Are you on your own?'

'Yes.'

She provided me with an address and ended the call. The location was an hour's walk away, but I couldn't take the risk of hailing a taxi. So instead, casting wary glances everywhere, I double-checked nobody was watching me before setting off through the downpour.

I trudged through the waterlogged streets, my jacket wrapped around me, attempting to blend into the bustling crowd. The relentless deluge pelted my face and soaked my hair, yet the discomfort barely registered. The weight of recent events consumed me as the rain thrashed against the pavement. Lost in my thoughts, the world seemed blurred, and the people passing by were mere phantoms detached from my existence.

As I walked, I passed alleyways, doorways, and shops, their windows barricaded and abandoned. Some souls had sought refuge within those neglected spaces, huddled against the unforgiving night and terrible weather. The glow of streetlights cast an ethereal orange hue upon the rippling puddles. In their shimmering reflection, the fires that had devoured my life this past decade seemed to dance, their fiery tongues licking at my consciousness.

Despite the chill in the air, every fibre of my being simmered with internal heat. Seraphina's hidden notebook had to be important. Why else would she have concealed it in her flat?

The bridge loomed ahead, and I paused, gazing into the expanse of the river. The rain continued its descent, tapping against my hood like a drum and bass playlist on a loop.

Cool droplets cascaded upon my skin, soaking my clothing and sending shivers through every inch of me. The water flowed with restless energy, a turbulent mass reflecting the city lights like an infinite array of glistening diamonds.

The steady pattern of rain provided a constant backdrop to my tortured thoughts. Closing my eyes, I inhaled deeply, allowing the crisp fragrance of the deluge to cleanse my senses. It carried a purity and freshness, washing away the urban pollution and grime, granting a momentary respite.

Suddenly, the wind roared, thrusting my hair across my face. Brushing it aside, I surveyed a labyrinth of streets, buildings, people, and vehicles sprawled everywhere. Somewhere within the vast expanse, those who wanted me dead lurked. Their identities had to be concealed inside Seraphina's precious book.

I removed it from my bag and opened it, huddled over to keep the rain off the pages. There were six names and addresses, all of which were local. Why were they important to her?

The closest was half a mile away from where I was heading.

And on the way.

I rushed across the bridge, increasing my pace while disregarding the scattered presence of weary souls who occasionally obstructed my path. A stray dog became my brief companion for a few miles before darting off in pursuit of a rat. I empathised with it, for I also chased an elusive prey.

As I jogged through the rain with the notebook pressed against my chest, the freezing wind nipped at my face, injecting ice into my flesh and bones. My empty stomach growled, a reminder I hadn't eaten since God knows when.

Then, a tantalising aroma of sizzling, fried food saturated the air. A street van beckoned me from a few hundred yards away, and I hastened towards it. The vendor, once a skilled Syrian surgeon adept at saving lives, now plied his trade by offering warm grub to city dwellers. He told me his life story as I ordered and waited, listening to a tale even worse than mine. I bought a burger and inquired about the first address recorded in Seraphina's book.

'Sure, I know it. It's just around the corner on the next street. It's an old church.'

I shovelled warm food into my eager mouth. 'Church? Is it closed?'

He nodded. 'They had to shut it down. There were too many scandals they couldn't cover up anymore. Nobody would go there.'

I thanked him and headed for the church. I'd never been religious, but with hot food in my belly and renewed vigour in my bones, I finally found my faith.

Chapter 22

Redemption Song

I woke with aching limbs and a throbbing head, lying in a lumpy, uncomfortable bed in a damp room. My legs shook as I crawled from the sheets and into the bathroom, standing on cracked tiles and peering at the lines on my face. I stumbled into the shower and turned it on, attacked by a jet of icy water, unable to increase the temperature no matter what I did.

The cold brought me to life, and I couldn't complain too much. When I arrived after midnight, the woman at the door could easily have sent me away. However, she didn't, and I was grateful.

I lurched out of the shower and brushed my teeth, waiting for the over-excited drilling in my head to fade. Then I dressed and sat on the bed, checking the news on my phone. The police had confirmed the fire at Bits & Bytes as arson and were treating it as murder. I skipped past the online details about my colleagues, finding it impossible to look at the photos of Ted, Dave, and Sid. They'd died because of me.

Nathan Beck's death was the main story in the news,

with every site calling it a tragic accident. The theory was he'd stumbled into the stand while confused by too much drink and drugs and knocked the tank over. That had resulted in it falling on him, spreading water and piranhas everywhere. Then, the inevitable happened. There was no mention of the stab wounds in his legs, so I assumed the deadly beasts had done an excellent job covering those up.

Many online comments said it was his fault for having the illegal fish. Then there were the posts accusing him of decades of sexual assault. I peered at his photo and remembered his expression when he threatened me.

Finally, there were the Meads, their deaths described as a murder-suicide by the chief constable. There was no reason given why John Mead would do such a thing, but I found plenty of rumours on social media about how he'd resented his wife leaving him for a woman.

Best of all, nobody had connected the three events. Yet. I wondered how DI Jenkins was doing with her investigation. I considered calling to tell her where I was when the aroma of fried food crept into my room and attacked my senses. I jumped off the bed and went downstairs, stepping into the kitchen as a purple-haired woman with a Bob Marley t-shirt cooked bacon and eggs.

'Nice top,' I said.

She smiled at me. 'Same for you.' I was wearing my *Never Mind the Bollocks* shirt. 'You must be the one who turned up late last night.'

'Enola.' I didn't see any point in lying about my name. I wasn't a spy.

'I'm Raeni,' she said. 'Are you hungry?'

A thousand tiny fingers clawed at my guts. 'Starving.'

'Sit then, and we'll have a chat. Tea or coffee?'

'Coffee.'

She placed a steaming mug before me, followed by bacon, eggs, and toast. My eyes widened at the food. 'What if I was a vegetarian?'

Raeni laughed. 'Then you'd be out of luck.' She sipped at her drink. 'You don't have to tell me why you're here, but I have to know if anybody will come looking for you. There are others we must protect.'

Would the killers be searching for me? I wasn't sure, but it seemed likely considering what they'd done at the computer shop. So, I'd made another mistake. I couldn't put more people in danger.

I bit through a delicious piece of bacon. 'I won't be here long.' I removed Seraphina's notebook from my pocket. 'Can I ask you about the church nearby?' I hadn't dwelled outside it last night, staying just long enough to notice it had been shut for a while, with its boarded-up broken windows and overgrown weeds covering the front.

'You look a bit young to be a journalist?'

I laughed. 'A journo? God, no. Why would a reporter be interested in a run-down church?'

'Why are you?'

The coffee warmed my throat. 'My father used to go there.' A lie. 'Before he died, he said I should visit the place as it meant so much to him.' Another lie.

I was good at lying.

Raeni buttered a slice of toast. 'That must have been a while ago. St Peter's has been closed for ten years at least.'

St Peter's? I opened the notebook and looked at the names, this time paying more attention.

Peters, Cooks, Stanway, Toon, Daly & Palmer.

I'd assumed they were all surnames, none of which I recognised.

I showed her them. 'Do you recognise any of these?'

She ate her toast and scrutinised the text. 'St Peter's is the church. Cook was the local funeral parlour; then there was the Stanway Community Centre. Toon is the nickname of the estate pub, the George and Dragon, because Geordies run it, but only locals call it that. Daly was likely the corner shop, the Daly Daily. I guess Palmer is probably the Palmer Nursing Home. They're all buildings within a three-mile radius of here, though only two are still open.'

My heart raced like a freight train as I used my tongue to loosen the bacon stuck in my teeth. 'Which ones?'

'The nursing home and the pub. Conveniently, they're right next to each other. Unfortunately, a shit government and failed economy did for the rest.'

'Including the church?'

She shook her head. 'Well, no. I didn't want to mention it since you said your father was part of the congregation, but....'

'There was a scandal?'

Raeni sighed. 'It's terrible how such horrible things can happen in your community, and you know nothing about it until it's too late.' She placed her hands on the table. 'More than one priest was involved, lasting over thirty years. Did your dad mention any of their names?'

'No. Was it child abuse?'

Her fingers trembled as she put one hand on the other. 'Yeah. I tried not to read about it in the news, but sometimes you can't help yourself, can you?'

I finished breakfast, and we sat in silence. There wasn't much else to say.

Then, a teenage girl walked in, chewing gum as if it was her first meal of the day.

'All right, Raeni.' She stared at me. 'Another newbie?'

I smiled at her, and she scuttled off upstairs. Was she in danger because I was there?

My stomach rumbled with satisfaction as I stood. 'I guess you get all ages here.'

She grabbed the dirty plates and put them in the sink. 'You got any plans for today?'

I slipped the notebook into my pocket. 'Just a bit of sightseeing.'

She was whistling "Redemption Song" when I left the house.

Chapter 23

Like A Prayer

I inserted my headphones, their cords tangling in my fingers, and with a press of a button, the Dead Kennedys were having a holiday in Cambodia.

The church was a three-minute walk away, and I strode along, passing stray dogs and truanting kids who should have been confined within the walls of a school. Twelve-year-old boys catcalled me, their audacity met with swift retaliation as the girls delivered resounding slaps to their heads. Last night's rain still lingered on the streets, forming scattered puddles containing discarded cigarette packets and used condoms.

As I neared the church, a scraggy black cat perched on the wall, its emerald eyes glaring at me. If I'd believed in such things, I might have thought it was a witch's familiar, judging every step I took.

Approaching the worn-out structure, I resisted the urge to delve into the scandalous details of its history through online searches, saving that for later. I pushed open the unlocked door. The pale wood groaned in protest, echoing through the corridor.

Inside, deterioration and decay had seized their domain. Once vibrant and enchanting, the stained glass windows were dirty and cracked, casting fractured light upon the grimy and graffiti-laden walls. Everywhere smelt of damp and rot, irritating my senses.

I had little experience of visiting religious places. Only one of my former children's homes could have been described as spiritual, and I think that was because the woman in charge was a Wiccan. She was nice but didn't last long. Having to deal with forty troublesome kids every day must have frazzled her nerves. No amount of well-being could have dealt with that.

The cracked windows let a dim, filtered light seep into the desolate space, casting elongated shadows that danced across the peeling paint and crumbling stone. A sense of eerie stillness enveloped me as I stood there, broken only by the scurrying sounds within the walls and the occasional haunting echo of dripping water.

In disarray, the pews lay smashed and overturned, with fragments of torn Bibles scattered amidst rat droppings. Yet, traces of its former grandeur remained visible in the intricate carvings and ornate designs that adorned the building. I reached out, my hand brushing against the rough stone, tracing the weathered ridges and deep grooves with my fingertips. The tactile connection to the past brought me a mix of emotions.

A tremendous crashing sound from the back made me jump. My heart raced as I peered into the shadows, trying to determine what caused the noise. I touched the knife in my jacket and strode to the rear of the church, walking over the crushed stone and other bits of rubble until I reached a half-open door.

'Is anybody there?' I said.

I removed the blade from my pocket when there was no answer. Sunlight snuck in through the broken window above me, shimmering off the knife as I saw my reflection. It was half my face, iridescent in the steel. It didn't look like me, as if I'd been replaced by a pod person ten years ago, and I only realised it now.

Pod people had no emotions, so I couldn't be one. I had enough anger burning in me to light the sun during an eclipse.

Then I heard something behind me, and I twisted around with the blade pushed out before me. It was no protection as a set of bookshelves tumbled forward. My reflexes took my hands up and caught the shelves. Small figurines of Jesus and the Virgin Mary slid off, hitting me in the head and chest as the weight forced me down. They crashed on top of me as I hit the floor, a surge of pain shooting through my back. I still held the knife as I flung the shelves off me and searched for an attacker while Jesus and his mother rolled across my ribs.

I jumped up, seeing nobody.

That was until something landed on my shoulders and stuck its claws into me.

I yelled as the cat shrieked. I stumbled into the wall, and the moggie dropped and stood on Jesus's head. The porcelain cracked, and the animal hissed at me.

I put the knife away. 'What did I ever do to you?'

Its jade eyes shimmered as it ran out of the room. I followed it, wiping the dust from my clothes. There was a twinge in my neck as I sat in the only pew left upright. It wasn't comfortable, designed to inflict pain on whoever was unwise enough to use it, but I needed to rest my legs. The cat gazed at me from a few feet away. I rubbed my head, feeling foolish for thinking the moggie was sent to the church to kill me.

Yet, it still seemed likely someone would look for me. That had to be the reason someone torched the computer shop.

And that meant I'd put those at the safe house in danger. I'd have to get my bag and find somewhere else to stay.

But where?

I removed the card from my pocket and called DI Jenkins's number.

'It's Enola Gray,' I said when she answered.

'I've had officers at your flat twice. Where are you?'

I glanced at the cat and the broken Jesus. 'In a house of God. Do you have any news about who attacked the computer shop?'

'No. Tell me where you are?'

'Do you believe the Mead's deaths were murder-suicide?'

'That's what my superiors say.'

'That's not what happened.'

'How do you know, Enola?'

I paused. 'Because I was there.'

'Where are you?'

'Can I trust you?'

'Why wouldn't you?'

'It's simple, Detective Inspector Jenkins. My parents were in a witness protection program, but John Mead betrayed them. I don't know what his rank was in the police force ten years ago, but he was a chief inspector until a couple of days ago. He was the one who gave their location away. I still don't know who to, though.'

'How do you know this?'

'Gemma Mead told me. She had evidence of what happened that she got from Seraphina. So that's why both of them were murdered.'

'Seraphina Shaw died of cancer.'

'No, somebody killed her and then covered it up. John Mead admitted that to me. You should see who signed her death certificate since I'm guessing there wasn't an autopsy. You must also get her body dug up and checked for foul play.'

'Sounds like I need to do a lot.'

'More than you know, DI Jenkins. Do you want to hear the rest?'

'Go on.'

'Gemma revealed some of this at Seraphina's funeral. Then Sid drove us to the chief constable's place.'

'You lied about that.'

'Gemma instructed me to stay outside while she confronted her estranged husband, but I didn't. He confessed to his involvement in my parents' deaths before shooting his wife. Then, before I could do anything, three masked men burst into the house and attacked him. I fled and told Sid to drive away, but whoever was in charge of all this must have known I was there, which resulted in the attack on the computer shop. When you left me yesterday, I realised they'd come after me, so I quit the flat.'

And I hoped they wouldn't go there and put Ginger and Bruce in danger.

'This sounds like a conspiracy long in the making, maybe a decade.'

'Probably more since my parents changed their names before I was born, so at least twenty years.'

'And there is police involvement high up the command chain?'

'Absolutely. I can't believe John Mead was the only one.'

Another pause.

'How do you know you can trust me?'

'I don't, so I won't tell you where I am. Not yet. I need to discover who's trying to kill me first.'

More silence.

'So why are you telling me this?'

'It's a test of your honesty, Detective Inspector Jenkins. That and your loyalty. All of this might be news to you and have nothing to do with you, but that doesn't mean you'll do the right thing if it means grassing on your colleagues. The only person more corrupt than a police officer is a politician.'

'But you want me to do something?'

'As I said, get Seraphina's death certificate and see who signed it. There are plenty of dishonest doctors available.'

'Anything else?'

'Yeah, have a sniff around your colleagues, especially those investigating the Mead's deaths. Anyone who looked at John Mead's body would have seen it wasn't suicide.'

'How do you know that?'

'Because I heard him screaming.'

Sometimes, I still did.

'When should I ring you, Enola?'

'You won't. I'll call you.'

Then I hung up.

The cat had buggered off, leaving me with the heads of Jesus and the Virgin Mary.

I stared at them and wondered what to do next, hoping for divine intervention.

Chapter 24

Down in the Park

I slipped into the safe house unnoticed, retrieving my bag without a sound. Leaving a note on the bed for Raeni, I expressed my gratitude before setting out on my mission to visit the other locations on the list. With the GPS on my phone, I navigated the streets, the Stranglers blaring in my ears, their rendition of "Walk on By" adding a sense of urgency to my steps.

'With the right music, you either forget or remember everything.' Seraphina's words echoed in my mind, one of her many insightful sayings that had stayed with me. I glanced up into the drizzle, peering into the misty clouds as if searching for her familiar face. I wasn't a believer in an afterlife or a higher power, but somehow, it felt like her spirit lingered, watching over me. She'd been my guiding light since our first meeting in the children's home, and now I was lost without her.

The weight of the what-ifs burdened my thoughts as I strode into the desolate expanse of a disused industrial estate, a shortcut suggested by the GPS. The once-thriving buildings loomed above me, their towering presence casting long shadows. Broken windows and graffiti embellished the walls. Discarded rubbish covered the ground, producing a bitter odour of decay.

I surveyed the factories, garages, and workshops, reduced to dilapidated shells. Ghostly figures seemed to linger in the shadows, haunting reminders of the past. Above me, a gathering of dark birds soared, their presence resembling vultures on the hunt, scavengers in search of justice for a lost soul.

Leaving them behind, I ventured into another housing estate, where once affordable council houses and flats now belonged to those trapped in an endless cycle of ownership. Walking along the deserted street, my footsteps reverberated off the decaying buildings, creating an eerie symphony of echoes. Amongst the desolation, I noticed an elderly woman seated on a weathered bench. She peered at the ground, her eyes vacant and distant. As I drew closer, she slowly raised her head, meeting my gaze with a blank expression. It was unclear if she was truly alive or only a mere shell of her former self. Strands of her hair bore the hue of a wounded stray dog. Her lips parted, revealing a mouth garlanded with only a few remaining teeth, like a crumbling facade.

'Are you lost, love?'

'I'm fine,' I said. 'Are you okay?'

She removed a slice of bread from her purse and nibbled on it. 'I am since I visited the food bank. I don't know what I'd do without them.' We were in one of the wealthiest countries in the world, and this poor woman had to survive on the generosity of others. 'I like your shirt. You better watch out that the rats around here don't try to take it from you.'

I assumed she was talking about the two-legged kind.

'Thanks for the warning.'

She leaned closer to me. 'Everywhere you look, smog obscures the sky. The once lively waterways are stagnant, shit fills the rivers, and harsh reality suffocates our dreams. The town is built of concrete and steel, and the buildings are crumbling, lacking the harmony and beauty depicted in song. Danger lurks in every corner, and injustice is a constant presence. Meanwhile, the struggles of daily life persist, leaving little time to pause and enjoy a cup of tea.' She reached into her bag and removed a small teapot. 'Would you like a cuppa, love?'

I shook my head. 'No, thanks. I'm on my way to the Stanway Community Centre. Do you know it?'

'Do I know it?' She patted the empty spot on the bench next to her. 'I worked there for years before the bastards closed it down. Come and sit here, and I'll tell you about it.'

I thanked my luck for bumping into her, removed my backpack, and sat.

'When did it shut?'

She scrunched up her face. 'What year is it?' I told her. 'Then it was a decade ago.'

'What happened?'

'Well, it was like everything else once owned by the council until the government forced them to sell it to a private company. They arrived and said it would all be sweetness and light, unicorns and roses, but soon enough, they started cutting jobs and wages. I went there for the Book Club and the Bridge afternoons. Lovely it was, what with all those young blokes in their 50s reading from the latest novels. I always made them read the juiciest bits from *Fifty Shades of Grey* and all those terrible sequels. That certainly warmed you up on a chilly afternoon, I can tell you.'

I guessed what must have happened. 'So, they eventually closed it.'

'Aye, with tall tales of building a bigger and better community centre, but that never materialised. So now it sits with the rest of them, concrete dinosaurs waiting to collapse into nothing.'

'Do you know the Daly Daily corner shop?'

'Of course. I used to shop there, even though it was more expensive than the supermarket.' She winked at me. 'You have to support your local community, don't you? Otherwise, we're all fucked.'

I laughed at her language. 'You got that right, but what happened to the shop?'

'The Daly Daily? Same as the community centre; it was bought out so the new owners could convert it into posh flats.' She snorted laughter out of her nose. 'Can you imagine posh flats around here? The scumbags would ransack them the first night.'

'The property developers went bust?'

She shrugged. 'Who knows? Probably. All it is now is a haven for druggies and creepers.'

'And the funeral parlour, Cook?'

'Ah, poor old Henry Cook. He inherited that place from his father, but I don't think he wanted it. He was too much of a sensitive soul to spend all his time around death, not that he worked as a mortician. He left that to others. Henry and I went to the same school. I can tell you he feared his own shadow. I guess all the rumours finally got to him, and he sold up. He died ten years ago, hit by a car while coming out of the boozer. And the coppers never found the bastard who did it.'

'Was it the George and Dragon pub?'

'The Toon? Aye. It's a right shitting dump, one of those

places where they give you a weapon as you go in. You should keep well away from it.'

'You mentioned something about rumours.'

She threw bits of bread at her feet, and a group of pigeons descended for a feeding frenzy. 'Oh, yes, they really hurt Henry's business, all those tales of his staff getting bodies mixed up in the back room and of missing limbs. All nasty stuff, it was. And there was that creepy doctor always hanging around there. I'm sure he was a necro.'

'Doctor?'

She nodded. 'Somebody from the local hospital. I don't recall his name. I think he worked in the mortuary.'

'Do you know anything about the Palmer Nursing Home?'

She laughed and wiped the spit from her lips. 'That place? Only that I don't have enough money to stay there. Anyway, I'd not want to live with those poor buggers who look in the mirror and can't recognise themselves.' She gazed wistfully at the birds. 'Still, my first-ever boyfriend is there now. I visit him for old time's sake.' She put one hand on my leg. 'Eddie loved me, you see, but his family were snobs, and I was just a girl from the wrong side of the tracks, and those Wood bastards always had their noses stuck up their arses.'

I jerked forward, scaring the pigeons, so they burst into the air in a flutter of feathers and beaks. 'Wood?'

'Aye, the Woods of Waverley Street we called them when they started thinking they were better than the rest of us because they won some cash on the lottery and flashed it around on big houses and fancy cars.'

'Do they still live here?'

She bit her fingernail, and a yellow piece of it came away.

'Oh no, they moved a while back. Eddie's the only one here now, in the nursing home. You'd think they'd look after him better with all their money, but I guess he upset them, so they dumped him with the other old duffers who can't remember who they are.' She touched my arm. 'You must promise me, love, that you won't let me end up like that. Just find me in the park and put a pillow over my head; that'll do.'

I smiled at her. My brain was overloaded with everything I'd heard. I'd intended to visit all the buildings on Seraphina's list, even the closed ones, but now I had to get to that nursing home and speak to Eddie Wood.

Could the Woods on the list be this family the old woman mentioned?

'What's your name?' I asked her.

'Why, it's Lizzie.'

'I'm Enola, Lizzie. How would you like to see Eddie right now?'

Lizzie discarded her broken nail and checked her surroundings.

'Why not, Enola? It's not like I'm doing anything important, is it?'

She laughed, and I joined in as I helped her off the bench.

Then we set off to see a man about murder.

Chapter 25

Secret Life

I thought it might be a problem getting past the security at the nursing home, but it wasn't since they didn't have any. The receptionist smiled at Lizzie and believed the lies about me being her granddaughter and that we were there to visit Eddie.

'So she can see the first boy I ever kissed.'

The woman with Mary on her name badge shook her head. 'I don't think he'll remember you, Lizzie, but you can try. It might dislodge something in his noggin.' She pressed a buzzer, and the door opened. 'You know where he is.'

The strong scent of disinfectant and old age hit me as I walked down the sterile, white-walled halls. The musty smell of decline and neglect filled my nostrils as Lizzie led the way, taking us past a large area where residents sat staring into space.

We arrived at Eddie Wood's room, my heart clawing at my chest as I stepped inside. Bright-coloured paintings of flowers dotted the walls, and the surroundings reminded me of ten years in several children's homes. The age groups were different, but I saw the similarities: one group waited for the freedom of age, while the other understood how it was a prison.

'This is Eddie's room,' Lizzie said.

She pushed open the door without knocking. Eddie was sitting on the bed as we approached. Confusion filled his yellowing and wrinkled face as he gazed at me. His cloudy blue eyes squinted in suspicion, his voice trembling.

'Who are you?'

'Don't you know?' I asked.

He shook his head and sighed. 'I remember little these days.'

Lizzie sat near him and took his hand in hers. 'What about me, lover?'

Drool dripped over his lips as he smiled at her. 'Oh, I'll never forget you, darling.'

I watched them hold each other, their grins as wide as the horizon, and I wondered what I was doing there. How could an old man who'd lost his memory help me? He hadn't ordered people to set the Bits & Bytes shop on fire. It wasn't him trying to kill me.

I turned to leave, only stopping when he spoke.

'I know why you're here, Enola.'

My legs froze as my heart transformed into a block of ice. I put a hand on a table to steady myself and looked at him.

'What?'

'Show me your hands,' he said

I did. 'Is this your fault, Eddie?'

Tears streamed down his cheeks. 'They knew you were in the house, but they didn't care. Then later, I read about you in the papers, about how you tried to pull your mam and dad out of the burning building even though they were already dead. So when I found out you were going into an orphanage, I said I'd adopt you, but he wouldn't let me. And he sent me away. That's why he keeps me locked in here.'

The pressure on my chest was unbearable, as if the moon had crashed out of the sky and was inside me, desperate to burst through my ribs. My legs and arms trembled as my throat transformed into a desert. I fought to breathe and grabbed the glass of water on the table, downing it in one, but I felt no better.

I gazed at him. 'Who?'

'Jack, it was my brother Jack who did it all. And then he punished me because I wanted to help you.'

I struggled to keep my anger under control. 'Why? Why would he do that?'

The tears congealed on his lips, slipping over and down his shirt.

'I don't know. Mum and Dad ran the business; Jack was the one they trusted. I was only there to do as commanded and never ask questions. They said it was better that way if the coppers spoke to me.'

I dug my nails into my palms and bit my top lip. The blood tasted sweet, and I wanted more of it. But not my own. 'Did you know my parents?'

His eyes glazed over, and I thought his memory had gone again. Lizzie squeezed his hand, and I wondered if she'd known about what he and his family were involved in.

'I saw their photos,' he said. 'Of the ones with you.' He gazed at me. 'You looked so much like the daughter I'd lost, and I wanted to help you.' He turned to Lizzie. 'Doesn't she look like our little Tina?'

Lizzie wiped the tears from his eyes and kissed his forehead. 'She does. I thought that when I saw her in the street.'

He beamed at her. 'It's a sign, love. God sent her here as an act of forgiveness and redemption.'

The blood slipped from my palms and onto the carpet. 'Who requires forgiveness, Eddie?'

His smile only made him seem more fragile. 'Why, all of us. Forgiveness and redemption, that's all there is in this life.'

'Should I forgive you?' I said.

He wiped the snot from his nose across his arm, and everything vanished from his eyes. He jerked his hand from Lizzie and stared at her like a sheep staring at a fox.

'Who are you? What are you doing here?'

I watched him piss himself and shook my head. Then I stepped out of the room as the stink of urine drifted over me.

Lizzie followed me outside. 'I'm sorry about that, Enola.'

I scowled at her. 'How long have you known what he did?'

Darkness covered her face. 'Since it happened. We've kept no secrets. He couldn't do anything to prevent it. His parents and brother were too strong for that, but he wanted to help you afterwards. Yet he couldn't do that either.' She wiped away tears. 'And now he can't even wipe his own arse.'

I had to stop myself from reaching over and strangling her. 'He could have gone to the police and told them everything.'

She shook her head. 'Of course he couldn't. The Woods had bent coppers falling out of their pockets. They still do.'

I slammed my hand into the wall and disturbed a painting of a cat licking a dog's nose. 'They're alive?'

'Eddie's brother, Jack, and his mother, Mel, yes.'

'Good,' I said as I left her and stormed out of the building. I'd finally learned something valuable. The clouds had burst, and the rain soaked me as I got my phone out, deliberating whether or not to call DI Jenkins.

That's when somebody punched me in the side of the head.

Chapter 26

Red Rain

As my bag fell off me, I hit the ground, sprawling into frozen, murky puddles. A thunderous blast pulverised my ears as a dull ache sped through me. Amidst the ringing in my head, somebody swore at me. I recoiled as a hand reached for me, springing to my feet. Blood trickled down my face, mingling with the raindrops, adding a crimson sheen to my vision.

I blinked rapidly, staring at three giant apes. 'Which one of you twats did this?'

A teenager wearing Manchester United shorts and a shirt with David Beckham's face on it waved a bony finger at me. 'Who said you could speak to my grandad?'

'Eddie Wood?' I replied.

'I'm going to skin you for that.'

I shook the confusion from my head. 'You're too little to make that big a mistake, kid.'

He ran at me, and I stepped aside, kicking him in the back of the knee as he went. The pavement gave him a warm welcome as he swan-dived into a shit-stained puddle. I ignored him and studied the other two. They were much older than him, not moving and just watching me.

'That's funny what you did there to Billy,' the dark-haired one said. 'That made my fucking day.' He wiped long, wet yellow hair from his face. 'It might even make it worthwhile coming out in this piss storm.' He spat a huge, green thing at my feet. I thought he could have some fungal disease for a second until I realised it was chewing gum. 'But he's right. You shouldn't have spoken to our Eddie without permission.'

Billy crawled through the rain to his relatives. 'Is your name Wood?' I asked.

The big fella shook his head while the other one kept quiet. 'Our names don't matter. What you were doing bothering Gramps is the important thing.'

'It was no bother. Eddie loved the company and said his family never visited him now, especially his brother. He gave me a message to deliver to Jack. Do you know where he is?'

Chewing Gum Guy popped another piece in his mouth as the other bloke helped Billy. 'What message?'

The rain increased and swam down my nose. 'He told his brother to give me a job. I'm one of the vast unemployed now since somebody burned down my place of work, ready to do anything to make this country great again. Do you need a general house worker with plenty of experience cooking terrible meals and never cleaning the shower? How about a quiet, refined travelling companion who speaks fluent gibberish? Or an assistant dog-walker? Or a private tie straightener? Or a lady car-washer? Because if you do, I'd appreciate you giving me a trial. My resume is typed in invisible ink, and my references can be contacted at HMS Strangeways, but only on weekends.'

The three of them gazed at me as if I was unhinged.

'She's mad,' Billy said. 'Not playing with a full deck of marbles, that one.' He flexed his hand. 'Should I hit her again?'

Chewing Gum Guy nodded to the Silent Bloke. 'Get her on film, and we'll add it to the collection.'

The thug pointed his phone at me and started recording.

So I did the same to them with my mobile. 'Since we're having a movie party.' The rain bounced off my head. 'We'll have a TikTok competition later.'

'You're fucking nuts,' Billy said.

'You remind me of a little dog, Billy.'

He narrowed his eyes. 'Eh?'

'One of those hapless pups once loved by the family, the neighbours, and strangers, who, for some reason, lost everything. All joy, all excitement, all fun, and friendliness. He just sits miserably, making low, growling, discontented noises, shitting everywhere, wanting direct attention, and then snapping at the hands that try to cajole. They'll soon put you out of your misery.'

'What do you want to talk to Jack for?' Chewing Gum Guy said.

'I told you, I need a job.'

'Jack retired a long time ago. Our Bianca runs the business now.'

'Bianca?'

'Jack's daughter.' He narrowed his eyes. 'What are you? A brickie?'

'A bricklayer? No. I'm good with computers.' Dirty water swam over my shoes. 'What sort of business is it?'

'Don't you know?'

'Can you fix my laptop?' Billy asked. 'It's got a virus,

and Michael said it's my fault for downloading too much porn.'

Chewing Gum Guy groaned, and I guessed he was Michael. The Silent Bloke and I continued filming each other.

'Sure, Billy. Take me to your grandad, and I'll sort it for you.'

He moved his head like a shaggy dog trying to get dry. Instead, the water went everywhere, hitting Michael's legs and covering Silent Bloke's phone. And he ended his vow.

'You fucking idiot, Billy.'

He lowered his mobile, and I did the same. 'Look, I only need a few words with Jack, that's all. It'll only take a couple of minutes.'

'Jack's not well,' Michael said. He tapped the side of his skull. 'Dementia. He can't tell you anything useful.'

I glanced at the building nearby. 'He's in a home?'

Michael shook his head. 'Fuck no. Bianca wouldn't put him in one of those zombie places. That's fucking terrible, that is.'

'His brother, your grandfather, Eddie, is in the place near you.'

He shrugged. 'Yeah, well, that's different. They fell out long ago, and nothing will change now.' Michael slapped Billy on the top of the head. 'Come on; we're done here.' Then he pointed at me. 'Don't speak to Eddie again. We won't go easy on you next time.'

They walked away. I grabbed my bag and stood there, getting soaked by the second, wondering what to do. Then I saw the pub through the rain, the George and Dragon.

The Toon.

And it had a sign outside with rooms to rent.

It was as good a place as any to get dry.

Chapter 27

Tubthumping

I stepped into the George and Dragon, and everything fell silent. The music on the jukebox stopped as if by magic, the darkest kind going by the décor that greeted me. Not that there was much greeting for me. The blokes playing darts paused mid-throw, their eyes fixed on me as if I were about to be the dartboard. The women in the corner gripped their dominoes, the air heavy with oleander, two-day-old fish, and sea mist collided with mould, wood polish, disinfectant, and the sugary aroma of a cheeky Vimto and the alcoholic stew of generations of dockers in Hai Karate aftershave.

The floorboards creaked as I went to the bar, smiling at the stout, middle-aged woman with greying hair and a stern appearance. She was drying glasses with a rag, but stopped when she saw me.

'You look like a drowned rat, love.'

Her charm shattered the silence, the blokes snorting laughter while the women cackled, resembling rejects from *Macbeth*.

The water dripped from me and formed a pool on the cracked floor. 'I need a room for a few nights.'

She scrutinised me before turning her head and screaming like a banshee.

'Barry! Get your fucking scrawny arse up here now!'

My ears throbbed as the rest of the punters returned to their business, having lost interest in the stranger in their midst, more intent on playing games as a distraction from the real world. A small, weedy bloke built like something you'd stick in your ear to get the wax out popped up from a hatch in the floor. His hair was thick and dark, falling below his shoulders and unwashed in several days, going by the bouquet of sweat drifting from it. He rubbed grimy fingers on a greasy rag and answered the siren's call.

'Whadda ya want, Gracie?'

She swivelled her hips and slapped him across the cheek with such a whack they must have heard it in the nursing home I'd just left.

'Don't talk to me like that, you fucking melt. Not in front of guests. Do we have a room for this young lady?'

His eyes blazed as his skin turned violet, and he stared at me. Barry rubbed at his face. 'Rooms? Well, let me think.' He grinned at Gracie, the pleasure in his expression telling me he'd enjoyed the slap she'd given him. 'We have the Queen Room available. Fit for a princess, that is.'

'Does it have a shower with hot water?' I asked.

Gracie's howl made the glasses vibrate and forced a bloke to miscue his throw, so his dart hit the door just as an old woman with a ferret on a lead entered.

'Shower?' she said. 'Of course, it doesn't have a fucking shower. We're not the bleeding money-grabbing royal family in here.' She slapped her hand on the bar, and all the customers flinched. 'What it does have is a gorgeous, big bath.' She grinned at Barry. 'Big enough for two it is, splashing around with all the lovely soap and bath salts we provide in every room at the Toon.' Neither of them sounded like Geordies. 'It also has fresh sheets and a TV with all five channels. There's no internet for your porn viewing, but Barry can deliver some traditional magazines if you want.'

I smiled at her. 'I'm fine with my imagination.'

She slapped Barry on the back, and he stumbled into the bar. 'Ha! That's what I tell this little shit all the time. Leave me alone, I say, and go play with your imagination.' She leaned closer to me. 'Mind you, he's got a fucking big imagination, has that lad. Now, how many nights would you like in the exclusive Queen Room?'

'How much?'

Gracie rubbed at the delve on her chin. 'Twenty quid a night. Cash only. We have none of those fancy bank card things here.'

'Government spying,' Barry said. 'That's what all those microchips and micro ovens do to ya. Bloody fucking politicians.'

I removed two twenty-pound notes from my pocket and placed them beside the dead fly on the bar. Gracie snapped them up like an alligator devouring a baby.

'Right, I'll show you where it is, and you can dry out. Do you want something to eat in your room?'

She made it sound like she was offering me a freshly baked infant.

I glanced around the pub. Decades of smoke and grime stained the walls, and the paint peeled in several places. The floor groaned with every step, and the bar was scarred and dented from years of use. The stools were unsteady, and the red vinyl seats were torn and faded. The lighting was dim and flickering, casting eerie shadows everywhere. An old jukebox sat in the corner, spitting out a torturous Elton John ballad. All I wanted to do was fall into the room, remove my wet clothes and plug the playlist into my head. Then, I could gather my thoughts about what happened at the nursing home.

'No. If I get hungry, I'll pop back here later.'

Gracie led me up a narrow set of stairs and opened the door. A single bulb hanging from the ceiling, casting eerie shadows on the walls, lighted the room. The window was dirty and smudged, letting in only a tiny amount of light. The curtains were torn and tattered, fluttering in the draft that leaked through the glass.

There was a loud buzzing from the lightbulb, with voices and laughter filtering in from outside. The air was thick with the smell of alcohol and smoke, and I could taste the bitterness on my tongue.

'This is the Queen Room?'

Gracie beamed at me. 'Aye, the finest we have.' She pointed to the door at the end. 'The bathroom is through there. Let me know if you need more towels.'

Then she left without giving me a key. I dropped my bag to the floor and went to the sagging old mattress. The sheets were stained and rough, but it didn't matter. I closed the curtains before stripping off my wet clothes and hanging them over the bath. I dried myself and flopped onto the bed naked, gazing at the stains on the ceiling, trying to find something in the intricate cobwebs that would guide me towards the next step in my quest for revenge.

And the spiders peered back at me.

Chapter 28

Wrote For Luck

I took Seraphina's notebook from my bag, glad the paper was dry. I opened the pages and peered at those six names again, with a thousand different things rushing through my head. Downstairs, the jukebox was playing music from *The Wicker Man*. Not the terrible remake with Nicolas Cage but the original classic where the woman who wasn't Britt Ekland takes all her kit off to dance and bang on the wall to tempt the bloke in the next room.

Fuck! And there I was, naked on the bed, while that tune seeped through the walls from the jukebox downstairs in that fucking bizarre pub. No spoilers, but in *The Wicker Man*, a virgin copper is tricked into visiting a weird community while he searches for a missing girl. All so the locals can burn him alive in a ritual pagan sacrifice.

I was no copper and not a virgin, but the similarities suddenly struck me as fucking odd. More than crops had failed this community. I'd seen poverty and depravation to put the island of Summerisle to shame.

My spine jerked forward as I sat up, trying to shake the nonsense from my mind. I'd spoken to Eddie Wood in the

151

nursing home, and Edward Woodward played the copper in the movie. And it looked like the Woods had murdered my parents ten years ago. Then set them on fire.

I jumped off the bed, shaking my head hard enough to get the craziness from my brain. Fatigue and stress were playing tricks on me. I grabbed my bag and retrieved the only dry clothes I had left. After getting dressed, I sat on the bed and checked Seraphina's notebook to scrutinise those names again. I'd lose the nonsense in my mind if I focused on what I'd discovered.

Four of the six buildings on the list were closed: the church, the local shop, the community centre, and the funeral parlour. Was there a link between those closures? Remembering what Lizzie had said, it didn't seem so. The community centre and the shop appeared to have been bought by property developers, whose plans went kaput when the bottom dropped out of the economy. Something similar must have occurred to whoever purchased the funeral parlour. The church was a different prospect. More than one scandal had forced the clergy out, but the same had happened to numerous churches nationwide, and they never shut their doors for good. So why that place? And what was their connection to the pub and the nursing home?

Could the names be meaningless, just random things Seraphina had written when she was ill? Did John Mead lie to me about her death? How easy would it be to murder someone and fake their death certificate? Mead was upset Gemma had left him for Seraphina, but that was ten years ago. They'd never divorced. She'd kept his name, and they were still in contact. And he didn't intend to kill her. The chief constable meant that bullet for me. Gemma sacrificed her life for me. Why? And why did somebody set the computer shop alight? Was it really an attempt to murder me? But I knew nothing worth killing for.

Did I?

I grabbed the notebook and threw it across the room, where it bounced off the wall and fell into a heap on the carpet. My guts ached as I sat on the bed and peered at the book, hoping some magical revelation would appear from its pages like a genie from a bottle.

Somebody put Slade's "Merry Xmas Everybody" on the jukebox downstairs, even though we were six months from Santa's big red bag. The lyrics annoyed the hell out of me, reminding me of my first Christmas in the children's home, sitting in the common room, surrounded by music and laughter, when I felt like I was a million miles removed from it all. The smell of pine from the Christmas tree and the sweet aroma of sugar cookies had filled the air, but I could only taste the bitter sadness in my mouth.

I remembered staring at all the other children as a woman approached and kneeled beside me. She had a warm smile, but I didn't trust her. 'Merry Christmas, Enola,' she said. I didn't reply and just looked down at my lap. 'I know this is difficult for you, but we're here to make it as special as possible. Would you like to help me decorate the cookies?' I shook my head, and she gently touched my shoulder. 'It's okay. Take your time. We'll be here when you're ready.'

I watched as she walked away and joined the others in their festivities. I was so alone, knowing I'd lost everything that mattered. The soft fabric of the couch underneath me felt rough against my skin, and everywhere was too bright and overwhelming. At that moment, I made a vow to myself. I'd let no one make me feel that alone ever again. I'd fight to create a new life for myself, no matter what.

Yet, years later, I was in that room above the pub, lonely and lost, not knowing what to do. I gazed at Seraphina's notebook, and nothing made sense. I rolled onto my back and stared at the ceiling. Maybe it would be better to go to the police and leave myself at the mercy of DI Jenkins.

Then I moved to my side and saw the paper I'd discovered in Gemma's flat, and the words floated before me: the Woods and the NCA.

The Woods had to be Eddie and his brother Jack. Eddie had said his brother was involved in the murders of my parents, and even though his mind couldn't be trusted, Lizzie had confirmed everything he'd said to be true.

But could I trust her?

I thought of it as my stomach rumbled. I wouldn't get anywhere without something to eat. I jumped off the bed and left the room, heading downstairs and wondering what culinary delights the Toon offered, trying to ignore that fucking Elton John song bleeding through the walls.

Chapter 29

Food for Thought

The bar stank of greasy chips and stale beer. The dart players had disappeared, but the domino women were still there, throwing pound coins down as they gambled, giving me only cursory glances as I sat in the corner. Flickering lights cast long shadows on the rough-hewn walls.

Gracie sidled over to me. 'How's your room?'

'Great,' I said. 'Can I order food?'

She removed a broken pencil from behind her ear and a notebook from her pocket. 'Fire away, love.'

'Do you have a menu?'

She lifted her arm and pointed at a poster on the wall near me. I studied its limited choice and picked the least likely to give me food poisoning.

'I'll have the chicken salad, a plate of chips, and a pint of cider.'

The light glinted off her yellowing teeth as she grinned. 'No problem. I'll stick it on your tab.'

She shuffled off, and I settled into my seat, peering at a picture of kangaroos boxing. I had to find an address for

Jack Wood, so I got my phone and searched online. It didn't take long to discover the details of Phoenix Property Developers, created twenty years ago and run by his daughter, Bianca, for the last two.

His photo on the website showed a sixty-five-year-old grey-haired man with narrow eyes and a cold stare. There was no mention of his dementia. Bianca Wood was thirty, single, with a business degree and five years of experience running her own financial services company before taking charge of Phoenix.

The family had money, there was no doubt. So I searched for what they were doing a decade ago, discovering that Jack Wood ran the company while Bianca was at university. I couldn't find any mention of Eddie.

Barry brought me my cider and cricked his neck to see what was on my screen.

'The Woods are the big wigs around here, a local family who did good.'

'Do you know them?'

He took that as an invitation to sit near me. He had eyes like burnt cigarettes and smelled of an ashtray. 'Eddie and Jack were a few years above me in school, but everybody knew them, especially Jack. He was the apple of his mum and dad's eyes. Eddie was more the idiot son, but Jack looked after him.'

I sipped the cider, the sweet liquid tickling my throat. 'What line of work did they do?'

He narrowed his eyes and scrutinised me. 'You don't look like a copper. Are you a reporter?'

It had to be my hair or how I dressed for two people to think I might be a journalist.

'No, I'm only curious. I'm a bit of a local historian.'

That seemed to satisfy him. 'Well, let's just say that Jack

was in charge and knew how to get folks to do things for him.' He touched his nose. 'Let's leave it at that.'

'And he started a property development company?'

'Oh aye, Phoenix, something or other. I think his daughter Bianca runs it now. Hard as nails she is, just like Jack was back in the day. I saw her break a bloke's arm in here once.'

'What did he do?'

Barry grinned. 'The daft bugger put his hand on her leg without permission. He didn't make that mistake again.'

'Do you know where this company does its property development?'

He got up and shrugged. 'Nah, that's far too boring for me. Won't you find that information online?'

I smiled. 'I guess so.'

He left, and Gracie brought my order over. 'I hope that little wanker wasn't bothering you.'

I slipped a chip into my mouth. 'No, he's no problem. Thanks for the food.'

'You're welcome, dear. Let me know if you need anything else.'

She returned to the bar, and I scoffed a fair amount of the chicken and chips before opening a web browser and searching the land registry. I expected lightbulbs to go off and discover that Phoenix Property Developers owned all six buildings on Seraphina's list, but they didn't. A Chinese business owned the funeral home and the nearby store, and somebody registered in the Cayman Islands owned the former community centre. The church belonged to the Catholic diocese. A private company owned the nursing home, and the local brewery ran the pub.

So that was a dead end.

I sighed and had a drink as someone slipped into the

seat near me and stole a handful of chips. 'Cracking grub this,' Lizzie said.

I grinned. 'Help yourself.'

She did. 'Are you getting the round in?'

I signalled Gracie for another pint of cider. 'And whatever Lizzie wants.'

'You're a darling, you are, Enola.'

I chewed on a chip. 'Did you and Eddie tell me the truth at the nursing home?'

She looked insulted. 'Of course. Why would we lie?'

'Why does anybody lie?'

She studied my face. 'Sometimes we have to lie to spare people's feelings.' Gracie brought a pint of cider and a Guinness to us. 'Eddie had been going in and out of the hospital for a year before the doctors recommended the nursing home. I tried to keep the worst from him, so I lied. He couldn't work in his workshop in the basement anymore, not with those tools and his memory dying. I always remember him working on something or other in that place. A set of shelves, a chair, or stuff I wasn't familiar with. I would watch him toil away. And then he couldn't anymore.'

She sighed.

'Some days were better than others, but I coped with the bad times until he started getting violent. The last time we lived together, I was watching a documentary about Jack the Ripper when he came screaming into the room and said I'd killed people. He flew at me, beating my arms and shoulders, and the neighbours had to drag him off. Bruises covered me when I called Bianca, but she wouldn't have anything to do with Eddie; she wouldn't have anything to do with us. I begged her, but she put the phone down on me.'

I touched her hand. 'It must have been terrible.'

'I remember the last time I saw him in our house. He was in the hallway, looking away from me. The lights were dark, though not enough to be pitch black. The shadows overtook the hall, but I could still see him. It wasn't the glare in his eyes or the brooding shape his mouth made. It was how he held himself. He sagged rather than stood tall. He didn't look at me, though I saw his face. He looked weak, like he was on the verge of the end. And in one way, he was.'

She took a long drink of her Guinness.

'I'm sorry, Gracie.'

She put the glass on the table. 'The reason I'm telling you this, Enola, is to make sure you understand that Eddie and I never kept secrets from each other. I know about his participation in what happened to your parents, his limited involvement, but he told me what Jack did, and I believe him.'

I started on my second drink, and Lizzie helped me finish the food. My belly was full at the end, but my head was still half-empty.

'I've a message for you,' Barry said as he offered me a bit of paper.

I opened it and read the note.

My driver will be outside in five minutes if you want to meet. Bianca Wood.

I slipped it into my pocket. 'News travels fast around here.' I stood and walked to the door.

'Don't do anything I wouldn't,' Lizzie shouted as I left.

At least it wasn't raining.

Chapter 30

You Can't Always Get What You Want

I stepped out of the car in front of a grand house. The rain had stopped, and a delicate haze hung over everything, creating an aroma of damp flowers. As I approached the entrance, the fountain in the garden burst into life, the gentle sound of trickling water filling the surroundings. A maid dressed in a crisp uniform opened the door and ushered me inside. It all felt very Beverley Hills, but without the glorious weather. I was unsure what I'd expected, but that wasn't it.

To the left of the entrance was a living room decked with opulent velvet sofas and chairs arranged around a polished grand piano. Light slipped in through the expansive floor-to-ceiling windows, offering a panoramic view of the meticulously maintained gardens. A spacious dining area awaited on the opposite side of the foyer, boasting an enormous mahogany table big enough to accommodate two football teams. A shining crystal chandelier hung from above, casting a radiant glow everywhere. Bianca Wood, dressed as if prepared for a high-powered business meeting, sat at the heart of this luminous ambience.

'You've been prying into my family's affairs, Ms Gray.'

She didn't ask me to sit, but I did anyway, sinking into the nearest seat. It embraced my legs like a warm glove, and I knew I'd struggle to get up.

'I need to speak to your father.'

Her gaze never left me. 'Regarding what?'

'Didn't those relatives of yours tell you? One of them hit me in the head for the sake of it.'

She rolled her eyes. 'The men in this family have barely a dozen brain cells between them.'

'Including your old man?'

She went to the mirror over the ornate fireplace, gazing at her reflection and adjusting her hair. 'Would you like to know my father's worldview, Ms Gray?'

'Is a drink included with it?'

She laughed before ringing a small bell that made me think I'd fallen through a time vortex into the 1920s, and a bunch of flappers and soused sops would come running in at any second. Instead, the maid from earlier entered and looked at me.

'A non-alcoholic double gin and tonic, if you have it, please.'

She turned to Bianca. 'One for each of us, Daisy, and bring some nibbles. I haven't eaten since breakfast at the mayor's house.'

'You mix with only the best folks, then?' I said.

She sat opposite me, smelling of roses. 'Oh no, all politicians are truly awful people. Just awful. They present a façade to the world, but behind closed doors, they're no different from any animal. Actually, I take that back. Animals have more nobility about them. They aren't driven by greed or anger.'

'And your father?'

'Yes, the great Jack Wood. He likes to wax forth on many concepts. Still, his particular favourites include: the government is a swamp, welfare undermines self-reliance, tax is an infringement of personal liberty, might is right in interpersonal as in international affairs, global warming is a socialist conspiracy and abortion and gay marriage offend God. So, you can imagine how entertaining our nights were around the family table.'

'You don't get on, then?'

She laughed. 'You could say that.'

The maid returned with the drinks and a tray containing nuts and crisps, which she placed between us. I grabbed my glass and raised it to Bianca.

'Cheers.'

'Has my father wronged you in some way?'

'That's what I'm trying to find out.'

'Which is why you were at the nursing home.'

'Yes. Information led me to speak to your Uncle Eddie. He then told me I needed to see his brother, your dad.'

She shook her head. 'Eddie hasn't been in his right mind for a long time, well before his dementia appeared. So, you should take anything he says with a pinch of salt.'

'I spoke to Lizzie. Do you know her?'

'Ah, poor Elizabeth. Again, her faculties are not to be trusted. What did they say to you?'

I put the glass on the table. 'Do you know who I am?'

'No. Should I?'

'My name is Enola Gray. Ten years ago, I hid in a wardrobe and watched three masked intruders murder my parents and then set the house alight.' I showed her my scars. 'Even though they were dead, I tried to drag my mother and father from that inferno. Recently, I discovered information that leads me to believe that your old man, Jack

Wood, was behind the killing of my parents. Your Uncle Eddie and his friend Lizzie confirmed Jack was to blame. That's why I need to talk to him about it. Is he here?'

'Why would anybody want to kill your parents?'

'I don't know. They were in a witness protection program, so I assume it had something to do with that.'

'As much as I dislike my father, Ms Gray, he's not a criminal, never mind a murderer.'

'I'd still like to speak to him.'

Bianca didn't move. 'If your parents were in a witness protection program, I assume they were relocated and given new identities.'

'I guess so.'

'Then how did their killers discover where they were?'

'A police officer, John Mead, betrayed them.'

She raised her eyebrows. 'John Mead? The recently deceased chief constable?'

'That's him.'

'Somehow, I don't think you're telling me everything, Ms Gray.'

She was right. So, I did, starting from meeting Gemma at the funeral.

'That's why I need to speak to your father, Ms Wood.'

'I'm sorry for your loss, Ms Gray, and I wish I could help you.'

I jerked out of the chair, spilling my drink. 'Then why can't I talk to him?'

Bianca Wood finished her non-alcoholic gin and tonic, downing it slowly. 'Because, Ms Gray, my father died six hours ago.'

Chapter 31

Revelations

Bianca's driver dropped me off outside the pub. The rain had stopped, but it felt like I was under a downpour. The moonlight flickered in the puddles as I heard a noise behind me. I turned, expecting the Wood boys again, ready to give me trouble, but surprised to see DI Jenkins there.

'How did you know I was here?'

'It's easy to trace a mobile phone, Enola. How are you?'

I told her about my failed meeting with Bianca Wood. 'It's all been a waste of time.'

'Jack Wood is dead? Wow.'

'Do you think he might have ordered my parents' murders?'

She shrugged. 'He was a well-known businessman in the area, but as far as I'm aware, the police had no interest in him for criminal activity.'

I slumped to the ground and leaned against the pub wall. 'Then I don't know where to go next. Seraphina's list and Gemma's note have led nowhere.' The moon sank into my back, and I had to stop myself from pushing my head into the pavement. Then I looked at her. 'Is there an update on the investigation into the fire?'

'Yes, but I can't speak about it.'

I jumped up. 'What? Why?'

DI Jenkins glanced over her shoulder. 'There's a lead I'm following nearby, but it might be dangerous.'

I grabbed her arm. 'You didn't come here just to tell me nothing, did you?'

She looked me up and down and sighed. 'I guess not. After everything you've gone through, I thought you deserved to know.'

'What is it?'

'I could lose my job over this.'

'Please, DI Jenkins.'

'Catherine. Call me Catherine.'

'Please, Catherine.'

'Okay. I had a tip from an informant that the people who set fire to the computer shop are working out of the old funeral parlour nearby.'

'The Cook place?'

'That's the one. I'm meeting uniformed officers there when I've finished with you.'

'I have to come with you.'

She took a long look at me. 'Only if you stay in the car.'

'Of course.'

'Okay, give me a second while I ring Davis.'

She stepped away and got out her phone. I turned from her and steadied my breathing. The conversation with Bianca Wood had been a waste of time, but this might be something. She finished the call.

'Where did the tip come from?'

Catherine shook her head. 'You know I can't tell you, Enola. Now, are you ready?'

'As I'll ever be.'

I got into the passenger seat and strapped myself in.

'Did you enjoy Gracie's food?'

'You've had it?'

She laughed. 'Oh aye, Gracie does a mean fish and chips.'

I remembered what I'd eaten as she drove through the estate, our only illumination coming from the flickering streetlights. Then my stomach rumbled.

'Maybe I shouldn't have had that chicken.'

Catherine grinned as she parked outside the funeral parlour. I saw no other officers as she got out. 'Stay here.'

I watched her go inside and rubbed my belly.

And I waited.

Five minutes later, I entered the building. The reception was dark, littered with tattered brochures and leaflets on the floor. I strode to the rear and stepped into the back room, my senses assaulted by the pungent odour of formaldehyde. The fluorescent lights hummed overhead, casting an eerie glow on the stainless-steel tables that dominated the space. It didn't look like it had been closed for years. The coldness of the tiles seeped through the soles of my shoes, sending shivers up my ankles.

There was a sheet on the middle table, but no sign of DI Jenkins.

'Catherine?' I said to no answer.

Then I glanced at the sheet and noticed the hand sticking out from underneath. The breath rushed up my lungs and clutched at my brain. I moved forward and pulled the sheet back.

'Fuck!'

Michael Wood's dead eyes peered at me, fresh blood on

his throat, with a blade next to him on the table. My knife, the one I'd left in the room at the pub.

Then, I saw the photo underneath the blade.

I used my elbow to push the knife aside, even though I assumed my fingerprints were on it and picked up the picture.

'His real name was Karl Moore, but of course, you knew him as someone else.'

My father's smile beamed out of the wrinkled photo.

DI Jenkins moved out of the shadows as the image shook in my fingers.

'What have you done, Catherine?'

I noticed the blood on the back of her hand. 'It started with Karl but didn't really take off until I met the priest.'

'The priest?'

'Yes. My parents were religious, but I never was. Not until I joined the force and everything became too much for me. I was stationed near here, and one day, I walked past St Peter's and popped in. It's strange how the atmosphere in a church can overwhelm somebody like me, a non-believer. I got to know the priest well, a generous and kind man, so imagine my surprise when a local came to me and accused the priest of abusing him thirty years before. I should have gone straight to the station and spoken to a superior officer, but I didn't. I still don't know why. Instead, I confronted the priest, and he broke down and confessed. I thought I'd be heartbroken and disgusted, but I wasn't. I felt nothing. And I still didn't tell anyone. Perhaps that's where it all began for me. The next day, a dog walker found the man who'd come to me hanging in the woods. There was no note, nothing, so my colleagues concluded it was suicide. And nobody knew why. John Mead investigated that death.'

'The chief inspector?'

Catherine laughed. 'He was a lowly detective inspector a few years into his marriage to Gemma. And he was my lover.'

'What?'

She smiled in the gloom, her perfect teeth sparkling in the moonlight creeping through the cracks in the boarded windows.

'Yes, we had a few things in common, John and I, and not just the sex. So I told him what the priest had done. Similar crimes were in the news then, and it was an educated guess there would be more victims.' She rubbed at her chin. 'I'm not sure who first suggested blackmail, but since we both needed money – him for his gambling debts and me for my drug use – it seemed a natural progression. And the priest was more than willing to pay, considering the alternative. I think he saw the whole thing as Divine intervention, of God saving him from jail and shame with the suicide and me demanding cash as his rightful punishment for his conduct. Still, it worked well for a while. Then more victims crawled out of the woodwork, and we had to ensure the priest never mentioned our actions to our superiors.'

'You killed him?'

She nodded. 'It's amazing how easy you can make a murder look like something else when you have certain medical professionals in your pocket. It was the same with Seraphina Shaw.'

I had to stop myself from rushing across the room and grabbing her throat.

'How do you get a doctor to help you do that?'

Catherine laughed. 'It's simple with the right leverage, and as a copper, you see everybody's dark side. And sometimes, you get to keep it hidden if certain palms are greased enough. So John and I turned it into a nice little business. The doctor with a cocaine habit, the community centre manager with the embezzlement problem, the shop owner who liked underage prostitutes.' She glanced around the room. 'And the funeral director who enjoyed fucking his corpses.' She sighed. 'It was all profitable for a while.'

I dug my nails into my palms. 'What has any of this got to do with my parents or me?'

Catherine gazed at me. 'I can't believe how much you look like your mother at the same age. It's quite remarkable. And disconcerting, giving me all kinds of mixed feelings.'

'You knew my mother?'

She smiled at me. 'Oh, Enola. I'm the one who killed her.'

Chapter 32

As It Was

I rushed at Jenkins, my vision filled with volcanic explosions and end-of-the-world scenarios. I got to within two feet of her when she swung the pipe and hit me in the head. My legs crumpled, hitting the floor and rolling into a container of stained needles and tubes.

'You should calm down, Enola. Don't you want to hear the rest of the story?'

My fingers trembled as I gripped a table and pulled myself up. The room spun around me, with the smell of formaldehyde infecting everything.

'What did you do to my mother?'

'Her name was Anna, and we met in primary school, bright-eyed and bushy-tailed, two eight-year-olds, unaware of the adult world's terrors waiting for us. Anna Dove. It was such a lovely name, and I knew I loved her from that first moment. It took her another seven years to realise she felt the same way about me, but the daily torture I endured was worth it.' Darkness crept out of the shadows and slunk over her face. 'And it was only another five years for her to think she loved *him* instead.' She spat the word *him* to the floor. 'She met *him* at university while I was a new police recruit. I begged her to stay with me, got on my knees, and fucking begged.' The increase in her voice gave me hope someone might hear her outside the building. 'But of course, she just dismissed me, dismissed everything we'd had.' She stepped closer to me, and the pipe trembled in her hands. 'To her, it was all a mistake, nothing more than a trivial waste of her time. She returned all my letters to me and continued with her life, telling me to do the same. "You're only twenty, Cath," she said. "You'll meet somebody else." And she was right because that's when I bumped into Mead at work.' She shook her head. 'And the rest, they say, is history. Only it wasn't since there was more to come. The blackmail and the murder, the sex and the drugs kept my mind occupied until John came to me and told me about his latest placement on a witness protection assignment. He knew about Anna and me, but we never talked about it. Cheery, emotional conversations were what his wife was for. I didn't care what had happened to Anna, but then John showed me the photo on his phone, and the hate erupted inside me.'

'Photograph? Of my parents?'

Catherine spat at my feet. 'Them? Fuck no. It was a picture of you, Enola, looking so cute at ten. That's what destroyed me. And, ironically, it's what ultimately destroyed her.'

My head was ready to explode. 'Why? Why would a photo of me lead to all this? You killed my parents and all the others because of a picture of me?'

She roared at me like a wounded lion. 'You don't fucking get it, do you?' She shook the pipe at me. 'You should have been our daughter, Enola; my child. I was the one who wanted a kid, but Anna said no, she couldn't. "I could never be a mother, Cath." She said that every time I told her I wanted a child with her.' She lifted the pipe and smashed it into Michael Wood's dead chest. 'Then she fucking had you with that worthless piece of fucking shit.' A fire blazed in her. 'And he was the one who got her killed. How fucking funny is that?'

It was so hilarious I craved to stick my thumbs in her eyes. 'Why?'

'Why? Because they were in the witness protection program because of him. He saw something he shouldn't have outside a nightclub a few months before leaving for university. A man running a county lines drug operation picked up one of his young kids and smashed the lad's head against the wall until nothing was left. Your father witnessed it all, and like a good little boy, he went straight to the police. Most sane people would have fucked off and kept quiet, but not your saintly father. So, he got a new name, a new location, and a new university. And that's where he met Anna. My Anna, who didn't want a child.' Her laugh chilled my bones. 'Then, ten years after, Mead discovers where they are and shows me the photo. That sealed all our fates.' She nodded at Wood's body. 'Michael was already working for us collecting the blackmail cash. He, John, and I made up the team that killed your parents and started the fire.'

I struggled to control my breathing. 'Who torched the computer shop?'

Jenkins tapped the pipe on Wood's chest. 'Michael wanted that job. I knew you'd be at home.'

My fingers trembled as I dug my nails into my scars. 'So why do it? Why kill three innocent people?'

She grinned at me. 'Why? To hurt you, of course. I knew you'd blame yourself.'

'You're evil,' I said.

She shrugged. 'Probably, but who isn't deep down?'

'Eddie Wood confessed about how his brother killed my parents.'

She raised her eyebrows. 'Did he? How strange. Eddie was never right in the head. Michael told me plenty of tales about him.' She smiled. 'The only question is, how do I kill you and make it look like self-defence?' She glanced at the blade. 'You could lunge for the knife.'

I studied my surroundings, searching for a weapon. 'I don't believe you, Catherine. You're not capable of murder.'

She laughed. 'Have you forgotten what you saw while hiding in that wardrobe?'

'What?'

'Yes, I knew you were there, watching us. I could have strangled you, and John wanted to. He hated leaving witnesses, but I didn't want you dead. I needed you alive and carrying your suffering for the rest of your miserable fucking life.'

'You killed my mother.'

'Of course. I did them both, two nice slices across their throats. I whispered in Anna's ear before I did, telling her you were next. That was fun, seeing the horror in her eyes.' She pointed at the corpse on the table. 'And Michael filmed it all on his phone. I still watch it every weekend with a glass of wine.'

I bit into my top lip and tasted the blood.

'Is this the book club?'

Lizzie stumbled into the room, bumping into Wood's body and distracting Jenkins. It was enough for me to step forward and kick her in the knee. It snapped with a crunch, and she dropped to the floor, the pipe rolling from her hand as I put my foot on her chest.

'It's a good job you have no balls, Catherine, or you'd be in even more pain.'

She twisted under my weight and scowled. 'We'd make a great mother and daughter team, Enola. You should consider it before doing anything rash.'

I pressed harder on her throat. 'Rash? Do you mean like killing you?'

'You'll have to if you want your revenge. My colleagues will struggle to find evidence for what I've told you.'

Butchering her would have been easy, and I'd have no qualms about doing it.

Then I saw Lizzie standing beside the corpse with a mobile in her hand. She lifted it to show me it was still recording.

'Will this help, Enola?'

I grinned at her. 'It's perfect, Lizzie.'

My toes itched, pressing more as I got my phone and called the police. While we waited, I showed Lizzie how to send a video file as an email attachment.

Chapter 33

No More Heroes

The wind swept through my hair in the cemetery. I placed fresh flowers on Seraphina's tombstone, with a note from me on the back of a postcard showing the cover of The Stranglers *No More Heroes* album. Then, I took the narrow path through the graveyard and walked a hundred yards to where my parents lay.

'Did you consider changing the names?' Ginger said at my side.

I wiped a tear from my cheek. 'No. Whoever they were before they had me was a different life for all of us.'

She held my hand. 'How do you feel?'

'I'm not sure. I should be relieved, but I'm not there yet. Maybe it will come later.'

I'd expected that burning desire for revenge to have vanished since my parents' killers were dead or imprisoned, but something dark still lingered inside me.

And perhaps it always would.

Ginger gripped my fingers. 'Things will get better now, Enola.'

I let go of her and laughed, removing a piece of paper

from my pocket. 'Oh, I don't know. This arrived this morning.'

She took it from me and read it. 'The landlord can't evict you just because you're a few weeks behind with the rent.'

I shrugged. 'Apparently, he can.'

Ginger shook her head. 'We'll give you the money, Bruce and I.'

'Maybe,' I said. 'The eviction proceedings haven't started yet. I'm assuming it's a good way for them to hike the rent before they get a new tenant.'

So there I stood: no job and possibly soon to be homeless, with that darkness still festering in the shadows of my mind.

What would I do next?

The Hanging Garden

An Enola Gray
Mystery

Chapter 1

Get Off the Stage

The soundtrack for my life was the shriek of nails driven into my coffin.

The guy with the broken bottle lunged at me, so I punched him in the throat. He resembled a cartoon drawn by a child with a faulty crayon as he hit the ground and wriggled like a worm towards me. The crowd cheered on the band as the angry man waved a fist at me. I stepped over him and admired my new shoes. The fresh leather gleamed under the palpitating lights as the man at my feet grasped his neck and made pathetic gurgling sounds. I gave him a swift kick in the ribs to shut him up so I could better appreciate the handiwork. Craftsmanship like that didn't come cheap after all.

I glanced around the venue, glad to be at a gig for the first time in months. The place stank of sweat and stale beer, and my heart pushed against my ribs. I soaked in the atmosphere, watching the writhing mass of bodies pulsating along with the pounding music. It was good to feel alive again after being cooped up for so long.

'I'm a diva in a dress, and you're a fucking mess,' the

lead singer sang through a cloud of dry ice. My friend Bruce was the gig's promoter, and things had been going well until the moron with the broken bottle had upset me.

Bruce had found his day job unfulfilling for a while, so getting the chance to organise the concert was a big deal. Our love of music was one of the many things we had in common despite him being ten years older than me. We were also both frustrated artists. He aspired to be a rock star, and I wanted to write a novel to change the world.

We were never going to realise those ambitions. The third part of our gang was Ginger, Bruce's flatmate and my only other friend. Human one, at least. I had my pet tarantula, Dirty Harry, as well. Ginger's dream was to have her own TV show reading tarot cards. However, she told me that fame wasn't important to her.

'What gets me is when you reach some success - no longer needing the money - and suddenly you're slapping your name on a perfume or hawking coffee machines. It makes it hard to focus on the artist and art.' Ginger had said that earlier in the night, before the venue filled up to the brim and sweat poured out of the walls like a river ready to burst.

I surveyed my surroundings with adrenaline pumping through my veins. Ginger was pressed against the wall, eyes wide with fear. Bruce was nowhere to be seen, probably counting the takings somewhere. Suddenly, the music stopped, and the room went quiet. The musicians looked at each other, confused.

The crowd surged towards me, a river of drunken, sweaty music lovers. Hands grabbed at me from all sides, but I rushed through the throng and made it to the stage. I jumped up, snatched the microphone, and shouted for everyone to calm down. My voice echoed through the venue, and for a moment, there was silence.

As everybody took a collective breath, the bloke I'd punched got to his feet, brandishing the broken bottle. He was a big man with broad shoulders and a scruffy beard, who looked like the villain who has his mask taken off in the final scene of a *Scooby Doo* cartoon. He roared angrily, and the band stepped back, leaving me alone on the stage.

Then, someone screamed, 'Fight!'

'Fuck off before you get hurt,' I said.

He dashed forward and placed his free hand near my feet, ready to push himself up. I sighed and kicked him in the jaw. He staggered backwards and dropped the bottle. It smashed on the floor, sending broken glass everywhere. Silence engulfed the venue for ten seconds before the punters howled, cheering and clapping as the bouncers dragged the man outside. I jumped down, and the band returned. They were Daffokill, Bruce's first job as a promoter. It was a terrible name, but the music was good. The drums and guitars sprang to life as I marched to the bar, with people patting me on the shoulder and complimenting me for dealing with the moron.

'What happened?' Bruce asked.

'The baldy twat grabbed my arse, so I poked him in the eye. That's when he smashed the bottle and came for me.' I still had his blood on my fingers.

'That sounds fair to me,' Ginger said as she joined us. 'He's throwing up in the gutter, so he should be okay.'

I wiped the blood on my trousers. 'That's a shame.'

'Apparently, he's well known for that here,' she replied. 'He's part of a biker gang.'

Bruce grimaced. 'Oh, fuck. That's all we need, a load of angry bikers turning up for revenge.'

I tapped his shoulder. 'Don't worry, mate. He'll be too embarrassed to show his face in here again. So let's enjoy the gig.'

As the musicians broke into a heavy riff, I returned my attention to the band. The female singer's booming voice filled the room, competing with the screeching of the guitar. The bass vibrated through my chest, and every beat was like a train thundering over my ribs. I swayed to the rhythm, getting lost in the noise. Music had helped me through a lot of shit in my life, but it was also my greatest joy. It had value beyond an instantaneous, fleeting interest, a crucial part of my being.

I examined Bruce's nervous face, guessing how he felt on his first night as a promoter. His slender build and explosive dark hair seemed like pure energy distilled into a person. His entire personality stemmed from passionate creativity, making it difficult to imagine him doing anything without a deeper purpose. He approached everything with intense focus, giving the impression that every action was a carefully planned project.

Trying to be heard above the noise, Ginger leaned into me, her eyes shining with excitement. 'How good are these?'

'Excellent.' People were dancing wildly, moshing and jumping in time with the beat. The air was thick with the scent of sweat and alcohol. I could taste the dryness in my mouth from shouting over the music. The band finished their song, and the crowd erupted into cheers.

Bruce grinned from ear to ear as he took in the response. 'I told you they were fantastic!' he bellowed at me. I smiled, feeling grateful for the moment of distraction from my troubles. The room's energy was just what I needed to escape my problems, even if it was only for a little while. I'd run out of money, and all my savings were gone, only a few days from being kicked out of my flat. I'd booked an appointment with the Department of Work and Pensions for the morning, hoping they could help me, though I'd heard it could take up to five weeks to get any financial assistance.

At least I had the music and the company to wash away my worries. Bruce and Ginger had offered to let me sleep on their sofa, but I couldn't accept their generosity. Their flat was smaller than my old one, and they already had a whippet, Kronos, living with them, so having another stray would only complicate matters for all of us. And I was worried the dog would try to eat Dirty Harry.

The perfect solution would be finding a job, but I hadn't worked in six months, and the trauma of what happened at my last employment still lingered. However, I'd have to get something soon. I glanced around the venue, wondering if I could ask about a position behind the bar. Bruce had dealt with the manager about the gig, but it was rumoured a local gangster owned the building. And I didn't want to be drawn into that. I'd warned Bruce about it, but the Raven Club was the only place that would put the band on. Going by the crowd numbers, it appeared to be a success, which Bruce said would probably lead to more gigs if he could find the artists to play in such a run-down part of the town.

I admired his dedication for wanting to do something innovative with his life – his regular work was sitting in front of a computer for most of the day – and for adding a novel touch to the cultural wasteland we lived in. And as much as I enjoyed the night's events, it only highlighted my yearning to do something with my life. Perhaps it was time for me to leave town and see some of the world or at least explore the UK.

Sometimes, I looked into the sky and saw a plane, far above in the blue, flying to who knows where. And in that moment, I longed to be on that aircraft, travelling to some far-off destination, away from the earthly burdens and responsibilities I faced. That feeling of longing seemed to be with me from the time I fell out of bed until I crawled back into it.

Was it normal for somebody not yet twenty-one to feel like that?

That thought possessed my brain as the music increased and rattled the walls. My throat withered in the heat as I saw a young woman surrounded by two shady-looking men. She looked frightened and tried to push them away, but they dragged her towards the exit. When the bouncers ignored the commotion and didn't stop them from taking her outside, I knew my night was only starting.

And maybe it would fill the hollow inside me for a little while.

Chapter 2

Razor Blade Alley

Stepping out of the club into the rain was like being doused with a bucket of ice. The torrent pelted my skin, soaking through my clothes and making me shiver. The raindrops were tiny pinpricks, each one a sharp sting against my flesh. The water on the ground was slick and reflected the orange glow of streetlights, which made the world appear like a dreary dreamscape. The air was heavy with the scent of damp concrete and car exhaust.

I couldn't see the men or the young woman anywhere.

Then I heard her shouting in the alley.

As I ran, my shoes squelched against the pavement as if I was wading through mud. The rain intensified, becoming a deluge that obscured my vision and made it hard to see where I was going. White noise muffled everything else around me, disappearing into nature's embrace. I jumped over empty beer bottles and discarded pizza boxes, dodging the used condoms swimming through the puddles.

The streets were slick with oily rainbows, trash carried along in the swirling eddies. A rat darted by, seeking shelter, its matted fur dripping. In the distance, a siren wailed, likely for someone else having an even worse night than me. Through the haze, I saw them pushing her to the wall. She squirmed in their grasp, trying to escape. They surrounded the poor girl, gripping her arms, two against one. I took a deep breath and grabbed a piece of wood from the ground.

'Let her go, fuckwits.'

They towered over her with broad shoulders and thick necks, their arms rippling like bodybuilders in the gym. Their clothes clung to them like they were stuffed into sausage casings, barely able to contain the bulges of their muscles. One had a twisted sneer, revealing a row of crooked teeth. His hair was greasy and slicked back, glistening under the neon lights of the street. The other had a shaven head dotted with scars, with a wicked gleam in his eye as he stared at me.

'This doesn't concern you, sweetheart.'

I dragged the wood across the wall as I moved towards them. 'It does now.'

Crooked Teeth exposed his yellow-stained gnashers at me. 'Just 'cos you made a fool of Rex, don't think it will work with us.' He removed a large knife from his jacket. 'I'll cut you up like a fish, darling.' There was a slight Geordie twang to his tone.

I shook my head, sending rainwater everywhere. 'Let the girl go, and we can forget about this. I'll return to my gig, and you boys can scuttle back to the rock you crawled from under.'

Crooked Teeth laughed. 'She owes us money, that's all. Once we get it, she can bugger off. There's nothing for you to worry about.'

I caught my reflection in a puddle, my tired eyes and bird's nest hair shimmering in front of the moon. Well, I tried to be nice. 'Release her, or I'll break your knees.'

The one with the shaven head let go of her wrist and stepped towards me. 'I know you.'

I smiled at him. 'I doubt you know very much.'

He nodded like a jackhammer, and I thought his head might fly off like some crazed toy from the 1970s. 'No, I do. You're the girl who watched her mum and dad get killed.'

'Yeah,' Crooked Teeth said as the alley turned into a mini lake. 'Your picture was all over the internet. You were a kid when it happened, right? And you were hiding in a wardrobe when the killers set the place on fire.' He pointed the knife at the scars on my hands. 'That's how you got those. You tried to drag your parents out of the house even though they were already dead.'

Shaven Head turned to his mate and laughed. 'Fancy being that fucking stupid.'

Crooked Teeth laughed. 'I heard she was a witch, and she killed her parents as sacrifices.' He grinned at me. 'Is that right, little witch?'

'Are you a Geordie?' I asked him.

He shrugged. 'What's it to you?'

'Four hundred years ago, this country was gripped with paranoia because of the crazed belief that witches walked the land. Newcastle was one of the places that murdered innocent people during this fear, with the execution of fourteen women and one man for witchcraft in 1650. This was forty-two years before the infamous events in Salem in the US, yet hardly anybody nowadays knows about the Newcastle witches.'

They laughed at me like stereo hyenas.

'She's fucking mental,' Shaven Head said.

I ignored the insult. 'During the witch trials, women accused of witchcraft were often falsely blamed for causing harm or seeking wealth and revenge through supernatural means. In reality, the women targeted tended to be those who didn't conform to prevailing patriarchal norms and expectations. Their divergence from the strict social and moral codes of the time led them to be scapegoated, and their power and agency recast as dangerous and demonic. This says more about the fear of female empowerment in patriarchal societies than any supernatural evils.' I sighed. 'Not much has changed.'

They grinned at me as if halitosis was going out of fashion.

'Are you trying to put a spell on us?' Crooked Teeth said.

I lunged forward and slammed the wood into his shin. He screamed and stumbled into his mate, sending them into the wall.

The young woman looked at me. 'Go now,' I instructed her.

She ran as the goons glared at me.

'That fucking hurts,' Shaven Head moaned.

I shrugged. 'Do you want some more?'

He jolted forward, but Crooked Teeth pulled him back.

'No, don't bother. The Rook will deal with her later.'

Water dripped from my lips as I laughed. 'The Rook? Did you two fuckwits fall out of a comic book?'

'You've interfered in his territory, sweetheart, and now the consequences are on you. Don't say you weren't warned.'

'What did she owe you money for?' I said.

He shook his head and held onto his hobbling mate. 'You'll find out soon enough.' They staggered towards the other end of the alley before he turned back to me. 'And no piece of wood will help you next time.'

I watched them go as the rain transformed me into

something wetter than any creature at the bottom of the ocean. My dry clothes were twenty minutes away in my flat, but I couldn't leave without telling Ginger and Bruce what happened. And I wanted to speak to that young woman and get her side of the story. That's if she'd hung around, which seemed unlikely.

I pushed wet hair from my eyes and returned to the club. The bouncers had vanished from the entrance, so I couldn't even tell them off for being a pair of useless bastards. The music was still going, and I headed to the toilets to get dry, stepping into the crowded space as laughter filled the air. The place was thick with the smell of booze and perfume. Gloom filled the room, with flickering lights from the broken bulbs casting a yellow glow over everything, making the women look like over-excited zombies. A mess of discarded makeup and drinks cluttered the area around the sinks, the surface sticky with spilt alcohol.

They stopped what they were doing and gazed at me. Then they burst out laughing again. 'You look like a drowned rat,' the Beyonce lookalike said.

'I feel like one,' I replied, shoving my head under the hand dryer. The noise wasn't so loud that I couldn't hear them talking about the scars on my hands. I twisted my face beneath the hot air and stared at my warped flesh, wondering if there would ever be a day when I didn't hear people talking about my scars.

Water dripped from me as somebody called my name. 'Enola!'

I peered down at Ginger's red-striped shoes. Then I pulled my hand off the drier and looked at her. 'What's up?'

She thrust her phone at me. 'It's my uncle. Something's wrong.'

I read the text: *I can't take it anymore, Ginger. Say goodbye to Debs for me.*

'Do you know where he is?' I said.

She shook her head. 'I called him but got no answer.'

'Who's Debs?'

'His wife.' Her eyes widened. 'Wait, I added his number into the Find My Device option in his Google account. So, we can use that.'

We were out of the club five minutes later and running to the nearby woods.

Chapter 3

The Memory of Trees

The club was ten minutes from Harrington Woods, but we sprinted there through the wrong part of town. The rain-slicked streets were deserted, not a soul in sight. Our heavy breaths and frantic footsteps echoed off broken windows and graffitied walls. Shadows seemed to loom from every alley we passed, reaching out with spectral fingers to grab us. The smell of rot and piss mingled with the petrichor, assaulting my senses.

The buildings were decrepit and crumbling, windows boarded up or shattered. Graffiti tags marked the brick walls, and rubbish littered the alleyways. We dodged broken glass and slipped on food wrappers as we ran, our feet splashing through oily puddles. The streetlights flickered uncertainly, making the shadows dance. Somewhere nearby, a dog barked at the moon.

We arrived panting and out of breath. The rain had stopped, but the earthy scent of damp soil and decaying leaves filled my head. The mist clung to my skin, a thin, ghostly membrane resembling lizard flesh. The trees were tall and imposing, the branches rustling in the soft breeze, whispering beneath the pounding in my skull.

Ginger collapsed onto a nearby tree stump and peered at her phone. 'The signal is showing him here, but he isn't.'

I inhaled deeply, attempting to steady my thumping heart, and surveyed our surroundings. Having frequented Harrington Woods numerous times, I was well aware of its vast expanse. The sound of dripping water reverberated through the dense foliage, generating a rhythmic beat as spent rain dripped from the leaves and branches, creating a symphony of nature reminiscent of a Disney cartoon. A liquid landscape immersed my feet as water collected around my soles. The ground beneath me was slippery and soft, squelching under my toes with each step, leaving a sensation of mushiness.

I plodded towards the nearby river and stooped down, submerging my fingers in the cold water. As I gazed at my reflection, it danced and shimmered below the surface, trying to reveal another version of me. I cupped my hands and splashed the liquid over my face, letting it cleanse the sweat and fatigue clinging to me like a second skin.

Ginger's eyes reddened as I watched her rub at her cheeks. I knew her father was dead, and her mother was in a care home, but she'd never mentioned an uncle. I assumed they were close from the distress in her voice.

'What shall we do, Enola?'

'Come on,' I said. 'He must be here somewhere.'

I grabbed her hand and pulled her away from the stump, navigating through the dense thicket of trees, using my phone to light the way. The leaves crunched beneath our feet, releasing a satisfying sound, while twigs snapped with each step we took. The atmosphere was thick with the earthy fragrance of damp soil and decaying foliage. A delicate mist enveloped our surroundings, lending an ethereal quality to the scenery as if we were walking through a realm of dreams.

She shouted her Uncle Joe's name, her voice tinged with worry. I tried to keep up with her, but she was moving too quickly, and I struggled to match her pace, my feet dragging through the mud. Insects buzzed around my head, and I swatted them away as we stumbled through the undergrowth like jungle explorers.

'Ginger, slow down,' I panted. 'We need to stay together.'

She didn't listen and ran ahead. My chest ached with anxiety as I caught up with her. She was bent over, searching for any signs of her uncle.

'Do you see anything?' she asked, her voice shaking.

I shook my head, eyes scanning the ground, but all I saw were footprints leading deeper into the woods.

'Let's carry on,' I said, trying to sound reassuring. 'He can't have gone far.'

She used her phone. 'I'll call him again.'

Immediately, we heard the ringing from the other side of the river.

'Come on,' I told her.

We trudged through the river's shallow edge, the coldness soaking through my shoes. The whisper of moving water surrounded me as I scanned the dense forest for a trace of her Uncle Joe. Ginger's voice trembled as she called his name again. The scent of damp earth and moss overwhelmed my senses as I tried to steady my breathing and focus on our task.

We moved forward, our feet splashing through the shallow water. The sound of rustling leaves and chirping insects surrounded us, and the ringing continued. She held the phone in front of her like a compass. The moon hung below the trees, casting a shimmering silver light across the riverbank.

Ginger lunged through the undergrowth. 'There it is.'

She ran to it, and I saw the case shining under the moonlight. Ginger scooped it up and looked around us, but Uncle Joe wasn't with his phone.

I took it from her and switched it off. 'He must be here somewhere.'

She dropped to her knees and sobbed. I glanced over our surroundings, peering into the leaves and branches.

Then, I saw the shadow hanging from a tree a few feet away in the moonlight.

Ginger wiped the hair from her eyes, unaware of what I'd seen. 'What should we do, Enola?'

'You wait here. I'll be right back.'

I was thankful she put her head in her hands so she wouldn't see what I suspected.

Not yet, anyway.

I rushed through the mud and the grass, pushing through wet bushes, and took a deep breath. I remembered this part of the woods from my teenage years, seeing the large stones surrounding the tree the man was hanging from. My heart and legs ached as I climbed the largest rock, reaching up to check his pulse.

There wasn't one.

Every inch of me said I should take him down from that branch, but I knew I couldn't. I had to call the police.

'Oh no,' Ginger whispered behind me.

I turned and jumped off the stone, going to her and putting my arms around her shaking body.

'Don't look, Ginger.'

She trembled in my embrace, shivering and crying as

she placed her head on my shoulders. 'Oh God, no, Enola, please no.'

I pulled her into me, listening to the accelerated beat of her heart and the whispering of the leaves on the branches. I knew what it was like to gaze upon the body of someone you loved. I'd watched the murders of my parents and understood that the death of a loved one, no matter how it happened, never left you.

She stuck to me for a few minutes before pulling away.

'We should call the police,' I said.

She shook her head. 'Not yet. I need to see him.'

I stood in her way. 'That's not a good idea, Ginger. It's better if you don't see him like that.'

I had many memories of my parents and saw them in my mind all the time, but there was only one image on a daily repeat, one that I'd have given anything to wipe from my head.

'I have to, Enola. Please.'

Against my better wishes, I let her pass me, removing my phone as she went to him. I should have told her not to touch anything before she put a hand on his leg.

But I didn't stop her.

Instead, I called the police.

Chapter 4

The Hanging Tree

I was twelve when I ran away from the children's home for the first time, sneaking out in the middle of the night with all my worldly goods stuffed into my backpack. I slept in the woods, near where we would find Joe Jackson's body eight years later.

My escape wasn't because of ill-treatment. I'd left to search for my parents, even though I'd watched criminals murder them two years earlier. My mind had slipped into some strange places in the period after that, hence my struggles with adapting to my new, lonely, isolated world. I'd tried to fit in with the other kids, but most of them always looked at me with suspicious eyes, and the adults had little time to give me the help I needed.

So, I rewrote reality to tell me that what I'd witnessed, the murders, the house set alight, had all been faked so my mother and father could hide from those who wanted them dead. I didn't know who those people were, not then, and I couldn't understand why they'd leave me behind in such a cruel fashion, but I knew it had to be true because the alternative that they were gone was impossible for me to process.

Therefore, I gathered my plans together and ran away that fateful November evening. Under dark skies, the bitter, cold wind slipped inside my gloves and nipped at the scars along my hands, freezing my flesh, so the temperature matched that in my heart. I didn't know where I'd go after the woods, with fantasies in my head of staying there and living off the land.

My expedition in the forest lasted for two days, including meeting Devil worshippers who thought I was the reincarnated spirit of a murdered witch, and discovering what people did when they were naked in the dark. I'm still unsure which was the most upsetting experience. I'd visit those woods on many occasions in the future, the seasons in those trees matching my journey from child to young woman. The Satanists wore dark robes and animal skulls, chanting in tongues around a bonfire. When they saw me emerge from the trees, with my purple hair stuck up as if struck by lightning and my face covered in enough white powder to bake a cake, they fell silent in awe. Beckoning me forward, they declared me their resurrected goddess.

'They're drugged up,' my friend Amy told me as she dragged me away.

There were good and bad times, but I never encountered a dead body until that night with Ginger.

I stared across the throng of bodies and peered between the flashing red and yellow lights to see Ginger standing, shivering with Bruce. I'd texted him after I'd called the police, but he'd arrived before them. He tried to console her as an officer put a blanket around Ginger's shoulders and offered her a hot drink. Nobody had spoken to me since the boys and girls in blue had descended upon the scene, and I was happy with that. The police were not my favourite people.

My mind wandered as I avoided looking at Joe's body still hanging from the branch, instead remembering the times I'd had in that spot, discovering the things in life that had made my teenage world go around. Somewhere nearby was the tree where I'd carved my initials alongside those of my first kiss. Close to that was where a group of us had dallied with a tattered old Ouija board. It was when I'd finally accepted that my parents were dead and believed I could reach them from beyond the grave. I shivered at the memory, pushing the images from my mind, and stared at the forensic officers doing their jobs.

'Are you Ms Enola Gray?'

I looked into the sea-blue eye of a man ten years older than me and nodded. His expression was of somebody who hadn't slept in a long time, his hair unkempt and food stains on his shirt.

'That's me.'

He showed me a warrant card. 'Detective Inspector Jack Parker. You're the one who called the police?'

'Yeah. I came here with my friend Ginger Jackson after she got a text from her Uncle Joe, and she thought he might be in trouble.'

DI Parker removed his notebook and scribbled into it. 'Trouble?'

'Have you seen the text?'

'Yes, Ms Jackson showed it to me when I spoke to her.'

I glanced at Ginger as she trembled in Bruce's arms. 'I don't think she's in the right mind for an interrogation.'

He ignored the jab. 'Why did you think the message indicated Mr Jackson was in trouble?'

'You read it?'

'Yes, as I said.'

'And you're not an idiot?'

DI Parker lowered his notebook. 'It's best not to read too much into a single text, Ms Gray.'

'So, you don't believe the words "I can't take it anymore, Ginger. Say goodbye to Debs for me" implied he was in trouble?'

Those blue eyes cut into me like a sapphire blade. 'What do you think it meant?'

I shook my head and laughed. 'You're the fucking detective, not me.'

He glanced at his colleagues as they lowered the body from the tree.

'What did you discover when you arrived here?'

I turned my hands into fists and wondered if they'd arrest me if I broke his nose.

'Exactly what you lot did when you got here.'

'You didn't notice anybody else?'

'Nope.'

He wrote in his book again. 'Did you touch anything?'

I sighed. 'I climbed onto the rock closest to Joe to check his pulse. That's all.'

'So, you touched his hand?'

'I can see why they made you a DI, Parker.'

'And those are your footprints on the stone?'

'Brilliant deduction, copper.'

'We'll need to take your fingerprints and examine your shoes. Is that okay?'

I scowled at him. 'And if it isn't?'

He put his notebook away. 'I'll send a forensic officer over. I'm sorry for your loss.'

He went to Ginger, and I took a deep breath. My anger wasn't with him but with the police officers who couldn't discover who'd murdered my parents. It consumed ten years of my life, but I finally unearthed their identities, and it still angered me every time I saw a copper.

I checked my phone to see we were in the early part of Monday morning. I was soaked to the skin and had an interview at the DWP in eight hours in a desperate attempt to get an emergency loan. Because if I didn't, I'd be homeless tomorrow.

That thought bounced around inside my head as I watched the police carry Joe Jackson's body away, knowing there was always somebody worse off in this world.

Chapter 5

Picture This

I stepped into the Department of Work and Pensions office, feeling as if I was walking into a prison. The sterile white walls, buzzing fluorescent lights, and the sound of fingers on keyboards all added to the oppressive atmosphere. The smell of dust and ink lingered in the air, making me feel like choking on a lungful of rigid bureaucracy.

I glanced at the people who were trying not to look miserable and remembered Joe Jackson's body hanging from that tree. I approached the reception desk, and a woman scrutinised me through wire-rimmed glasses.

'Can I help you?' she asked, her voice as cold as the room.

'I'm here for an interview for an emergency loan.'

'Name?'

'Enola Gray.'

'Take a seat over there,' she said, pointing to a row of plastic chairs in the corner. 'Someone will be with you shortly.'

I sat down and took a deep breath, trying to calm my

nerves. My stomach was in knots, and I felt like throwing up. It was annoying, having to ask for help to maintain a roof over my head.

As I waited, I glanced around the room at the other people. Most appeared defeated, like they'd already lost the fight. Others looked angry, as if they couldn't believe they were in this position. I knew a few from my recent trip to the food bank: a woman who'd had a stroke and couldn't write, yet the DWP expected her to fill a form in to get the benefits she needed to feed herself and pay her bills. Then there was the man with PTSD, whom the DWP forced to come to their office three times a week to prove he was ill.

And there were the other horror stories I'd heard, how they'd sanctioned a man with learning difficulties for not completing his job search on the computer. So, he hand-wrote it instead because he didn't have the IT skills to use the DWP system. They also penalised a woman with mental health issues for missing a job centre appointment because her condition prevented her from leaving the house.

'They're only the tip of the iceberg, Enola,' Bruce had told me. 'Every day there are a hundred needless deaths in England resulting from government policy. Just think of that.' I did, and it chilled me to the bone, as it would to anyone to whom empathy was not an alien concept. 'New research shows how decades of welfare reform and DWP failings are linked to hundreds – and probably thousands – of suicides and other deaths of disabled people.'

I thought of what he'd said as I waited in that lifeless place, staring at the blank faces of the staff. Then, a man in a cheap suit approached me.

'Enola?'

'Yes.'

He pushed the glasses up on his nose. 'I'm Eric, your work coach. We've communicated through your online universal credit journal.'

'Right,' I replied as he led me to a tiny, cramped office. He positioned himself behind his desk before a computer screen, and I sat opposite him. A small plastic figurine of Winston Churchill glared at me as Eric spoke.

He glanced at my hands. 'I see from your form that you don't have a disability or a health condition. Is that right?'

I remembered what Bruce had told me. 'Yes.'

'So, you haven't worked for six months, and you're applying for an emergency loan.'

'My savings have run out. I must pay the rent today, or the landlord will evict me.'

'Do you have any friends or family who can put you up?'

I pictured Ginger in her flat, with Bruce and Kronos, and how she'd be suffering from her recent loss. I couldn't interfere on her grief.

'No. I want to stay in my current place. If I lose it, there's no guarantee I'll get one anywhere else, even if the loan comes through later.'

He peered at me and then at the screen. 'Indeed. What happened with your last place of employment? Your online journal lacks the essential details.'

'Somebody tried to kill me and set it on fire.'

'Oh. It's out of business, then?'

'You could say that.'

'Do you have references from the employer?'

'He died in the blaze, along with two of my colleagues.'

Eric typed those details into my file. 'Right. So, what type of work are you looking for?'

'I was an IT manager, but anything will do. I'm not fussy.'

He gazed at me. 'You're twenty years of age?'

'I'm good with computers.'

'Okay, did you bring the documents for your proof of identity?'

I reached into my jacket and handed him a bank statement with my address, last payslip, and National Insurance number.

'Will these do?'

He examined them several times. 'Very good. Now I just need to see something with your photo on it. Do you have a passport?'

I shook my head. 'I've never been out of the country.'

'Driving licence?'

'I don't drive.'

'Student card?'

'I left school at sixteen and haven't been back.'

Eric pushed the documents onto the desk. 'Then we have a problem, Ms Gray. The DWP can't do anything for you unless we have photographic proof of ID. I made that clear to you before you arrived for this interview.'

I reached into my other pocket, removed the two sheets of A4 paper that Bruce had printed for me, and placed them face up on the desk. He read the headline aloud.

'Ten Year Mystery Solved. Local Woman Finally Discovers Who Killed Her Parents.'

Below the text was a nice large black-and-white picture of me. They hadn't captured me on my best day, but it was clearly me. And my name was printed next to it.

I smiled at Eric. 'There you go, photo ID.'

The glasses had slipped like a snake to the edge of his nose, and he pushed them up again. 'I'm sorry, Ms Gray, but this won't do. I need an official document, not a photocopy from the local newspaper.'

I put my hands on the table. 'But you agree that the person in the photograph is me, Enola Gray?'

He nodded. 'Yes, but....'

'No buts, Eric. That proves who I am. You'd have to be an idiot not to know otherwise.'

That might not have been the best choice of words. He puffed out his cheeks as they turned a delicate shade of pink. 'As I said, Ms Gray, I can't do anything for you without an official photographic document.'

He pushed all the papers back towards me. I gazed at my image and considered how much easier it would be to kick the annoying twats in the balls.

'So I won't get a loan?'

'Once you have a photo ID, you can complete the process again.'

'What do I do now? Where will I live from tomorrow?'

He held out his hands as if I wasn't his problem anymore.

And I guess I wasn't.

I scooped up the documents and stuffed them into my jacket.

As I left the building, I glanced at the others waiting there, wondering how many would be tossed onto the streets because of petty bureaucracy and indifference.

Then I got a text from Ginger and knew I had friends who would help me.

And I needed all the help I could get.

Chapter 6

Cold Coffee

I sat at a small round table in the corner of the café, staring blankly at the menu. I didn't remember the last time I'd eaten, probably before the gig, but I couldn't face any food after my encounter with Eric at the DWP. The smell of freshly brewed coffee wafted through the air, but I couldn't even summon the energy to order a drink as I waited for Ginger. She hadn't said why she wanted to meet, but it didn't matter. I needed somebody to talk to, and I guess she did as well.

The place was busy, with a constant hum of conversation and the clink of cutlery against plates. Servers bustled past me, balancing trays of steaming food like jugglers in a circus. A couple at the next table whispered to each other over their lattes and croissants. I couldn't focus on any of it, my thoughts consumed by the weight of my situation.

I checked the time on my phone. Ginger was running late. She was experiencing her own struggles, grieving the loss of her Uncle Joe, and trying to find out what had happened to him. I didn't know how to help her, feeling guilty for even thinking about my problems when she was going through so much.

As I waited, my thoughts spiralled. Where would I sleep after tonight? What would happen to me if I lost my flat? I tried to push the questions away and took deep breaths, focusing on everything around me. Somebody with a sense of humour had adorned the café with film posters related to food. However, I wasn't sure if the other customers appreciated the *Delicatessen* and *Eat the Rich* images gazing down at them.

A barista called out orders, the sound of the espresso machine blending into the background. The bitter aroma of coffee did little to soothe my nerves. I watched the people chatting happily, envious of their trivial concerns. Didn't they see the walls closing in? How could they smile and laugh while I was drowning?

The door opened, letting in a damp gust of air. An elderly woman shuffled in, pushing a cart of bags full of her possessions. The baristas eyed her warily, ready to shoo away a potential bother. Ginger arrived, and I stood up to hug her. She looked exhausted, her eyes red from crying. She ordered a coffee, and we sat at the table.

'How did your interview go with the DWP?'

'About as well as that time an entertainment reporter thought Samuel L. Jackson was Laurence Fishburne.'

She cringed. 'Yikes.' She touched my hand. 'You know you can stay with Bruce and me until you get your own place.'

'Thanks, Ginger, I appreciate that, but you also realise it's the same landlord, and if he finds out I'm staying with you, he'll likely put your rent up.'

She shook her head. 'I'm not having you sleeping on the street.'

'I'm sure it won't come to that.' I wasn't. 'And anyway, I've slept rough before.'

'When and where?'

I was about to tell her when I remembered it was in the same woods where we'd discovered her uncle's body. I changed the subject instead.

'Enough about me. Why did you want to meet?' I squeezed her fingers. 'Are you okay?'

She gave me a tired smile. 'Oh, you know, still coming to terms with it. You understand how it is.' We sat in silence as the server brought Ginger her coffee. The aroma assaulted my senses, and the rumble in my stomach returned. 'I spoke to Joe's wife, Debbie, this morning, and she wants me to go to the house. I was hoping you'd come with me for moral support.'

'Of course. Whatever you need.'

'Great. Bruce has taken Kronos for a walk by the river. With everything that happened last night, he hasn't spoken about the Daffokill gig, but I know it went well. He was on the phone with the manager of the Raven about putting another band on soon. Bruce was calling local bands as I left, trying to arrange a performance for later this week. I guess it might take all our minds off things.'

'That's good news.'

She sipped at her coffee. 'Before everything went to shit last night, did something happen to you outside the venue?'

I told her what happened with the two thugs and the young women. 'They mentioned somebody called Rook? Do you know who that is?'

Ginger laughed. 'No. It sounds like a cartoon character.'

'Indeed, but I doubt it will be. Probably some small-time hoodlum involved with drugs. It doesn't matter now.'

'Maybe, but don't forget that biker with the bottle. You made quite a few enemies last night.'

'That's the story of my life, Ginger.' She smiled and seemed happier, so I broached a difficult subject. 'Have the police been back in touch?'

She shook her head. 'No. Do you suppose they will?'

'At some point, yes. That pinhead Detective Inspector Parker was interrogating me as if I was a suspect.'

'What? That's stupid. And anyway, don't you think that Joe, well, that Joe....?'

She didn't want to say it, so I did. 'Took his own life?'

'Yeah, that.'

I watched her drop four sugars into her coffee. 'It certainly looked like that, but you can never be sure.'

Ginger held a sugar cube between her fingers. 'What else could it be?'

'From what we saw and the text message you got, suicide looks the likely answer. DI Parker treated me as a suspect, but that's just because he's a jackass and not from anything else. How close were you to Joe?'

She crushed the sugar, and it crumbled all over the table. 'He was busy with his business, so I hadn't seen him for a bit, but if I didn't see or speak to him, we texted every day.'

'When was the last time you saw him?'

'A week ago, on Monday afternoon. I met him in the pub near his office. He and his staff were celebrating a new contract. He had everything to live for, Enola.'

'What was his business?'

She forced a smile across her face. 'You'll love this, with your IT background. Joe had a start-up tech company that designed AI apps. He always told me what they were working on, but it was too technical for me and went over my head. But I know they were doing well even before the new contract.'

I pictured the scene we'd stumbled into in the woods, seeing how easy it would have been for him to wrap the rope around the branch and then get up on that rock. And how simple it would have been for somebody else to be involved.

However, there was one big problem. If the police looked at the location and saw no evidence of foul play, they wouldn't investigate why Joe would take his own life. And with that, the coroner wouldn't take it any further, either.

'Finish your coffee, Ginger. We need to talk to Joe's wife.'

Chapter 7

Everybody Hurts

We strode up the path to Debbie's house, and Ginger rang the doorbell. Debbie answered, her eyes swollen and red. She looked like she hadn't slept in days and had messy hair. The smell of fresh flowers wafted in from the nearby gardens, and the chirping birds did their best to bring some sunshine into the melancholy mood.

Ginger hugged her, and I stood silently, hearing my heartbeat echoing inside my skull. I was not yet twenty-one, and I'd already seen enough death to last me a lifetime. I stepped back and left them to grieve, turning into the garden and gazing at how tidy it was. The flowers had died due to the arrival of winter, but someone still tended the garden. I assumed it was Joe and wondered why he'd cut the grass if he knew he wouldn't be around much longer.

'Come in,' Debbie said, her voice breaking. 'Ginger has told me all about you.'

I returned her smile and followed them in, closing the door behind me. The inside was just as immaculate as the outside. There were pictures of Joe on every wall and surface, most with his wife, but others of him in the garden and some which must have been from work. An aroma of lemon polish lingered everywhere, as if she'd been cleaning the house all night. I could see she was trying to erase any trace of decay, to preserve the illusion that her dear husband was still there. The house was a meticulously maintained shrine to their lost love. But beneath the antiseptic chemical scent was a whiff of something dank and rotten.

She led us to the living room, where a large bay window let in streams of sunlight. A vase of flowers sat on a polished wooden coffee table, and I admired the expensive furniture. Everything was neatly in its place, perfectly curated to project an image of prosperity and stability.

But peering closer, I noticed a thin layer of dust on the ornamental decorations. The flowers in the vase were made of silk, expertly arranged to seem lifelike but never changing. On the lacquered shelves, framed family photos showed frozen smiles that never faltered over the passing years.

'I'm so sorry for your loss,' I said, sitting on the couch beside Ginger.

Debbie sniffled and nodded, tears rolling down her cheeks. 'Thank you. Joe was a good man, a loving husband, and he didn't deserve what happened to him.'

Ginger grabbed Debbie's hand and looked at her with concern. 'We're here to help, Debbie. We'll do anything we can.'

She enclosed Ginger's fingers in hers and took a deep breath. 'I know you will. The police are coming here in about an hour, and I didn't want to be alone when they arrived.' She smiled at me. 'Would you like a drink?'

'I'm fine, thanks.' My stomach rumbled like Vesuvius before the explosion.

'Something to eat?' Debbie said.

'Enola's nervous because she has to move out of her flat tomorrow and has nowhere to live since she won't lodge with Bruce and me.'

Debbie's eyes lit up. 'Oh, why don't you stay with me? There's a large spare bedroom upstairs, you know the one, Ginger, and you'll do me a big favour. I hate being alone at the best of times, and now, well....'

I didn't know what to say, so my belly growled again.

Ginger laughed. 'God, Enola. When did you last eat?'

'It was that spag bol Bruce made yesterday before the gig.'

Bruce was an excellent cook, but the stress of preparing for the gig must have unnerved him because yesterday's culinary delight wasn't his best effort. Not that I told him that.

Debbie stood. 'I'll make sandwiches, and after the police have been and gone, we can order a takeaway. How does that sound?'

'It sounds great,' I replied.

She went to the kitchen. I spoke to Ginger. 'I shouldn't stay here.'

'Why not?'

I glanced towards the kitchen and heard Debbie humming. 'I can't take advantage of her situation.'

She shook her head. 'Don't be daft. You heard her; you'll be doing her a big favour. And that bedroom is lovely. I've stayed in it before.' She grinned at me. 'She'll even let you play your terrible music as loud as you like.'

'This is from a long-time Barry Manilow Fan Club member.'

Ginger waved a finger at me like a dart. 'Now behave. I won't have you disparaging Bazza.'

Invisible fingers stabbed me in the gut. 'I'll consider staying here. Should we help her with the food?'

Ginger stretched her legs on the sofa. 'No, she'll shout if she needs us. Why do you think the police are coming here?'

'Probably to give an update on the investigation. Did they come here last night?'

'Yes, to break the bad news.' She lowered her head. 'I should have gone with them, but....'

I touched her hand. 'You have your own grieving to do, Ginger.'

Having struggled through my own grieving process for my parents over the last ten years, I knew how each person had to deal with it in their own way. Grief is a strange thing. It creeps up on you when you least expect it. One moment, you're okay, and the next, you're overwhelmed with sadness. Even after all this time, sometimes, it just all comes crashing down, and I feel like I'm drowning.

'We all do, Enola,' she said.

Ghostly insects crawled over my skin. I stood, deciding to take an uninvited tour of the room. 'How long have they lived here?'

'Twenty years, I guess,' Ginger said. 'Joe moved his business north after my dad, his brother, died. He said there were better opportunities up here, but I think he wanted to be closer to me. So apart from Debbie, we were the only family we had.'

A sudden practical thought struck me. 'Did Joe have a will?'

She shrugged. 'I don't know. Won't everything go to Debbie, anyway?' She glanced around the room. 'There's nothing I need.'

I peered at the photos on the wall, examining the ones

of Joe suited up and shaking hands with prominent-looking people. 'Joe was the sole owner of the business?'

'Yes, but he had a partner originally until they fell out.'

'About what?'

'His name is Mark Fuller,' Ginger said. 'He accused Joe of stealing some computer code for an app that made the business a lot of money and got their name and reputation out there.'

'What kind of apps do they make?'

She considered the question for a few seconds. 'Joe said they were all to do with artificial intelligence, getting AI to make art or movies or write books and music.'

'I told him he should stop because it was unethical.' Debbie returned with a tray of snacks, sandwiches, and drinks. 'We didn't need the money, but he was excited by what the software could do.'

'What do you mean, unethical?' Ginger asked.

Debbie sipped on what smelt like red wine. 'Think about it, Ginger. Joe and his team created AI apps that will eventually replace people from making all kinds of art.'

I was about to engage her in that conversation when the doorbell rang. 'Let's get ready for Robocop,' I said.

Chapter 8

New Life

Detective Inspector Parker arrived with an officer I'd met before, Constable Davis. Davis acknowledged my presence as Debbie showed the officers into the living room. Parker gave me a curious look, but I ignored it. He stood before us, looking stern as he delivered the news.

'There are no suspicious circumstances surrounding Joe's death.' He looked at Debbie. 'And there was no evidence of anybody else's involvement at the scene.'

She sobbed and buried her face in her hands. I felt a knot in my stomach as I pictured what we'd discovered in the woods.

I scrutinised Parker, trying to read his expression. 'What about how he got there?'

'We found Joe's car at his office, a twenty-minute walk from Harrington Woods.'

'CCTV footage?' I asked.

'Of the cameras that are working,' he replied, 'we didn't find any clips of Joe for yesterday.'

'Why would he go to that place?' Ginger said.

Parker looked at Davis, who answered. 'Officers spoke to his work colleagues, who said he would frequently go there for lunch. Apparently, the fresh air and being around nature helped with his creativity.' He glanced at Debbie. 'Mrs Jackson confirmed that to us yesterday.'

Debbie dried her eyes and raised her head. 'That's true. Joe loved spending time in the garden and surrounded by nature. He knew the woods well.'

I didn't want to ask in front of Debbie, but I had no choice.

'Do you know why he'd take his own life?'

DI Parker glanced from Debbie to me. 'Some of Joe's colleagues have indicated he might have been suffering from depression. And Mrs Jackson said things in her interview which corroborated that.'

'What?' Ginger asked.

Debbie's face darkened. 'It's true. He'd been going through what you'd call a mid-life crisis for a while, questioning what he was doing and if anything he'd done was of any value. I think his work with artificial intelligence was his final pressure point. He could see AI replacing him and the rest of us and wondered why he was stuck in that work.'

Ginger was ashen-faced. 'He never told me any of this.'

Debbie touched Ginger's arm. 'He didn't want to burden you. He loved you too much for that.'

'You checked the area around the crime scene?' I said.

Davis looked at me as if he suddenly remembered why he didn't like me. 'It's not a crime scene.'

'Forensics went over it with a fine tooth comb,' Parker said. 'The monsoon weather last night washed everything away. So all we found were your fingerprints and footprints, Ms Gray.'

'Why do you have Enola's fingerprints on file?' Debbie asked.

Ginger answered. 'Because of what happened to her parents, Debbie. Remember?'

Debbie put a hand to her face. 'Oh gosh, I'm sorry, Enola.'

I shrugged. 'It's nothing.' I turned to Parker. 'So that's it, case over?'

He nodded. 'The coroner will complete their investigation, and a doctor will issue you a death certificate in due course.' He cleared his throat. 'If you have further questions, please contact me.'

Ginger showed them out, and Debbie came to me. 'I'm really sorry, Enola. I don't know what I was thinking.' She touched her head. 'Bloody hell, I wasn't thinking at all. Stupid old cow.'

I smiled at her. 'Think nothing of it.' I led her to the sofa and sat her down as Ginger returned. 'How do you feel about what the police said?'

'About Joe's death?' I nodded. 'I suppose it makes the most sense.'

Ginger sat on the other side of her. 'Why didn't he tell me there was something wrong?'

Debbie touched Ginger's face. 'He couldn't. You know what he was like, a typical bloke always keeping his feelings to himself.'

'Did he speak to you about it?' Ginger said.

Debbie shook her head. 'Of course not, but I could see that work was getting him down. He was working longer hours and sometimes didn't come home and slept in the office. He was burning out, and I wanted us to get away for a holiday and take a long break somewhere warm. A bit of winter sun would have done us both the world of good.'

We sat in silence for a while before my stomach rumbled. Then we all burst out laughing. My belly hurt, but seeing their smiling faces, I knew this would be the start of a complicated process for them.

Ginger got up. 'We should eat.' She removed her mobile phone from her pocket. 'I'm going to tell Bruce he's eating with Kronos tonight. What takeaway do we want? I'm fine with anything.'

'What about pizza?' Debbie asked. 'I haven't had one for a while, not since Joe went on a diet and cut out all fatty foods and alcohol.'

'Pizza's great,' I said. 'Something with pepperoni for me.' Ginger made the call, and I spoke to Debbie. 'When did Joe start his diet?'

'About two weeks ago,' she replied.

So why would somebody taking measures to improve their health suddenly take their own life? It made little sense to me.

'It should be forty-five minutes,' Ginger said. 'So, Enola, where are you sleeping tomorrow?'

Debbie gripped my arm. 'Oh, please say you'll stay here.'

How could I refuse such a plea? 'Okay, but I need to bring my pet with me.'

Debbie touched her face. 'Oh. I'm allergic to cats and dogs.'

Ginger grinned. 'Dirty Harry has more legs than that.'

'Dirty Harry?' Debbie said.

'He's a tarantula,' I replied. 'Named after the Clint Eastwood film.'

Her eyes lit up. 'I love his movies.' She grinned at me. 'Do you keep your spider on a lead?'

My gut ached as I laughed. 'No, he lives in a tank. Could I bring him here?'

She nodded. 'I want to meet him now.'

'Great, but you'll have to let me earn my keep.'

She dragged me into the kitchen. 'We can sort that out later. So, what would you like to drink?' She grabbed the open bottle of red wine. 'We have a choice of booze.'

'I don't touch alcohol,' I said.

Debbie's mouth opened wide enough to fit that wine bottle inside.

Ginger laughed. 'Yeah, Enola is quite straight-laced in some things.'

I winked at her. 'Only some.'

Laughter filled the kitchen, and it felt good to be alive.

Yet I had a sneaking feeling something wicked was coming our way.

Chapter 9

Living in Another World

Ginger drove us home. Once I sorted my meagre possessions out, she'd take me back to Debbie's place in the morning. Then I'd have to look for a job. What happened at Bits & Bytes, the computer shop where I was the IT manager before somebody burnt it to the ground, had left me unwilling to return to employment for the last six months, but there was no choice now. I couldn't stay at Debbie's rent-free without feeling guilty.

The conversation in the car had focused on only one thing: Joe's death.

'I don't care what Debbie, the police, or his work colleagues say. I'd have known if Joe was depressed. He would have come to me.' The fire burned in her eyes with a mixture of sadness and anger.

'I'm not so sure, Ginger. Some people are good at hiding their feelings. When the authorities were shifting me between children's homes, there were always kids who bottled up how they felt, and you only discovered how they were suffering when it finally boiled over. Sometimes, it was violence against others, but more often than not, it was against themselves. And adults are a lot more adept at keeping those emotions secret.'

She glanced at me in the mirror. 'Tell me to mind my own business if you like, but where you one of those kids?'

I peered out of the window as she drove, staring into the faces of the lost souls on the streets. 'Sometimes I was, yeah. But I always vented it on others, never myself.'

'And now?'

That was a tricky question. 'Well, it depends on the situation. I finally have some closure knowing who killed my parents, but there's still a raging injustice burning inside me for how it happened and why it took so long to discover the culprits.'

'Do you resent the police for that?'

'Of course. Wouldn't you?'

'Sure. I know how they let you down, which is why I think they've been hasty with their investigation into Joe's death. It's as if they don't care about it or him.'

'As it is now, death with no suspicious circumstances, they can close it on their books. If it were anything else, like a murder, they'd be under pressure to solve it. So, it's easier for them this way, but not so much for you and Debbie.'

'I don't know, Enola. I won't say a bad word about Debbie, especially as she's probably still in shock, but she seemed to accept DI Parker's conclusion quickly. I thought she might kick up more of a fuss.'

'Perhaps she just wants to put it behind her,' I said. 'And she knew him better than anybody else.'

'I guess so,' Ginger said.

She parked outside the building, and we got out. It was close to midnight, and I had to be out of the flat by eight, which meant I would be packing for most of the night. Not that I had much to pack: getting Dirty Harry's living quarters sorted was the most important thing. Apart from a meagre collection of clothes, there were a few books and CDs. And I didn't even own a CD player anymore. I kept most for sentimental reasons, ones that my friend Seraphina gave me or others I nicked from the houses of former lovers I now hated. I should have binned those, but sometimes, just looking at a particular CD made me feel alive because I knew there were still people around that I wanted to suffer. It was a peculiar way to derive pleasure, but I assumed I wasn't the only person to think like that.

As we approached the entrance, three figures crept out of the shadows. The air stank of dope and unwashed armpits.

'Go home, boys. I'm not in the mood,' I said.

The one sporting the haircut created by Edward Scissorhands spoke.

'You were warned not to mess with Mr Rook's business. So, you must pay for that.'

I kept a careful eye on them and laughed. 'It's Mr Rook now? What is he, a chess piece sprung to life?'

'It doesn't matter who he is. We're here to teach you a lesson. One you won't forget in a hurry.'

Ginger stepped forward and screamed in his face. 'Fuck off, you fucking ugly fucking cunt!'

The fierceness of her blast even made me waver. The two goons with Mr Terrible Haircut looked at each other for guidance. Then, all the lights came on in the surrounding flats, with doors and windows opening to see what the fuss was. The thugs had little to worry about because they knew that short of somebody being murdered, nobody would ever call the police for help. This wasn't that type of neighbourhood. And it was one of the many things I loved about it.

Terrible Haircut scowled at her. 'This has nothing to do with you, you stupid cow. Now fuck off.'

I'd known Ginger for three years from the first day I moved into the area, and she knocked on my door to give me a welcome to the community cake she'd baked herself. I got her life story over a cup of herbal tea, and she promised to map out my star sign and tell me my future. I politely declined, not wanting to know how many more terrible things were waiting for me.

We'd been firm friends ever since, and in all that time, I'd never seen her lose her temper once. Not when Bruce ripped and melted her favourite top while ironing it. Not when some moron had tried to set his Yorkshire terrier on Kronos. And not even when a customer lost one of Ginger's tarot cards during a reading.

'You should have seen that coming,' he laughed as he left without paying.

But now she was angry.

She lifted her arm and smacked her elbow into Terrible Haircut's nose. It exploded like an elephant with diarrhoea, his blood spurting all over his two hapless mates. He screamed and grabbed for what remained of his snout as she punched him in the balls. He dropped to the pavement like scaffolding poles falling off a lorry, with arms and legs going in opposite directions. People hollered and shouted from the windows and doorways. She stood there with her arm held high like an Amazonian warrior.

I grinned at Ginger. 'I'm impressed.'

She rubbed at her elbow. 'It's what you taught me. I didn't want to break my fingers on his ugly mug.'

The two monkeys helped the organ grinder, and I spoke to them.

'You can tell your Mr Rook if he wants a word with me, he just needs to knock on the door.'

We went into the building and left them to their obscenities.

'You won't be here after tomorrow,' Ginger said.

I smiled. 'Then he'll have a hard time finding me.' I hugged her. 'I'll see you bright and early in the morning.'

She pointed at her watch. 'Eight o'clock sharp. And I'll have Kronos with me, so no moaning.'

I stepped into my flat and closed the door.

Now, I had to sort my life out.

Chapter 10

The Unexpected Guest

We arrived at Debbie's at eight-thirty. Kronos had behaved himself in the back of the car, but he was due for his morning walk. Dirty Harry was safely in his plastic terrarium in the boot.

'Once I drop you off,' Ginger said. 'I'll take Kronos down to the river. You can join us if you want.'

I watched him salivating all over the seat and said I'd give it a miss.

'I better get my room sorted at Debbie's and work out how to repay her.'

She glanced at my backpack. 'Yeah, you've really got a lot of stuff in there.'

'Well, I gave Bruce all my books, and you took most of the CDs. So that's all of my valuables right there.'

'Valuables? I don't think you'll get much for that lot on eBay.'

I didn't argue as she pulled up outside the house. Instead, I stepped out of the car and opened the back door for the dog, grabbing his lead before he sprinted into some-body else's garden and shat over everything. That's when I

231

saw the front door was open and heard raised voices from inside. I gave Kronos to Ginger.

'If I ask you to stay here, will you?' I said.

She shook her head. 'Of course not.'

I shrugged and ran into the house, straight to the living room. A hulking man with greasy hair and a sneer towered over Debbie. Two goons were standing behind him, looking ready to attack at a moment's notice. Debbie was sitting on the couch, appearing scared and small.

The living room was in shambles - lamps broken, furniture overturned, shards of glass and porcelain scattered across the hardwood floor. Picture frames lay smashed, beloved memories ground underfoot.

'Move away from her,' I ordered them.

The brute turned to face me, his eyes resembling burning embers. 'Who are you?' he spat.

Kronos growled, and Ginger had to restrain him. I removed the phone from my pocket. 'I'm the one who's going to call the police if you don't get the fuck out of here.'

'I know you,' Ginger said. 'You're the loan shark, Tom Brown.'

'That's right,' he replied. 'And your good old Uncle Joe owes me forty grand. Topping himself means that debt transfers to the not-so-merry window here. And maybe to you two as well, whoever you are.'

Debbie's lips trembled. 'I don't have it.'

Brown stepped forward, his bulk filling the room. 'Then you'd better find it, or else.'

Ginger's hand gripped mine, her nails digging into my skin.

'Why shouldn't I call the police?' I said.

He laughed, a cruel sound that echoed off the walls. 'The coppers don't care about the likes of us. Joe was a deadbeat who owed me money. Now, she's going to pay his debt. Or one or both of you two can.' He smirked at his goons. 'How long do you think they'd take to pay off forty grand, boys?'

They grinned but didn't reply.

My body temperature increased enough to melt ice cubes on my face. Brown took another step forward, his thugs following suit, the stench of cigarettes and cheap aftershave coming off them. The floral wallpaper seemed to wilt as they advanced, their presence leaching the cheer from the room. Motes of dust swirled in the shafts of sunlight, agitated by the palpable menace.

Brown's heavy boots thudded against the carpet, leaving indentations like wounds. Debbie recoiled further into the couch, eyes wide and pleading. Behind Brown, his goons shuffled with barely contained violence, jackals awaiting the command to pounce. Meaty hands flexed, adorned with garish rings. Cruel mouths twisted in anticipation.

'I told you to fuck off,' I said. The dog growled again, and I was glad Ginger hadn't fed him before we left that morning.

Brown smiled at me. 'You're not in charge here, kid.'

I tried to defuse the situation. 'Show me the proof Joe borrowed forty grand from you.'

He laughed. 'It wasn't that type of loan.'

'Then we don't have to give you anything.' I stepped to the side and grabbed the poker from the fireplace. 'And you're right; we don't need the police to deal with fuckwits like you.'

Kronos growled, and I beamed. Brown glanced between the whippet and me. Then he nodded to his men. 'This isn't the last you've heard of this, girl.'

They slipped past us and left the house. Debbie

slumped on the sofa and put her head in her hands. When I thought things couldn't get any worse for her, this happened. I placed the poker back, knowing Brown would return at some point and he wouldn't be so easy to scare off next time. With this and Rook's goons from the previous night, I had to think of getting something more impressive for protection.

'What am I going to do?' Debbie asked.

Ginger put her arm around Debbie's shoulder, and Kronos jumped onto the sofa. I went to the window and watched Brown and his thugs drive away. He blew a kiss at me as they left. It was a good thing I didn't have a job to go to as a lot needed doing. And the first thing was to calm Debbie's nerves.

'What happened?' I said.

She stopped shaking and looked at me. 'They turned up and pushed their way in, saying Joe owed him, Brown, £40,000, and now I was responsible for that debt. I said I didn't have the money, so he told me I'd have to sell the house or Joe's business to get the cash.'

She sank further into the sofa, and Kronos licked her face. I hated asking her questions when she was upset, but there was no choice.

'Did Joe leave a will, Debbie?'

Her eyes glazed over as she stared at me. 'We both made wills, leaving everything to the other.'

'So, the business is yours?' Ginger said.

'I guess so,' Debbie replied. 'But what will we do about Brown? Shouldn't we go to the police?'

'He won't return here, and even if he does, I'm staying with you now. As for the police, we might need to contact DI Parker about the loathsome Mr Brown.' I looked at

Ginger. 'Will you stay here while I pop out? I have an errand to run.'

Ginger nodded. 'Sure.'

'Thanks,' I said. 'Debbie, can you sort all of Joe's papers together while I'm gone?'

'Yes,' she replied.

'Did he have a computer or a laptop?'

'It's upstairs,' Debbie said.

'Great, bring that here as well. Did the police give you his mobile phone?'

She shook her head. 'Not yet.'

'Okay, we'll have enough to go on for now when I return.'

'What are we going to do?' Ginger asked.

I stroked Kronos's cheek. 'We're heading on a journey into Joe Jackson's life.'

First, I had to see a woman about a gun.

Chapter 11

Stab Your Back

The Dog and Duck was one of the town's oldest pubs and had the worst reputation, one of those places your parents warned you about. If you stumbled into it as a stranger, you'd be cashless by the time you left. The exterior was dingy and worn, decades of pollution staining the walls charcoal grey. Grime coated the windows, obscuring the interior and giving the pub an air of ominous secrecy. It was my local for a while, but a falling out with a former friend meant I hadn't stepped inside its mangy walls for several years.

That was until now.

It was a dingy, dimly lit establishment in the seediest part of the town. The sour smell of stale beer and vape smoke hung thick in the air, and the sounds of raised voices and clinking glasses echoed through the room. The patrons matched the ambience: sullen men with prison tattoos and dead eyes, rakish youths itching for trouble. A desperate figure huddled over their drink here and there, seeking oblivion in the dirty glasses. Anyone not local stuck out painfully, attracting malicious stares.

I scanned the crowd, searching for Amy Sparrow, the queen of the underworld. It was a name she gave herself as a teenager, and after she'd skewered a few gormless thugs, it stuck.

A group of rough-looking men played pool, grunts and laughter ringing through the air. In another corner, a woman with bleached blonde hair and too much makeup flirted with a disinterested man. Feckless souls dropped dirty coins into flashing machines as if they were alien visitors ready to whisk them off to another world.

Amy was sitting at a booth at the back, surrounded by her usual entourage of shady characters. The Damned's "Stab Your Back" was blurting from the speakers, an appropriate tune considering my falling out with her. And all over a pair of shoes. I moved towards her, and she glanced at me with a twinkle in her eye.

'Supping whisky from the jar and swapping insults in the pub, stared down by a woman with eyes like Beelzebub.'

'That's nice, Amy. Do you speak in rhymes now?'

She laughed. 'I recall the last time we spoke, Enola, and how much pain you caused me. It is this matter of pain that separates us. Until the point when you no longer feel physically or emotionally sick from the pain you see or hear, until your pain no longer controls you, until the pain ceases to be the basis of your beliefs about life, I must inform you that you are still an animal, thinking only slightly more clearly about what an animal feels. Suffering is such a minor thing. Anyone with a truly open mind, guided by what science has revealed, should understand that it is a minor issue. Perhaps, outside of this small planet, this tiny particle of cosmic dust, so insignificant that it is not even visible compared to the nearest star - perhaps, I repeat, that pain does not exist anywhere else.'

'So, you're a philosopher now?'

'You stole my shoes, Enola.'

'They didn't suit you, Amy.'

'Well, you would say that since you always had terrible taste in everything.'

'Does that include friends?'

She grinned. 'These are your old mates. Don't you remember them?'

I'd tried to forget them all, but they were still fixed in my brain. On her right was cat burglar Jack, a born-again Christian and lifelong weirdo who was filmed eating his ear wax. Next to him was Tricia, the card shark, who talked like Marvin the Paranoid Android and dyed her hair red when she was twelve to attract attention. We'd spent time together in the same children's home with Amy. Opposite her was the explosive expert, Dave the Rave, a bloke who couldn't walk across a room like a normal human being and communicated like an AI-generated version of a primary school teacher. Finally, making up her little group was Ted, Amy's muscle, a man unable to smile without looking like a serial killer caught in the act.

'Send them away, Amy.'

'What? You don't want to reacquaint yourself with your old mates after all this time?'

'They were never my friends, Amy.'

She shook her head. 'And there was me thinking that your little message was all about contrition and regret.'

'I need to talk to you in private.'

'Sure, but I have a price.'

'What?'

'You stole my shoes, so you owe me a kiss.'

I shook my head. 'You'll get a kiss with a fist, that's it.'

She waved a finger at me. 'You know the price.'

I sighed and remembered why I was there. 'Okay, let's get it over with.'

She told them to leave, and her motley crew sulked to the bar as I sat beside Amy. She smelt of lavender and honey as she leaned into me. Then we kissed without me moving my lips.

She pulled away and looked disappointed. 'Your kiss is better with cocaine.'

'On your lips or mine?'

She smirked. 'On both, Enola, like the good old days.'

'Those days are gone, Amy, and they won't be coming back.'

'Your cheeks are bright with the soft vermilion of Snow White's poisoned apple mingling with Sleeping Beauty's virginity.'

'You should be given a nice new jacket, Amy, the one that fastens up the back.'

She frowned. 'Your cruelty wounds me, Enola. How many times did people pick on you for being different when we were younger, and now you're acting like them?'

She was right, and I still needed her help. 'I'm sorry.'

Amy sucked on a vape and blew orange smoke around us. It smelt as if somebody had stuck a tangerine up my nose.

'Reality is fundamentally an illusion, a constantly shifting amalgam pieced together by our brains rather than anything concretely real. You taught me that, Enola.' The smoke lingered above her like a living cloud. 'What did you come here for? Do you fancy having more of my shoes?'

I lowered my voice. 'I need a gun.'

She peered into my eyes. 'Oh, this is rich. Why do you want such a thing?'

I told her about my little difficulties with the loan shark and the thugs. 'Have you heard of a Mr Rook?'

'Isn't he a Batman villain?'

'Probably, but he seems to have several goons determined to harm me, so I'm outnumbered.'

'I could lend you, Ted, for a few days.'

I glanced at him at the bar, and he winked at me.

'No thanks. A gun will do.'

'No problem, my old friend. Do you have a particular pistol in mind? A derringer, maybe. They're all the rage now with the thirteen to sixteen age group.' She gazed wistfully beyond me. 'Though there is a rising demand from young girls for untraceable poisons. It's quite a lucrative market.'

I got up. 'Get me something light and small. And plenty of ammunition. When will you have it?'

'This time tomorrow. Don't you want to know the price?'

I turned from her and replied. 'Knowing you, Amy, it'll be something I can't afford.'

Laughter erupted behind me as I left the pub. Now, I needed a shower to wash the stench off me.

Chapter 12

In the City

Bruce rang me as I stepped out of the pub.

'Are you still at Debbie's?' The voices in the background told me he wasn't home.

'No, I had to pop out for a bit.' I didn't mention the commotion with the loan shark. Ginger could tell him about that. 'Is everything okay?'

'Yeah, great, never better,' he said. 'I've set up another gig at the Raven tonight. It's very last minute, and I need some help, which is why I'm ringing. Would you like to earn a few pounds, cash in hand?'

'Of course, Bruce. Every little helps. What's the deal?'

He spoke to somebody near him before returning to me. 'I'm over at the Edge Street food bank. Can you meet me there, and I'll tell you about it?'

'Sure. See you soon.'

It would keep me busy for the night, but we'd have to bring Debbie with us. I didn't like the idea of leaving her in that house alone with the loan shark sniffing around. And maybe I'd bump into those goons again or the young woman they were harassing.

I glanced at the Dog and Duck as I turned the corner, wondering how I felt seeing Amy after all this time. I recollected when we first met in the children's home, two teenagers craving excitement. We found that and more, sneaking out of the house to wander the streets and explore the town, often getting into trouble. We felt invincible then, brimming with reckless, youthful energy. Others we knew back then weren't so fortunate, swallowed up by the streets or addictions. Some wandered those same grimy pubs, lost souls unable to break free.

Then, Amy's idea was to add some danger to our lives by shoplifting from the most expensive stores. One of us would be the lookout or the distraction, while the other slipped luxurious perfume or fancy handbags into our coats. We'd hang onto the stuff for a few days before dumping it in the woods. We were a duo of teenage female Robin Hoods for a time, stealing from the rich but keeping it for ourselves.

It was a thrill to walk out of those polished boutiques with dozens of illicit goods, our hearts racing as alarms blared behind us. We'd run through the streets, giddy with adrenaline, before collapsing in each other's arms, breathless and exhilarated. For two nobodies from the home, beating the system and enjoying forbidden luxuries felt intoxicating.

It was fun while it lasted.

The thing about the stolen shoes was only a joke, a reference to our love of the *Wizard of Oz*. Often, when we couldn't get out of the home, we'd commandeer the TV and DVD player to curl up on the sofa in the common room and watch Dorothy and Toto wander down the Yellow Brick Road, constantly arguing over who was which character.

However, it wasn't stolen shoes that caused our falling out. We had two years of wild living, but my friend

Seraphina finally talked some sense into me when I turned sixteen. So I quit the drugs and the booze and gave up my life of crime. I tried to talk Amy around, but she wouldn't have it, heading in the opposite direction, embroiling herself deeper into the criminal lifestyle.

'I'm the queen of the underworld, Enola,' she bragged.

So I got away from that world, and we stopped talking until now. Still, it went better than expected, though what payment Amy would want from me would probably keep me awake all night. But for now, I focused on seeing Bruce and sorting out Debbie's situation when I returned to her place.

I headed towards Edge Street. The air was thick with the scent of gasoline and fried food mixed with the salty aroma of the nearby river. The sun was shining, but it did little to lift my spirits as I thought of everything on my mind. As I walked, I gazed into the river. The water flowed steadily, reflecting the buildings and bridges that loomed over it. Several boats of all shapes and sizes chugged along, their horns blaring as they navigated the busy waterway. The gulls swooped and cried overhead, yet when I glanced at them, I could have sworn they were vultures circling me, representing the troubles on the horizon: the mysterious Mr Rook and his reappearing goons; Brown, the loan shark; my search for full-time employment and a place to live that wasn't somebody else's sofa or spare bedroom; and the mystery of what happened to Joe Jackson.

I stopped momentarily, leaning against a railing and staring at the water. My thoughts turned to my childhood and my friendship with Amy Sparrow. We were trouble-makers, always getting into mischief and causing chaos wherever we went. And it seemed like nothing and every-thing had changed since then. I remembered the thrill of stealing and the adrenaline rush as we snatched what we wanted and ran away, of the times spent in those woods, just the two of us, when the only world we recognised was our own.

Did part of me want to return to that world?

Then I pictured Joe Jackson hanging in the same spot, dangling from a branch near where Amy had handed out our ill-gotten gains only a few years ago. If the police were convinced there were no suspicious circumstances in Joe's death, why did I have a nagging doubt at the back of my mind? Probably because I didn't trust the coppers. Their incompetence and rampant corruption were known to all, so I wouldn't trust them to organise a piss-up in a brewery.

But maybe I should tell Detective Inspector Parker about that thug, Tom Brown. Brown seemed unlikely to kill Joe if he were owed forty grand, but there was no accounting for how stupid some criminals could be. I should have asked Amy if she knew Brown, but I could do it when I picked up the gun.

The gun. I'd fired one before, several times during my two years of wild youth with Amy, but I thought I'd put that part of my life behind me. Hopefully, I wouldn't have to use it, so Brown, Rook and their goons would back off just by the sight of it. On the other hand, it could worsen things, and everything would go to hell and high water.

I pushed that image out of my mind, walking over the bridge and away from the river. The food bank was at the end of the street, with long queues outside. People smiled at me as I thought of Bruce's gig, looking forward to being at work for the first time in six months.

Fingers crossed, nobody would try to kill me.

Chapter 13

Food for Thought

I walked into the food bank and was immediately hit with the scent of spices and the noise of clanging pots and pans. There were rows of shelves filled with non-perishable items and a crowd of people shuffling about, volunteering their time to help those in need.

Bruce stood at the far end of the room, surrounded by children and adults. The kids looked happy, but the grown-ups appeared stressed and worn out. I waved at him, and he left the others, greeting me with a smile.

'I didn't know you worked here,' I said.

He nodded. 'I started as a volunteer a few months back. Two weeks ago, I thought we could see the light at the end of the tunnel, but the tunnel is never-ending now.'

'What do you mean?'

Bruce stepped away from those receiving their food parcels, the weight of the world possessing every word he said. 'Demand for food banks has grown since the start of the pandemic, but in recent months, the numbers have exploded. In addition to the regulars, we're getting twenty-five to thirty new people each week. What's happening regarding the volume we're receiving and the complexity of the problems and issues people are coming in with is scary. We're seeing folks who hadn't even had to contemplate using a food bank, who might have been donating to a food bank this time last year. And it's happening in every part of the country.' He gazed across the room. 'Before Covid, the reason most people used us was benefit sanctions. That's not the case now. Almost every referral is here because of low incomes or because they're waiting to be moved on to universal credit, which takes a minimum of five weeks.' He looked at me. 'Ginger said your DWP meeting didn't go well.'

'Yeah, I don't have any photo ID, so apparently, I don't exist.' A man behind a counter waved at us, so I told Bruce. 'I think you're wanted over there.'

'It's all go here,' he said. 'I'll be right back, and we'll talk about tonight.'

He left, and I sat at a table, watching the events around me. Then, after a few minutes, a young girl, maybe about eight years old, came over and showed me her doll.

'What's her name?' I asked.

She smiled at me. 'She's Daisy, and I'm Becky.'

I returned her smile. 'Well, I'm pleased to meet you, Becky and Daisy. I'm Enola.'

The kid grinned. 'That means alone backwards.'

'It does,' I replied. 'You're very clever, Becky.'

'I know, I tell everybody that.' She put the doll on the table, and I noticed how dirty its clothes were. 'Are you here because you have nothing as well?'

Before I could answer, a young woman rushed over.

'Becky, what have I told you about bothering people?'

The girl grimaced. 'I'm not bothering anybody, Mum. I'm chatting with Enola.'

Becky's mother collapsed into the seat opposite me, looking too tired to smile.

'I hope she's not disturbing you.'

I shook my head. 'No, she's fine. How are you?'

She spoke to me as if I was the first adult she'd spoken to in a while.

'Thank God for this place because I don't know what we'd do without it. I've gone from being an average working-class citizen to somebody who's in poverty. The soaring cost of food and fuel combined with rent, childcare costs, and the universal credit cut means I'm struggling to make ends meet. Without access to the food bank, my options would be just bread and butter, really. I make sure there's enough for Becky, but I'd be going hungry. And we can only afford to have the heating on three or four days a week. God knows what I'll do when the cold weather kicks in.' She glanced at her daughter. 'And there'll be no Christmas presents this year.' She leaned in closer to me. 'When I first visited here, I was ashamed, but luckily, the team is amazing, and they put me at ease very quickly. Especially Bruce. He's so kind.'

'Yeah,' I said. 'He's a good bloke.'

She laughed. 'And god knows there aren't many of them around.'

'Speak of the devil,' I said as Bruce joined us.

'What have I done now?'

'Mum said you're a catch,' Becky said.

'Becky!' her mother shouted.

He pulled at the top of his shirt as his cheeks turned pink. 'Eh, okay, but I need to borrow Enola.'

He dragged me away, and I didn't protest. 'You might have yourself an admirer there, Bruce.'

'I'm too busy for any romantic interests, Enola. And that's why I require your help.'

He handed me a leaflet. 'Hey Venus at the Raven. Doors open at 7. £10 entrance.' I stared at him. 'This is tonight?'

Bruce snatched the leaflet from me. 'Shit, I'll have to handwrite the date on fifty of these now. As if I didn't have enough to do.'

'So, what do you want me to do?'

He muttered something to himself before returning to me. 'Can you meet the band at the train station at four o'clock? There are only two of them, a husband-and-wife team. She plays the drums and sings while he's on the guitar. Like the White Stripes, but only better.'

'Sure, I've got nothing else to do. So then, what do I do with them?'

Bruce gave me fifty quid. 'Get a taxi to the Raven and see what they want to eat and drink.' He glanced at the clock on the wall showing 2 p.m. 'Stay with them, keep them entertained, and I'll meet you there at about five. How does that sound?'

'Fine. Would you like me to work at the venue during the gig?'

He rubbed at the spot growing on his chin. 'I could put you on the door for the tickets.' He reached into his wallet again. 'Would fifty quid be a fair payment for the work?'

I snatched the notes from his fingers. 'It looks like I might have some rent for Debbie Jackson.'

'Yeah, how did that go?'

'You haven't spoken to Ginger?'

He shook his head. 'Not since this morning.'

'It went fine. I have a few hours to kill, so I'm returning to Debbie's. Any messages for Ginger?'

'Just tell her I'll see her tonight.'

He slipped away, and I watched him go as a group of adults approached him. I put the money in my pocket and got my phone to call a taxi.

I had to ask Joe Jackson's widow if she fancied attending a rock gig in a sweaty dive bar.

Chapter 14

Messages

When I arrived, Kronos was sleeping on the sofa, and Dirty Harry was in his plastic abode on the coffee table. Debbie and Ginger were sitting at the dining room table, peering over a pile of documents. I gave them the good news first.

'You're going to a gig tonight, Debbie.'

She peered at me over the top of her spectacles. 'What?'

'Bruce got it sorted, then?' Ginger said.

I joined them at the table. 'Yeah, a duo called Hey Venus. I'm meeting them at the train station at four and then taking them to the Raven. That's why I need you to bring Debbie to the gig.'

Debbie looked at me with startled eyes. 'Why am I going to a concert?'

I didn't want to tell her it was because I suspected Tom Brown and his goons could return to the house when she was inside alone.

'Ginger told me you and Joe were keen concert-goers in your younger days, so we thought it might be a nice night out for you.' I glanced at Ginger. 'Maybe it will get your mind off things for a while.'

She put a hand to her cheek. 'Don't you think I'm too old?'

I studied her face. 'How old are you?'

'Forty-eight,' she replied.

I laughed. 'That's no age. My friend Seraphina was still going to live music in her sixties. You're just a spring chicken.'

'Will she be there tonight, Seraphina?' Debbie asked.

'No. She passed away a few months ago.'

Silence settled between us before Ginger broke it. 'What have you been up to apart from helping Bruce out?'

I picked up a few documents from the table, seeing bank statements and household bills. 'Not much. How far have you got with this stuff?'

She sighed. 'It's all routine paperwork. Joe must have kept his business accounts at the office.'

I glanced at the laptop. 'Have you checked the computer?'

'No,' Debbie said. 'Joe never liked me using his machine.'

I went and retrieved it, an expensive MacBook that started when I lifted the lid.

'Do you know the password?'

Debbie opened a drawer and removed a notebook. Then she gave it to me.

'Joe's memory was terrible, so he wrote all his passwords here.'

I flicked open the pages, seeing the details for everything from his bank accounts to all his internet and social media information. The password for the laptop was on the first page, and it was Ginger's birthday. I showed it to her as I typed the numbers into the machine.

'I thought the police would have looked at this,' Ginger said.

The screen flickered into life. 'They've moved on to other things now.'

The desktop image was Joe and Debbie smiling on a beach. I checked his email first, reviewing the sent, received, and deleted messages. Apart from the junk mail, everything was work-related. It took me fifteen minutes to read them all, searching for anything about his state of mind. They were all positive, with the last few about the new contract the business had signed.

'Anything useful?' Ginger asked.

I turned the screen around to show her the email about the contract. 'I don't see why Joe would borrow forty grand from a loan shark when he'd just inked a million-pound contract.'

Ginger whistled, and Debbie put a hand to her cheek. 'Joe told me it was good, but he never said it was that good.'

I scrutinised the details, memorising the name of the company – YellowBack Publications – and what they were paying for: an AI app that would produce novels and short stories from minimal input.

'We need to go to Joe's office,' I told them. 'Debbie, you're the boss there now. This contract and the others belong to you.'

'Oh my,' she said.

I moved beyond the email and searched through the files and folders, hoping something would jump out from the thousands on the machine. I started with the most recent ones Joe had looked at: work-related photos and videos of meetings. There didn't appear to be any personal stuff on the computer. I watched two clips, but nothing was illuminating.

Then, I went to the web browser and poured through Joe's internet history. Apart from trips to the BBC website, it was all about his business, mainly the Jackson Systems site and others to do with AI. After that, it was a trawl through his social media accounts. Twitter and Instagram were all about promoting the business, but Facebook was different. There was very little on his personal FB page. His last comment was three months ago when he'd liked a post about an AI art app, but the surprise came when I looked at his Facebook messages.

I lifted the laptop and got up. 'I'm going to the sofa to get more comfortable.'

Kronos woke up as I sat beside him, peering at me through huge eyes. I ignored his expectant expression and returned to the FB messages, more than a dozen, going back a month, from a woman called Sarah Bailey. I read them several times, hers and his, and discovered that she and Joe had been a couple at university thirty years ago but hadn't seen each other for over two decades. That was until three weeks ago when they'd met in town. The conversations between them weren't sexual, but the undercurrent of flirtation was unmistakable.

Ginger came into the living room. 'Would you like a drink?'

I pushed Kronos off the sofa, and the dog whimpered. 'Sit,' I said to Ginger.

I handed the laptop to her and nodded at the messages.

'What?' she asked.

I lowered my voice. 'Read them, but keep it between you and me.' There was no point in upsetting Debbie if we didn't have to. I observed Ginger as she went through the messages, watching her eyes expand with every word.

'Do you think...?' she said.

Then Debbie walked into the room. 'What are you girls whispering about?'

I grabbed the laptop and closed the lid. 'We're wondering what to wear for the gig tonight.' I put the computer on the sofa and got up. 'How about you, Debbie?'

She scrunched up her face. 'You'll have to show me what to wear. I wouldn't have a clue.'

Indeed, just like she didn't have a clue about her husband and his old flame.

The question was what to do about it.

Chapter 15

Hey Venus

When I arrived, the train station was full of people, a hive of activity and noise, five minutes before Hey Venus were due. I leaned against a pillar and studied the surroundings. The announcements echoed throughout the cavernous space, blending with the murmur of voices and the screech of trains. The old building smelt of oil and metal and the aroma of coffee from the café. I took a deep breath and tried to focus.

As I waited, I replayed those Facebook messages in my head. Was it only an innocent flirtation between two former friends reconnecting after thirty years? Or was there more to it than that?

The more I thought about them, the more I wondered what really happened to Joe. Was his death a suicide, or was something more sinister at play? And could this old flame of his, Sarah Bailey, be involved? Was he having an affair? Had his guilt driven him to such drastic action?

I straightened up as the train arrived. People busied themselves, ready to start their journeys. Young children ran around like excited bees as adults tried to pull them away from the platform's edge. I had a vague memory of my parents taking me to the seaside by rail for my fifth birthday, a lingering recollection of eating fish and chips and building sandcastles.

The train squeaked into the platform and hurt my ears. The doors slid open, and a flood of commuters poured out. Briefcases bumped against legs, and raised voices bounced off the station roof. The smell of coffee and perfume mingled in the air as I waited.

Then the two musicians stepped off the train and onto the platform, and I recognised them from the photos Bruce had sent me. The bloke held a guitar case, and I guessed she'd be using the drums at the Raven. He was tall, with broad shoulders and shaggy brown hair that framed his chiselled jaw. He had a confident stride, and his eyes sparkled with a hint of mischief. His wife was the opposite - petite and delicate, with a mass of curly locks that cascaded down her back in a golden waterfall. Her eyes were a brilliant blue, and her skin was like porcelain, giving her a fairy-like appearance. She moved with poise and fluidity, her gracefulness unexpected for a rock band drummer.

They were the epitome of a musical duo - yin and yang, the perfect balance of power and grace. I noticed the love between them, seeing their eyes meet and hold for a moment longer than necessary and how their hands would brush ever so slightly as they passed each other. I stared at them and thought of Amy, wondering what gun she would get for me. And how much it cost.

'Enola?' he said.

I nodded. 'And you must be Hey Venus, Pete and Amanda?'

She ran forward and threw her arms around me,

squeezing so hard that I understood how she could bash a drum set for hours.

I breathed again when she finally let go. 'We're excited to play tonight.'

'And I can't wait to see you play. Bruce has told me so much about you.' Of course, he hadn't, and I wasn't even sure how he'd ended up booking them. Pete must have read my mind.

'We have a huge following on TikTok and Instagram.'

'Great,' I said, leading them to the taxi rank. 'Bruce said to get you anything you needed, food and drink wise. Then we'll go to the venue where you can do a soundcheck.'

Amanda put a hand around my waist. 'That's fantastic, Enola. I can tell from your aura we'll be firm friends.'

She spent the journey talking to me about spiritual energy and how they knew playing at the Raven Club was perfect for their synergy. I nodded and stayed quiet, getting them safely into the dressing room before going to the corner shop for bottles of red and white wine and ordering a three-course Indian meal for each of them. Then I called Ginger.

She sounded out of breath on the phone. 'What should we do about those messages in Joe's FB account?'

'What do you want to do?'

'Hang on. I'm moving to the garden, so she can't hear me.' I heard her heavy breathing and Kronos barking as she stepped outside. 'Should we inform the police?'

'It would be a waste of time. We've got several choices, but it's up to you. Joe was your uncle.'

'What choices?'

'Well, first, we could do nothing. So don't tell Debbie and close Joe's FB account. That will be the end of it.'

'No,' she said. 'I need to sort this out.'

'Would you like to tell Debbie?'

Ginger paused. 'Not yet. We should speak to this woman.'

'Sarah Bailey.'

'Yeah, *her*.' The bitterness in Ginger's voice surprised me.

'How do you want to go about it?'

'I don't know. What do you think?'

'We don't even know if she realises Joe's dead.'

'Fuck, yeah.'

That gave me an idea. 'I could message her from Joe's FB account and ask to meet.'

'What, pretend to be Joe? Jesus, Enola, won't that be cruel when we turn up, and she discovers he's dead?'

'It's up to you, Ginger.'

I pictured the gears grinding in her head on the other end of the phone.

'Do it,' she said. 'But I'm going with you to meet her.'

'Right. As soon as I finish this call, I'll send a message saying it's important she meets me, Joe, tomorrow morning in the café where they met before. How does that sound to you?'

'Perfect. I want to know what she was doing with my uncle before he died.'

'Okay. On to other things. Have you got Debbie sorted for tonight?'

'Yeah, she had jeans and a leather jacket in her wardrobe; that will do. So how are the band?'

'They seem fine, though they look a little lightweight physically to be a rock band.'

'Well, Iggy Pop was skinny as fuck, and he did okay with The Stooges.'

'Yes, but he wasn't banging fuck out of the drums.'

'I guess we'll see tonight. We should get there between six and seven. What are you doing for food?'

'I'm sharing an Indian meal with the band.'

'Great. See you soon.'

Ginger hung up. I signed out of my Facebook account and into Joe's.

Then I pretended to be a dead man to message a woman who might have killed him.

Chapter 16

Sultans of Swing

I spent an enjoyable time with Pete and Amanda, eating curry and watching them drink. They told me about their musical journey, how they'd met in the final year of a failing school and had bonded over music – though she still couldn't believe he thought Queen were the greatest band ever. I recounted my discovery of punk and new wave as a teenager and how I spent most of my time discovering new music on the radio and the internet.

Amanda hugged me again at the end of it. 'You have to let me read your aura after the gig.'

I agreed and then watched them rehearse and do the soundcheck. Bruce arrived halfway through.

'How's it going?' he said.

'Great,' I replied. 'How did you find them?'

He grinned at me. 'I told you all that time watching TikTok videos would be worth it.'

I laughed. 'Right.'

'Can you go on the door for me and handle the tickets and payments?'

I nodded. 'Sure. I could do with a sit-down. Is it the same useless security as it was the other night?'

Bruce shook his head. 'I couldn't get anyone at such short notice. So, we're on our own tonight. Are you okay with that?'

'Great.' I left him as he went to speak to Amanda and Pete.

I sat in the booth and checked Sarah Bailey's Facebook. Bailey had not updated her profile in months, the last being an allegedly humorous photo of two cats wrestling. Her page had no personal pictures or details, and the account had only been created six months ago. Her avatar was a cartoon cat smoking a cigar. I searched other social media sites, Twitter and Instagram for her. There were dozens of accounts with her name, but none appeared to be the same woman. I gave up when Ginger and Debbie arrived.

'You need tickets to get in,' I told Ginger.

She scowled at me. 'For my mate's gig? I don't think so.'

I laughed and said hello to Debbie, telling her how good she looked. She touched her cheek.

'You don't think I look too old?'

I shook my head. 'You look great. Are you looking forward to it?'

Ginger intervened before Debbie could reply. 'She's already had half a bottle of wine, so she's well lubricated.'

Debbie ignored us to talk to a young woman standing behind her. I leaned into Ginger. 'Keep an eye on her until I can get away from here. I wouldn't put it past Brown to try something inside.'

'Okay. Speak to you later.'

She dragged Debbie into the venue as I dealt with the first customers. As I took tickets, I made small talk and answered questions. Everybody seemed in good spirits, and there was no sign of the moron from the other night or those two thugs.

Some punters were eager to know more about Hey Venus, but I couldn't tell them much. And all the while, I kept watching for Brown or any of Rook's thugs, knowing they would return to my life at some point. But as long as it was after I collected the gun from Amy, there would be no problems. Well, none that I couldn't handle.

Music drifted out of the venue as Bruce started the warm-up by shuffling a playlist through the speakers. He came to see me five minutes later as Suede's "Animal Nitrate" followed him.

'How's it going?' he asked.

I glanced at the numbers I'd jotted on a notepad. 'I've taken sixty tickets and twenty cash payments. A few wanted to use their cards, but I told them we don't have the facilities for that and pointed them towards the machine outside the supermarket down the road.'

'Great,' he said. 'Remember that the capacity is a hundred and fifty.'

'How many tickets have you sold?'

'A hundred.'

'Okay, thirty more walk-ins, and that's it. Unless you're counting the liggers like your flatmate in the numbers?'

He laughed. 'Nah, we're good for a few over if it comes to that.'

His confidence that we wouldn't have any problems with having too many people in the venue didn't ease my concerns.

'Is the manager here?'

'Ben? Yeah, he's behind the bar, pulling pints.'

'What's he saying about the crowd?'

Bruce shrugged. 'He's happy as long as they sell plenty

of drinks.' He checked his watch. 'Anyway, I've got to go. Hey Venus are due on in twenty minutes.'

He sloped off and left me to deal with the queue. In the end, everything went far smoother than I thought it would, especially as there was no visible security at the entrance. When I heard the crowd cheering for Hey Venus striding onto the stage, I'd let one hundred and thirty punters into the venue.

Then I didn't know what to do. I was reluctant to stay there to stop people from getting in without paying for tickets, yet if I went inside to watch the band, then anyone could enter.

'Fuck, Bruce, you didn't think this through.'

As the music erupted in the other room, I left the Raven and scanned the streets. The breeze was cool against my skin, and I shivered as a wind blew across my face. It would be a cold winter, and I thought of the people sleeping rough in the town. The distant sirens and the murmuring chatter of stray cats filled the air.

The road was poorly lit, the dim glow of street lamps casting long shadows over the pavement. The smell of trash and stale cigarettes surrounded me, mixing with the dampness of the night. On one side of the street was a row of dark, abandoned buildings, their windows boarded up and graffiti covering the walls. On the other side was a line of bars and nightclubs, the music thumping through the pavement and vibrating beneath my feet.

Then I heard a rustling sound behind me. I spun around, my heart racing, but all I saw was a stray cat darting down an alley. I sighed in relief and turned to go back into the club.

That's when somebody punched me in the side of the head.

Chapter 17

Midnight Rambler

I drifted in and out of consciousness, my vision blurred and a buzzing noise filling my ears. My head ached, and there was a wet sensation on my neck. I noticed my feet moving through a dirty street when I could see. Two people held onto my arms like puppeteers, with me their unwilling marionette.

'Did you knock her out?' A voice said. 'Mr Rook won't be happy if she's asleep when we get to him.'

'Nah, I only give her a little tap. You said she was tougher than that.'

'I don't care. I hope you've fucking given her brain damage. Her stupid cunt friend broke my fucking nose. I hope we're going back for her later.'

Mr Terrible Haircut? I recognised his voice, him and one other, as they dragged me over a weed-encrusted wasteland. Spots of light danced before my eyes, and I could have sworn I saw a fat rat following me.

'You don't think you're pretty anymore?'

One of them dug his fingers into my arm. 'Look at me. She's turned me into fucking Frankenstein.'

'The monster.'

'What?'

'Frankenstein was the doctor, and the creature he created was the monster.' They stopped moving as my vision cleared. 'And you were always fucking ugly, Stan, well before the tarot reader hit you.'

They relaxed their grips on my arms, and I took a deep breath.

'We should have got the other one as well,' Stan said.

'Why, so she could tell you your future? You don't need her for that, Stan. I'll tell you your fucking future if we don't get her to the boss pretty fucking quick. You'll end up like Harry Marsh. Do you remember what happened to Harry?'

'Nobody knows what happened to Harry. The dipshit just disappeared.'

'I swear to God, Stan, you're the stupidest fucking person I've ever met.'

That was my cue to jerk free from their grasp and run for it. I did the first part, wriggling away and heading into the dark. Then my legs gave way, and I hit the dirt with my nose.

'Fuck me,' the other one said. 'She's a slippery little eel.'

Pain shot through my face and then invaded every inch of me. I rolled onto my side and struggled to breathe, pushing my arms out to find grass and weeds between my fingers. Blood dribbled down my cheeks and onto my mouth. I tasted it, hoping it would re-energise my legs, which had turned into melted plastic. The moon hovered above me, and I waited for it to crash into my head. It couldn't have made me feel any worse than I did.

But it didn't.

Their shadows loomed over me, creating a chill wind that burnt into my cheeks.

'We could just do her here,' Stan said. 'Then we could tell Mr Rook she fell and broke her neck.' I heard the glee in his voice. 'Yeah, that will do.'

'You're going to lie to Mr Rook?'

Something fat and hairy crawled over my hand. I didn't have the energy to flinch away from it as it sniffed my fingers.

'He'll believe us if you tell him. You're his favourite.'

'You want *me* to lie to Mr Rook?'

Stan coughed. 'No, of course not. What I mean is, fuck, I don't know what I mean. I can't breathe properly with this fucking broken nose.'

'Breathe through your mouth – it's big enough.'

'Look, why don't you go off for a piss or something and leave me with her? Then, it'll be done when you return, and you won't have to lie to anyone.'

The rat stopped with my fingers and scuttled towards my face.

'Why are you bothered by her so much? She's not the one who made you a laughing stock with the boys. She's not the one who's disfigured you for life. She's not the one who's fucked you up forever.'

Stan whined. 'Fuck, you think this won't heal right?'

The other bloke laughed a vast throaty thing that reminded me of the death throes of the minotaur.

'You're a lost cause, Stan. I don't know why Rook puts up with you. Are you related to him?'

'So, are you buggering off for a piss, or what?'

The rat was an inch from my face when the other bloke stepped over and kicked it fifty feet into the air. It hit something in the distance with a screech. I twisted my head to glance up, but all I could see through the haze and the blood was a fuzzy shadow.

'I know why Mr Rook wants to make her pay, but what's your obsession with her, Stan?'

'I fucking told you. It's her fault I look like this.'

The big guy laughed like a horse. 'No, Stan, that was God having a bad day or your mother and father having the worst genes since one of the royal family fucked that goat. Now help me pick her up.'

They grabbed me again, lifting my useless body as if I were nothing. They'd stopped talking, and I found my voice.

'You guys are....' The wind blew across my cheeks. 'You guys are....'

I spat blood into the grass as they stopped walking.

'What are we?' the big guy asked.

His head was close to mine, but I still couldn't make out what he looked like.

'You guys are fucking cunts.' I swallowed my blood. 'Especially that fucking ugly twat, Stan. He makes the Frankenstein monster look like Brad Pitt.'

Both increased their grip on me.

'See,' Stan said. 'I told you we should do her here.' His nails dug into me. 'There's still time.'

The big bloke let go of me, so only Stan had my arm. 'Okay, Stan. Go on, then. I won't stop you.'

'What?' Stan said.

'Do what you said. Finish her off. There's a brick near your feet. Use that to crush her skull. That's unless you haven't got the balls for it.'

Stan let go of me, and I dropped to the ground. My shoulder thumped into the dirt, and electricity sped through my arm. I rolled onto my back and groaned. He reached down and picked up the brick.

'Are you sure?' Stan asked.

'Are you?' the big guy replied.
Stan crept over me and raised his arm.
Then the brick came down.

Chapter 18

Bad Medicine

I woke with a throbbing skull, and what felt like an elephant sat on my chest. A sandstorm swirled before my vision, and a thousand tiny flies buzzed in my ears. My mouth was as shrivelled as a Tory politician's heart. I tried to sit up, but a searing pain shot through my head, and I groaned, falling back against the pillows.

My neck ached as I opened my eyes and examined my surroundings. I was in a hospital, the walls a sterile white, the only sound was of a machine beeping. The place smelt of bleach and antiseptic.

'You shouldn't move too quickly. You had a concussion.'

I rubbed my eyes and peered across the room at Detective Inspector Jack Parker leafing through a copy of *Vogue*.

'What happened?' There were vague memories of two shadows dragging me through a jungle.

He put the magazine down. 'Somebody punched you in the head. A woman walking her dog found you on the industrial waste ground. The last sighting of you before that was outside the Raven Club at around 9:15. That was three hours ago.'

I reached for the glass of water on the table near me, downing it in one go, feeling the cold liquid tickle the back of my throat. 'Do you always work this late?'

'Crime never stops, Ms Gray. Do you remember what happened to you?'

'Yeah, somebody sucker punched me outside the club. There were two of them.' I wanted more water. 'One was built like a brick shithouse; the other was a scrawny git called Stan. You can't miss him since he has a broken nose.'

'Was that your doing?'

'No, it had nothing to do with me.' He peered at me as if he didn't believe me. I held up my hands. 'Honest, copper.'

'Have you any idea about the motive behind their attack and abduction?'

'They work for some guy named Rook. Have you heard of him?'

'Do you know what county lines are?'

I licked my lips for moisture. 'Sure. County lines is a term used for organised illegal drug-dealing networks, usually controlled by a person using a single telephone number, or 'deal line'.'

'That's correct. Serious organised criminals, often from big cities, recruit vulnerable children and adults, usually in rural and suburban areas, as 'runners' to transport drugs and cash all over the country, frequently using the rail network or taxis and other private hire vehicles, so the people behind it can remain detached and less likely to be detected. We believe that the person in charge of the county lines enterprise in this area uses the codename, Mr Rook.'

'You don't know who he is or what he looks like?'

Parker shook his head. 'Rook might not even be a he.'

'Great.'

'So why is he interested in you?'

I told him about my recent confrontations with various thugs. 'I obviously interfered with his operation at some point.'

'How old was the girl you saw them drag into the alley?'

I shrugged. 'Sixteen or seventeen. It's hard to tell these days, but she looked younger than me.'

Parker got up. 'When you feel better, come to the station to give a statement.'

'There's another thing,' I said. 'Do you know a loan shark called Tom Brown?'

'I've heard of him.'

'Well, he forced his way into Debbie Jackson's house and harassed her, claiming Joe owed him forty grand. Can you do anything about that?'

He nodded. 'I'll send some uniforms to have a word with Mr Brown.'

When he left, Ginger and Bruce rushed into the room.

'Oh God, Enola, you look terrible.'

I gave her a weak smile. 'Thanks, mate.'

She grabbed my hand. 'We were so worried about you. I came out to the desk at the club, but you were gone. What happened?'

I told her the gruesome details. 'The guy whose nose you broke is called Stan. I didn't get a good look at the other one, but he's a big fucker.'

Bruce bit his fingernails. 'Does this mean they're coming after Ginger as well?'

It probably did, but I didn't want to worry them more than they already were.

'It's okay; DI Parker is on the job. I'm sure we won't have any more trouble.' I didn't believe that for a second, but I'd have a gun for protection soon enough.

Ginger squeezed my hand. 'Oh, Enola, this is all my

fault. I was the one who hit that bloke. If only I'd controlled my temper.'

I smiled at her. 'Don't blame yourself. They wanted to teach me a lesson after what I did to those two goons harassing that young woman outside the club.'

Bruce ran shaky fingers through his unkempt hair. 'They could have killed you.'

When I saw that brick heading for my head, I thought they would. But that was another thing not to tell my friends.

'It was only a warning. The big bloke told me that when he towered over me.'

'What did he say?' Ginger asked.

'He warned me to stay out of Rook's operations without explaining what that meant. I was too busy pushing the rats away and lying in pain to argue.'

'So, he's running a county lines drugs gang?' Bruce said.

I shrugged. 'That's what Parker claimed.'

He rubbed his chin. 'Shit! What are we going to do?'

I swivelled my legs out of bed and grimaced at the gown the hospital staff had dressed me in. 'Don't worry about it. Do you know where my clothes are?'

As I spoke, Debbie stumbled into the room. 'I brought you some fresh things from home.'

I smiled and took the bag from her. 'Cheers, Debbie. Did you enjoy the gig?'

A nervous tick affected her eye. 'Well, it was great until I heard what happened to you.' She stared at my face, and I wondered how bad it looked. 'Is this my fault because of that loan shark?'

'No,' I answered. 'This is unrelated. It's nothing for you to worry about.' I looked at my friends. 'It's nothing for anyone to worry about.'

'You can't go home now,' Ginger said.

I emptied the clothes onto the bed. 'Why not?'

She removed a small mirror from her bag and shoved it in my face. 'Look at you. You had a concussion.'

It wasn't a pretty sight: half of my face was a lovely shade of purplish blue, and it looked like somebody had dropped the moon on my eye. However, on the other hand, it didn't feel too bad, so I assumed the medics had pumped me full of painkillers. That must have been why my legs moved as if they were underwater.

'I had a concussion, past tense. I'm fine now.' I glanced at the wall clock. 'And we've got a meeting to go to in a few hours.'

'What meeting?' Bruce said.

I changed the subject. 'And anyway, I've had lots worse than this. First, I fell off a roof when I was fourteen, which was bad. Then, there was the time some kid smacked me in the head with a cricket bat and broke my jaw. After that, I had to eat through a straw for months.' I still had nightmares about vegetable soup. I picked out the clothes I wanted and turned to Ginger. 'Can you help me get this gown off?'

She scowled at me. 'So, you're well enough to leave but can't dress yourself?'

'I'll ask Bruce if you're not up to it.'

He gulped. 'I'll leave you to it. I must check that the band got to their hotel, okay?'

He scampered out of the room, and I laughed, which hurt like hell. Ginger crossed her arms and frowned while Debbie stood there, open-mouthed.

And I thought about how much pain I'd feel when meeting Joe's fancy woman in a few hours.

Chapter 19

Little Lies

I chewed on strong painkillers while we waited in the café. Ginger still wasn't happy with me.

'We should have postponed this, Enola. Your face looks terrible.'

'So you keep telling me.' We garnered several curious glances on our way to the café. Usually, the stares were at the scars on my hands, but today, people didn't know where to look when they saw me. And it wasn't much better when we entered the café. The smell of coffee and baked goods wafted towards us, a stark contrast to the sterile hospital from earlier. The place was busy, with people coming and going, their laughter and conversation bouncing around me, accompanying the occasional glance in my direction.

My breakfast arrived while we waited for Sarah Bailey. Ginger kept flexing her fingers, glancing everywhere before peering at the door.

'I don't know how you can eat; my guts are on butterflies.'

My jaw throbbed as I ate, but I needed sustenance. I stuffed a fat sausage in my mouth. 'I haven't eaten since the curry with Amanda and Pete.' The server placed a steaming mug of tea in front of me. 'You haven't said much about the gig?'

Ginger narrowed her eyes into pinpricks. 'I've had other things on my mind.'

'Well, we've time now, so go on.'

She relaxed her shoulders and put her handbag on the table. 'It was great. They were really, really good and are such lovely people. I got on so well with Amanda. Did she tell you she's a healer?'

Eggy yolk dribbled over my lips. 'She mentioned something about my aura. I think it might be out of whack.'

Ginger stared at my face and shivered. 'If it wasn't before, it must be now. So anyway, Amanda and I will organise a spiritual gathering, maybe run an event somewhere if we find a venue.'

'Use the Raven.'

She shook her head. 'No, we want something for during the day which is crisp and bright.'

'Ask Bruce about the food bank building. They've got plenty of space in there.'

Ginger smiled at me. 'Hey, you can have good ideas sometimes.'

'Did he make any money from the gig?'

Her smile increased. 'Oh, yeah, enough to put Hey Venus on again. He's really getting into this promoting lark now.'

'What about his proper job? Between the gigs and the volunteering at the food bank, he won't have much free time.'

She shrugged. 'He does his consultancy work from home on the computer and only needs a few hours a day. He's very good at time management.'

'Okay.' The tea warmed my lips, and I stared at my phone, checking if Sarah Bailey had sent any Facebook messages to Joe and reminding myself what she looked like from the few photos she'd messaged him.

'What do we do when she arrives?' Ginger said.

'We'll ask her what she was doing meeting a married man.'

'Should we tell her what happened to Joe?'

'Of course.'

I tucked into the rest of my breakfast and studied our surroundings. The walls were bright, vibrant colours, with murals and paintings decorating every inch of space. The lights were low, casting a warm glow over the room, with the aroma of freshly brewed coffee and baked goods every-where. The place filled up by the second. There were artists with paint-splattered clothing, chatting animatedly with a bunch of musicians, their instruments stacked against the wall. A group of bohemian-looking women were huddled in a corner, their laughter ringing above the din.

Then she strode through the door. Sarah Bailey, dressed in a sleek, black dress, perfectly styled hair, and a nervous expression, looking entirely out of place.

I nudged Ginger. 'Right,' she said and got up. I watched her march over to Bailey as I finished my toast. My head throbbed, and the room twisted around me if I turned too quickly. Instead, I fixed on them as Ginger brought her over.

'What is this?' she asked. 'Where's Joe?'

'You better sit down, Sarah,' I replied. 'We have bad news.' So I told her.

'I'm Joe's niece,' Ginger said. 'And we found your messages on his Facebook account.'

I studied her face, expecting a mixture of shock, horror,

and anger, but nothing. On the contrary, she was as emotionless as the speaking clock.

'How did it happen?' she asked.

'You haven't seen the news or read the papers?'

Bailey shook her head. 'I never bother with things like that.'

'How did you meet Joe?' Ginger asked.

She glanced around the café with a strange look on her face, as if she expected reporters to stick a camera in her mug. 'We met at university long ago, drifted apart, and then I found him on Facebook. That's all.'

'When was the last time you saw him?' I said.

'Last week, in here.'

'Did you know he was married?' Ginger asked.

Bailey finally expressed a little bit of emotion and dropped her eyelids. 'Yes.'

I grabbed my fork and thrust it into a sausage. 'Were you having an affair?'

She looked startled. 'What? No.'

I didn't believe her. 'You weren't meeting for sex?'

Bailey lowered her voice. 'Joe wanted to, and I was interested, but then he mentioned some things and I....'

Now, it was getting interesting. 'What things?'

She moved closer to me. 'My husband died last year, and I was lonely. I needed to be close to somebody again, emotionally and physically.' She gazed at me. 'You're too young to know how it feels to be abandoned and lonely. And then I found Joe online, and we met a few times, and we fooled around a bit, but then he asked for things that scared me.'

I heard Ginger grinding her teeth next to me. 'What things?'

She blushed. 'Kinky things, whips and chains, leather and studs. And other stuff. S&M, he called it.'

Ginger's lips trembled. 'Uncle Joe? Never.'

Bailey got up. 'You don't have to believe me, but it's true.' She stared at me. 'Will you tell his wife this?'

'I don't know,' I replied. 'Where did you fool around?'

'What?' she asked.

'You said you and Joe fooled around. Where was that?'

She used a tissue to wipe a tear from her eye. 'Oh, some woods near his office. He liked it there.'

I watched her leave as Ginger destroyed a sugar packet on the table, sending the grains everywhere.

And my head throbbed like an exploding supernova.

Everything was leading back to those woods.

Chapter 20

Raw Power

'What the fuck?' Ginger said as I ordered a cream cake. The server frowned at her.

The throbbing in my temple had increased. 'Do you think she was telling the truth?'

She pushed her half-drunk coffee to the side. 'About Joe? No fucking way. I'd have known if he was like that.'

I grimaced as I laughed. 'I thought you were into the kinky stuff? I've seen what's in your wardrobe. And what you keep in your bedroom drawer.'

She turned to me. 'I don't care what people get up to in their sex lives. They can fuck whoever they want as long as it's consensual, but you know....'

Even though my parents died ten years ago, I knew what bothered her.

'You don't want to think of your Uncle Joe getting up to things like that, especially if he was having an affair.'

'Do you think he was?'

I shrugged. 'Probably, and if not with her, then likely with somebody else before that. These things don't just pop up overnight.'

She shook with laughter. 'Was that a pun?'

The server brought me my cream cake, and I thanked her. 'Maybe. So, what do you want to do with this information? Tell Debbie?'

'God no, tell her that her dead husband liked kinky sex and was probably having an affair before he hung himself.'

'If he hung himself.'

'Yeah, that too. No, we can't tell Debbie. I'm unsure if she's started grieving, so we can't dump this on her.'

'Has she sorted the will or the funeral yet?'

'I don't think so. I need to help her with both. And there's the business to sort out.'

'Yeah, there's still plenty to do.' I bit into the cake and got cream all over my chin.

'Fuck, this is a mess.'

I wiped the mess from my face. 'I'll go through his laptop again, see if I missed anything, and we must visit his office. If he was hiding secret sex stuff from Debbie, it might be there.'

'God, secret sex stuff,' Ginger said. 'Why is this never easy?'

I got stuck into the rest of the cake as my mobile vibrated with a text. I checked it, reading the message from Amy.

I've got what you need. We can't meet in the pub as it's too open. I'll see you in the old spot at lunchtime. It's your turn to bring the sandwiches.

'Fuck,' I said.

'What's wrong?' Ginger asked.

I put the phone away. 'Nothing, I just forgot I had a meeting.'

'A meeting? Who with?'

That was a good question, and I couldn't tell her the truth. So, I lied.

'It's a follow-up with the DWP.'

'I thought they turned you down for the loan?'

'They did. This is about my application for universal credit.'

'But you don't have a photo ID.'

'I know. That's what the meeting is about.' I didn't like lying to her, but I had no choice. Now, I had a few hours to kill before seeing Amy. 'Do you fancy a trip to the record shop around the corner? I need new music to play at Debbie's house.'

'Aren't you skint?'

I got up. 'I was, but Bruce paid me for last night. And he gave me a twenty quid bonus for getting banged on the head.'

She laughed. 'Think of how much you might have made if those twats had broken a bone.'

We spent an enjoyable hour in the record shop, and I left with a CD of *Raw Power*, having lost my original a few years ago. Then I walked to the rendezvous, my stomach churning at another excursion into Harrington Woods.

I stepped into the trees, the rustling of leaves underfoot and birds chirping the only sounds there. The air smelt of pine and damp earth, and a light haze hung everywhere. The police had removed their bits of plastic and warning signs, returning the spot to nature. I strode along a narrow path, searching for any sign of Amy.

As I walked, a fine mist crept out of the undergrowth as if I was in some '80s horror movie, and the memories flooded back to our teenage years and when we used this place like modern-day Robin Hoods.

'There can only be one Robin Hood,' Amy told me. 'You'll have to be Maid Marian.'

I laughed at her. 'Why me? You're the youngest.'

She spat laughter into the leaves. 'Yeah, only by six days.'

The memory made me smile as I spotted her ahead, her silhouette barely visible in the mist. She was leaning against a tree, her arms crossed and a wistful look on her face.

'You're still younger than me,' I said as I approached.

She smiled, and all the trouble between us fell away. 'The memories always hit me as soon as I set foot in these woods.' Her eyes sparkled. 'We had so many good times here, existing in our own little world.' She touched a nearby leaf. 'It was such a simpler time.'

'Is that why we're meeting here?'

'You know how much I love nature.' She pointed at my empty hands. 'I don't see any sandwiches.'

'I've already eaten.'

She gazed at my face. 'I can see. It seems the rumours are true, then?'

'Rumours?'

'That you've got yourself into a spot of bother. I assume that's why you want what I've brought you?'

'What do these rumours say?'

She stepped away from the tree, and the mist swirled around her legs like waspish fairies worshipping at the feet of their goddess.

'Do you remember when we first came here, and the other kids refused to join us because the woods were supposedly haunted?'

I shook my head. 'No, but I recall us playing with that Ouija board, which was useless. No spirits spoke to us then.'

Amy rubbed at her top lip. 'Ah yes, that's when you were still trying to communicate with your dead parents.'

I tried not to think about that. 'Don't remind me.'

She smiled at me. 'Supposedly, the ghost of a young woman who vanished near the river twenty-plus years ago haunts these woods.'

I shrugged. 'I don't believe in ghosts. Tell me about these rumours.'

'You've upset important people and their trade, and there will be no more warnings.'

'Do you know this Rook?'

'Only by reputation as somebody not to be messed with.'

I arched my eyebrows. 'You're afraid of him?'

Amy laughed. 'Shadows don't scare me, Enola. I stopped fearing the dark a long time ago. You know that better than anyone.'

'So, what is it with Rook, then?'

'You're aware that I don't handle drugs. If it doesn't interfere with my operation, then I don't care what Rook or the thousands like them do.'

'People die because of it, Amy, including kids. You used to care about that.'

She reached down and plucked a small yellow flower from the ground. 'I used to care about many things, but we all grow up, eventually. You will, too, one day. That's if you get that far.' She removed a plastic bag from her jacket. 'Which is why you need this.'

I took it from her and peered inside, seeing the revolver and a box of bullets.

'Thanks. What do I owe you?'

'Do you have money?'

'No.'

She pulled the petals from the flower and dispersed them into the wind. I watched them drift towards the tree where I'd found Joe Jackson's body. Perhaps there were two ghosts in the woods now.

'Well, you can owe me a favour, then.'

'A favour?'

She grinned. 'Yes. Do you remember them?'

'What type of favour?'

Amy shrugged. 'Oh, I'll think of something.' She walked past me and touched my cheek. 'There's no need to worry about it.'

She left me, and I put the bag into my jacket.

'Aren't you worried?' I shouted at her back.

She stopped and turned, the sun glistening behind her like a halo. 'Worried about what?'

'About me.'

She shook her head and laughed. 'I've never stopped worrying about you since the day we met, Enola. You were pulling at poor Bobby Smith's hair so hard I thought his eyes would pop. Do you remember that?' I did. 'And you were enjoying it so much. If Rook kills you, at least I can stop worrying.'

I watched her go and hoped she'd given me enough ammunition.

Chapter 21

Career Opportunities

Ginger was waiting for me when I got to Debbie's. 'Have you eaten?'

My stomach rumbled, and I wished I'd bought those sandwiches. 'No. What do you have in mind?'

She grabbed her bag. 'Debbie spoke to someone at Joe's office, and we're going over to tell them what's happening. Then we'll go for food.'

The weight of the gun pressed against my heart. 'What's happening?'

Debbie entered the room looking as happy as I'd seen her since her husband's death.

'I'm going to give one of Joe's staff control of the office while I sort his affairs out.' I saw Ginger grimace at the use of that word. 'He always talked about a young woman called Sally and said she was his best worker.' Ginger glanced at me, and I wondered if we had the same thought. 'Then I need to arrange the funeral. How is your face?'

I touched my cheek and winced. 'It's getting there. At least it doesn't hurt when I eat if I stick to the other side of my mouth. Are we leaving now?'

Ginger nodded. 'Yes. Are you ready?'

'Just give me a few minutes in the bathroom, and let me feed Dirty Harry.' And time to hide my illicit weapon and ammunition in the bedroom the widow had kindly let me use. Of course, she could get into trouble if the wrong people discovered it there, but I had little choice since I wouldn't take it to Joe's office.

I rushed upstairs and hid the bag at the bottom of the wardrobe under a pile of Joe's clothes. I had a quick leak before giving my pet tarantula his daily treat. Then I rejoined them downstairs.

Ginger spoke to me as we went to the car. 'You feel up for a day out? No problems with your face?'

I got into the passenger seat. 'No more than usual. You two have been busy, then?'

'Yeah. Debbie contacted the bank to get Joe's name removed from their joint account, and her solicitor said there should be no problem with the will as he left everything to her, including ownership of Jackson Systems. So all she has to do is assess the staff and hand the running of the business to one of them.'

'That's with your help,' Debbie said from the back.

Ginger started the engine. 'Well, I am a good judge of character.'

As she drove off, I left them to talk about it, more concerned with what I'd dumped in Debbie's house and what I might have to use it for. We passed tall buildings and small shops, most boarded up or closed. I spied a former ice cream parlour where I'd spent my thirteenth birthday and a derelict pub where I'd got drunk on my fifteenth. The shops where Amy and I had stolen our clothes were no longer there, replaced by bookmakers or vape emporiums. The kids wandering the streets looking lost or lonely seemed no different than in my wasted youth. It was strange peering at them as if it was a lifetime ago, yet I was only a few months from my twenty-first birthday.

Twenty-one. Wasn't that supposed to indicate a certain coming of age, a stepping away from childhood and into adulthood? If it was, I think I must have rushed ahead about ten years ago, the night I saw my parents murdered.

I gazed from the window as we drove past the river, the water sparkling in the sunlight. There was a memory of a cruise with my mother and father, of the weather turning foul and the three of us huddling together in the cold below deck. Then we'd gone for pizzas afterwards.

Ginger pulled into the parking lot of a large industrial building, and I saw Joe's company name on a sign above the entrance. My head throbbed as we got out and went inside. Jackson Systems was on the fourth floor, so we took the elevator up, stepping aside to let a man with a mop and bucket get out.

'I'm nervous,' Debbie said.

'Don't be,' I replied. 'Just introduce yourself and ask them who has been in charge for the last few days. Then talk to them individually, with Ginger, and I'll have a look round.' I patted my jacket. 'I've got Joe's passwords here, so I'll examine his work computer. Okay?'

She nodded as we exited the elevator and saw the sign for Jackson Systems. Ginger went and opened the entrance. The hum of the machines and people chatting filled the room, punctuated by the occasional ding of an incoming email or the beep of a scanner. Six staff were in the office, and they all turned to us as I closed the door.

They stopped what they were doing. A tall woman in a bright red dress rushed over. 'Mrs Jackson, we've been expecting you.' She held out her hand. 'I'm Sally Reed. I'm so sorry for your loss.' She looked at her colleagues. 'We all loved Joe here.'

Debbie gripped Sally's hand. 'Thank you, thank you all.' She smiled at them. 'I don't want to disturb what you're doing or interrupt the running of the business, but I need an idea of what goes on here.' She glanced at Ginger and me. 'This is my friend Enola and Joe's niece, Ginger.'

Everybody nodded and said hello. I studied them and guessed they were all in their mid to late twenties.

'Shall I show you Joe's office and explain what we're working on?' Sally asked.

I replied. 'Actually, Debbie wants me to go through Joe's computer and his desk, so if you can take her and Ginger to another room for the business update, that would be great.'

She stared at me like I'd just escaped a reform school. 'Sure, of course, no problem. Would anybody like a drink?'

'Yes,' Ginger said. 'I haven't had a coffee all morning.'

Sally escorted me to the office and took care of Debbie and Ginger. It was a spacious room with large windows overlooking the other businesses on the industrial estate. From the window, I saw the trees in Harrington Woods. I pictured Joe in that same spot, wondering if he'd gazed from his office to the woods and considered how it would all end for him.

I sat at his desk and switched on the computer. It sprang to life, with the company logo filling the desktop. I removed the notebook from my jacket and found the password, dancing my fingers over the keyboard as my head ached. I needed to refuel on painkillers.

As the machine sprang into action, I examined the contents on his desk, the photos and the trinkets. There was a picture of him with Debbie, a small cartoon character figurine of a computer with a human face, and a stress ball in the shape of a globe.

The ornament stared at me as I used the mouse to go through the files and folders and check Joe's internet browsing. If I was expecting to find an avalanche of S&M documents on the machine, I was disappointed. Fifteen minutes of searching left me better informed about how Jackson Systems created AI apps for a demanding market, but there was nothing to indicate that Joe was in a fragile state of mind. And there was no evidence of an affair with Sarah Bailey or anybody else. So, it was another dead end.

I shut the machine down and searched the desk drawers. All I discovered were paper versions of what I'd found on the computer. That was until I reached the last drawer, full of bank statements. I pulled them out and scrutinised the details, seeing it was Joe's business account. Nothing seemed out of place until I saw the six payments over a two-week period before he died, a hundred pounds each time. The amounts weren't what interested me but who Joe had paid them to: the Park Regency Hotel. It sounded upmarket, but I knew it wasn't.

I slipped the papers into my jacket and left the office. I went to the others, wondering how to tell Debbie her dead husband had visited a hotel where you rented the rooms by the hour.

Chapter 22

Heartbreak Hotel

Ginger drove us to an Italian restaurant near Debbie's house after we left Jackson Systems.

'How did it go?' I said as I sipped a Coke.

Debbie beamed at me. 'Sally was brilliant. She's upset about Joe's death, as they all are, but she's more than capable of taking the company forward and completing the latest contract.'

Ginger nodded. 'Yeah, I think the business is in good hands with her. Did you find anything on Joe's computer?'

'Nothing out of the ordinary,' I replied. 'It looks like a very well-run and efficient place. So I don't believe you have anything to worry about, Debbie.'

'Great,' she said. 'Things are moving on now.' She drank half a glass of wine and appeared to relax.

I turned to Ginger. 'I'm nipping outside to make a quick phone call. Do you want to ring Bruce while I'm at it?' She peered at me as I raised my eyebrows and hoped she got my message as I stood. 'I'll be back soon.'

A group of smokers had gathered outside the restaurant, shivering and blowing smoke at each other to keep warm.

Ginger followed me out as I inhaled their tobacco, and I remembered two years of injecting poison into my system.

'You found something on Joe's computer, didn't you?'

'No, but something interesting was in his desk.'

She grimaced at the woman lighting a cigarette nearby. She grabbed my arm and pulled me away from the group. 'I've got news as well.'

'Go on,' I said.

She leaned in closer to me. 'Debbie doesn't know this.' She glanced over her shoulder to ensure the widow hadn't followed us outside. 'Sally told me while Debbie was chatting with the rest of the staff. Did I mention the name Mark Fuller to you before?'

I shrugged. 'Maybe.'

'Well, Joe and Fuller set up Jackson Systems five years ago. Sally was there at the beginning, and she says it was Joe's money and Fuller's ideas. Or at least that's what Fuller claims. The first few years were a struggle for the business, and Fuller left. Nobody knows why, but soon after, Jackson Systems got their first big contract, and everything has been on the up ever since. But, get this: a few months before Joe died, Fuller turned up at the office and got into a heated argument with Joe. Sally claims they couldn't hear what it was about but assumes it was over money. Fuller never returned, but she heard Joe on the phone with him several times, and those conversations usually turned into arguments. Now Joe's dead, she thinks Fuller will return to the office at some stage.'

'He wants some part of the business?'

'But she also said something strange about Fuller and Joe.'

'What?'

Ginger took a deep breath. 'Sally said she always

thought there was something else between them under all the arguments and the tension, as if there might be a, you know, romantic undercurrent.'

'Between Joe and Fuller?'

'Sally thought she was probably being foolish, but you never know.'

'Indeed.' It was another thing to consider and probably not the right time to ask Ginger if she thought her uncle might have lived a secret life. 'Did you get the financial documents for the business?'

Ginger nodded. 'Debbie has them. What did you find?'

I removed the bank statements from my jacket and gave them to her. 'Check the repeat payments.'

'The Park Regency Hotel?'

'It's a knocking shop.'

'What? How do you know?'

'Some kids I hung around with at the last children's home would use the place.'

'Fuck! Didn't any of the adults know? Social services or the police?'

'Not at first. Seraphina put an end to it, and the hotel was closed. But now it's open again.'

She returned the documents to me. 'What should we do?'

'After the meal, you'll take Debbie home and stay with her. I'll go to the hotel and speak to the staff.'

'I should come with you.'

'You don't think I can look after myself?'

Ginger pointed at my bruised face. 'No.'

'Do you want to leave Debbie on her own?'

She thought about it for a second. 'No. But you better be careful.'

I smiled at her. 'Of course. Now let's get something to eat.'

Two hours later, I stood outside the Park Regency Hotel with a full belly. I shouldn't have had the ice cream for dessert, but I couldn't help myself. It was like being a kid again, remembering how my mother would feed my father so much chocolate ice cream his chin would be covered in it. It was a happy memory, enhanced by watching Debbie and Ginger enjoy themselves during the meal. I guess it took all our minds off the recent tragic events, even if only for a few hours.

But now I had a job to do. The building was in dire need of a paint job, with peeling walls and dirty windows. Litter and empty beer cans lined the street, and screeching cars and barking dogs filled the air with an overpowering odour of smoke and garbage hanging over everything. A group of young men scrutinised me from the other side of the road, huddled under hoodies and hawk-eyed. Perhaps I should have got the gun from Debbie's wardrobe.

I stepped into the hotel, the inside no better than the outside. It stank of sweat and bad breath. The dim lighting made it difficult to see, but I noticed the stained carpet and the flaking wallpaper. The desk clerk was a gruff-looking man with a scowl, and he barely glanced up from his magazine as I approached.

'I require information,' I said.

Yellowed fingers pushed his mag away, and he glared at me, his face resembling a melted muppet. A fly crawled across the shoulder of his dirty jumper as he picked something from the few teeth remaining in his gob.

'What?' he asked.

'I need to know who stayed here on certain nights.'

He looked me up and down as if he was a farmer at a cattle market. 'Do I look like a fucking library?'

'Actually, you look like a man whose only bed folds up in the wall.'

He flicked the debris from his mouth at my feet. 'I'll show you my bed if you like.'

I removed the bank statements from my jacket. 'You must have a register, so show me who stayed here on these nights.' I pointed at the name of the hotel on the papers.

He ignored them and touched my fingers. 'Sure, love, and what do I get in return?'

I placed the statements on the desk and put my other hand on his. 'I'll show you the house.'

'The house?' he said.

'Yeah, the house of pain.' I bent his fingers back, close to breaking, but not quite. He screamed like a baby dropped into boiling water. He jerked his other hand around to hit me, but I pushed harder, and he wilted.

'Fuck, fuck, fuck! Stop it, lady.'

'Are you going to behave now?'

The tears streamed down his face as he nodded. 'Yes, yes.'

'Where's your register?'

He continued crying. 'It doesn't matter. Nobody uses their real names here.'

Shit. I hadn't thought of that.

I considered that as a seven-foot-tall brick shithouse strode into reception and glared at me.

Chapter 23

Blue Hotel

The big fella looked at me and then at the bloke with tears on his cheeks.

'Did you clean the toilet like I said, Johnny?'

Johnny's lips trembled. 'Yeah, it's all done, no problem.'

The giant gave me one last look before taking the stairs, the floorboards creaking under his weight. I breathed a sigh of relief and considered what to do next. Then I saw the camera high above Johnny's head with its flickering red light. I nodded at it while maintaining the pressure on his fingers.

'Does that work?'

'Yes, yes. All the videos are stored on the computer in the back room.'

I let go of him. 'Show me.'

'I'm not allowed to take people back there.'

I gave him my best smile. 'Pretend I'm a health inspector.' I nodded at his bruised fingers. 'And it's your health I'm worried about.'

He whinged as he took me through. However, for a dump of a hotel, it was a pretty modern digital setup, and he found the clips quickly, six of them corresponding to the dates on Joe's business bank statements.

'Where do you want to start?' he said.

'Play the latest one.'

It was silent, grainy black and white, but Joe's face was clear on the screen, looking nervous and excited simultaneously. The person with him was tough to make out, with a hood pulled over their head and wearing bulky clothes that made it impossible to discern if they were male or female. It was the same in all six clips, as if they intentionally avoided the camera, whereas Joe didn't care.

'That's all there is,' he said while nursing his hand.

I pointed at the other person on the screen. 'Do you know if this was a man or a woman?'

He shook his head. 'It's best not to pay attention.'

I removed a data stick from my pocket. 'Copy the videos onto this.'

He stared at me like a dog desperate not to get into the bath. 'I'll break the law by doing that.'

I laughed. 'Better than me breaking your fingers.'

He did it and handed it to me. 'There. You can go now.'

'Do you remember which rooms they used?'

'Sure. He always wanted the same one and paid extra for it.'

'Show it to me.'

I waited for his protests, but they didn't come, grabbing a set of keys and limping away. We took a creaky, dangerous lift up four flights, and he let me into the room, a study in decay and neglect. The musty scent of mildew hung heavy everywhere, causing my nose to wrinkle. Cobwebs draped the corners of the ceiling, and dust coated every surface. Pornographic magazines lay scattered over the floor, and I tried to ignore the stains on the sheets.

The yellowed curtains were drawn tight but did little to block out the outside sounds. Cars honked, and people shouted, creating a discordant symphony that filtered through the thin walls. I stepped forward, my foot sinking into the stained carpet, which gave off a muffled squish. The soles of my shoes stuck to the floor, making it difficult to move. Looking at the bed, I knew it was somewhere to steer clear of. I used my phone to take some photos.

'I don't know why he liked this room, but he always asked for it.'

I went to the window and peered outside, seeing Harrington Woods in the distance.

And I knew.

I took a taxi to Debbie's, finding Ginger staring at her mobile when I arrived.

'Debbie finished another bottle of wine when we got back.' She'd had two large glasses in the restaurant. 'So she's sleeping it off.'

I slumped in the seat opposite Ginger. 'Is she okay?'

She shrugged. 'Who knows? Even though I was close to Joe, I didn't know Debbie well. She might have been a heavy drinker before this, or this could be her coping method.' Dark shadows crawled across her face. 'Or maybe I wasn't as close to Joe as I thought, considering how many secrets he kept from me.'

I touched her hand. 'Don't think of him like that. Remember all the good times you had together.'

Ginger nodded. 'How did it go at the hotel?'

'Pass me the laptop, and I'll show you.'

She got it and sat next to me. I put the drive into the

machine, and we watched the clips together. On the second time around, Ginger pulled the screen closer to her.

'It's impossible to say who that is. It could be Sarah Bailey.'

'Or Mark Fuller. Or Sally from the office. Or anybody.'

She passed the laptop to me. 'I guess this confirms he was having an affair. Should we tell Debbie?'

'Do you want to?'

'Fuck no.'

We sat in silence until Ginger's phone rang. It was Bruce, and she put it on speaker.

'Are you staying at Debbie's tonight?' he asked.

Ginger yawned. 'No, I'm coming back. I haven't seen Kronos all day.'

'I was going to walk him, but I'll hold on, and we can do it together.'

'I'd wait until the morning,' I said.

She frowned at me. 'Why?'

'Because Rook's goons are still out there, and it's best if we all stayed sensible until the police deal with them.'

'You're saying I can't take my dog for a walk at night?' she said.

I shrugged. 'No point putting temptation in their way.'

'You go jogging in the dark,' she said.

'That's different.'

Ginger's frown increased. 'Why?'

'Because I can handle myself.' And I'd have a gun with me the next time I went out at night. Not that I would tell them that. Bruce would worry, and Ginger would tell me off for being so stupid.

'So can I, remember. I'm the one who broke that ugly fucker's nose.'

'Yes, and look where that's got us.'

Bruce sighed over the phone connection. 'Ladies, let's not argue amongst ourselves. We'll save Kronos's walk for the morning.'

Ginger ground her teeth and stood. 'Fine.' She went to the door and turned to me. 'What will you do about those videos?'

I gazed at the monitor, seeing Joe's grainy, frozen black-and-white face.

'I'll take them to the coppers tomorrow. I have to give them a statement about the other night, so it will kill two birds with one stone.'

Ginger left, and I peered at the screen, still seeing Joe Jackson and his unknown companion striding through that dingy hotel.

And I wondered if I'd need to use Amy's gun soon.

Chapter 24

Dream Police

Debbie was cheerful the following day, with no sign of a hangover.

'What would you like to do today, Enola?'

I finished my coffee. 'I must visit the police station to give them a statement.'

She peered at my bruised head. 'Of course. I have to go into town as well.' Her face lit up. 'I haven't been shopping for ages. How about I drop you off, and we can meet for lunch when you're done?'

There was a sparkle in her eyes that wasn't there before. 'Sure, that sounds good.'

She dropped me outside the police station as I gripped the copy of the hotel videos I'd made. Part of me wondered if I should give them to DI Parker, knowing that if the police investigated the clips, they'd eventually have to tell Debbie about them. And maybe it was best if she didn't know about them. Yet, I knew we couldn't keep it from her forever. She

304

deserved to know the truth about her husband, whatever that was.

I entered the building, my heart thumping against my ribs, still irritated about how many times the police had let me down. The sterile environment irritated my nose, the smell of disinfectant overpowering and the harsh fluorescent lights making my eyes water. Shuffling feet and muffled voices surrounded me as I strode to the front desk. A suited man sat there, his expression uninterested.

'Can I help you?' he said.

'I need to see Detective Inspector Joe Parker.'

'What for?'

I pointed at the purple part of my face. 'I have to give a statement.'

He shook his head. 'DIs don't lower themselves to that level.' He handed me a clipboard with a form on it. 'Take a seat over there.'

'I've got something important to tell him.' His face was unmoving. 'It's about a murder.'

He thought about it for five seconds. 'Fill out the paperwork, and I'll let him know you're here. What's your name?'

'Enola Gray.'

He shuffled off, and I sat. I gripped the pen and recounted the events of my attack, every detail fresh in my mind. Yet, as I wrote, I couldn't help but feel a sense of unease. The bland, concrete walls seemed to close in on me, the buzzing of the lights grating on my nerves. The hum of conversation and the clack of computer keys formed invisible hands surrounding my head. The occasional flash of blue and red from the lights outside added to the chaotic ambience. My brain was underwater, submerged in the river near where Joe Jackson died. And then I was out on dry land again, dragged through the weeds as those two thugs punched me.

I scribbled down the descriptions, reliving the whole thing and picturing what might have happened if I'd had the gun with me then. Would I have fired if I'd been on the ground with the two of them above me and Stan ready to crush my skull?

'Too fucking right.'

'What?' Detective Inspector Parker said as he approached me.

I grinned at him. 'Oh, nothing, just thinking aloud.'

'What's this about a murder?'

'Joe Jackson was murdered.'

Parker sighed. 'I thought we were done with this?'

'Is there somewhere we can talk in private?'

He hunched his shoulders. 'Follow me.'

He led me back to the desk and a different copper.

'You need a visitor's pass, Joe?'

Parker nodded. 'In the name of Enola Gray.'

The bloke laughed. 'Like the song?'

I smiled. 'No, like the bomb that's about to go off.'

He stopped laughing, entered my details into his computer, and handed me a lanyard to hang around my neck. 'Return this on your way out.'

'Yes, sir.'

I took it and followed Parker down a corridor and into a room. The walls were a pale grey, and the only furniture was a metal table and two chairs, one for the suspect and another for the interrogator. The table was scratched and dented, evidence of its use in countless examinations. The environment was familiar to me, and it made me think of Amy.

'Take a seat,' he said.

'Couldn't you have found somewhere warmer?'

He took the nearest chair. 'Everywhere is full right now. This was the only place available. So, what's this about Joe Jackson and murder?'

I sat opposite him. 'Busy day for the force?'

He glared at me, and I noticed lines under his eyes that weren't there the other day. 'Actually, yes, so I don't have time for any nonsense.'

I removed the data stick from my pocket and put it on the table.

'There are six videos on there taken from the Park Regency Hotel. Do you know it?'

'I'm aware of its reputation. What's on the videos?'

'Joe Jackson and one other, person unknown, spending hours at the Park Regency for illicit assignations.'

He grabbed the stick. 'How do you know this?'

'Why does anybody use that hotel once, never mind six times?'

'How does it prove somebody murdered Jackson?'

'It doesn't, but it proves that a lot was going on in his life before his death, which would warrant a further police investigation, don't you think?'

'Maybe,' he said, 'but we now have a witness who saw Mr Jackson in those woods, who observed him climb onto the rock, throw the nose around his head, and then jump.'

All the air was sucked out of the room and my lungs. I sat with my mouth wide open and struggled to breathe.

'What?'

'The witness came forward last night.'

'Who is it?'

'I can't tell you that, Ms Gray.'

'What was this person doing in the woods that late? Did you ask them that?'

Parker sighed. 'Yes. The witness is a bird watcher with a special interest in owls.'

'Fuck. And you believe him?'

'No evidence indicates foul play or another person's involvement in Mr Jackson's death.'

'Why did he wait this long before coming forward?'

'It doesn't matter, Ms Gray. Now, are we finished?'

'Will you at least look at the videos from the hotel?'

He lifted the USB stick, peering at it like Hamlet and that skull. 'If I get the chance. Is there anything else?'

'The loan shark, Tom Brown; did you speak with him?'

'Two of my colleagues spoke to Mr Brown, and he denied ever visiting Mrs Jackson's house or talking to her.'

'Of course he did. Did your officers warn him off?'

'I believe you know Constable Davis.' I nodded. 'He assured me that Brown will be no trouble to your or Mrs Jackson.' He stood to leave.

'I'm not finished.'

He sat again. 'Go on.'

'Rook and his goons. Did you find the one called Stan?'

He settled into his chair as if he would be there for a while. 'Stan Fletcher, small-time hoodlum and petty criminal with a record of house burglaries and intimidation.'

I moved forward. 'So you've got him?'

Parker shook his head. 'Mr Fletcher has gone the way of Lord Lucan and Shergar.'

'Huh?'

'Sorry, before your time. Stan Fletcher has vanished from our streets. None of his known associates have seen him since the day of your attack.'

'Fuck. What about the big bastard?'

'Do you know how many "big bastards" are around here?'

'No luck then?'

He got up again. 'I'll see you out.' I followed him, and he stopped at the door. You haven't told me everything, Enola.

'Haven't I?'

'You have a juvenile criminal record.'

'Doesn't everybody?'

'No.'

'Have you looked at it?'

'Not yet. Should I?'

I pushed past him. 'That's up to you, Parker. If you get bored one night and need something to enlighten your life, look and learn how the system lets down the children in this country.'

I dropped the visitor's pass at the desk and stepped outside.

Then I texted Debbie and realised I wouldn't have to tell her about Joe's indiscretions.

Chapter 25

Good Times

Debbie dropped me at Ginger's after we'd eaten. Kronos bounded towards me as I entered the flat, which stopped me from lingering outside my old place to see who was living there instead of me.

'Do you want a coffee?' Ginger shouted from the kitchen.

I struggled to stop the dog from slobbering all over me. 'You shouldn't leave your door unlocked, not with Rook's goons on the prowl.' I lost my fight with the hound, and he knocked me onto the sofa, primed to lick me to death. My face had stopped aching, but my legs throbbed.

She entered the room. 'We don't need any locks with Kronos around.'

He was on top of me, dribbling snot everywhere. 'Yeah, I can see that. A bit of help wouldn't go amiss here.'

Ginger laughed and dragged him off me. 'I took it as a yes for the coffee.'

I tried to brush the dog hairs from me and failed. 'Cheers. Where's Bruce?'

She flopped into the chair opposite. 'Volunteering at the

food bank. It's a good job we're not a couple, or I'd think he was cheating on me with somebody there. Speaking of illicit assignations, how did it go at the cop shop?'

I told her what happened. 'At least we don't have to worry about Stan returning.'

'I thought you weren't bothered by him, anyway.'

She was right. 'Yes, it's the big fucker we must watch out for.'

Kronos came to her side, and she stroked his head. 'How do you feel about this alleged witness to Joe's death?'

I removed a dog hair from my cheek. 'It's all rather convenient, don't you think?'

'Yeah, a birdwatcher in the woods at night seems a bit suspect. But, if it's true, it has to be a bloke.' She removed a pack of tarot cards from her pocket and put them on the arm of the chair. 'Most women don't have time for hobbies.'

'Indeed. I tried to trick Parker into revealing something about the witness, but he never did.'

Ginger grinned. 'He must be cleverer than you thought.'

'Well, he couldn't be any stupider than the rest of them.' I glanced at the tarot cards. 'How are the new neighbours?'

'Much better than the last person. At least they don't play punk music full blast in the middle of the night.'

I touched my chest. 'Oh, how you've wounded me.'

She jumped up. 'I'll get the coffee, and then you can tell me how it's going with Debbie.'

I watched her enter the kitchen as Kronos gazed at me with watery eyes.

'I should have gone to Debbie's for the gun, shouldn't I, boy?'

'What?' Ginger shouted.

'I said I've got some surprising news for you.'

She returned with the drinks. I took mine and warmed my hands on the mug.

'What news? Are you pregnant?'

I spat hot coffee all over the carpet and scared the dog away. 'Fuck! When have I had the time to get pregnant? Not that I want to.'

She gazed wistfully at me. 'Oh, I don't know, you're always sneaking off to places without telling me and then with all these revelations about Joe and your disclosure about the knocking shop hotel, my mind drifted into a strange place.'

'Yeah, very fucking strange. Your aura must be all out of whack.'

Ginger clapped her hands. 'Speaking of which, Amanda called me this morning, and we've had more thoughts about our spiritual event.'

'Surprise me.'

'No, that can wait. You said you had news.'

I put my coffee on the table between us. 'Debbie picked me up outside the police station and took me for a lovely dinner in a posh restaurant. And that's where she made me a proposal.'

'Oh, I'm intrigued.'

'Well, she said that with all my experience running the Bits & Bytes computer shop, she'd like to offer me the position of office manager at Jackson Systems.'

'Wow, that's excellent, and you'd be great for it, but won't that put Sally out after their conversation yesterday?'

'No, she said Sally doesn't want to be responsible for the day-to-day running of the office as she'd rather stick to her normal job of creating apps. So it would be a win all around.'

'You don't sound too happy about it.'

'I am, especially when she told me the salary, but don't you think it might be a bit awkward?'

'Why?'

I drank more of the coffee. 'Think about it. Debbie would be my boss and landlord. What happens if we fall out?'

Her laugh was raucous. 'You, fall out with somebody? Never.'

I grabbed the dog's chew toy and threw it at Ginger. 'Sarky cow.'

'So?'

'So I said I'd consider it.'

She patted the sofa, and Kronos sat next to her. 'New place to stay, new job, the loan shark warned off by the police, and one of the thugs who attacked you has vanished. So it's all going well, then.'

'I suppose so.' However, it didn't feel like it. 'Who's moved into my old flat?'

Ginger shook her head. 'Nobody yet. I believe the landlord has to fumigate it first.'

I looked for something else to throw at her, preferably bigger and harder this time. That's when Bruce walked in.

'Hello, ladies.' Kronos ran to him and jumped into Bruce's arms. 'And to you, boy.' He sat next to me, and I told him all the news. 'I guess the Joe Jackson investigation is concluded, then.'

I wasn't so sure, but I didn't want to say. 'I assume so.' I looked at Ginger, trying to gauge her reaction.

'Yes,' she replied. 'We have to focus on Debbie now and help her through this. And with Enola working at the office, we won't need to worry about the business.'

'And with the salary,' Bruce said, 'you'll get a place of your own in no time.'

Ginger's face lit up. 'Hey, why don't you contact the landlord about your old flat?'

I grinned. 'Fuck no, not with those neighbours.'

She threw the chew toy at me, and we all laughed. Even Kronos smiled.

Finally, it seemed like everything was going well for me.

Chapter 26

A Forest

It was dark when I left Ginger's, telling her I needed to pop to the shop on the corner before getting a taxi to Debbie's. She offered to drive me there, but I said no since she'd had two large glasses of wine. Bruce was out walking the dog.

So I headed for the woods.

The moon hid behind a veil of clouds, leaving the streets shrouded in darkness. As I approached the brink of the woodland, the buildings gave way to trees and undergrowth. The pitch-black surroundings enveloped me as I searched for the flashlight on my phone. It was a long shot expecting the birdwatcher to be out, but if what Parker had said was true, the witness would eventually revisit that spot. And I needed a word with them.

A biting wind whipped across my bruised face, and I took a deep breath. The torch's beam on my phone sliced through the gloom, illuminating the path ahead. The trees were tall and menacing, their branches reaching out like bony fingers. Things were rustling through the leaves at my feet and moving through the foliage around me.

But the darkness had never scared me. I used its ebony grip to warm my bones and conceal me from the things I didn't want to see.

As I moved further into the woods and away from the urban sprawl, the dimness lifted, revealing the stars twinkling above. The shrubbery gave way to a clearing, and I stopped, staring at where Joe had died. Perhaps it would be best to forget about everything now that Debbie seemed okay and the police had closed the investigation.

However, tiny voices were still nagging away at the back of my head. Was the dalliance with Sarah Bailey just an innocent flirtation? If Joe had borrowed forty grand from the loan shark, why did he need the money when his company was doing so well? Was there something more than a disagreement between him and his old business partner, Mark Fuller? And who was with him in that hotel?

I strode to where we'd found Joe, peering at the large rock. I touched the surface and examined the branch above me. Could somebody have forced him to climb up and put the noose over his head?

Of course they could. I'd witnessed many similar things when people were forced or manipulated into acts they'd typically hate. Getting somebody to do something they wouldn't normally consider wasn't difficult. All you needed was the right motivation.

Then there was the witness. Why didn't they rush to help Joe? Why hadn't they contacted the police immediately or phoned the emergency services? I couldn't stop looking into Joe's life until I spoke to this so-called observer. And it didn't matter if I had to return to the woods every night because I wouldn't give up until that nagging voice at the back of my head disappeared.

Memories swirled around me of the times in the woods,

with Amy and the others, playing with the Ouija board and hoping to talk to my parents. Were kids still doing stupid things like that amongst those trees and bushes?

Amy didn't believe we could talk to the dead.

'I'm just sick of listening to the living,' she'd say as we escaped from the children's home.

I pictured Amy giving me that gun, wondering why I kept leaving it in the house. The whole point of getting it was for my protection, so why didn't I have it with me?

That question perplexed me as I heard the owl hooting.

Parker had said the witness was a birdwatcher observing owls, so maybe they were in the woods. I turned and gazed into the branches, peering at the leaves and waiting for the noise to return.

And it did.

It was just ahead of me, near the river. I jumped over broken twigs and ran, pushing through bushes and trees, being scratched and cut with no concern for my safety. The owl hooted again, only this time, it seemed like there was more than one.

I stumbled through the undergrowth and ignored the fox with the searing red eyes, silently judging me as I ran. My heart rate increased as oxygen rushed into my lungs, my head throbbing as my bruised cheek vibrated. Then I kicked a broken branch and tumbled forward, my elbow smacking into a tree as my knee hit a rock. My body twisted, and I crashed into a carpet of leaves. Insects scuttled everywhere, over my hands and face, as I rolled through damp mud to land near wild mushrooms.

Damp leaves touched my lips. Spiders fell from their webs and settled on my face. The touch of their many legs calmed my nerves. The moon gazed down at me through the leaves as I panted for breath. A wispy strand of air drifted out of my mouth like ectoplasm, swirling from me and into the trees. A group of extravagantly patterned moths fluttered their wings around the wisp, and for one second, I imagined I'd fallen through a portal into another world.

Perhaps the moths were my parents watching over me. If so, I wondered what they must have thought of my life without them.

Then I heard the bird again.

I shook the spiders from my face and jerked up. Pain possessed my knee, and a bolt of agony crawled up my arm to settle in my skull. Nevertheless, I moved onward, startled to see a massive owl near the river's edge. It dipped its huge head to drink the water, and that's when I saw the man a few feet away pointing a camera at the creature.

My legs ached, and my brain throbbed as I rubbed at my eyes, sure I'd seen the bloke before.

But where?

I stumbled forward, stomping through branches and making enough noise to wake the dead. The owl beat its wings and flew off.

'Fucking hell,' the birdwatcher said. He turned to me, and I saw the recognition in his eyes.

He knew me.

Still, I struggled to remember where I'd seen him from.

I spat wet leaves onto the ground. 'Are you the one who told the police about Joe Jackson?'

I couldn't get a good look at his face in the gloom, and my throbbing head interfered with my vision, but he stared at me for ten seconds.

Then he turned and ran.

Fuck!

Every inch of me screamed in agony, but I sprinted after

him, my legs moving as if somebody had sewn anchors into my feet. I loped through the mud, kicking away leaves and branches and keeping my gaze on him. He stuck to the river's edge, and I hoped he'd slip and fall in. Not to kill him, but to slow him down.

And I searched my memory for where I'd seen him before.

I found strength from somewhere and picked up speed, gaining on him as he struggled in the mud. I spat as I ran, clearing the crap from my mouth as a freight train shot through my chest. I'd have him soon enough.

Then something whacked into my side and sent me flying into the river.

Chapter 27

Moon River

I hit the water hard.

The cold punched me in the face. I gasped for air, the shock of the fall and the drop in temperature disorienting me. Then, the current grabbed me like invisible fingers from nowhere and dragged me into the inky blackness. Panic set in as I struggled to swim against the momentum, pulling me deeper. I reached out, trying to grab anything to steady myself, but my hands only met water. Reflex thrust my mouth open, and the river forced itself in, diving down my throat and clinging to my lungs. A dread possessed all of me, my body jerking in every direction, arms and legs pushed out in desperation.

Then I relaxed and went limp, my mind accepting that this was it and my life was over, but I would reunite with those I'd lost to see my parents and Seraphina again.

It would be worth it for that, wouldn't it?

An explosion of voices boomed through my head, of people telling me to fight, never to give up. Ginger, Bruce, and Debbie shouted at me while Amy wagged her finger.

Even Kronos barked, his long tongue licking my face, so it was soaked.

But it wasn't the dog. It was the river.

I opened my eyes, gazing into the abyss and seeing pinpricks of light above me, little stars glittering not so far away. Then I thrust my arms out and pushed, kicking my legs behind me. Push, push, push.

Up I went as the current tried to drag me back down into its cold embrace.

Push, push, push.

But the voices in my head drove me forward, and I gathered my last strength to burst through the veil of darkness above me.

Water gushed out of my mouth, and air dived in, swimming through my throat and into my chest. The moon hung close to my face, just out of my reach, but I grasped for it. I missed and hit mud and weeds, hanging onto them to drag myself from the river. The smell of damp earth and decaying leaves packed my head. I saw the silhouette of trees and bushes along the bank in the darkness, but they seemed so far away. I felt so small and helpless, my mind racing with thoughts of what might happen if I couldn't get to shore.

My arms ached as I kept moving forward, my legs forcing me on and out of the water. I crawled onto my side and rolled through the sludge and filth, gasping for breath and pushing wet hair from my eyes.

That's when I heard them.

'Where did she go?'

'I don't know. Into the fucking river where you pushed her.'

'Christ, if we lose her, the boss will have our nuts.'

'Who was the other twat she was chasing?'

'Fuck knows. Probably some creepy cunt looking to molest someone.'

'Shame he didn't wait a bit for you, then. That's right up your street, ain't it?'

'Ha fucking ha. Now help me find that bitch.'

I slipped between the reeds and inched my head up. There were two of them a few feet away, strangers to me. I assumed they were Rook's goons, but neither was the big bastard from the other day. And I guessed the drug lord was done handing out warnings.

The murky liquid slithered over my hands as I searched for something to use as a weapon, cursing myself again for leaving the gun in Debbie's wardrobe.

'Maybe she drowned. You hit her pretty hard.'

They were close, only a few feet from where my head rested in the mud.

'Nah, we'd see her floating in the water.'

'I dunno, that current is fucking strong. Some woman got pulled under there a few years back, and they never found her. The pigs sent divers down and everything, but she was just gone. It's fucking spooky, I tell ya.'

'You fucking moron. You'll tell me it's the creature of Harrington Woods next, slithering out of the river to pounce on unsuspecting cunts to fuck 'em up the arse.'

'You can laugh, but that bloke killed himself in here the other day. Hung himself from a tree he did.'

'Nah, I heard somebody murdered him and made it look like that. You know how fucking stupid the coppers are.'

'Yeah, that's good for us, though, right?'

They laughed together, still unmoving and close to my throbbing head. An insect crawled over my hand and up my arm, skittering over my shoulder and onto my neck. There it stopped, its tiny, hairy legs brushing against my skin. Then it moved over my chin. I kept my mouth shut as it scuttled over my lips and past my nose. It settled on my cheek, its several eyes peering into mine.

'What will we do if we can't find her? We were instructed to bring her back.'

'Who told you?'

'You know, the boss.'

'Yeah, but not the Big Boss, right?'

'Grunts like us don't hear from the Big Boss.'

'Yeah, so we don't know who we're doing this for, do we?'

'Of course we do. We're following orders from the bloke who pays us, the guy who will break our bones if we don't find this girl. Unless you want to end up like Stan.'

'Stan? What happened to Stan?'

'Don't ask. Can you see anything from where you are?'

'Yeah, the fucking moon.'

The bug moved towards my eye, and my nails found broken glass. It cut my skin and drew blood as I grasped it.

'Hey, she's here!'

He reached down as the insect flew from my face, and I thrust the glass into his calf and dragged it down. It sliced into my hand, my blood dripping into his as he collapsed into the sludge, and I rolled away from him.

I let go of the glass and jumped up, just in time to see the other one running straight for me. I put my head down and smashed into him, my skull connecting with the fat of his belly and sending us both backwards. He grabbed me and went down, so I landed on him.

'You fucking cow!'

I stabbed my fingers into his throat, hitting his Adam's apple, so he gasped for breath. I leapt off him and looked for the other bloke, expecting him to be bleeding out in the reeds.

But he wasn't there.

Then I heard his roar, turning to see him hopping on one leg to throw himself at me. I stepped out of the way, and he hit the dirt face first. He groaned in the mud as I put my foot on his hip and kicked him onto his back.

'Who sent you after me?'

His eyes bulged like a deranged puffer frog. 'I'm going to fucking kill you for this.'

I turned from him, searching the ground and finding what I wanted. My hips throbbed as I retrieved the glass, seeing his blood glisten in the moonlight.

'Do you want me to slit your throat?'

He put a hand on his thigh to stop the bleeding. 'You haven't got it in you.'

'Tell me again what you were about to do to me.'

He grinned through his pain. 'You're going to die, bitch, but first, me and the lads will play with you for a few days. You'll be begging to die then.'

'Have you done that before to other women and girls?'

'All the fucking time, you stupid fucking cunt.'

'Well, you won't be doing it again.'

I plunged the shard into his groin, slicing through his thin pants and dragging it over his cock and balls. He screamed and screamed, but I kept cutting, only stopping when he blacked out.

My legs throbbed as I stood, returning to the other thug. He was on his back, clawing at his throat. I left him there and threw the glass into the river.

I guessed it wasn't over after all.

Chapter 28

Sister Surprise

I hadn't dried out when I arrived at Debbie's and was about to creep upstairs when voices came from the living room. I thought Ginger might have made an unexpected visit when I heard a man speak.

Fuck! What if the loan shark was back?

I burst through the door, still fuelled by adrenalin from the river, but stopped by the suave-looking bloke beside Debbie on the sofa, sitting very close to her. And his hand was on her knee.

Debbie's fingers shook, and she spilt wine from her glass. 'Oh, Enola, is it raining?'

'What's this, Debbie?'

She put her drink on the table. 'This is my old friend, Mark.' She smiled at him. 'Mark, this is Enola.'

He smiled at me. 'Ah yes, the young woman who has moved in with you.'

'Mark? Mark Fuller?'

His grin resembled a worm wriggling in the dirt. 'Have we met?'

'You used to be Joe's partner in Jackson Systems?'

'Yes, well, that was a while ago.'

'You argued and fell out, right?'

He stopped smiling. 'As I said, that was in the past. I'm only here to offer Debbie my condolences.'

I remembered his hand on her knee. 'Yeah, I noticed.' Dirty water dripped off me onto the carpet. Someone else's blood stained my fingers.

'Well,' he said. 'I should be going.'

I stood in front of the door. 'Did you threaten Joe just before he died?'

'What? Of course not. Who told you that?'

I didn't answer. 'Why did the two of you fall out?'

He waved his hand at me, but I didn't move. 'Oh, it was such a long time ago, and it doesn't matter.' He glanced at her. 'Everything is different now.'

I moved to the side to let him go.

'I'll see you out,' Debbie said, following him through the door.

I went to the window and watched them, seeing her squeeze his arm before he got into his car. Then I moved to the fireplace and waited for her.

'Did you know he was coming tonight?' I asked when she returned.

She grabbed her wine and drank it. 'What happened to you, Enola? You're soaking wet. Are those worms in your hair?'

I ran my fingers through the thick clumps on my shoulders. 'Somebody pushed me into the river.'

'What?'

'Have the police contacted you today?'

She wrapped her hands around the glass. 'Detective Inspector Parker called me.'

'He told you about the witness.'

She nodded. 'I guess that settles the matter.'

'Why was Fuller here?'

'Like he said, to tell me how sorry he was to hear about Joe's death. They were best friends once.'

'But they had a falling out?'

'Yes.'

'Over what?'

She laughed. 'What do most people fall out over? It was money.'

'In what way?'

She stood and went to the window, her back to me as she spoke. 'Oh, I don't know. I never got involved with Joe's business dealings.'

'Did you know Fuller before you met Joe?'

She turned to me. 'No. Why?'

The river was still stuck to me like a second skin, and my head was full of images of what I'd done to those two goons. I still heard their screams, mixing them into the chorus of The Clash's version of "Police and Thieves."

'Because his hand was on your leg, and you seemed to enjoy it.'

An inferno blazed behind her eyes. 'What right do you have to question my behaviour?'

'Where were you the night Joe died, Debbie?'

She shook her head and laughed. 'You want to know where I was when Joe took his own life? I was here, alone, like always.'

'Fuller wasn't here?'

That fire increased inside her. 'I think you should dry off, Enola. You're dripping all over the carpet.'

'Are you familiar with a woman named Sarah Bailey?'

I noticed the tension in her fingers as she gripped the glass. 'No. Who is she?'

'An old friend of Joe's. Where did you meet Joe?'

'At university. He was two years above me.'

'And Fuller?'

'Yes, he was in Joe's year group, but I didn't meet him until after Joe and I got together.'

'Sarah Bailey was there at the same time.'

Debbie shrugged. 'There were over a thousand students at that university when I was there. Who is this woman?'

'I've met her, this Sarah Bailey. She told me she and Joe were an item at university.'

'Jesus, Enola, what is this? Joe had many girlfriends before me. This was nearly thirty years ago. Joe's dead, for Christ's sake.'

'When I checked his laptop, I found that he and Sarah had sent messages to each other through Facebook.'

'What sort of messages?'

'I guess you'd call them flirting and mild sexting. They'd also met in town, and she claims Joe asked her for sex.'

Debbie finished her wine and went to the bottle for a refill. Then she returned to the sofa. I continued to drip onto the floor.

'What's this all about, Enola? Are you upset you came back and found me with Mark? Is that it? Are you troubled because I'm not more visibly distraught over Joe's death? What has made you so furious?'

Many things got me angry, but discovering Debbie had quickly moved on to another bloke wasn't one of them. Joe was dead, and the police and his wife didn't seem to care. So why should I?

Why? Because Ginger cared, and I cared about her.

But I needed to focus on Rook and the thugs he kept sending to hurt me.

Had I interfered with his drug operation that much just

by stopping those blokes from harassing the young woman outside the Raven? It seemed a bit of an overreaction for one incident. How substantial was the debt that woman had with those goons? Was it similar to what Joe allegedly owed Tom Brown?

'I'm not angry, Debbie. I'm tired and wet. I'll see you in the morning.'

I left her and went to my room. I opened the wardrobe to make sure the plastic bag with the gun was still there. After tonight, I'd have to carry it all the time.

Chapter 29

Policy of Truth

A thousand heavy metal drummers were practising in my head when I woke. I pulled the pillow over my eyes, but the noise wouldn't go away. It was only when I heard Ginger calling my name that I realised she was banging on the bedroom door.

I tossed the pillow to the floor. 'Fuck!'

I looked at the door, unable to remember locking it when I'd crawled up to bed.

'Are you awake, Enola?'

My fingers trembled as I opened up and glared at her. 'I am now.'

She pushed past me. 'Where's Debbie?'

The skin was burning under my eyes as I touched it. 'Not in here. What's wrong?'

Ginger thrust her phone into my face. I had to blink three times before my vision returned to normal and I could read the text.

It's all too much. I've had enough.

'Fuck,' I said again. 'Have you rang her?'

'Of course I've called her. She's switched her mobile off.'

I staggered back and flopped on the bed. 'Or somebody else has.'

'What does that mean?'

I told her what I'd found when returning to the house. I didn't mention what happened at the river. That could wait for later.

'So Fuller might be behind all this.'

Ginger sat next to me. 'Why?'

I shook my head, but the pain didn't go away. 'Fuck knows. Maybe he's convinced Debbie to change her will, and he's the beneficiary.'

'Fuck!' she said. 'What are we going to do?'

I got off the bed. 'I need a shower before I can do anything. You go downstairs and make breakfast. There's no point rushing into this.'

She left the bedroom, and I threw my underwear into the damp clothes from the river. I examined myself in the mirror before showering and saw the new bruises alongside the one on my face. I was going to need a long holiday once this was over.

If it was ever over.

What was I to do about the mysterious, vengeful Rook?

Hot water drenched my head, and I had a flashback to being in that river, dragged by invisible hands deep into the abyss. Years ago, a young woman about my age vanished from that spot. Some people thought she must have drowned. Maybe that was her spirit pulling at me in the inky depths.

Spirits in the woods, ghosts in the water.

I increased the temperature and shook the memory from my mind, considering paying another visit to Detective Inspector Parker. As much as I distrusted the police, he seemed the best bet for getting the drug dealer off my back.

I finished showering, got dry, and grabbed fresh clothes. As I strode into the kitchen, the smell of fried bacon and eggs kick-started the adrenalin in my blood.

'Here you go.' Ginger placed a full plate in front of me. The eggs broke between my teeth, and a delicious yolk swirled inside my mouth. I ate with only the fork and put my phone beside the drink, searching online for anything about last night's river confrontation, expecting to see headlines about more bodies discovered in the woods.

However, there was nothing.

I checked the national and local news sites and got the same results. Then I browsed social media, thinking there might be some gossip, but again, there was no mention of people hurt or dead near the river. I wasn't sure if that was a good thing or not.

'This is a great breakfast, Ginger. You should cook for me more often.'

'Cheers.' She joined me at the table. 'What are you looking at?'

I'd moved on to something else with my online search. 'An address for Mark Fuller.'

'Fuller? Why?'

The toast crunched between my teeth. 'After last night's shenanigans, I'd assume that if Debbie is anywhere, it's with him. So that's where we should check once we finish this.'

'I suppose so, but maybe I should call the police.'

'You could, but I doubt they'd do anything about a woman who hasn't answered her mobile for a few hours.' I pointed at my phone. 'I've got his address.'

She peered over the butter dish at the screen. 'Are you sure it's him?'

I turned the screen to her. 'The photo on his LinkedIn account matches the bloke I saw here. He lives near Echo Park.'

'That's forty minutes away,' she said.

I downed my coffee. 'Less the way you drive.'

Ginger shook her head, finished her breakfast, and stood. 'Get your jacket, then.'

I ate the last of the bacon and pushed the plate from me. Two minutes later, we left the house, with me wondering if I should have gone upstairs for Amy's gun.

As she drove, I flicked through the radio stations, my ears tuned to anything that might mention bodies in the woods, but it was the same as I'd found online: nothing. So, instead, I settled on the station playing the latest from Young Fathers.

'You're hiding information from me,' she said as we left the estate.

I peered out the window and saw the kid from the other day, the one I'd met at the food bank.

'What do you mean?'

'I can tell from the look on your face that you're keeping something from me. So, what is it?'

My bruise vibrated as I touched it. 'How is it possible to determine anything from this?'

'It's about that, isn't it? You've met more of those goons, haven't you?'

'No,' I lied. 'Last night, I went to the woods after I left you.'

She slammed on the brakes at a red light. It was a good job I had the seatbelt on, or I would have smashed into the dashboard.

'For fucks sake, Enola. Why did you do that?'

'I hoped I might see the birdwatcher, the supposed witness to Joe's death. And I did.'

Ginger sat open-mouthed as the light turned green and the cars behind us honked their horns. She stuck her hand out the window and gave them the finger before leaving.

'What happened?'

'He saw me and ran off when I shouted at him. If that's not suspicious, I don't know what is.'

The music on the radio changed to First Aid Kit.

She laughed. 'Yeah, some crazed woman with a bruised face shouts at you in the woods in the middle of the night, and you just stay around for a chat. I'd have been surprised if he hadn't scarpered.'

'The thing is, Ginger, I'm sure I've seen him somewhere before, somewhere recently.'

'Where?'

I thumped the seat. 'I can't remember. My head's been all fucked up since the beating.'

'Maybe we should take you back to the hospital. The bruise doesn't seem to be getting better, and, honestly, you looked like you weren't walking properly at Debbie's. I'm worried about you.'

'I fell into the river last night while chasing the bloke.'

'What? Fucking hell, Enola. I can't trust you to go anywhere on your own, can I?'

My jaw ached when I smiled. 'That's why you're with me now.'

She took a deep breath. 'Okay, what do we do when we get to Fuller's house?'

"We Are Glass" by Gary Numan blasted out of the radio.

'It's simple. We make him tell us the truth.'

Chapter 30

House of Fun

Fuller's house was nestled on the edge of a park, surrounded by lush green trees and rolling hills as far as the eye could see. The exterior was a beautiful, grand, two-story building with bright emerald vegetation crawling over the yellowing stone. The front of the house featured a wrap-around porch with ornately carved columns and railings. Wicker furniture with floral cushions beckoned visitors to sit and admire the view. Stone steps led to an imposing double front door of heavy oak and iron fittings. The door knocker was a bronzed lion's head, mouth open in a silent roar. Tall, narrow windows flanked the entrance, their panes glinting in the sunlight. Along the sides of the house, ivy blanketed the weathered brick walls like a living tapestry.

'This must have cost a lot,' Ginger said as we exited the car.

The lawn was perfectly manicured, stretching out from the house in all directions. A cobblestone pathway meandered through the garden, leading to a charming pond with a small wooden bridge that crossed it. On the far side of the water, a gazebo offered a shaded place to relax and enjoy the park's natural beauty.

'Fuller's LinkedIn page said he was an IT consultant and had recently worked with the government.'

Ginger laughed. 'Bent as a nine-bob note, then.'

'I bet this is all bought on borrowed money,' I said as we strode up the path.

She lifted her hand to knock on the door. 'We'll ask him.'

I stopped her and touched the entrance. It swung open with no trouble. 'I guess we're invited.'

'We can't just walk in.'

Then we heard loud noises from inside, sounding like somebody was being murdered.

'Fuck,' I said as I stepped in.

'He's killing Debbie upstairs.'

I grabbed her arm before she ran up. 'That's not murder?'

'What?' she asked. Then we listened closely to the sounds above us. 'Oh fuck, they're....'

I smiled. 'Yes, they are.'

We crept upstairs and followed the grunts and groans to the bedroom. I pushed the door open to a sight I'll never forget: Sarah Bailey dressed in full dominatrix gear, including leather corset, lingerie, high heels, and wielding a whip, while Mark Fuller was bent over the bed, completely naked apart from the giant vibrator sticking out of his arse.

Ginger gasped. 'Fuck!'

Bailey offered her the whip. 'Do you want a go? You can hit him as hard as you like. He loves it, and I need a break.'

He rolled over and spat a red plastic ball from his mouth. It trundled across the sheets and landed at my feet, looking like the one Kronos chewed on.

'What are you doing here?' he demanded.

I lifted my hand to block out the sight of his withered penis. 'How long have you two known each other?'

Fuller jumped off the bed, and the dildo fell out of his arse. 'That's none of your business. Now get out of my house.'

'Is Debbie here?' Ginger asked.

Bailey twisted the whip between her fingers. 'Debbie? She never gets involved in our games. That's why Joe had to look elsewhere, the poor love. I told him at uni she was a waste of time.'

The gears started clicking in my head. 'You were all together at university.'

'I told you to leave,' Fuller said. 'Or should I call the police?'

I kicked the dildo out of the way and went to the window, gazing over the expensive exterior. 'Perhaps you should, Mr Fuller; then you can explain how you black-mailed Joe Jackson for forty grand.'

'What?' Ginger said.

Fuller puffed out his reddening cheeks. 'That's nonsense.'

'Is it? Is that why Joe left photos of you two on his work computer?' I glanced between Bailey and Fuller. 'They must have been taken when you were at university, but who sent them to Joe, and whose idea was it to blackmail him?'

They glanced at each other before Bailey threw the whip on the bed.

'I didn't care about the money; that was Mark's plan. I only wanted to repay Joe for what he did to me.'

'Shut up, Sarah,' Fuller shouted.

'What did Joe do to you?' Ginger asked.

Sarah pulled at the side of her corset, which looked like it was crushing her ribs.

'He left me. That's what he did, and all for that miserable cow.' The heat was simmering on her face. 'And years later, he contacts me through Facebook, desperate to get back together. He claimed he'd always loved me, but he just wanted to hook up and fuck. I was with Mark and wanted to tell Joe to go fuck himself, but Mark had a better idea.' She smiled at him. 'Didn't you love?'

Fuller sat on the bed and put his head in his hands. Ginger grabbed a towel from a chair and threw it at him.

'Cover yourself up.'

He left it on his groin and stared at me. 'I needed the money to pay the debt on this place. So, I begged Joe to lend it to me, but he refused and said I should go to my mates in the government if I was desperate. Well, I was desperate and sent him the photos. I knew he had a new contract on the line and asked him what the clients would think if the pictures were plastered all over the media.'

'Nobody cares about stuff like that anymore,' Ginger said.

Fuller shook his head. 'You'd be surprised how many people still do, especially in business. And that contract was for an AI app for schools, helping kids create art. Those photos getting out would have ruined that for Joe.' He sighed. 'I just wish I'd known how much it was worth, and I would have demanded more than forty grand.'

I spoke to Bailey. 'You didn't go to the Park Regency Hotel with Joe?'

She shook her head. 'I met him a few times in that café where I saw you, but that was it.'

Fuller glared at me. 'Now get the fuck out of my house before I shove that dildo up your arse.'

I smiled at him. 'You wouldn't be the first bloke to try that with me.' I stepped forward. 'And he'll never come out of that coma.'

Ginger got her phone. 'We should call the police.'

He laughed at her. 'And tell them what? You have no evidence of blackmail or that Joe gave me money. The photos were only something for two old mates to share of their university days. And as you said, nobody cares about that sex stuff anymore.'

I stopped her from lunging at him. 'He's not worth it.' I looked at him. 'Why were you at Debbie's last night?'

'She called me and asked me to go over. So, I did. That's all.'

I had to stop myself from punching him. 'Come on, Ginger. We've still got to find Debbie.'

I bundled her out of the house, feeling the anger in her, ready to burst like a volcano.

She wriggled from my grasp. 'Fucking fuck!' She reached down, grabbed small stones from the path, and hurled them at the windows. 'Those fucking cunts might have made Joe take his life.'

'They'll pay for what they've done.' I wasn't sure how.

She was about to grab more pebbles when her phone rang. 'It's Sally,' she said. Ginger put the call on speakerphone.

'Debbie's here at the office. She seems okay.'

'Great, we're coming over,' Ginger said, ending the call.

At least, that was some good news.

Now I had to decide how to tell Debbie about what we'd seen at Fuller's house.

Chapter 31

Busy Earnin'

We talked briefly on the way to Jackson Systems, but she had one important question for me.

'Why didn't you tell me you'd found those photos on his computer? It wouldn't have bothered me.'

Grace Jones was pulling up to the bumper on the radio as we approached the industrial estate, and Ginger parked the car.

'There were no images on Joe's computer.'

'What? But you told Fuller you found some.'

I shrugged. 'It was a bluff.'

'Then how did you know he'd blackmailed Joe for the forty grand he got from the loan shark?'

I turned to her. 'I could never understand why he'd need the cash if the business were doing so well. Then I figured maybe it wasn't making any profit and was just keeping above water, which was why they needed that new contract. So, Joe had to get the money from somewhere else. We'll probably never understand why he chose Brown, but that's where he went.'

'Okay, but how did you know Fuller was the blackmailer?'

I grinned. 'It was two things. Noticing that house and his garden, plus what Sally said about Fuller going to Joe's office and arguing with him, I knew it had to be about money.'

'What was the second thing?'

We got out of the car. 'Bursting into that bedroom and seeing that giant dildo in his arse, I knew there wasn't anything he wouldn't do.'

She laughed and shook her head as we entered the building to find the lift out of order. 'Fuck. Now we have to climb four flights.'

'I thought you were fit?'

She pushed open the door to the stairs. 'I'm not the one who goes jogging, missus.'

'I haven't done that for a few days.'

We strode up, and a voice was nagging at the back of my head, telling me I was missing something. Ginger was out of breath when we reached Jackson Systems, leaning on the wall like an asthmatic chain smoker.

'Give me a second,' she said.

'Sure, no problem. What are you going to tell Debbie?'

'About what?'

'About her scaring you shitless because you thought she'd followed in her husband's footsteps.'

'I won't mention that. What will you say about Fuller?'

'Well, I could say he's a cheating twat, but I assume she already knows.'

I entered the office, and Sally rushed over as the rest of the staff continued their work.

'Oh great, you're here. Debbie's in Joe's old office.' She smiled at me. 'I guess it will be yours soon.'

'How's she been?' Ginger said.

'Fine, fine, asking everyone about what they do, wanting a better feel of the place.' She moved closer to us and lowered her voice. 'At first, when she arrived, she seemed quite agitated. And when she started talking about the business, needing to see the books again, I thought she'd tell me she was selling up.' She put a hand on her chest. 'That gave me a real fright.'

For no reason, a picture formed in my mind of Joe and Sally enjoying S&M sex in the office. I tried shaking the image from my head, but the bugger wouldn't let go.

Ginger pushed open the door. 'I've been calling you all morning, Debbie. Is your phone off?'

Debbie got up from behind the desk. 'It ran out of battery. I'm charging it now.' She peered at me. 'I had to get out, to be alone for a bit. It was driving me mad being cooped up in there.'

'Okay,' Ginger said. 'Sure, I understand.' She glanced at the papers strewn everywhere and then at me. 'Mark Fuller was at the house last night. Did you call him?'

'Oh God, no,' Debbie replied. 'Mark was always Joe's friend. I never really got on with him. I didn't know he was coming. He just turned up to pay his condolences and ask when the funeral was.'

'It's sorted?' I asked.

She gazed at me. 'It's next Friday. Family and friends only.'

Ginger slumped into the chair in the corner as I went to the window and looked outside. 'Well, at least things are moving forward.'

Debbie grabbed documents from the desk and put them in the top drawer, reminding me of the bank accounts I'd found there and what they contained.

Who was with Joe at the seedy hotel?

'I just need to clean everything now,' Debbie said.

Then it hit me like an atomic bomb. 'Fuck!'

'What?' Ginger asked.

'I recall where I saw him.'

'Saw who?' Debbie said.

I glanced out of the window and then back to them. 'The eyewitness, the birdwatcher, he was here the other day when we came.' I looked at Ginger. 'As we got into the lift, a man stepped out with a mop and bucket. Do you remember?'

She scrunched up her eyes. 'I think so, short bloke, pudgy face and a terrible haircut.'

'That's the one.' I asked Debbie. 'Do you recall seeing him?'

She shook her head. 'I don't. What's this about?'

'Ginger will tell you.' I rushed out of the office and found Sally. 'Do you know the janitor for this building?'

'Can't say I do. Why?'

'Will any of the other staff?'

She shrugged. 'I'll ask.' She clapped, and they all stopped their work, staring at her like seals waiting to be fed. 'Does anybody know the name of the janitor for this building?'

They all appeared bemused until a bloke who looked younger than me spoke.

'The building manager has an office on the ground floor. He'll know.'

I left without an explanation, cursing as I remembered the lift was out of order. I sprinted down four flights, taking two steps at a time, lucky not to break my ankle. My chest throbbed like a bastard when I reached the bottom and burst through the exit. The building manager's office was straight ahead, and I banged on the door. A middle-aged man with glasses too big for his face opened it.

'Yes? Can I help?'

'The janitor for this building. Is he here?'

'George? No, he never came in today.' He narrowed his eyes at me. 'He's probably obsessing over that hobby of his again.'

'Birdwatching?'

'Yes. Are you one of his friends?'

'No. What's his surname?'

'I can't tell you that. Who are you?'

I grabbed his shirt and pulled him to me. 'I'm the woman who's about to break your glasses if you don't tell me George's surname.'

'Wilson,' he spluttered. 'It's George Wilson.'

I pushed him away as Ginger strode through the door. 'What's happening, Enola?'

'Where's Debbie?' I said.

'She's staying here for a bit, chatting with the staff.'

'Did you say anything about Fuller?'

'Fuck no. You can do that.'

'Maybe later. Come on.' I exited the building and went to the car.

Ginger caught up with me. 'Tell me what's going on.'

I took a deep breath. 'Detective Inspector Parker's eyewitness to Joe's death, the midnight birdwatcher, is George Wilson, the janitor for this building, the bloke who probably cleaned Joe's office.'

'Wow, that's some coincidence.'

'Ginger, come on. That's no fucking coincidence.'

She nodded. 'Yeah, you're right. Fuck. What do we do now?'

'Get in the car,' I said. 'We're going to the coppers.'

Chapter 32

Walk on By

Detective Inspector Jack Parker wasn't happy to see us at the police station, but he ushered us in anyway. The smell of leather and old books hit me as we walked into a different room from where he'd taken me last time. A stack of papers, folders, and a black telephone sat beside a computer.

'Why didn't you bring me here before?' I said.

'What do you want, Ms Gray?'

Ginger took a seat, but I stood over the desk. 'Your eyewitness to Joe's death is George Wilson.'

He narrowed his eyes and peered into mine. 'Who told you that?'

'Did you know he works as the janitor in the building where Jackson Systems is?'

'Do you think I'm stupid, Ms Gray?'

'Would you like an honest answer, Inspector Parker?'

He crossed his arms. 'Why are you here?'

The bruise on my face throbbed. 'Are you fucking stupid? Your only witness to Joe's death is a bloke who used to clean Joe's office. Don't tell me that isn't suspicious.'

'Mr Wilson never set foot anywhere inside Jackson Systems. His job is to maintain the parts of the building outside of all the offices. And yes, we checked the staff rota to verify that. We also spoke to everybody at Jackson Systems, all six of them, and none of them recalls ever seeing Mr Wilson in their office.'

'Come on, Parker. You don't see how this is problematic?'

He picked up a paper and offered it to me. 'Would you like to read the coroner's verdict on Joe Jackson's death?'

I didn't but snatched the document from him anyway, scanning the details and tossing it back to him. 'So that's it, death by suicide?'

Parker returned the paper to the pile on his desk. 'Have you had any more contact with those thugs?'

I sneered at him. 'Which ones? You'll have to be more precise, as criminals surround me wherever I go.'

He pointed at my bruise. 'Those who did that?'

'Yeah, two jumped me and shoved me in the river when I was chasing George Wilson through the woods last night. When I finally stopped myself from drowning and crawled out of the water into the mud and reeds, they tried to kill me. Then I beat the shit out of them and left. How does that sound?'

He gazed at me. 'I can never tell if you're lying or not.'

'The feeling's mutual.'

'I hope you won't harass Mr Wilson.'

'Would there be any point? If I brought proof that other people were involved in Joe's death, would you even look at it?'

'Do you have evidence?'

I glared at him for five seconds before storming out of the office and the station and throwing my visitor's pass in the bin. I stepped into the street, blood boiling in my veins and my heart about to rip my chest apart.

'Was any of that true?' Ginger asked.

'What?'

She punched me in the shoulder. 'Don't fuck about, Enola. What you said about being in the woods last night and getting attacked. Was any of that true?'

I rubbed at my aching flesh. 'Most of it. I left some bits out.'

'Which bits?'

'The violent ones.'

Concern consumed her face. 'What?'

'Don't worry. It was violence against them.'

'What did you do?'

'I defended myself.'

'There were two thugs?'

'Aye. I left them near the river, bloodied and in a state of distress. I thought it would have been in the news or all over social media, but there was nothing. So that's why I told Parker, thinking I'd get a response from him.'

Cars whizzed past, spewing out smoke and noise that increased the throbbing in my head. A woman with two small kids trundled by, glancing at my bruised face as if I'd just got off the boat and she was desperate to put me on a plane to somewhere else.

'What do you want to do now, Enola?'

I stared across the street, peering into the empty shops and boarded-up buildings. An old bloke dragged a guitar from his bag, cleared his throat and belted out a decent impersonation of "Walk on By", though I preferred The Stranglers' version. Ginger was still talking to me, but I wasn't listening, my mind having drifted back to my fifteenth birthday in the children's home and what Amy gave me as a present.

'I did it myself,' Amy said as she handed me the bag with The Stranglers' name painted in their distinctive red style across the front. 'It took me ages.'

I beamed as I grabbed it from her. 'Thanks! I didn't know you were an artist.'

She shrugged. 'It's in the genes. My mother was a painter.'

I shouldn't have asked, but I did. 'What happened to her?'

'She's in prison.'

I didn't explore further, but she'd tell me the details later. That bag was my most prized possession until it got damaged in the first place I lived alone, with rain leaking through the roof and destroying the art Amy had created for me.

Ginger's voice brought me back to the present. 'Are you listening, Enola?'

'What?'

'I said, what do you want to do now?'

What did I want to do? I was unsure. The mystery of Joe's death was apparently cleared up, but there was still Rook and his thugs to think about. However, I had the gun at Debbie's, so I needed to start carrying it.

'Take me to Debbie's.'

'Sure,' Ginger said. 'And then what?'

I thought about my future. 'I suppose I should prepare for my new job at Jackson Systems.'

Perhaps I'd bump into George Wilson while I was there.

Chapter 33

Red Red Wine

Debbie was still out when I got back. I went to the kitchen for a drink of water, sat at the table, and checked my phone. No news about my river antics told me that Rook's goons had cleared everything up. Were both still alive? I didn't care. Actions had consequences, and they'd wanted to hurt or kill me.

But how was I going to resolve the issue? Rook wouldn't give up; there would be another attack on me or my friends in the future. So, even if I carried the gun permanently, it wasn't an answer to my problem. I had to get ahead and turn the situation around, so I became the hunter, not the hunted. But I didn't know how.

County lines. That's what Parker said this was all about. I must have disrupted Rook's operation with what I did outside the Raven, so that's where I had to focus my attention. The local police or the National Crime Agency might not view dealing with it as a priority, but it certainly was for me.

I went to the Raven's website, scrolling through it to see if they had any forthcoming events. Bruce wasn't the only promoter to use the venue for gigs, and they seemed the best times for dealers to target customers. Bruce didn't know who owned the Raven, but the manager was notorious for his lax attitude.

My eyes lit up when I noticed a gig for that night, a local group I didn't know but who would likely attract a large crowd. That would be perfect for me to assess the potential for criminality in the club.

I put my phone away as a car pulled up outside. I assumed it was Debbie, and I was in no rush to see or talk to her with the tension still between us. She entered the house as I went into the bedroom, closing the door and waiting to hear if she called for me. She didn't, and I heard her enter the kitchen, guessing it was to open a bottle of wine.

As she did that, I went to the wardrobe and reached for the plastic bag with the gun and ammunition. Joe's clothes sat on top of it, so I had to push them out of the way to get what I wanted. Then I hauled it out, finally ready to use it if necessary. As I did, a pair of Joe's trousers got tangled up in the plastic and came out with it. When I pulled the bag out, a mobile phone fell from the trouser pocket and landed on the carpet.

I left it there and sat on the bed, removing the pistol and box of bullets. I'd used a gun before, but it was a while ago, so I felt the weight of it in my hand, checking the trigger and the barrel. Then I replaced it in the plastic and picked up the phone. I pressed the button on the side and switched it on. When the screen sparked into life, it asked for a code. I put it next to the bag and reached for my jacket, getting the notebook with Joe's passwords. There were two pages at the back with several combinations of four digits, but without indicating what they were for. I looked at them all and knew which one it would be.

Debbie was singing downstairs as I entered Ginger's birthday into the phone. The security prompt vanished, revealing icons for the internet and various apps. I checked the text messages, finding nothing. Then, I did the same for the email and got the same results. There was no history of web browsing or app use.

However, the camera function provided different outcomes. There were hundreds of photos and dozens of videos. I flicked through the pictures first, seeing images of Joe I'd never show to Ginger. Then I plugged the headphones from my bag into the phone and my ears. I trawled through the dates and started with the earliest one, a three-minute clip. I watched it twice to ensure I didn't mistake what I saw. The other clips were of a similar length, featuring Joe and the same person in the same place. After watching them all, I put the mobile into my pocket and headed downstairs.

Debbie was in the living room, singing along to an Oasis CD and drinking red wine.

'I thought you were out, Enola.'

'Did you know George Wilson before you entered the woods that night, Debbie, or was that the first time you met him?'

She held the glass before her face, the red merging with her ruby lips. 'What?'

'Or perhaps Wilson wasn't even there, and you paid him to lie to the police because you thought Ginger and I were getting too close to the truth.'

'You've lost me, Enola.'

'The sex in the dingy hotel – was that because Joe wanted to add spice into your lives? And was that also why you were in the woods, because of the danger? I guess so from the look on your face. I can't decide if you panicked when he strangled himself, that it was a sex game gone wrong, or that you knew exactly what was happening and left him to die on purpose.'

Debbie emptied the glass down her throat and put it on the table. 'You know, Enola, I don't think it will work out with you living here.' She smiled at me. 'You should move out in the morning. And as far as the job is concerned at Jackson Systems, I've decided to give it to Sally after all. So, I hope there are no hard feelings.'

'What was it, Debbie? Were you just sick of him, or was it about the money and the business? Did you see that million-pound contract and want it all for yourself?'

Her grin increased. 'I guess you're still suffering from concussion, Enola. You should go back to the hospital. I'd drive you there, but I've had a drink.'

'I don't know how well you know George Wilson, but once the police get him into an interrogation room, he'll crack and tell them everything. It's only a matter of time, Debbie.'

She refilled her glass and drank half of it. 'It's a nice little story, Enola, but let's say some of it is true, and I was there when Joe died; who's to say I didn't just panic and run away? And I've been in shock and suffering from grief ever since. So, I'm sure an excellent defence lawyer would do well with that.'

'Let me get this right: theoretically, you saw Joe put the noose over his head as part of a sex game, and you didn't know what to do when it all went wrong? Then you panicked and ran. Is that correct?'

Debbie cradled the glass in her hands. 'It could be.'

I removed the phone I found upstairs from my pocket and put it on the table between us. 'I suppose that might work, but for the fact, there are two dozen videos on that device showing you and Joe partaking in the same sex game. You watch him strangle himself in them, and then you help him survive every time. How strange is that?'

Debbie lunged for the device, and I smashed my fist into her hand. She screamed like a baby and rolled onto the table, knocking the glass and bottle over the carpet. The red stain spread out from it in the shape of the human heart. I watched it glisten as I got my phone and made a call.

'I want to speak to Detective Inspector Parker, please. Yeah, tell him it's about Joe Jackson's murder.'

Chapter 34

Money for Nothing

The warehouse was on the far side of the town. I took a taxi there and made the driver wait.

'Where are you going?' Ginger had asked as I grabbed my jacket. I was sleeping on her couch for now. The true nature of Debbie's betrayal of Joe was something we wouldn't fully know until the trial, but I could see that Ginger was struggling with the revelation. And she still didn't trust me to leave the house alone.

'I've got an errand to run?'

'What errand?'

'It's a surprise for your birthday.'

I was outside and in the taxi before she could protest. Now the driver was waiting for me with the engine running. The sky was overcast, and a chill wind blew through the broken windows, carrying the scent of rust and decay. I stepped into the factory, the air thick with the smell of oil and grease and a hint of an acrid substance that made my eyes water. Flickering fluorescent lights overhead lighted the place, casting long shadows over the rusted machinery. In the centre, a man leaned against a worktable, arms crossed over his chest. He was big and burly, with a rough-hewn face and a scowl that said he didn't like surprise visitors.

'Who are you?'

'Where's Brown?' I replied.

Brown emerged from the shadows and glared at me. 'What are you doing here?'

'Do you still want your forty grand?'

He stepped closer to me. 'Have you got my money?'

I removed the paper from my pocket, scrunched it into a ball, and threw it at his feet.

'The man who has your cash, his name and address are on there.'

I left them to it and returned to the taxi, telling the driver to take me to the Raven.

I was homeless and still unemployed.

And Rook was out there somewhere, waiting for me.

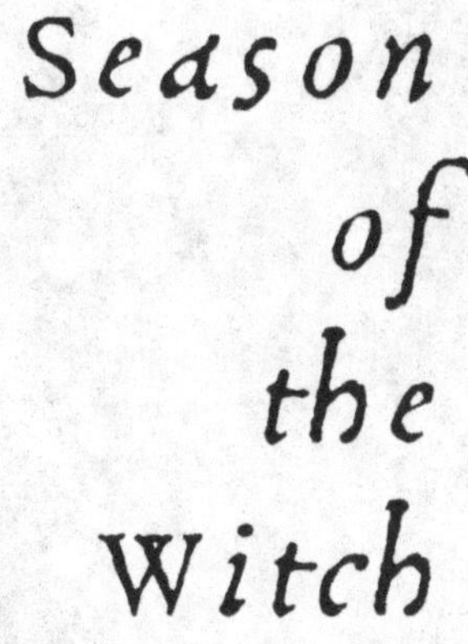

Season of the Witch

AN ENOLA GRAY MYSTERY

A. S. FRENCH

Chapter 1

Happiness Is a Warm Gun

It had been a good day until the gunman arrived.

I wore my new jeans, a leather jacket and my favourite Louise Brooks T-shirt, with her head back and eyes closed. Gathered ahead of me were a bunch of local dignitaries, including our newest surprise MP after the recent by-election, ready for the grand re-opening of the community food bank. I was there as a volunteer, joined by fellow volunteer – and friend – Bruce, plus his flatmate and my best mate, Ginger. I was homeless, sleeping on their sofa, unemployed and without money, but still feeling good.

That was until I stepped into the building and observed people worse off than me, including the refugee families, smiling as they spoke to Bruce. He organised not just food for them but clothing and bedding. It warmed my heart to see their smiles, but my blood also boiled at how it had come to this in one of the wealthiest countries in the world.

A small hand tugged at my sleeve. I removed my headphones, pausing Killing Joke in mid requiem, and listened to my newest friend, ten-year-old Becky Cross.

'I'm bored, Enola. Can we break some more windows?'

One of the ways I occupied my free time was by caring for Becky while her mother, Julia, was at work. This included showing the kid how to enjoy herself in the bits of the town kept out of the tourist guides: abandoned factories, disused playgrounds, crumbling hospitals, and the derelict shopping mall. It was my way of educating Becky on how to find entertainment away from her mobile phone.

I glanced across the room to see Julia flirting with Bruce and wondered what she'd think if she knew I was trying to toughen up her daughter. Becky was having a difficult time at school, and my first instinct was to advise her to deal with the bullies directly, violently, before Ginger told me off.

'You can't tell a ten-year-old kid to hit other kids, Enola,' Ginger said.

'It didn't harm me at her age,' I replied.

She shook her head and frowned. So, I took Becky to break things instead. And she seemed to enjoy it so far, though I'd made her promise not to tell her mother.

I pointed to the tables in the corner. 'They have cakes over there.'

She pulled a face as if somebody had dropped a worm in her throat.

'I had a scone. It was harder than a whore's heart.'

'Becky! Who taught you to talk like that?'

The kid twisted her bottom lip to the side of her mouth. 'You did.'

I scratched my chin as Julia and Bruce approached us. 'Okay, but don't tell anyone. Especially your mother.'

Bruce rubbed his hands. 'The ceremony and speeches will start soon. Have you tasted the cakes?'

I put my hand on Becky's shoulder before she could speak. 'We haven't had time. Who made them?'

He pointed at our newest member of Parliament. 'Kate's assistant brought them.'

I laughed. 'Kate? Are you on first-name terms with our MP, the honourable Kate Frost?'

He nodded. 'I need to be if I'm going to wangle any funding out of her for this place. We desperately need money here, and I'm running out of options. You know I distrust all politicians, but this is different. As an independent MP, she doesn't have the financial support of the traditional political parties, but she has several contacts with local businesses.'

'Yeah,' I replied. 'It's a welcome change for the area, but I still don't see how she could overtake a 5,000 majority to win by over 4,000 votes. I know the country's a shitshow right now, but that's some swing for somebody with no political experience.'

Bruce shrugged. 'I don't care as long as we got the previous idiot out who wanted to sell the NHS to the Americans.'

'I voted for Frost,' Julia said. 'Who did you vote for, Enola?'

I was approaching my twenty-first birthday fast, so the by-election was the first time I could legally vote. However, I hadn't.

'I abstained,' I replied.

'You're full of stains,' Becky said. 'There's mustard on your jeans.'

She was correct. 'I had a hot dog for breakfast.'

Bruce scowled at me. 'Everybody should use their democratic right to vote, Enola.'

'What if you don't believe any of the candidates are worth a vote?'

'You must vote,' he said.

I shrugged. 'It would be worth it if they replaced the first past the post system with proportional representation. Otherwise, it's a waste of time in many constituencies where you get die-hard supporters of the big two who would vote for a corpse as long as it was wearing the right coloured rosette.'

'He looks like a dead man,' Becky said as she pointed at Kate Frost's assistant. 'And he smells like a fart in a spacesuit.'

'Becky!' Julia shouted at her daughter, and I wondered if the kid had been spending too much time with me.

Bruce sidled over to me. 'Is Ginger okay?'

'Why?' I asked.

'I'm not sure. She seemed a bit down when I spoke to her.'

'We watched TV late last night, a horror movie marathon, so she might be tired.'

He scrunched up his nose. 'I was curious what that noise was. I thought Ginger didn't like horror movies.'

'She uses them as research,' I said. 'But don't worry, I'll find my own place soon.'

'Hey,' he said. 'That wasn't a hint. You know you can stay as long as you want. And anyway, you'll need a job first to pay for a flat.'

That was true. 'If the landlord discovers I'm staying with you, it might cause you and Ginger problems. He might increase the rent.'

He patted me on the shoulder. 'It'll be fine, Enola. Forget about it and enjoy today. It's not every day that the community comes together like this.' He waved at our MP. 'Would you like me to introduce you to Kate?'

Julia harangued her daughter. I pulled him to the side. 'Are you flirting with her?'

He frowned. 'Who? Kate? She's recently separated from her husband.'

I laughed. 'As if that makes any difference. I was thinking more about you and Julia.'

He glanced at Julia as Becky stuck her fingers in her ears. 'I like Julia, but, you know.'

Growing up as an orphan since I was ten, I knew how he felt. 'You don't want to bring a kid up.'

Bruce grimaced. 'It's not that I don't like Becky because I do.' He fidgeted next to me. 'I feel unprepared for the responsibility, which would be unfair to her or Becky.'

I didn't argue with him, watching the kid as she ran from her mother and jumped on the climbing wall at the far end of the room, a remnant of the food bank's former life as a gym. She scrambled up like an Olympic athlete, and I knew getting her to climb those trees in the woods had really helped her. Then Bruce cleared his throat, preparing the stage for Kate Frost's big speech.

That's when the bloke burst in, waving his gun in the air.

Chapter 2

Beans

There was a loud crash at the entrance. Then came the screaming and shouting as I saw the gunman. I stepped forward when he lifted the pistol and fired into the ceiling. I looked for Becky, seeing her halfway up the climbing wall behind him.

'Get on the floor!' the bloke screamed.

Most people did, apart from me, Kate Frost, and Julia. I studied the man, with his hand trembling on the trigger. His face was pale with dark hair and a cold stare detectable at any distance.

I put my hands up slowly and took a cautious step towards him. 'Hey, take it easy,' I said gently. 'No one needs to get hurt here. Just put the gun down.'

The guy was freaked out. His eyes kept ping-ponging around the room, all shifty and weird. I could tell he was scared but also getting angry. Like some rabid raccoon backed into a corner - you know he will come out claws slashing if you mess with him.

'Stay back!' he shouted, jabbing the gun in my direction. I froze.

'Becky!' Julia screamed.

He pointed the gun at her. 'Get down!'

I grabbed Julia and pulled her to the floor. Kate Frost followed.

'I have to get Becky,' Julia said to me.

'You will,' I replied. The kid had stopped climbing, hanging on by one hand, but I didn't think he was even aware of her. He was too busy staring at the rest of us.

'I know him,' Ginger whispered to me. 'That's Nigel Craig, the former librarian.'

'Former?' I asked.

She nestled up to me. 'The council sacked him last week. I don't know why, but I saw online rumours about him spreading conspiracy theories around the council.'

Craig used his free hand, reached into his jacket and removed a handful of leaflets. Then he threw them into the crouching people. I snatched the one that landed near me, its headline screaming in red ink and all capitals about a SILENT WAR. I didn't need to read it to know it was all conspiracy theory nonsense.

Nigel Craig told everybody about it, going on a tirade about how the 5G phone network was responsible for COVID-19, climate change was a hoax, the earth was flat, the pharmaceutical industry was suppressing a cure for cancer, vaccines caused autism, the royal family murdered Princess Diana, and lizards ruled the planet.

It was impressive how he got so much crap into a five-minute rant but saved his real ire for the silent war.

'Generations of politicians have taken total control of the people to impose a one-world government. They're controlling you with the microchips in vaccines and using your mobile phones to spy on you. Our so-called leaders are replacing the natural-born citizens of this country, swapping them with illegals to take all of our jobs.' He shook the gun at Frost. 'None of them will help you because they're all the same.'

His voice echoed through the building as everybody else silently held their breaths. Was he there only to spout his nonsense, or did he intend to hurt people? I watched him wave the pistol around, expecting it to go off any second. He was twenty feet away from me and not looking in my direction. Could I get to him before he realised what I was doing? Even if I did, might he shoot somebody before I reached him?

I wondered what to do when Becky jumped off the climbing wall and ran at him.

'Fuck!' I said.

The kid stood before him with her hands on her hips and gazing straight into his eyes.

'My mum says people like you are gammon-faced morons.'

His cheeks burned red and grew to the size of mutant oranges. He lifted his arm, turning the gun towards Becky. Julia screamed as I pounced, rushing forward to jump on him, taking us both into the wall.

He hit it first, but dug his elbow into my stomach, knocking the wind out of me. I struggled to breathe as he wriggled off me and swung the pistol close to my face. Craig pulled the trigger as I jerked my head away. The bullet burst past my cheek, sending a crashing cascade of thunder into my ear. The universe exploded in my skull as I thrust my arm up and knocked the gun from him. It went scuttling across the floor, but freed up his hand so he could get both around my throat and his knees on my chest.

An excruciating weight pressed down on me like the

moon had collapsed onto my ribs. His fingers dug into my flesh, squeezing all the oxygen from my lungs.

The buzzing in my ears increased, but I heard him speak as he choked the life from me. 'You are a soldier in the silent war, and I'm your assassin.'

My arms flailed before my eyes like a drunken marionette and were just as useful. He pushed deeper into my ribs, and it was impossible to breathe. Parts of my life flashed before me: seeing my parents murdered when I was ten, my first night in the children's home when the other girls beat me to the floor, and I ran away with tears streaming down my face. A night spent dodging the street predators and hiding in darkened doorways, meeting my best friend Amy and all of our shoplifting trips, the first time I killed a man, and, strangely, the last occasion I shared an ice cream with Becky.

I suppose it was as good as anything to see before I left this world.

Then I saw Becky again, striding towards Craig, carrying a tin of baked beans. She lifted them high above her head before smacking him in the face with the tin. His fingers slipped from my throat, and he gurgled before falling off my chest.

I coughed and jerked up, my eyes watering as Becky moved to me.

'See, Enola. I told you beans were bad for you.'

I rolled onto my back and laughed. Nearby, people had wrestled Craig to the ground, and I heard sirens approaching.

She offered me her hand, and I took it. 'Thanks, kid.'

Julia, Bruce and Ginger rushed over.

'Are you okay?' Ginger asked.

I touched the marks on my neck. 'A drink of water wouldn't go amiss.'

'I'll get one,' Bruce said.

I pushed my back against the wall. 'That's not how I expected to start the day.'

Craig was ranting a few feet away from me, proclaiming that all women were evil and that everybody was part of the new world order.

Becky sat next to me. 'That's one of your favourite bands.'

Speaking caused a throbbing sensation in my throat. 'Who?'

'New world order.'

It hurt to laugh, but I couldn't help it. 'No, kid, that's New Order.'

She leaned her head on my shoulder as the police arrived, and I recognised the first two faces through the door.

Becky whispered to me. 'Trust the pigs to turn up late.'

My throat throbbed as I laughed, but the event had taught me a valuable lesson.

I had to modify my language around the kid in the future.

Chapter 3

Pumped Up Kicks

Detective Inspector Jack Parker and Constable Davis stood over me while their colleagues removed Nigel Craig from the building. Craig continued to rant against the world as Davis got out his notebook. I'd met him several times in the last few months, and he'd never spoken more than a few words to me.

'What happened here, Ms Gray?' Parker said.

My throat ached as Kate Frost answered for me.

'The man your colleagues are taking away stormed in here and fired a gun.' She gave Parker one of the leaflets Craig had thrown around the room. 'Then he ranted about several conspiracy theories before Ms Gray disarmed him.'

I rubbed my neck. 'I think a ten-year-old girl with a tin of beans did more than me.'

Parker glanced over the paper and shook his head. Then he handed the leaflet to Davis. 'We might need to call in NaCTSO.'

'NaCTSO?' I said.

'The National Counter Terrorism Security Office,' he replied. He looked around the room as the police escorted people out of the building. 'Do you know the man with the gun?'

Ginger answered. 'His name is Nigel Craig, the former librarian.'

Davis scribbled in his notebook. 'Former librarian?'

'Yeah,' Ginger said. 'He was well known in the community for his forthright views.'

Parker pointed at the leaflet. 'Those types of views.'

She shrugged. 'I guess so.'

Frost cleared her throat. 'He might have been here for me.'

Everybody looked at her.

'Why?' I asked.

Frost nodded to her assistant, who went to the back of the room.

'I receive many threats, online and in letters. Some things these people accuse me of, of betraying the country and wanting to replace, in their words, "the white race", are in those threats. They are never signed, but Craig's words in that leaflet echo what I've received.'

'Have you reported the threats to the police?' Parker said.

Frost smiled. 'The police are far too busy to deal with such things, Inspector.' Her assistant returned with a handful of letters. 'Thank you, John.'

Davis took the letters as Parker spoke. 'I'll send uniformed officers over for your statements.'

He moved away, but I grabbed his arm and dragged him to the side. 'Have you got anything to tell me?'

Parker gazed at my hand, and I let go. 'Such as?'

'You promised to keep me updated regarding the county lines investigation. Rook still has a grudge against me, remember?'

'We don't even know if Rook exists, Enola. They might be an urban myth.'

'Someone runs the operation, Parker.'

'Indeed, and we're working with the NCA to discover who that is. So when we catch them, I'll inform you.'

I puffed out my cheeks. 'That's great. And I'll tell you when Rook sends somebody to attack me again.'

I turned from him and returned to my friends, who Becky and her mother had joined.

Julia Cross touched my arm. 'Work called and asked me to take a shift.' She was a care worker, visiting vulnerable people in their homes. It wasn't well-paid, and she needed every penny she could get. 'Can you look after Becky for me?'

I glanced across the room, seeing the kid grabbing a copper's helmet and putting it on her head. 'Sure, Julia, no problem.'

She smiled and handed me her flat keys. 'There's money in the kitchen for a takeaway. I'll call you later.' She hugged me. 'And thanks again. You're a true friend, Enola.'

I watched her rush off and wondered how she juggled so much in her life and stayed sane. The first time I met her and Becky was in the food bank a few months back, and I'd surprised myself with how close we'd become. Julia kept many things close to her chest, so I still knew little about her, but the relationship was one of the few good things in my life.

'You're a changed woman, Enola Gray,' Ginger said.

'Give me your mirror,' I said to her.

She dug into her bag, removed a small compact, and handed it to me. I peered at the bruises forming on my throat and winced. Maybe the police should have dusted my skin for Craig's fingerprints.

'I can help you cover that up.'

I returned the mirror to her. 'No thanks. What do you mean, I'm a changed woman?'

'Well, look at your work in this place and all the help you've given Julia, looking after Becky as if you were a big sister.'

'How does that mean I've changed? I'm still the same person I was before.'

Ginger scrunched up her face. 'You're not as self-centred as you were a few months ago.'

'Self-centered? You cheeky cow. I'll have you know I always put others before myself.'

Bruce joined us. 'What are we talking about?'

She laughed. 'About how wonderful Enola is.'

He was about to laugh until he saw my expression. 'Now, Ginger, Enola just saved us from a lunatic gunman.'

Ginger removed one of Craig's leaflets from her pocket. 'How do people get away with printing shit like this?'

Bruce shook his head. 'It's called free speech.'

She scowled. 'I know, but have you read this stuff? Global warming is a hoax. The Holocaust never happened. Vaccines are used as population control. It just goes on and on.' She scrunched the leaflet into a ball and tossed it into a bin to join the others.

'I saw some people taking those leaflets away with them,' I said.

'Maybe they've run out of toilet paper,' Bruce replied.

Becky ran over with a police helmet hanging half on her head. 'Can we go to the funfair, Enola?'

She danced around me as if she were at a disco, and I was amazed at how she could just ignore the seriousness of what had happened in the centre.

I caught her arm and took the helmet off her. 'Funfair?'

'The one near the river,' Bruce answered. 'There's a shortcut to it through the woods.'

'That closed last year,' I said. I'd jogged past it several times on my nightly runs, noticing how it looked like something from a Stephen King novel.

Becky made a grab for the helmet, but I held it away from her. 'Yeah, but all the rides are still there, and you can sit on them.'

I stared into her eager eyes. 'Why would you want to do that?'

She stopped jumping up and down. 'Because that's where my dad used to take me.'

I glanced at Bruce and Ginger. Julia had told us how Becky's father had died in a road accident when she was five.

'You don't want to go to the park and feed the ducks?'

The kid scowled at me. 'The ducks are no fun.' Then she grabbed her stomach. 'And I need something to eat before those birds do.'

Her enthusiasm was infectious. 'Okay, Becky. We'll get some lunch on the way.' It might be good to take her mind off how much danger she'd been in.

She bounced around again. 'Yeah!'

Before we could leave, Kate Frost's assistant approached me. 'Ms Frost would like to speak to you, Ms Gray.'

'About what?'

His smile reminded me of a worm crawling through mud. 'About a job.'

Becky grabbed my hand, and I felt excited about being employed again.

Maybe I was a changed woman after all.

Chapter 4

Career Opportunities

The room was cramped and overflowing with papers, books, and various knick-knacks. The musty scent of old paper filled my nostrils, making me sneeze. I stumbled over a stack of file folders, nearly tripping on my way in. A box full of tinned food was in the corner, and a tattered poster for *The Maltese Falcon* was on the wall.

Faded yellow wallpaper covered the rest of the walls, peeling at the edges and dotted with thumbtacks holding documents and pictures. A mountain of papers and a vintage lamp buried the desk in the centre of the room.

The stacks of books and documents on the windowsill mostly blocked it, but a small window let in a sliver of light. Dust motes danced in the beams of sunlight, and I heard the traffic from the busy street outside. I squeezed myself into the rickety wooden chair to avoid the piles of paper and books. It creaked under my weight, and I felt a twinge of concern that I might end up on the floor. The handle of a stapler dug into my side, and I shifted, trying to get comfortable.

Kate Frost, MP, sat opposite me. 'You look surprised, Enola.'

I had trouble feeling at ease in the chair. 'I thought a Member of Parliament would have their constituency office somewhere slightly more upmarket than in the back room of a food bank, a former school gym.'

'As I said before the excitement earlier, as an independent MP without the backing of the majors, I have to take the help where I can. And by being here, I get to speak to my constituents daily. Those living in the Westminster bubble with lifestyles funded by wealthy donors don't see how most people have to live in this country.'

I laughed. 'I'm shocked you think a government of millionaires doesn't know how those on the breadline struggle to exist day to day.'

'You sound disillusioned with the country's current state, and you're not the only one. Millions are fed up with the two-party political system. For example, in the 2019 elections, nearly eight million voted for candidates not in the two major Westminster parties, and over fifteen million failed to vote. That's over twenty-three million people, just under fifty per cent of the electorate, who would like an alternative to the two main parties.'

'Did you ask me here to give me a party-political broadcast?'

Frost grinned. 'I'm not part of a political party, Enola, remember?'

'I saw you on the TV during the by-election. You were impressive.'

'How so?'

'With what you said, promising to dedicate your time to improving things for the people here, living in one of the most deprived parts of the country. Most locals feel that the main parties have let them down, so I guess that's how you achieved such a surprise victory. But I don't see how you can improve anything here if you do everything independently.'

'That's why I need others to help me, Enola. That's why I want your help.'

'Yeah?'

Frost pointed to the massive pile of papers near her computer. 'The death threats are increasing, and after what happened this morning, it's probably time I brought somebody in as my personal security.'

I put a hand on my heart. 'Me? Why? Because of what I did to Craig?'

'That was impressive, but not only for that, no. Bruce had told me much about you before today, how you solved the enigma of your parents' murders and the riddle of the man who died in the woods a few months ago.'

'You make me sound like Batman.'

She laughed. 'Wouldn't that be Batwoman?'

'You can't offer me a lot of money, can you?'

She grinned. 'No, but it will look good on your CV. And working for me has other benefits.'

'Such as?'

'Free trips to London and other parts of the country, plus you can claim for food and travel on expenses.'

I frowned. 'Don't all MPs fiddle their expenses?'

Frost narrowed her eyes. 'No, not all of them.'

I dredged an image from my shaky memory. 'I remember my parents telling me about a bloke who had an expenses claim for an island to house the ducks in his pond.'

'Yes,' she said. 'It wasn't a good time for British politics. A lot of people lost trust in the parliamentary system then.'

My laughter hurt my ribs. 'And you think it's better

now? We've had a decade and a half of incompetence, corruption, and downright nastiness. Most folks think Westminster is a cesspool.'

She sighed. 'I know, which is why I want to change things from the inside. But I can't do it on my own.'

The determination in her eyes impressed me, and she spoke well. Maybe she was one of the rare politicians who did want to help people. And it would be nice to earn some money since my last place of employment burnt down after a murderous arson attack.

'What would you want me to do?'

Frost got up and strode around the desk. 'Stay at my side. Watch for anything out of the ordinary or suspicious. Be cautious of any eventuality.'

'Surely you'd need someone with experience for such an important job? A former military person or ex-copper? Jack Reacher or that warrior woman from *Game of Thrones*?'

She sat on the edge of the desk. 'What message does that send, me moving through the community with some hulk at my side?'

'It tells people not to hurt you.'

'You think that would stop somebody like Nigel Craig?'

I shook my head. 'No. What's the pay?'

'John will sort the contract with you. So, do you have any other questions?'

I reached past her and grabbed the first few letters from the death threat pile. 'Do you want me to go through these?'

'That's up to you, but I don't think you'll glean anything useful from them since none are signed. They'll only give you nightmares if you read too many of them.'

'Tell me the gist of them,' I said.

She sighed. 'Hatred of women, gay and trans people. Believing I'm a spokesperson for replacing the white race. Calling me a socialist, Marxist, Trotskyist, or Stalinist. Saying I hate white men and I'm plotting against them. A hatred of refugees, immigrants, and most foreign people. I'm sure there are others, but I've tried to push them from my mind.'

'The world is a hateful place.'

'Not all of it. The good people outweigh the bad, but unfortunately, the worst of us have the loudest voices. And easy access to the internet and social media doesn't help.'

'Do you want to ban people from getting online?'

'It depends on what they say. I would like to end anonymous hate posts.'

'Good luck with that. Are any of those threatening letters from your ex-husband?'

'The divorce hasn't gone through yet, but none are from Jeff. He's too busy enjoying the Bahamas with his new girlfriend.'

'Okay. How can you help this community as a lone voice in Parliament?'

The sparkle in her eyes lit up the room. 'Investment. I have contacts with influential and wealthy people, and I'm always fostering more. Bringing money into the area to create jobs, housing, and other resources to develop the infrastructure is the only way to improve people's lives.'

'What about crime?'

'What about it?'

'Do you have any plans to reduce it?'

'That's the police's job, and I'll work closely with them.' She got up and returned to the other side of the desk. 'The best method to decrease crime here or anywhere is to elevate people out of poverty and degradation. So, are you with me?'

I stood and offered her my hand. 'Why not?'

It would be nice to have a paying job again.

And I might get paid to hit somebody.

Chapter 5

Hymn of the Big Wheel

Becky rushed ahead of me in the woods.

'Come back!' I shouted at her. She turned and ran through broken twigs and leaves.

'You're so slow, Enola.' She kicked dead wood at me. 'Does your new job mean you'll spend less time with me?'

'Maybe,' I replied.

We strode past where I'd found a dead man hanging from a tree a few months ago, with the river ahead of us. The cool spring air nipped at my cheeks while the scent of pine and decaying leaves filled my nostrils. The memory of that grim discovery still turned my stomach, but I tried to push it from my mind as we moved through the woods. It was better to focus on the beauty around us - the shafts of sunlight filtering through the canopy, the birdsong, the lush ferns sprouting up from the underbrush, and the sound of the nearby river.

I glanced at the kid, remembering what she'd said about the abandoned funfair and her dead father.

'Or I could come to work with you,' she said.

'You'll be at school.'

She scowled. 'I hate school.'

Becky had made that plain to me, her mother, and her teachers for some time without specifying why. So perhaps this was the occasion to explore it.

I put my hand on her shoulder. 'What happened this morning and the bloke with the gun – how do you feel about that?'

She fidgeted under my fingers. 'What do you mean?'

I stared into Becky's eyes, seeing my ten-year-old self reflected in her as I crouched in that wardrobe while thugs murdered my parents.

'Weren't you worried because he had a gun?'

The kid shrugged. 'I knew he wouldn't use it.'

'How did you know?'

'I saw it in his face, Enola.'

'What did you see, Becky?'

'His fear. He was scared. That's how I knew.'

I sighed. 'Frightened people sometimes do the most harm. What you did was very dangerous, and you could have got hurt.'

'So I shouldn't have saved you?'

It didn't feel like I was talking to a ten-year-old but to somebody with more life experience than me.

'Thank you for what you did, Becky, but don't do anything so risky again, okay?'

'My mum told me you lost your parents when you were my age.'

'That's true.'

'And you had to go into a children's home.'

'It was a long time ago.' Yet it didn't feel like it. Sometimes, I woke up in the morning and thought I was still there.

'What was that like? Did you get on with the other children?'

'Some of them. Is that why you hate school, because of the kids?'

She hung her head and lowered her tone. 'They call me names and laugh about my dad. They point at me and say I have terrible clothes.'

'Do you miss your dad?'

I expected tears when she looked at me but saw the opposite: a fierce determination that reminded me of me at the same age. She pointed at the funfair nearby.

'Yeah, he used to take me to the fair when I was little. We'd go on the rides, play games, and win stuffed animals. They're all gone now. Just like him.'

'Do you want to go home?'

Becky put her hands on her hips and puffed out her cheeks. 'No.'

I grabbed her hand. 'Come on, then.'

The sandwiches we'd had after leaving the food bank weighed heavy in my guts as we ran past the river, though perhaps I shouldn't have given her half of my coffee as it seemed to have injected her with even more energy than usual.

'Come on, slowpoke!' she called over her shoulder. Her eyes were bright, cheeks flushed pink from exertion and the chill. It was good to see her spirits lifted.

'All right, speed demon, take it easy,' I huffed, stride lengthening to catch up. The coffee sloshed uneasily in my stomach, but I pushed on.

We continued along the path, the river beside us. Ducks fluttered away indignantly as Becky chased them, giggling. The heaviness from the food bank visit began to lift.

Then she stopped at the edge of the water. 'Can you swim, Enola?'

An image flashed through my mind of a thug knocking me into the river not long ago. And then he tried to strangle me when I crawled out of the water. I stared at Becky, worried she might throw herself into the river.

I grabbed her hand. 'Sure. Can you?'

She wriggled from my grasp. 'Of course. I go to the swimming baths every week with school.' Her expression darkened, and I knew she was thinking of those bullies. 'Mum told me that somebody drowned in there before I was born. Do you remember that?'

'It was before my time as well, Becky. A young woman disappeared near the river, but nobody knows what happened to her.'

'Didn't the police find her?'

'No.'

She glanced into the rippling water. 'How can somebody just vanish like that?'

Her switch from wanting to go to the funfair to dwelling on the town's dark past concerned me. 'Come on, Becky – let's look at the rides.'

I put my arm around her and led her away from the water. As we got to the funfair entrance, where somebody had smashed the locks from the gates, she wriggled free from my grip. She darted inside, and I should have paid more attention to her safety, but all I could remember was what I was like as a kid. What trouble could she get up to if I was with her?

When I got inside, it was as if time had stopped. The rickety rides were rusted and broken, the once bright paint faded and chipped away. The musty, decaying wood and metal smell was overpowering, mixed with the aroma of the overgrown, weed-encrusted land. A rabbit ran through the grass, and I suddenly saw Alice in her Wonderland.

Weeds sprouted up through the cracked pavement, overtaking once vibrant rides. The carousel horses stood frozen mid-gallop, their paint faded and peeling. In the distance, a rusted Ferris wheel loomed like a skeletal giant. I remembered riding something similar when I was Becky's age, sitting at the top of the world with my parents and staring at the ants below.

I shook the memory out of my head and gazed across the funfair. It must have been magical in its heyday. I could almost hear the joyful screams of children and the clanking of rides in motion. It was hard to fathom it all slipping into this advanced state of decay, but a crumbling economy had crushed the life from many things.

Wandering deeper in, I paused by a teacup ride. The seats sat empty and lifeless, spider webs spanning the spaces between them. I ran a hand over the cold metal, flecks of paint chipping off beneath my fingers. A few tiny spiders emerged from the cracks, and I let them crawl onto my palm, skittering over my scars and resurrecting the memories of me in that wardrobe, watching my parents die.

Then Becky rushed to me, and her beaming smile banished the past back into my shadows, gazing at the dereliction surrounding us. What stories would these rides tell if they could talk? How many wide-eyed kids had climbed into these teacups, giddy with excitement? I could picture them spinning and laughing, not knowing that the funfair's days were numbered.

'This place looks different now,' Becky said, her voice tinged with sadness.

'It does,' I agreed, 'but your memories of what you did here with your dad will always be with you.'

The wind whistled through the broken rides, and she rushed between them, running her fingers over the distressed attractions.

'Did you come here with your parents, Enola?'

I stared at a dilapidated booth that would have once tempted customers to win a prize by throwing a small ball into a bottle.

'No, they used to take me to a bigger place in town. There was a bigger Ferris wheel, a carousel, and a roller coaster. And even a haunted house.'

I'd buried all the memories when they became too painful to recall, but they were creeping back.

Becky grabbed my hand. 'Are ghosts real?'

I squeezed her hand. 'No, kid. It was just fake spooks to scare the Rubes.'

She gazed into my eyes. 'Sometimes I think I see my dad in the house, looking at me from the shadows. Does that happen to you with your parents?'

I glanced beyond her at the dodgems, picturing me sitting between my mother and father as we screamed at each other.

'Sometimes.'

She let go of me and ran towards a sign for toffee apples. 'I'm getting hungry!'

I caught up with her, and we strode around the funfair, discussing the different rides and imagining what we'd do if it were still open. Despite the eerie atmosphere, I was happy to be there with Becky, sharing a moment of joy. And it was good to see that the morning's excitement with the gunman didn't appear to be negatively affecting her.

My phone rang, and I answered it, watching Becky as I did.

'Are you on a break, Julia?'

It sounded as if she was walking as she spoke. 'Sort of. I'm going from one client's place to another, and I have to walk through the estate to get there. How is everything?'

The kid picked stones from the floor and threw them at the colossal clown head in front of a building. It looked like the cover of a horror novel.

'We're fine. We got something to eat, but Becky's getting hungry again, so I'll probably take her to a burger place.' I didn't want to concern Julia unduly, so I didn't tell her where we were.

'That's great. I should be home between six and seven. I hope that's okay?'

'Sure, Julia, no problem. I'll see you later.'

She ended the call, and I knew she'd be disappointed when I told her I might have to see less of Becky because of the job with Kate Frost. I would as well.

I put the phone away and looked up to tell the kid to stop throwing stones.

But she wasn't there.

She'd vanished.

Chapter 6

Helter Skelter

'Becky!' I shouted.

There was no answer except for the wind whistling through the damaged wood and metal. I looked at the giant clown grinning at me and ran into his open mouth. My heart and head throbbed in unison on the brink of panic.

'Becky!' I shouted again when I got inside.

The noxious scent of rot filled my skull as I searched for the kid. The building was dark and cluttered, with broken-down carnival games and rusted metal attractions littering the space. The only light came from a few cracks in the roof, casting eerie shadows on the peeling wallpaper. Illustrations of clowns covered the walls. Time and decay had eaten bits of them, removing their eyes, cheeks, arms, and legs so they resembled zombie jokers. They peered at me, seemingly judging my lack of adult responsibility.

I removed my phone and switched the torch on, sweeping it in front of me, the light shaking through the shadows as my hand trembled. I called out Becky's name, my voice echoing in the emptiness, hearing my footsteps moving through the debris and the rustling of old paper and garbage underfoot. The air was thick and hot, making it difficult to breathe.

Dread washed over me as I searched everywhere, my hands trembling as I moved aside broken tables and desks. I couldn't believe I'd lost her, my chest suffocating, trapped in a maze with no escape, turning my heart into a heavy, throbbing beast ready to explode.

I smacked myself on the forehead. 'You stupid fucking cow!'

A million images of what might have happened to her flashed through my head, picturing the police dragging me away as Julia wept at my feet. I tried to squeeze the image from my mind as a voice slithered out of my memories.

'You'll never be a mother, Enola.'

My friend Amy spoke to me as we watched the younger girls playing with the dolls in the children's home. We were fifteen years old.

'What do you mean?' I asked her.

She bit into her fingernails and spat a bloodied part onto the floor. 'You only care about yourself, too self-centred to think about others.'

I was an orphan whose parents were murdered in front of me. What did I know about how to care for other people? Or shouldn't that have come naturally to me?

Amy's words stung. I stared at her, mouth agape, as she gnawed her nails and flicked the bloody remnants. The other kids played innocently behind us, oblivious to the tension.

'How can you say that?' I finally managed. 'After everything I've been through...'

My mind flashed back to that horrific night. My

parents' screams. Their broken bodies. The blazing inferno. The spiders crawling over me.

Amy scoffed. 'We've all got sob stories. You're not the only one who's suffered.'

'But...' I faltered. Maybe she was right. I'd been so focused on my trauma since coming to the home that I hadn't considered the other girls. Most were orphans, too, with their own agonising pasts.

A sound shook me from the past, a noise in the corner, what sounded like breathing. My fingers trembled as I moved the torchlight, seeing a massive tank of dirty water.

Oh, fuck! Had she fallen in there?

I ran to it, sweeping the torch over the surface. It was about three feet high, six feet long and wide, resembling a giant watery coffin. Empty beer cans floated on the top near a grey, leathery bat corpse. I held the light over the surface and peered into the shadows. The liquid was murky and thick, the colour of embalming fluid, far too dark to see inside. I put the phone down and grabbed the wooden pole leaning against the wall. Then I shoved the stick into the water and dragged it through the gloom. Dead things rose to the surface: rats, mice, birds, and a small cat.

But no Becky.

Thank fucking God!

I threw the stick away, got my mobile, and called her name again.

'Becky!'

Ahead of me, I saw several miniature cars shaped like clown heads. I searched each one, finding only crushed beer cans, dirty shoes and old newspapers. One of the headlines screamed at me: LOCAL GIRL GOES MISSING. It was from twenty-five years ago, and I kicked it away from me as

I moved further inside, wondering how big the building was.

I combed every corner of the place, my heart racing as I repeatedly called out Becky's name. The musty smell of mould filled my nose as I stumbled over scattered rubble. The dim light filtering in from the broken windows only added to the chill gripping my bones. I heard my breathing and the shuffling of my feet echoing against the peeling walls.

'Becky! Can you hear me?'

Silence.

Then the sound came back to me.

'Becky! Can you hear me?'

Was that an echo?

'Becky! Can you hear me?'

No, it was all twisted, as if somebody was cruelly impersonating my voice.

'Who is that?' I said.

They stepped out of the shadows: three blokes with bloodshot eyes, sores on their lips and hands, puffy cheeks, and dead expressions. The one at the front wore a dirty, tattered vest, his bare arms covered in needle marks, his yellowed fingers on Becky's shoulders.

He opened his mouth to reveal a space with more gaps than teeth.

'Is this your mummy, Becky?'

I looked at her, expecting to see fear or tears, but it was the opposite, the same expression as when she stared down the gunman.

Fuck! What a day the kid was having.

'Let her go,' I demanded.

'Oh, we will,' the Vest said. 'We won't hurt her once you pay our finder's fee.'

'Finder's fee.'

He ran dirty fingers through Becky's hair, but she didn't flinch.

'Yeah, for finding your kid. She nearly fell into a big dark hole if we hadn't saved her. Isn't that right, lads?' The other two laughed. 'Surely that's gotta be worth a reward?'

I removed a ten-pound note from my pocket. 'Sure, of course it does. Now let her go.'

He spat something green near my feet. 'Ten quid? Is that all your kid's worth?'

'It's all I've got.'

The one with the skull tattooed on his neck spoke. 'It's better than nowt, Billy.'

'Think of what the money will buy you, Billy. Enough to get you through today, at least,' I said.

He spat again. 'Fuck! She knows my name now, you stupid twat.'

'Just let the girl go,' I said, wishing I'd kept that stick.

He glared at me before pushing Becky from his grasp. She didn't run to me; instead, she turned to give him the finger. He grasped for her and missed. Then she ran to me, laughing.

'This is much better than some silly haunted house, Enola.'

'The money,' Billy demanded.

I turned my hand into a fist with the notes scrunched inside.

'Sure, but I need you to tell me something first.'

'What?' he asked.

'Where do you normally buy your gear from?'

He narrowed his eyes and gazed at me. 'Are you the filth?'

I laughed. 'Do I look like a copper?'

Billy rubbed at his chin. 'I dunno. The pigs are getting younger every day.'

'What does it matter?' I asked. 'I'll give you the cash, anyway.' I opened my hand, and the plastic ten-pound note sprang up like petals on the first day of spring.

'Do you know the Coronation pub?' Billy said.

I nodded. 'Sure.' It was a hive of criminality, where they gave you a weapon on the way in. 'What about it?'

He stared at the money in my palm. 'There's a guy there. I don't know his name, but he's a local dealer. He'll give you what you want.'

'Describe him.'

His lips shook as he spoke. 'Six foot tall, thick build, cropped hair like a squaddie. Looks a bit like Elton John but without the specks.'

'Thanks.' I threw the note to the ground and grabbed Becky's hand.

'Hey!' she said.

I dragged her outside and into the light, struggling to contain my anger and relief.

'What have I told you about going out of my sight?'

She wriggled from my grasp. 'Yeah, but you have big eyes like a frog.'

We stood facing each other, a few yards from the giant grinning clown head. If I looked at it the wrong way, I could have sworn it was winking at me.

'Are you okay?'

Becky crossed her arms. 'I'm hungry.'

'Did they hurt you?'

The kid laughed. 'Those three? I could have got away any time. I only stayed there because I was bored. He had no strength in him. They were zombies without the bite.'

'Do you know what was wrong with them?'

'Yeah, they were junkies. Mum told me about people like them. Will you tell the police?'

'I should. Will you tell your mother?'

'Do you want me to?'

Her stomach rumbled, and I laughed. 'I'll think about it. McDonald's?'

Becky threw up her arms and ran around me, singing some pop song I didn't recognise.

We left the funfair, and I texted Detective Inspector Jack Parker, knowing he already regretted giving me his phone number.

And I thought about going to the pub later.

Chapter 7

I Ran

Kronos was my wake-up call on Sunday. He slobbered all over my face as I wiped the sleep from my eyes. Every part of me ached; my body was still unused to sleeping on a sofa. I flexed my fingers, inhaling the aroma of coffee from the kitchen. My throat had shrunk in the night, and I was desperate for a drink.

The dog's wet tongue dragged across my cheek again, prompting a groan. I gently pushed his muzzle away and sat up, my back protesting from another night of fitful dreams. Sleep still fogged my brain as I stretched and cracked my stiff joints. I scratched behind Kronos' ears as memories from the past week flickered through my brain.

'Don't forget you're helping me this afternoon.'

I shoved the dog off me and sat up. 'Mystic Meg and her assistant?'

Ginger slipped cards into envelopes. 'Don't be sarky. This is how I make a living.'

I got off the sofa and yawned. Ginger was a tarot reader, astrologist, and healer. We'd met at a psychic evening when I was seventeen, and I thought I could communicate with my parents in the next world. I soon realised it was all shit but became firm friends with her.

'Who wants breakfast?' Bruce asked from the kitchen. Kronos jumped up at me, and I grabbed him to stop me from falling over. There was lead in my veins, and I needed to shake the lethargy from me.

'I'm going for a run,' I said as I went to the bathroom to change into my running gear. The dog tried to follow me, but I pushed him out. Then I checked my phone while on the toilet, seeing yesterday's events at the food bank all over the news, local and national. The tabloids and the social media gossip had spread Nigel Craig's life all over the internet, including his recent sacking from the library. He was a loner with no friends or family. One of his unnamed work colleagues claimed that Craig spent all of his time listening to Pink Floyd and obsessing about how the world was out to get him.

He'd driven the mobile book van through the community for the last five years before the council relieved him of his duties. Some theorised that must have triggered his attack, but others, a vocal minority, defended and supported his conspiracy views. I flicked through some of his online posts, knowing it was all nonsense, but I always found that reading shit helped me empty my bowels.

I finished up, brushed my teeth, formed my hair into something that didn't resemble a bird's nest, and dressed. Dirty Harry, my tarantula, peered at me from his enclosure, so I fed him. Then I went to the kitchen to fill my water bottle.

'You were snoring again,' Bruce said.

I flexed my fingers. 'Are you talking to the dog or me?'

He laughed. 'Kronos makes a lot less noise than you, my friend.'

'Well, I probably won't disturb you much longer as I've got a job.'

His eyes widened. 'What?'

'Oh, yeah,' Ginger said. 'I forgot to tell you in all the excitement yesterday. Enola will be working for our new MP.'

'And it's all thanks to you, Bruce since you put a good word in for me.'

'Excellent,' he said. 'But that doesn't mean you have to move out. You know we enjoy having you here.'

I laughed. 'Yeah, apart from the snoring.'

'You'll be working for Kate?' I nodded. 'Doing what? Her new IT expert?'

'Not quite.' I told them about the death threats and my security position for the honourable member of parliament.

Ginger stared at me, resembling a confused cat. 'You're her bodyguard?'

I grinned at her. 'Impressive, right?'

Bruce frowned. 'That sounds dangerous, especially after what happened in the community centre.'

I patted his shoulder. 'Don't worry, Bruce. I'll put in a good word for you with Kate.'

He raised his hand, but I hurried off before he could reply, stepping into the fresh morning air. An hour's run would clear my head before breakfast and helping Ginger with her nonsense at the community centre. Not that it would all be nonsense as it was advertised as a Community Day with many activities free for the public.

My legs throbbed as I headed into town. The smell of freshly baked bread wafted over me, but it only made the emptiness of the area more pronounced. Storefronts with faded "For Rent" signs cluttered the street, and weeds grew through cracks in the pavement.

The poverty was palpable, with groups of people huddled together on street corners, trying to keep warm in the crisp morning air. Children in tattered clothes played hopscotch on the sidewalks, and mothers pushed strollers past boarded-up buildings. A baby cried while its mother vainly tried to soothe it, her threadbare clothing and sunken cheeks mirroring the infant's distress.

It was once a thriving community before the collapse when jobs and opportunities evaporated like morning dew. Now, it was a ghost town haunted by the spectres of poverty and hopelessness. But still, people persevered. Maybe Frost could help the community.

Despite the run-down parts of the neighbourhood, I couldn't help but feel a sense of pride for the resilience of its people. They had little, but they still made the best of their situation. Seeing a small community garden filled with vibrant flowers and vegetables on my route was a beacon of hope amidst the decay. It was a fragrant oasis in the concrete jungle, a blend of freshly turned soil and the sweet, earthy perfume of blossoming flowers.

The likes of Nigel Craig and his supporters were anomalies, outliers who had the loudest mouths, who should have been protesting against an uncaring, incompetent, corrupt government but instead turned their rage against the marginalised and those set up as scapegoats by a hate-filled media and the petty-minded.

I jogged through the woods and past the river, letting the fresh air clear my mind. I didn't go near the abandoned funfair, not wanting a repeat of yesterday's antics. Parker had texted me a few hours after the event, as I was handing Becky over to her mother, and told me he'd sent uniformed officers into the fair, but they'd found nothing.

It was in the distance as I turned to go back, my legs and

lungs vibrating with exertion and my belly calling for food. I stopped in the middle of the woods for a drink of water and considered what to do about Becky. I didn't tell Julia what happened with the addicts, but I should have. The girl was emotionally strong, but I was worried she was only storing up future troubles. And I was a significant contributor to them. So perhaps it was good I'd see less of the kid now I had the job with Kate Frost.

I looked forward to new employment and a steady wage, but it wasn't what excited me the most; that was the thought of what I'd do when I visited the Coronation pub for the drug dealer Billy had described. If what he said was true, and you never knew with junkies, then the bloke had to have a connection to Rook because you don't run a county lines drug operation without knowing who was dealing on your patch.

It was a start. I'd waited months for Rook to make another attempt on my life after the assault near the river, always looking over my shoulder and jumping at shadows, but nothing had happened. So far. And I couldn't keep living like that, waiting for the unexpected attack.

The police and NCA had been unsurprisingly useless in finding Rook and shutting down the county lines gang, so I knew it was up to me.

That would start at the Coronation once I'd helped Ginger with her tarot cards.

Perhaps I should ask her to tell my future.

Chapter 8

Fortune Teller

I helped Ginger carry her stuff into the centre while Bruce took Kronos for a walk. The atmosphere was energetic and happy. Posters and banners advertising community events and services adorned the walls while music and laughter filled the air. My legs throbbed, and my head ached, but the event lifted my spirits.

Ginger and I hauled armfuls of donations into the bustling community centre, greeted by a wave of cheerful chatter and lively music. A young girl skipped past playing a handclap game with a friend. Teenagers on ladders hung motivational banners on the walls. At a back table, seniors taught a small crowd to crochet baby hats for the nearby hospital. The smell of freshly baked cookies wafted from the kitchen.

Ginger set up at the far end while I surveyed the room. People from all walks of life gathered there - native residents, immigrants, homeless, disabled, young and elderly. Everyone had a place, with no judgement or exclusion. It was a sanctuary of belonging.

Across from us were several tables where refugees from

different communities handed out samples of their traditional food. The delicious aromas wafted through the air, making my mouth water.

'I know what I'm eating later,' Ginger said as she laid her tarot cards on the table.

I rubbed my stomach. 'Me too.'

Further into the room, children gathered around a table where a woman painted their faces. Their giggles and squeals of delight were contagious. A man created balloon animals for the kids; their eyes lit up like fireworks. Towards the back was a wine and cheese tasting station, with people chatting and sipping their drinks. The sound of glasses clinking together increased my need for a soft drink to quell the irritation in my throat.

'This is what it's all about, the community uniting in celebration.'

I turned to see Kate Frost. 'Are you here in your official capacity?'

She shook her head. 'No, today I'm just an ordinary citizen.' She pointed at Ginger's table. 'Maybe I'll get my cards read. What do you think?'

I grinned. 'Go ahead, but be warned that Ginger takes it very seriously.' Then I thought better about it. 'What if somebody takes a photo and it appears in the media? How will that look for your political career?'

I could just picture the headline in one of the red-top rags. "MP Turns to Mystic Meg For Help."

She touched my arm. 'Perhaps you're right. We don't want to give ammunition to the opposition, do we?' I nodded. 'Are you looking forward to tomorrow?'

'Sure, but I haven't received a contract yet.'

Frost narrowed her eyes. 'That's strange.' She took out her phone. 'I'll text John.'

As she moved away, I nearly told her not to bother him on a Sunday, but I didn't. I'd got the distinct impression he disliked me for some reason, so him having to work on the weekend amused me. Then Becky and her mother approached me.

'Becky says she had a wonderful time yesterday,' Julia said. 'I think she enjoys your company more than mine.' The kid grinned at me before rushing off to get her face painted.

'About that,' I said before telling Julia about my new job.

'That's great, Enola. I'm happy for you.' She smiled at me without mentioning who would look after Becky when both of us were working. 'Now I'm getting my cards read.' She sat opposite Ginger, and I watched my friend go to work.

'This is the Celtic Cross,' Ginger announced as she placed the cards in a ten-card layout.

'My surname is Cross,' Julia said.

Ginger laughed. 'That's just a coincidence. Each card represents different aspects of the person whose cards are being read and their life. Although readers use different layouts or techniques, every tarot is a narrative in which you are the hero - and the card in the middle - and the surrounding cards represent issues or people affecting you and your life story. Any given tarot deck comprises seventy-eight cards sorted into the minor and major arcana.'

I'd heard it all before, but Julia seemed fascinated by it. 'I've always wanted my future read,' she said.

'That's not really how it works,' Ginger replied. 'At its most basic, tarot tells stories about the cycles of our lives. Shuffling the deck, picking out cards and laying them out in order reveals what different trials and tribulations we may face during any journey. However, the cards in the major arcana don't necessarily represent us in a given reading; they might represent someone else in our lives or symbolise more general issues. Tarot is a complex language, and every reading is different; similarly, every reader and the methodology they use to interpret how the cards interact is different.'

Ginger was in her element, and Julia's eyes sparkled like UFOs over a nuclear power plant. So I left them to it and wandered through the centre. Becky waved at me as she got her face painted, and Kate Frost was talking to a Syrian woman while tasting some fantastic smelling food. I was about to have some myself when Bruce came barging over, hanging onto Kronos by his lead.

His cheeks bulged like a puffer frog. 'Christ, just when you think the world can't get any worse.'

I patted Kronos's head. 'What's up?'

'There's a group protesting outside,' he said. I didn't ask what about. 'As a rule, I make a strenuous effort in attempting to see the best in people and making excuses for them. So it is with sadness and after many years and a lot of wasted intellectual and emotional energy that I've come to learn there exists a subset of deplorable humans whose mindset simply can't be fixed. They are now too brainwashed and too far gone.' He took a deep breath. 'There truly exists in this country monstrously pathological, grotesque and broken people, subsisting on lies, outrage, racism, fear and delusion who are irreparably toxic and damaging to everyone and everything around them.'

Kate Frost joined us. 'Are you talking about the protesters outside?' Bruce nodded. She sighed. 'I'm afraid it's a worrying sign of our times, driven by those who should know better. And that's why I decided to stand as an MP.'

I scrutinised her, wondering if she was there just to give a party political broadcast even though she didn't belong to one. I'd taken her job offer, but was still unsure what her game was. No matter the little speech she'd given me in her office, I didn't see how she could make a difference in this community when she had no organisational backing to help her.

'You're right, Kate,' Bruce said. 'Our current leaders want completely unconstrained capitalism, minimal public services and limited workers' rights, and the devil takes the hindmost while the rest of us go squat. So let them put that on their election manifestos and see how far they get.'

I was about to interfere before it got too heated when I heard the screaming behind me. My body ached as I turned to an unusual sight: Ginger was leaning over the table with her hands around some bloke's throat.

Next to her was Becky, grinning with a flaming skull painted on her face.

Chapter 9

Everyday People

I dragged Ginger off the bloke, her fingers cutting into his neck as he spluttered and fell into a chair. They tumbled to the floor as Becky stared at me with her skull face.

'You always spoil the fun, Enola.'

I ignored her as Ginger wriggled from my grasp. 'What are you doing?' I asked.

She wiped the spit from her lips. 'That twat said terrible things about my mother.'

The bloke untangled himself from the chair and got up. He stumbled around, resembling a drunken bumblebee, hands flailing towards any unfortunate bystanders, with a face to launch the *Titanic*. He stood there, a puzzle with missing pieces, trying to decipher the cryptic riddle before him. His furrowed brow resembled a tangled thicket, with lines etched deep like the roots of a tree searching for sustenance in barren soil. His mouth hung open like a trapdoor, as if waiting for an answer to fall into his lap.

He pointed a shaky finger at Ginger. 'You're just like her.'

I moved between the two of them. 'Who are you?'

'Paul,' he said. 'Paul Robinson. I knew Ginger when she was younger and not taken in by this rubbish. It was her mother who filled her head with all this nonsense, tarot cards and astrology.'

She scowled at him. 'I don't know you.'

He touched the marks on his neck. 'It was thirty years ago. You were only a baby.'

I looked at Ginger. 'Is this your...?'

Her cheeks were a fiery crimson. 'No, he's not my father. My dad died years ago.'

I turned back to him. 'I think you should leave.'

His lips trembled as he spoke. 'I was more of a father to her than David ever was.'

'Why are you here?' I asked him.

He stopped shaking, and determination replaced the fear in his eyes. 'I'm getting reacquainted with my old neighbourhood. What's that to you?'

'You upset my friend.'

He rubbed at the bruise forming on his throat. 'Ginger is on the Devil's path; somebody must set her straight.'

I laughed. 'And that's you?'

'Of course. I know her better than she knows herself.' He glanced around the centre. 'Ginger needs to get away from this den of deviance.'

There was a crash behind us before I could respond to his nonsense. I swivelled around to see a group of ruby-faced people barge into the community centre.

'Oh fuck,' Bruce said.

'There should only be locals in here,' the bloke at the front stated. Their eyes were flame-red, and they waved their arms like manic octopuses. All they were missing were the flaming torches.

Kate Frost approached them. 'Everybody is welcome here, even you.'

'No,' he said. 'Our taxes are paying for them.' He pointed at the refugee families handing out their free food.

Bruce stepped forward. 'You're expressing your anger in the wrong place. If you stop voting for the wrong people, there's more than enough money and resources for everyone.'

I studied the group, wondering if trouble was following me around.

'He's a socialist,' somebody shouted. 'Stick him in a dress and call him a woman.'

They all laughed, and I expected it to turn ugly.

Then Julia spoke. 'You should all be ashamed of yourself, barging in here and ruining this for everybody.'

The torchless mob grumbled amongst themselves as the face painters, jugglers, craft makers, bakers, tarot reader, and skull-faced Becky joined the refugee families in solidarity and stared down the intruders. The tension simmered in the air as I watched the octogenarian knitters sharpen their needles while the kid stuck out her tongue at the prime moaner.

Paul Robinson slithered by me on his way out. 'We're wasting our time with them,' he told the gammon-cheeked interlopers. 'Mumbo jumbo and lies have brainwashed them.'

I heard Ginger grinding her teeth behind me and got my phone from my pocket, ready to call the police. Then a surprising voice shouted from the doorway.

'What's happening here?'

Everybody turned to face him, a man I didn't recognise until I realised it was the first time I'd seen him in regular clothes.

'Constable Davis,' I said. 'How nice to see you here.'

There was another bloke with him, someone I didn't know. Davis beamed at me, which was unnerving as I'd never seen him smile before.

'Somebody told me I could taste *samaka harra* here, and I like nothing better than spicy fish on a Sunday afternoon.'

A small boy ran out from a table and handed Davis a plate and cutlery. The aroma was divine, and my stomach rumbled loud enough to scare the intruders.

Becky marched to the front. 'I'm starving!'

Seeing her screaming skull face, the mob broke up and slithered out of the community centre. The last thing I saw of them was Paul Robinson scowling at me before disappearing into the group.

Constable Davis and his friend grabbed some food, followed by Becky, Julia, and others. I was about to join them when Bruce and Ginger approached me.

'I told you,' Bruce said. 'This whole place is going to shit.'

'They're only a minority,' Ginger added. 'A loud, ignorant minority, but they can't harm us if we stick together.'

I glanced at Becky chatting with Davis. 'It's not us I'm worried about.' Then I turned to Ginger. 'What happened with that bloke, Robinson?'

She sighed. 'After I finished with Julia, he sat at the table. I thought it was for a reading, but he ranted about my mum, insulting her and saying what I was doing was blasphemy.'

'Blasphemy?' Bruce asked.

Ginger nodded. 'Yeah, he bragged that he's a born-again Christian, and I was going straight to hell where my father was if I didn't mend my ways. So, I wrapped my hands around his throat until somebody intervened.' She frowned at me.

I grinned. 'I thought he was one of your ex-boyfriends.'

Her frown turned into a scowl. 'He's at least thirty years older than me.'

Bruce laughed. 'Don't be ageist, Ginger.'

'Does he live near here?' I said.

Ginger shrugged. 'Who cares? Let's forget about him and get some of that delicious-smelling food before it all goes.'

I agreed, and we wandered over to join Becky and Julia. The kid pulled on my hand and dragged me to the side to whisper to me.

'I didn't tell Mum about yesterday.' She nodded at Davis, chatting to a woman refilling his plate. 'Did you tell the coppers?'

'I did, but I didn't mention you, Becky. I don't think that's why he's here.'

Davis left the table and came over. 'DI Parker sends his apologies. He would have come but had to visit his mother.' He introduced me to the other bloke, a stocky man with eyes like burnt coal.

'I'm surprised to see you here, Davis,' I said.

He showed me his food. 'I never turn down a free meal, especially when it's this good. And I wanted to bring my American friend Chris here to show him all the great things about the community.'

Chris doffed an imaginary hat to me and spoke in an American drawl. 'Pleased to meet you all.'

'And you,' I said before turning to Davis. 'Did you know those people were coming here?'

He shook his head. 'Seeing them when I came in was a complete surprise.'

'What will happen to them?'

He replied as he ate. 'Nothing. Did they do something criminal before I arrived?'

'No, but it wasn't for want of trying.'

'Well, Ms Gray, we don't have thought crime in this country yet.'

'That's probably a good thing considering what I'm thinking right now.'

Becky dragged me away before he could reply. 'Mum says she's happy for you about the new job.'

My guts grumbled again, and I still had no food. 'Yeah, I start tomorrow.'

Sadness seeped out of her painted skull face. 'That means I won't see you as much.'

'No, it doesn't. I'll be working when you're at school.'

Becky stuffed a handful of chips into her mouth, and I grabbed a piece of fried lamb from her plate. 'Oh, that's okay then.'

She scampered back to her mother before I could steal more of her food. Then I glanced across the room to see Bruce talking to Kate Frost. After the events of the last two days, I was looking forward to a quiet life in my new employment.

First, I had a dodgy pub to visit.

Chapter 10

Happy Hour

When I thought my life was threatened recently, I acquired a gun from an old friend. I still had it, hidden at the bottom of my bag in Ginger and Bruce's flat – for which I felt guilty – and I considered taking it to the Coronation but eventually thought it wise not to. It would only be an exploratory visit to see if I could identify the drug dealer the junky at the funfair had mentioned.

I'd visited the pub several times before, but not for ages. The first time was just before my sixteenth birthday when I lived in the children's home. The Coronation's reputation was well known as a place to avoid unless you were looking for trouble. But back then, trouble was my hobby. Plus, I had my friend Amy with me, and we were a formidable pair.

Our reputations proceeded us when we marched into that dive bar for the first time. The regulars stared as we went to the bar, trying to look older than our years. Amy ordered a couple of ciders with a fearless confidence I envied. We found a corner table where we could watch the room, a silently agreed-upon strategy. Safety in numbers and all that.

The jukebox was blaring some AC/DC song I didn't recognise. A few shady-looking blokes played pool in the back while casting furtive glances our way. The bartender, a burly guy with tattoos covering his arms, kept a wary eye on us like he expected trouble. Maybe our youth and innocence would disarm any real threat.

Everything went swimmingly for a while, and we mixed with the locals like long-lost friends: playing darts with the ladies' team, taking money from drunks at the pool table, and filling the jukebox with punk classics. It was our go-to place for weeks, an escape from the children's home and somewhere warmer and drier than the woods. We even played a game of inventing our own imaginary cocktails.

'Gin and marmite for me,' Amy said as she nibbled on a piece of cheese like a mouse.

I grimaced. 'They won't like you bringing your own food in here.'

She laughed. 'They don't care, Enola, as long as we spend enough.' The profits from our shoplifting trips were keeping us economically active. 'Tell me what drink you'd have.'

'I'd call it a Brain Burst,' I said.

Amy nodded. 'I could do with that. What's in it?'

I removed the notebook from my bag, opening it to where I'd kept all the scribbles of interesting stuff I found online. 'In the seventeenth century, sixty drops of lavender and a mouthful of gingerbread was thought to cure memory loss. So I'd mix that with a shot of vermouth and a dabble of gin.'

She narrowed her eyes, scrutinising me as if I was under a microscope. 'Is this because you're still trying to remember what happened to your parents?'

I shook my head. 'No – that's a night I'll never forget. It's the times before my mum and dad died that I'm starting to lose.'

I didn't think then that the drinking might have been causing my memory problems.

Amy shrugged. 'Some things are not worth remembering.'

I watched her go to the bar for more drinks, wondering when she'd open up to me about her family problems.

We had a grand time at the Coronation for a while.

Then it all changed when the landlord's son groped Amy one night in front of his laughing mates. It might have been partially my fault for encouraging her, but she responded to his unwanted overtures by stabbing him in the eye with a pool cue. I'd heard they still couldn't get the blood out of the carpet.

That was my Amy. Amy Sparrow.

We experienced much during our two years together, including inspiring each other to experience the things teenage girls were supposed to avoid: criminality, recreational drugs, illicit romances, and alcohol. It was the booze that convinced me to change my lifestyle.

We drank beer, cider, lager, cocktails, shots, and spirits – but I never liked the taste of any of it. I did it really to fit in with Amy, not that I blamed her for my drinking, but I soon associated alcohol with medicine.

'It's medicinal,' I heard the adults say around me, and it certainly helped me suppress the bad memories, even if it was only for a short while. When I drank, the images of my parents' deaths vanished into the shadows, and a huge weight lifted from my shoulders.

Yet it was enjoyable, living that carefree, uninhibited, rebellious lifestyle. And doesn't every teenager need to rebel? It was always harmless fun, which gave me happy memories and maybe a sore head the next day. Then, the fun dwindled at some point, and I found myself riddled with anxiety, often wondering what I did and who I was with the night before. I could be out all evening and not remember much the following morning. I knew this was not a great path to be on, but I made constant excuses for my behaviour.

Finally, my only other friend – Seraphina – helped me change my life. She was the only adult in the care home I got on with, and a few hard-hitting truths from her set me straight soon after my sixteenth birthday. Nearly five years later, I hadn't touched a drop of booze since, though there had been several times when I'd had to resist the over-whelming temptation to drink.

Amy's friendship and mine had fractured not long after I stopped drinking, but that wasn't the main reason we fell out. Maybe we just grew apart. I hadn't stepped inside the Coronation after the pool cue incident. Perhaps I wouldn't have to again if I could recognise the dealer from Billy's description before he entered the building.

The night embraced me as I strode through the town to the pub. I walked past derelict houses and closed shops, their windows and doors covered with metal grates. The buildings were old and decrepit, with peeling paint and broken glass. In the occasional doorway, I'd see people huddled against the cold, their only protection being a tattered cardboard box or a dirty blanket. There seemed to be more homeless every time I took that route, and I wondered if Kate Frost and all her grand ideas could do anything to improve their lives.

Seeing them also made me thankful for friends like Bruce and Ginger, for without them, I'd have had to curl up in one of those doorways. And that only added to my guilt. If the landlord – the same bloke who kicked me out of my flat – discovered I was sleeping on their sofa, it wouldn't go down well for them. Yet it would be even worse if the police turned up for some spurious reason and found the gun in my bag.

I had to get my own place soon. That or lose the weapon. Or maybe do both.

But then Rook was still out there, and so was his threat against me. I wouldn't have been marching to the pub if it wasn't.

It was a thirty-minute walk there, and I was freezing when I arrived, slipping into the shadows opposite the Coronation. I rubbed my hands for warmth and wished I'd brought a scarf and gloves. I pressed my back against the wall, and the door opened across the street, the smell of stale beer and cigarette smoke rushing over to hit me like a wave. The stink of alcohol clung to me like a blanket, working through my skin and attaching itself to my heart and lungs. I took a deep breath, inhaling tobacco and nicotine to combat the drug that was trying to flick that switch in my brain again. The government had banned indoor smoking years ago, but that didn't bother the Coronation's landlord. None of the punters was likely to complain, and there was more chance of Harry Potter walking in there than a police officer.

A woman lingered in the doorway, talking into her phone, and I heard people laughing and rowdy singing from within. Discarded cigarette butts lay scattered on the ground like bodies in a Quentin Tarantino movie, while piss and blood stained the pavement.

She finished her call and returned inside as I stood and watched, waiting for the man. People came and went, the noise increasing in the pub. I shivered in the cold, moving around to get warm, recalling my times in the Coronation to distract my brain from the bitter chill biting at my flesh. I thought of gigs and the bands I saw in there: the punk girls who only played speeded-up versions of Abba songs, the one-armed bloke who sounded like Jimi Hendrix, and the synth-pop duo who wouldn't take off their Halloween masks even when the punters threw stale sausage rolls at them.

I got bored and checked my phone, searching for information on the afternoon's events in the centre. There was nothing on the news sites, but social media was full of gossip, mostly untrue. I found a link to a group called Progressive Britain, who claimed they were behind the interruption of the event. I scanned their website but stopped after two minutes of reading hate-filled garbage. I was about to leave the site when I saw a post from a name I recognised: Paul Robinson. There was no photo with the text, but the comments about spiritual fraudsters and cheats indicated it must have been the same bloke Ginger tried to strangle.

I put the phone away and shoved my hands into my pockets in a futile search for warmth. A group of lads entered the pub, and I considered it a waste of my night. Billy might have lied to me, or perhaps the dealer had arrived before I got there.

Then I saw him through the window, tall, thick build, cropped hair like a squaddie, resembling a young Elton John but without the glasses. I removed my phone to check the time, seeing it was nine-thirty. He could be in there all night, and I was freezing.

There was only one thing for it.

I marched across the road and strode into the pub as "Babylon's Burning" by the Ruts burst out of the speakers.

And the booze crawled all over my memories.

Chapter 11

Babylon's Burning

The pub had changed since my last visit, resembling the insides of a disused factory, with rusty sewing machines in the corners, fake Victorian books on the shelves, and pictures of the old industrial town hanging over the bar. Somebody thought giving the place a themed look was a good idea. I half expected to see urchin chimney sweeps swigging jugs of ale.

Ragged furniture cluttered the joint while flickering lights illuminated the dingy decor. The stench of alcohol and cigarette smoke lingered with the overpowering scent of sweat. Somebody was singing along badly to the Ruts as I went to the bar. A few people shot me harsh looks, but that was it.

Tattered old movie posters and photos of dead celebrities hung haphazardly on the walls. The floors were sticky, and I could feel the grime and dirt on the soles of my shoes. I ordered a soft drink, trying to blend in with the crowd. The bartender, a burly man with a thick beard, slid a glass towards me, and I sat at a small table in the corner. The atmosphere was tense, with people arguing and shouting at each other. I glanced across the room at the pool players, peering at the carpet and seeing the same bloodstains from five years ago.

'I always said they'd never get that stain out.'

I turned to the woman who'd slipped into the seat opposite, surprised to see Amy smiling at me.

'You're the last person I expected here.'

She raised her pint of Guinness. 'I could say the same about you, my old friend.' Somebody smashed a glass at the other end of the bar, and a group of people laughed. 'So what brings you here?'

'I was desperate for a drink.'

Amy smiled. 'There are two other pubs close by, but you came here for an orange juice that, by its appearance, looks like its only association with orange is having once stood on a photo of Donald Trump.'

I tasted it and grimaced. 'Yeah, I know what you mean. So, what are you doing here? Is it the same landlord? The place looks totally different. I thought they'd string you up when you stepped inside.'

She shook her head. 'Deflect if you want. I have business here tonight, that's all.'

I looked around the bar, searching for the drug dealer. 'What business?'

'Why should I tell you, Enola? Four years ago, you made it perfectly clear you wanted nothing to do with my alternative lifestyle.'

I coughed loud enough to bother the smokers near the jukebox.

'Alternative lifestyle? Is that what you're calling criminality now?'

'Criminality? My, Enola, how your mind has shrunk since we went our separate ways. Is it criminality when our government overlords wipe billions off the economy and make the most vulnerable pay for it? Is it criminality when the wealthiest manipulate the system to steal taxpayers' money? Is it criminality when the most privileged in our country lie and cheat and get away with it? Is it criminality when the schools and hospitals are crumbling, but the wealthiest are getting richer?'

'That's not the same, and you know it. Those are piss poor excuses.'

'Was it criminal to take that gun from me a few months back?'

I shrugged. 'Probably.'

She parted her ruby-red lips and grinned. 'Are you aware that, long ago, people used urine to tan animal skins, so families would all pee in a pot, and then once a day, they sold it to the tannery? So, if you had to do this to survive, you were "Piss Poor". Worse than that were the unlucky folk who couldn't afford a pot and didn't have a pot to piss in and were the lowest of the low. The next time you wash your hands and complain because the water temperature isn't just how you like it, think about how things used to be.'

'Have you become a social historian since I last saw you?'

Amy grinned. 'I'm a woman of many talents, Enola, or have you forgotten already?'

I sipped the juice and imagined what it would be like with some vodka. 'I remember.'

'Many years before we met in that children's home, Enola, baths consisted of a big tub filled with hot water. The man of the house had the privilege of the nice clean water, then all the other sons and men, then the women and finally the children. Last of all was the babies. By then, the water was so dirty you could actually lose someone in it. Hence the saying, "Don't throw the baby out with the Bath water!"'

I sighed. 'Are you trying to tell me something, Amy?'

She laughed like a docker. 'I've been trying to tell you things since our first meeting, Enola, but you never listen.'

'I'm listening now.'

She nodded. 'Do you see the tall man at the bar?'

I saw the bloke I'd come to the pub for. 'Yeah, what about him?'

She grabbed an ashtray. 'If I was messing around with this and it slipped out of my fingers, flew over there to hit him in the head and killed him, society would class that as manslaughter. But, on the other hand, if I went over there on purpose and killed him, that would be murder.'

'So?'

'Yet when society creates circumstances that result in the premature and unnatural death of hundreds of people, deaths just as violent as being killed by a weapon, should it not also be considered murder? This happens when governments deny us access to the necessities of life, places them in unsurvivable conditions, and uses the law to force them to remain in such situations until death is the inevitable outcome. This type of murder is disguised and malicious; however, it remains murder.'

'Well, Amy, I guess I'm not the only one who's changed since we were teenagers. I don't disagree with what you said, but what's it got to do with the bloke at the bar?'

She supped her drink. 'I watched a documentary the other night that described part of the sea squirt's life cycle, outlining how it drifts around as an adolescent, looking for something to attach itself to as its home for life. Once it has found somewhere suitable, it glues itself to its chosen rock, and then, having no further use for its brain, it consumes it.

That's a pretty good description of Larry at the bar. Unfortunately, Larry has damaged several people, including those I care for. So, you know what that means.'

'Okay, Amy, I have no problem with that, but I need information from him first.'

'What information?'

'I think he might be a link to Rook. You remember him?'

'Him? I thought we decided Rook could be he or she?'

I pushed the crappy orange juice out of the way. 'Whatever. I only need to know if Larry over there is connected to Rook. You can do what you want with him after that.'

'Do you still have that gun I gave you, Enola?'

I grimaced at the reminder. 'Not with me, why?'

'The pirates are coming.'

I glanced over my shoulder to see four blokes approaching us, with the one in front wearing an eye patch.

'Shit!' I said.

'I can't believe you bitches have the fucking nerve to come here after what you did.'

Amy finished her Guinness with a dab of white foam on her lips. 'Didn't you get that parrot I sent you, Robbie?'

He grunted and tugged at his eye patch. 'There's no pool cue to help you.' He glared at me. 'I remember you as well, the little witch.'

'You're getting hysterical, Robbie,' I said. His one good eye bulged, and I wondered if Rook supplied the drugs in his body through Larry. 'Once upon a time, physicians treated hysteria with a brew of breast milk and the blood from an amputated tomcat ear. However, it was only for women, of course. Hysteria didn't affect men.'

Amy put her glass on the table. 'Indeed.' She nodded at me. 'Our friend is leaving.'

I looked at the bar, watching Larry slip out of the pub.

'Time to go,' I said.

Then I grabbed my orange juice and threw it into Robbie's good eye. He screamed as if it was acid and staggered backwards into his mates. Amy and I got up together, and she spoke to the goons as Robbie clawed at his face.

'Do yourself a favour, lads.' She tossed a twenty-pound note on the table. 'Have a drink on me, and don't bother following us, or it'll be more than orange juice in your mugs next time.'

She pushed past them, and I went with her, stepping into a delicate drizzle of rain and seeing Larry walking fifty yards ahead.

'What if they come after us?'

Amy shook her head. 'You should have brought that gun.' She marched off after Larry as I stared at the pub door, expecting the goons to burst through at any second.

Then I turned and ran after Amy.

And I wished I'd brought the gun.

Chapter 12

Teenage Kicks

The aroma of garbage and the stink of dog shit assaulted my senses as we followed Larry, heading away from the well-lit main street and into a maze of dark alleys. We kept a safe distance from him, trying to blend in with the shadows. Amy and I hugged the grimy brick walls, moving from one pool of darkness to the next. The merry din of the main drag faded behind us, replaced by an ominous silence.

The homeless denizens of this hidden underworld glanced up from their fires with suspicion as we passed them. Larry seemed oblivious, muttering unintelligibly to himself as he shuffled ahead.

'What will you do to him?' I asked Amy.

She stepped over a discarded pizza box. 'Do you care?'

'I suppose not.'

All I cared about was getting information about Rook. What Amy did with him wasn't my concern.

Or was it?

'You can ask him your questions and be on your way. You don't need to see what comes next.'

We dodged an old woman asking for money and shooed away a stray dog.

'What did he do to you, Amy?'

'It wasn't to me,' she said as we walked. 'He hurt a friend of mine.'

'Drugs?'

Even in the gloom, I saw the sorrow in her eyes. 'Yep.'

I didn't ask again. She could tell me in her own time.

We followed him for half a mile, over the bridge and across the river, moving past those people for whom the night provided comfort or a cover for them to do terrible things. Nobody else approached us, and I didn't blame them when observing Amy's expression. Outside of my friend and mentor, Seraphina, Amy was the kindest, most generous person I'd ever met. But she was also the most ruthless if you got on her wrong side. I had no doubt what she'd do to Larry when I'd finished questioning him; the problem was whether I should try to stop her.

She grabbed my arm. 'Wait.'

Larry stopped in front of a dilapidated building and disappeared into it.

'There could be more in there,' I said.

Raindrops had settled on Amy's hair like tiny wet dots.

'You can leave if you're afraid, Enola. I don't need your help.'

'That's not it, Amy, and you know it. We have no idea what's waiting for us inside. And it's not like you to do anything without a plan.'

She reached into her jacket and removed a flick knife. 'This is my plan. Now, are you coming or not?'

I pushed past her and went first, jogging across the street and through the entrance, forgoing any caution I'd warned her about. The building was a set of flats converted from an old house. Damp and dirt clung to everything, with a smell that made my eyes water. The only light came from the moon shining through broken windows, creating eerie silhouettes on the walls.

Graffiti tags covered the peeling wallpaper. Empty beer cans and cigarette butts littered the floors. Others had been there before us, seeking their own cheap thrills. We stepped over broken glass and piles of rubble until we reached the top landing.

A deathly silence hung over the surroundings until I heard voices up ahead. My heart skipped a beat as Amy gripped the knife, catching a glimpse of my reflection in the blade as she went. We moved further into the building, disturbing rats and mice that skittered between the shadows. The floorboards creaked under our feet, and I held my breath, waiting for someone to discover us. She pushed the knife to her lips and pointed to the open door ahead and the voices coming from it. Larry had company. We crept forward, watching where we stepped and listened to what was happening in the room.

'That's all I've got,' a man said.

'They won't be happy,' a young girl replied.

I peered inside, seeing Larry and two teenage girls, probably no older than fourteen. One of them wore a school uniform.

Amy barged in. 'Are you corrupting more kids, Larry?'

He stood there frozen like a victim of Medusa, but the girls sprinted faster than an Olympic gold medallist. I grabbed one by the arm, pulling her to me.

Then she kicked me in the shin, and I collapsed like a drunk on New Year's Eve.

'Fuck!'

Pain shot through me and settled in my chest as I struggled to get up. The two teenagers were gone, but Amy had the knife at Larry's throat. I hobbled on one leg and hoped the agony would vanish, but it didn't.

'Don't,' I said. 'I have to talk to him.'

Amy pressed the blade into his Adam's apple, and he pissed himself. She swore and pushed him into the wall. He slid down it and sat in a pool of his own urine.

'He's all yours, but make it quick before he shits his pants.'

I loomed over him and held my nose. 'Who do you work for?'

He shed tears. 'I don't know.'

I resisted the urge to punch him. 'How can you not know? Who supplies you with the drugs? What were those girls doing here?'

Amy lit a cigarette. 'We could torture him for a bit. I find that always loosens the most stubborn of tongues.'

Larry wiped the tears from his cheeks. 'I'll tell you everything.'

She laughed. 'They don't make petty criminals like they used to.'

'Go on,' I said.

He took a deep breath. 'Those girls or other kids bring me the gear, and I give them most of what I earn. I don't see or meet anybody else. There's no phone contact or anything. That's how it works.'

'Who recruited you?' I demanded.

'A bloke in a pub. He mentioned somebody I shared a cell with and asked if I wanted to make some easy money.'

'And you said yes,' Amy said.

'Sure.'

I studied the room. 'Do you always meet the couriers here?'

He nodded. 'Twice a week, but they won't return now after seeing you here.'

'So what will you do?' I asked.

Larry shrugged. 'I don't know.'

I grabbed his shirt and pulled him to me, smelling stale tobacco on his lips.

'Do you know the name Rook?'

Fear shimmered behind his eyes. 'Only by reputation. Those girls said if I fucked up, then Rook would make me pay.' He took a deep breath. 'I've heard rumours of Rook kneecapping people or having them shot if they cheated him.'

Amy blew smoke in my direction. 'Okay, have you finished with him?'

I released him, disappointment speeding through me. 'Sure, go ahead.'

She waved the blade before his nose. 'Unless you came from wealth or privilege, Victorian society was designed to ensure that a woman without a man was redundant; from birth, a female's entire function was to support their fathers, brothers, sons, and husbands.'

Confusion gripped his face, and I wondered what she would do to him.

'Working class women and girls began their lives in arrears,' she continued, 'less important than their brothers and other male relatives. Education was irrelevant to them since they would never earn as much as a man. Domestic service was the highest they could wish for, of twelve-hour days hoping to become a cook or house-keeper. If not, the sweatshop beckoned and beyond that was the workhouse. If a woman had none of those, she would likely live on the streets with all the dangers that entailed.'

His mouth quivered as he spoke. 'I don't know what you mean.'

'Of course you don't.' Amy moved the knife close to his eyeball. 'Have you ever experienced watching someone die slowly in front of you?'

Larry's lips trembled. 'No.'

'Well, my friend over there watched people like you murder her parents. It took hours, and she had to keep quiet during it because she was hiding from the killers.' Amy turned from him to gaze at me. 'I felt terrible for her when she told me what happened, but I could never truly understand what it did to her because how could anybody know what that was like without going through it?' She inched the blade closer to his eyeball. 'And then I had to watch somebody I love suffer and die, not over hours, but for weeks. And that was all down to you, Larry.'

Tears streamed down his face. 'It wasn't my fault. There are loads of people selling drugs, not just me.'

Amy took the knife and ran it over his forehead, drawing blood. 'Indeed there are, but it was you who sold this specific batch of heroin that got my friend hooked. And for that, you have to pay. Actions have consequences, Larry, and your actions have produced these consequences. So, you have nobody to blame but yourself.'

'Don't do it,' I said.

She snapped her head to me, eyes blazing with an unholy heat. 'Do what?'

'You're going to kill him.'

Amy laughed. 'Eventually, probably, but I'll have some fun first.' She moved from him and towards me. 'Do you remember when we used to have fun?'

'It wasn't like this.'

'No, I guess it wasn't.' She returned to Larry and

cleaned his blood from the blade on his shirt. 'Perhaps this is progress.'

He raised his hands. 'Wait, I'll tell you something about how this works.'

She waved the knife at him. 'Tut, tut, Larry; were you keeping things from us?'

'I know where the kids get the drugs and take the money.'

'How?' I said.

I watched his chest pumping against his clothes. 'I followed them one night to see what they did.'

Amy placed the blade against his cheek. 'That's very naughty, Larry, stalking teenage girls. I had a stalker once. Do you know what happened to him?'

His lips shook so much that he struggled to get one word out. 'No.'

Amy laughed. 'Strangely enough, nobody does.'

'Where do the girls go?' I asked him.

'I followed them to the old abandoned Globe cinema on Stork Street. Are you familiar with it?'

'Yeah.' It was another blast from my past, where my father used to take me every Saturday morning for the cartoons and the Disney double bill.

Amy grabbed my arm. 'Okay, that's great. Now you can bugger off.'

'What will you do?' I said.

She whispered in my ear. 'Enola, I'm pretty sure you know what I'm about to do. The same thing you've done to several people. Now, do you want to stay and watch?'

I pulled back from her and headed for the exit.

The rain had returned as I got outside. Then, as I hurried away, I heard a low sob coming from behind me.

Or maybe it was all in my head.

Chapter 13

Protection

When I left for my first day in a new job, Ginger and Bruce were busy beavering away in front of their computers; Bruce with his consultancy work and Ginger with her online tarot readings. I thought having a job where you could work from home was curious, but I wouldn't fancy being stuck in the house all day.

So I said goodbye to Kronos and stepped outside. I didn't know what to wear from my less than extensive wardrobe, so I chose a white top, black jacket and dark blue trousers, with my most comfortable shoes.

It was a fifteen-minute walk to the food bank, with no interruptions and nobody protesting. I said hello to the volunteers as I walked through the building to Kate Frost's office at the back. Her assistant, John Tate, greeted me with a silent glance at the clock on the wall when I arrived. I was two minutes late.

'Where's the boss?' I asked.

Frost entered before he could reply, carrying a tray with three steaming cups of coffee and half a dozen doughnuts.

'Good morning, Enola. How are you feeling after yesterday's shenanigans?'

I thought she was talking about my dalliance with Amy until I remembered the events in the community centre.

I grabbed a coffee and a doughnut. 'I'm ready and raring to go, Ms Frost.'

She laughed. 'God, you make me sound like my mother. And I hate my mother. Call me Kate.'

I burnt my lips on the drink. 'Okay. I bet you got teased a lot at school.'

She sat on her desk while Tate scowled at me. 'Why?'

'Oh, you know, with that musical *Kiss Me Kate*.'

'Is that why people were always trying to kiss me? I thought it was because of my charm and good looks.'

She laughed, and Tate joined in, like when somebody laughs at an unfunny joke because they think it's expected of them. I just stood there and ate my doughnut.

Then Tate finally spoke. 'Do you want today's itinerary, Kate?'

'Send it to my phone, John. Did you get Enola's contract sorted?'

He didn't look at me. 'I'm waiting for her references.'

She grabbed a doughnut. 'No need for those. Go and get it done now; otherwise, my new security specialist might refuse to protect me today when we go for a walkabout.'

I watched him slip behind a computer desk while I licked sugar from my lips.

'Walkabout?'

She beamed at me. 'Yes, I like to wander around the community to meet my constituents on Mondays. Then, after lunch, I have my MP surgery in the library where anybody can talk to me about local issues.'

'Great. Do I have to be on high alert?

Kate sighed. 'After the weekend's events, we all must be extra vigilante when dealing with the public.'

'Perhaps I should have a taser or some pepper spray.'

She looked at her phone. 'I don't think that will be necessary. Now, are you ready?'

I finished my drink. 'Sure. Is it just the two of us?'

'And John,' she said, grabbing her bag and jacket.

Marvellous. I smiled at the miserable man, but he didn't return the gesture. Kate led the way through the food bank as it was filling up, including people I'd seen at the community centre.

We wandered down the high street, and I felt like somebody you see in movies protecting the US president, but without a suit and dark glasses. It didn't take long for my inherent cynicism to kick in, viewing every person as a potential serial killer or terrorist. In my mind, the old man selling fresh fruit was ready to pounce and attack Kate with a dangerous-looking aubergine. The young kids on the corner playing a guitar and singing were a front for some fundamentalist religious group preparing to smother her in hate crime lyrics.

When Kate rushed across the road to speak to a bunch of ladies in colourful hats who were draping knitted cartoon characters over the community centre gates, I pictured them swarming all over the country's newest MP and stabbing her with knitting needles.

Then we strode into an outdoor market, and a young woman tapped Kate on the shoulder. 'Would you like some homemade jams and chutneys?'

'Oh, thank you; that's lovely.'

I had to stop myself from intervening before she spread jam on a slice of bread and ate it. How easy would it be to poison her like this?

'Are you okay?' I said.

She beamed at me. 'You must try this, Enola. And you, John.'

He scuttled over and dropped a few free jars into his bag before shoving bread and chutney into his unsmiling gob. My gut was still digesting the doughnut, so I gave it a miss.

Or maybe I was suspicious of the food.

After that, we strode through the market, and she got a friendly welcome from everyone. It seemed she was well-liked by everybody, regardless of their politics. A woman said she was a lifelong Tory voter but switched to Kate in the by-election.

'I can't vote for them anymore. They're all greedy and corrupt.'

I smiled at the woman, wondering why it had taken her so long to recognise the bleeding obvious. John stuck to Kate like glue, and I followed behind, scanning everywhere and everyone as we went. When it got to lunch, I realised how stressful the job would be; suspicious of everybody and ready to jump at my own shadow. Yet Kate's effervescence and boundless energy were contagious, reminding me of an adult version of Becky.

I thought of the kid and what she'd told me about the bullies at school. Should I tell her mother about it? Or her teachers? I wasn't sure. I'd dealt with my tormenters the only way I knew how with force. But those were different times, and Becky was different from me at her age. Watching my parents die had toughened me up, but the death of Becky's father had probably affected her differently. Still, she'd shown bravery with the gunman at the community centre and the druggies at the funfair. So why was she scared of a few kids?

And what was I going to do about it?

'A quick bite and then to the library,' Kate said. 'How have you found it so far?'

I didn't tell her about the several times my heart rate had increased to breaking point during the walkabout. 'A doddle,' I replied.

She put an arm around my soldier while John snorted disdain. 'Don't worry about him. He's a natural grump and thinks my protection is down to him.'

Kate pulled me into a coffee shop, and I glanced between them, wondering if Bruce might have a rival for our glamourous Member of Parliament's affections.

And one other thing surprised me.

I really liked my new job.

Chapter 14

Read it in Books

The library looked like it had been through a war and lost. The walls were shedding paint like a snake with a skin condition, and the carpet had more stains than a Rorschach test for coffee addicts.

But, despite its sorry state, that library had character. The rickety chairs in the corner had probably been around since the invention of the printing press, and they were more welcoming than a grandmother's hug. The books on the shelves might've had a layer of dust thick enough to write a novel on, but their stories were just waiting for someone brave enough to blow off the cobwebs and dive in.

John was talking to a librarian as Kate and I sat at a table, waiting for somebody to come and speak to her.

'Few people grow up dreaming about becoming politicians,' I said.

'Oh, this was never my dream,' she replied. 'My ambition was to become the first woman on the moon.'

'What happened?'

She removed her jacket and put it on the back of her chair, revealing a dark blue top.

'I fell off a roof when I was twelve and discovered my fear of heights. So that was that for getting into space. Then I thought about being a doctor until I realised how long it took. But I grew up in a working-class family near here and saw people's daily struggles first-hand in this town. So I knew I wanted to make a difference, to give a voice to those who felt they didn't have one.' She grinned at me. 'It would have been nice to stand on the moon and gaze at this planet, but my voice wouldn't have achieved much down here from up there.'

'I don't know; you might have inspired other women and girls.'

'Don't you think I can do that now as an MP?'

I shrugged. 'Possibly, but considering how disastrous our female prime ministers have been, I'm unsure.'

'I never claimed I wanted to become PM.'

'Then what do you want?'

'My goal is to improve the lives of the people in this community, in my community. My mother was a cleaner at the hospital, working the graveyard shift, and my father worked in a factory, putting in long hours to provide for us. Yet, despite the hard work and time away from our home, they were always there for me, supporting and encouraging me to reach for the stars. I saw the same from my friends' parents and the other kids where we lived. However, for many of them, no matter how arduous their work was or how much they struggled, they could never lift themselves beyond their born position.'

'That's because the system is stacked against most people.'

'Yes, and that's what I want to change.'

'How old are you?' I said.

'Thirty-two.'

'Well, you didn't get to be an MP overnight.'

Kate laughed. 'No, that's right. I left school at eighteen and went to work in the local café, cleaning dishes and serving tables. Then, I moved on to an office, admin jobs, and typing. Finally, I took night classes to further my education and get a political degree. After that, I spent five years in the local Labour office doing every job going.'

'Why didn't you stay with them?'

'Why? Because they didn't want a local to stand for this constituency but to ship somebody in from down south. This had been a safe Labour seat for fifty years, but then....'

'2019 happened.'

'Yes, and we got our first Tory MP, a bloke who wanted to bring back the death penalty and said food banks were a sign the government was working.' She shook her head. 'And then he had to resign.'

'Watching tractor porn in the House of Commons?'

'No, that was one of the others. This bloke fiddled his expenses and forgot to pay his taxes. Once I knew he'd resigned, I decided to stand as an independent.'

'That must have made your former Labour colleagues happy.'

She shrugged. 'Most of them had lost touch with what was happening here, unwilling to admit to their own failures as well as the government's.'

'Sure, and I hope you don't mind me saying this, but I didn't know who you were when the posters went up and the leaflets came through the door.'

'I understand, which is why I had to do a lot of canvassing and get John to spread me all over social media, if you pardon the expression.' Her laugh was warm and welcoming. I could see how people would have warmed to her on their doorsteps.

'Where did you get the campaign expenses from?'

She grinned at me. 'I thought you might have asked that question earlier.' She removed a piece of paper and handed it to me. 'This is all on my website, but that's a list of donors to my campaign. Have a look.'

I gave it a cursory glance, seeing if any alarm bells jumped out - like pharmaceutical companies, oil barons, or right-wing media organisations. I recognised a few local businesses, including the pet shop where Ginger bought Kronos's dog food, but nothing was alarming.

'What do these donors get for financing you?'

'Only my eternal gratitude. This isn't cash for favours, Enola. Those people want the same as I do, and if things improve here economically, it also benefits them.'

'Everyone's a winner.'

'Hopefully,' she said. 'Do you feel better now?'

'What makes you think I wasn't feeling good about this?'

'Oh, perhaps the fact you haven't signed the contract John sent you and returned it.'

I took my phone from my pocket. 'You know, I forgot about it. I'll do it now.'

'I never forget where I come from,' Kate added, looking around the library. 'I know what it's like to struggle, to work long hours to make ends meet. I want to use my position to make a difference and help those in the same position I was in. And I hope you can help me do that, Enola.'

I signed the digital contract and sent it to miserable John. 'Well, Kate, I can't promise to take a bullet for you, but I'm here to stop anybody who shouldn't get too close to you.'

'Brilliant, thank you. But does that include Bruce?'

I nearly choked on my surprise. 'What?'

'It's just that I've become quite fond of him the last few weeks, and I thought maybe you and him....'

'He's my friend, that's all. And he's ten years older than me.'

She laughed. 'Oh, Enola, age is only important if you're a cheese.'

We grinned together as I discovered how open she was. Which meant I could ask a tricky question.

'What happened with your marriage?'

I thought she'd deflect and talk about something else, but she didn't. 'Whenever someone decides to poke the hornet's nest and ask about my marital status – or, more precisely, my glorious entry and exit from the institution of marriage – I can't help but indulge in a little mental math. It's like a game show where I calculate the financial and emotional cost of spilling the beans versus the cost of maintaining a blissfully ignorant silence.'

She smiled at a passing librarian before continuing. 'In that awkward pause that follows their question, my mind goes into overdrive. I'm running the numbers, folks! Should I reveal the sordid details of my matrimonial rollercoaster, complete with lawyer fees and emotional trauma, or should I just slap on a smile and deflect with a well-timed joke?'

'I shouldn't have asked, sorry,' I said.

Kate gripped my hand. 'Oh, no, really, I should talk about it.' She glanced at Tate munching on a sandwich out of earshot. 'And, truth be told, I don't have a lot of female friends, so this will be good for me.' Her laugh added warmth to her face. 'So, I'm picturing my ex-husband's face bursting into flames. What a sight that would be! But alas, I cannot speak such diabolical wishes out loud. Especially in a library.' She let go of me. 'So there's nothing between you and Bruce?' I shook my head. 'What about him and Ginger?'

'No, they're only friends.'

She seemed happy at the news, and I wondered if she'd only employed me as a way to get to Bruce. I tried to get the idea of him and me out of my head as a little old lady shuffled over on her walking stick, and I watched Kate go to work.

And I kept an eye on that walking stick.

Chapter 15

Looking At You

'How was your first day working for the honourable Kate Frost, MP?' Bruce said, putting the food he'd cooked on the table, a delicious-smelling curry.

I didn't mention how she'd questioned me about his romantic life.

'Nobody stabbed or shot at her, so I guess it was okay. One moment in the library, I thought an old granny would stab her with a knitting needle. It turned out that her walker was wonky. But apart from that, it was fine. What was it like at the food bank?'

Ginger joined us from the bathroom, drying her hair as she sat down. 'It was a nightmare. I went over in the afternoon, and the queues were horrendous.'

I shoved curried peppers into my mouth. 'What was wrong?'

Bruce poured wine for him and Ginger. 'The demand has increased as the donations have reduced. People who were donating a few months ago can't afford to do so now. The price of everyday foods, from baked beans, biscuits, and long-life milk, is rising. There's been a considerable increase in the costs of our food packages. Food banks are supposed to be a short-term fix, giving people time to sort themselves out when they've suffered a financial shock, but for most of our clients, it's turning into a long-term thing.'

A sense of gloom hung over the meal, and even Kronos seemed depressed. Things didn't improve when Amy rang me.

'When are you going to the Globe?' she said.

'What makes you think I am?'

'Come on, Enola. You want to track down Rook, so I know you won't wait around. I thought you might like some company.'

'I saw nothing in the news about Larry.'

'Why would you?'

I lowered my voice. 'I don't need your help, Amy.'

'Okay. Are you taking the gun with you?'

'No.'

'Christ, I don't know why you even asked me for it.'

'It doesn't matter now, Amy.'

'You still owe me a favour, Enola.'

'What's that got to do with this?'

'Nothing. It's only a reminder.'

Then she hung up. I told Bruce and Ginger I was going for a run. Kronos stared at me like an expectant child.

'I believe he wants to go with you,' Bruce said.

I patted the dog on the head. 'Not tonight, boy.' I turned to Bruce. 'What's this with you and Kate Frost?'

'What?' Ginger said.

'What?' Bruce echoed.

I shrugged on the way to the door. 'Oh, just something she mentioned today. I think she might have her eye on you, Bruce.'

I left as Ginger laughed at him, setting off on my usual route. The cold had kept most people indoors apart from those who didn't have an indoor and those flitting between pubs and clubs. Twenty-five minutes in, with my heart pounding and my legs aching, I took a detour through the park and ended up in the shadows of the old post office building opposite the Globe Cinema.

I considered my options. I wouldn't make the same mistake I did outside the Coronation. There would be no waiting. I was ready to cross the road when a car pulled up, and four blokes got out, smoking and drinking beer. The car drove off and left them there, standing near the entrance to the old cinema.

Were they part of the drug gang?

And if they were, what could I do against the four of them?

I should have brought that gun.

The men shuffled toward the end of the street. I could still see their lit cigarettes and hear their obscene jokes, but if I were careful, they wouldn't see me entering the cinema.

Then somebody tugged on my shirt.

'Are you going to watch a movie, Enola?'

I nearly jumped out of my skin as I stared at the kid. 'Jesus, Becky, what are you doing here?'

She wore a bobble hat, gloves and a scarf. 'Mum had to go to work, so I was alone.'

I put a hand on my chest to control my breathing, but failed miserably. It was as if a high-speed train was rushing through my body and had got stuck in my lungs.

'But what are you doing here, Becky?'

'I was outside the flat when you came out, so I followed you here.'

'I ran most of the way. How did you keep up?'

She smiled at me. 'I'm a good runner, Enola.'

I checked my phone. 'What time is your mum due home?'

'After ten, she said.'

I had two hours to take her to Bruce and Ginger and come back.

I held her hand. 'Come on; I'll take you home.'

She pulled away. 'I thought you were going to the pictures?'

I glanced at the old cinema. 'No, that place closed ages ago.'

'So why are you here?'

'It's part of my nightly run, that's all.'

'Is that your kid, Enola?'

I turned to see Amy behind us. 'What a fucking night this is turning out to be.'

'Enola!' Becky shouted.

Amy grinned. 'Yeah, Enola, fancy using that language around your kid.'

'Becky's ten years old, Amy. How could she be my kid?'

She shrugged. 'It's hard to tell how old she is in the dark. Sorry.'

'Enola's like my big sister,' Becky said.

'Is that right?' Amy answered. 'Did she teach you how to escape from your house?'

Becky narrowed her eyes, glancing between Amy and me. 'What?'

Amy put her hand on the kid's shoulder. I expected the kid to flinch from her, but she didn't, peering at my old friend as if she were a celebrity.

'Enola and I grew up in care homes. Did you know that?'

Becky nodded. 'She told me all about it.'

Amy smiled at me. 'All of it? Really?'

'Stop messing around, Amy,' I said. 'The girl needs to go home.'

Amy shook her head. 'I think she'll learn more about life with us.' She grinned at Becky. 'What do you think, kid?'

'It's boring at home,' Becky replied.

'Of course it is,' Amy laughed. 'It was the same for us in the children's home, which is why Enola was always helping me to break out of that place.'

'Could you take her home for me, Amy?'

'Is this another favour you need from me?'

I sighed. 'Sure, anything you want.'

Becky crossed her arms. 'I can't go with her. Mum said I shouldn't go with strangers.'

'She's not a stranger,' I replied. 'She's strange, but you'll be okay with her.'

'And what will you do while I play at Mary Poppins?'

'You know what, Amy.'

'Or,' she said. 'We could take her with us into the cinema.'

I grabbed Amy and dragged her away from Becky. 'Are you out of your fucking mind, taking a kid in there?'

'From what I understand, Enola, there are kids already in that building.'

I let go of her. 'You take her home, and I'll deal with the rest.'

'That might be a problem, Enola.'

'Why?'

She pointed across the road, and I saw Becky enter the Globe.

'Fuck!'

Chapter 16

Over the Rainbow

'You're a bad influence on that kid,' Amy said.

I didn't argue since I'd lost her twice in a matter of days.

'Becky's safety is the most important thing here, Amy.'

'Of course.' As we crossed the road in the gloom, I saw the glint in her eyes. 'You never struck me as the mothering type, Enola.'

I ignored her jab and scanned the surroundings as we entered the cinema through a broken door. Moonlight bounced off the walls, slipping through cracked windows as we strode into the foyer. Dust covered everything, and a strong smell of dampness and decay pounded in my skull. The sign had fallen from the sweet stand, landing on top of a humanoid M&M and cracking its chocolate head open. One of its inhuman eyes stared at me as we moved past it, beyond the ticket booth with its broken glass and rat droppings, and into the section leading to the screens.

Amy's barbed words hit their mark. She was right - I'd been reckless with Becky's safety, wrapped up in my own life.

I swept my gaze around the dilapidated theatre, searching for the child even as I avoided Amy's glare. Dirt and decay choked the once grand lobby as a discarded sweet wrapper crumpled under my shoe, a reminder of my failure to protect the kid.

Guilt gnawed at me as we crept past the deserted concession stand. Its shattered glass stared like an accusing eye. This was no place for a vulnerable little girl. What if she'd been hurt - or worse?

'Where is she?' I whispered.

'The last time I was here was to see *Parasite*,' Amy said.

I heard her but couldn't focus on her words, my brain throbbing with the thought of what happened to Becky. We moved inside, staring at the entrances for multiple screens. Ripped and faded movie posters clung to the walls, including one of a huge green face staring at me.

You're bad news for the kid, it seemed to say to me.

'We should split up,' I said.

'Sure, you take the ones to the right.' She stopped in front of the door. 'Should we call out to her?'

I recalled the events from the old funfair, and as much as I was worried for Becky, I didn't want to alert anybody else who might be there to our presence.

'Not yet,' I replied.

Amy nodded and disappeared into screen eight as I entered number seven. I held my breath, passing rows of dilapidated seats with the odd dead rat on them and seeing a broken projector at the back, film reels strewn across the floor. The blank screen loomed over the room like a giant tombstone.

Somewhere in the shadows of my mind, I heard my father's voice when he brought me to that cinema for the first time, telling me to eat my popcorn quietly, as if that was possible. I stood before the giant screen, picturing what I watched that day as many strange and colourful toys came to life and had extraordinary adventures. It was a wonderful world of excitement, and I loved it. Dust and cobwebs covered the screen now, but I only saw the flickering frames of my past before it changed forever.

My parents did their best to give me a safe movie education: the *Toy Story* films, *Tangled*, *Kung Fu Panda*, and many other Disney flicks. Even then, before the psychodrama of their deaths, I was drawn to more grown-up fare. And it was always the villains I focused on: Heath Ledger's Joker, Darth Vader and Palpatine, Buffalo Bill in *Silence of the Lambs*, Mrs Carmody in *The Mist*, Kevin Spacey in *Se7en*, Joaquin Phoenix in *Gladiator*, De Niro in *Cape Fear*, DiCaprio in *Django*, Daryl Hannah and David Carradine in *Kill Bill*, Jack Nicholson in *The Shining*, Joe Pesci in *Goodfellas*, Al Pacino in *The Godfather*, Brad Pitt in *Fight Club*, Anthony Perkins in *Psycho*, Margaret Hamilton in *The Wizard of Oz*, Bette Davis in *Baby Jane*, Robert Mitchum in *Night of the Hunter*, Kathy Bates in *Misery*.

Most of those movies were too 'adult' for me to watch, but there were always ways around such restrictions. One good thing I could say about that last children's home was that they had an excellent DVD collection. They weren't for the kids but something for the staff to while away the hours on the night shift. Somebody had locked them in a cupboard, but Amy was an expert lock picker.

Images flashed before my eyes, a rush of scenes that dragged me out of my current situation and the fear I felt for Becky, of Amy and me sneaking into her room and putting a contraband DVD into her laptop. I remembered the first time I watched *Aliens* and knew I wanted to be like Sigourney Weaver. Strong. A survivor.

Amy laughed when I told her. 'Better to be the alien queen: ruthless, determined and showing no mercy.'

I thought of that as I noticed the shattered glass and debris before the screen, moving closer to see broken beer bottles, chocolate wrappers, damaged popcorn boxes, and human shit. The smell invaded my nose, and I put a hand over my face.

Somebody touched my shoulder, and I jumped out of my skin.

'Jesus, Enola, calm down.'

My heart clawed at my chest. 'Fuck, Amy, give me a warning next time.'

'I did. I called your name, but you were in another world.' She glanced at the destruction near the screen. 'I heard voices from number six. Are you coming with me?'

I followed her into the corridor and moved to the next screen, hearing what she had.

'It's people talking,' I said.

'At least two of them. Did you bring that gun?'

'Of course not.'

She shook her head. 'I don't know why you even asked me for it. Have you used it since I gave it to you?'

'None of your business.' I nodded at the entrance to the screen. 'What do we do?'

Amy removed the flick knife from her pocket. 'Now we find your kid.'

She went first with me close by, the voices louder as we approached the screen. We stuck to the shadows as two figures appeared, their backs to us as they spoke to each other.

Then I saw Becky with them.

Amy stopped me from rushing to her. 'Wait.'

Moonlight splintered through the cracked roof, illuminating the people with Becky, the two teenage girls we'd seen with Larry.

Amy stepped forward. 'You girls are having a party and didn't invite us?'

The kid noticed me. 'Enola!' She ran over and grabbed my hand. 'This is my friend Debbie and her mate, Glory.'

I gripped tight to make sure she wouldn't get away. 'Your friend?'

'Yeah, Debbie goes to my school, the big part.'

I stared at the teenage girls. 'What's going on?'

They looked at each other, and I thought they'd sprint again. Instead, Debbie spoke.

'What are you doing here?' She glanced nervously around the room. 'You don't want to be here when Josh turns up.'

I peered into the shadows, checking if anybody else was there. 'Josh?'

Glory, the younger-looking of the two, pulled on Debbie's hand. 'You can't tell them anything. We'll get into trouble.'

Amy rolled the knife between her fingers. 'Why don't you girls tell us everything, and then we'll decide who's getting into trouble.' She smiled at them. 'And don't think of running again.'

Debbie looked at me. 'I'm sorry for kicking you, but we didn't know who you were. You might have been rival runners.'

'Runners?' I asked.

'The runners handle the distribution of drugs from the urban areas to the rural ones,' Amy replied. 'Isn't that right, Debbie?'

'We don't have a choice,' Debbie answered. 'They threatened our families.'

'You're at the same school as Becky?' I said.

She nodded. 'We're next door to each other, primary for her, secondary for me.'

I looked at Glory. 'What about you?'

She crossed her arms and glared at me. 'I'm excluded. The staff teaches me at the children's home.'

My heart sank. 'Children's home?'

'Glory's dad ran off, and her mother's in the nick,' Debbie asked. 'Why are you here?'

'We're looking for Rook,' I said.

Fear filled both their faces.

'We should leave, Debbie,' Glory said. 'He's not coming.'

'Josh?' I said.

'He should have been here two hours ago,' Debbie replied. She showed me her phone. 'And he hasn't called or texted. Something's wrong.'

Any snatched the mobile from her. 'We can go now, Enola.'

'Hey!' Debbie shouted. 'Give that back.'

She jumped at Amy, who pushed her out of the way.

'Wait,' I said. 'What's that noise?'

It was footsteps behind me.

Becky screamed, 'Enola!'

I turned as four men rushed towards us.

Chapter 17

Smells Like Teen Spirit

Paul Robinson and three bug-eyed loons glared at us. 'I knew you were up to something.'

They wore badges with the letters PB stamped on them. 'You followed me?' I said.

Robinson grinned like a demented clown. 'Not so clever now, are you?'

Amy put her arm around my shoulder. 'You're losing your touch, Enola. It's bad enough the kid trailed you here, but letting these rejects from humanity track you is beyond careless. No wonder the army rejected you at sixteen.'

I shoved her off me. 'No, that was you.'

She laughed. 'Of course, yeah.'

'What do you want?' Debbie said.

Robinson rubbed his hands with glee. 'Progressive Britain knows what you're up to here, selling drugs to fund your plan for the Great Replacement.' His mates lined up near him like two deformed KitKats. 'But we won't let that happen.'

Amy sighed. 'Great, fucking Progressive Britain. You know, I scarred my brain scouring your website, and for the life of me, I couldn't find anything progressive, so why don't you enlighten me?'

He seemed happy to have the opportunity to impress us. 'Progressive Britain works alongside local people across the country to amplify their voices and concerns regarding the lack of facilities and resources for them compared to those provided to outsiders, invaders, and degenerates.' He scowled at Debbie and Glory. 'This trash prostitutes themselves to pay their unclean masters.'

Debbie grabbed a dead rat from a seat and threw it at him. 'Fuck you!'

It bounced off his forehead and landed with a splat.

He howled in pain. 'Animals!'

I kicked the rodent corpse towards the human vermin. 'You should fuck off now, Robinson, before somebody gets hurt.'

He touched the bruise forming on his head. 'We want to know who those brats are working for.' He glared at me. 'And you work for that horrible woman, Kate Frost.' He grinned at his mates. 'This will look good when we post it online.'

Amy lit a cigarette and blew smoke at them. 'You're right; it will.' Then she got her phone and took photos of them. 'Let's see. Four middle-aged blokes stalk a group of teenage girls into an abandoned cinema and threaten them. How do you think that sounds, lads?' She snapped several more pictures as they stood there, open-mouthed and wide-eyed.

'No one would buy that,' Robinson commented.

'I'm struggling to believe you can walk and talk simultaneously,' Amy said.

He sneered at her. 'I'm a member of Mensa.'

I put a hand on my chest and laughed. 'Paul, I could paddle in your intellect and not get my toes wet.'

He growled at me. 'I'll make you pay for that.'

I shook my head. 'You're too little to make that big a mistake, Robbo.'

He lunged at me with a move that could have been seen from space. I stepped to the side and tripped him so he sprawled into the seats. The others seemed ready to pounce, but Amy waved her knife at them.

My focus was split between them, making sure Debbie and Glory didn't run for it. I needed that phone number for Josh from her. And there was Becky to worry about, though she had a huge smile as if she was eating a box of invisible popcorn. The last few days around me had given her a distorted view of the world, and I thought a ten-year-old shouldn't spend so much time with me. Not that I'd dragged her to the cinema.

Fuck. I had to have her home by ten, and these idiots were holding me up.

Robinson hauled himself up, and there was blood dripping from his chin.

He pointed a shaky finger at me. 'We'll get to the truth about you and Frost, mark my words. And you won't intimidate us next time.'

I laughed at him. 'Yes, bested by three girls and two young women. What brave souls you are in your Progressive Britain. Now fuck off before I set the ten-year-old on you.'

His mates helped him away, their obscenities lingering in the air behind them. I checked my phone to see I had an hour to get Becky home before her mum returned.

Debbie and Glory stared at me with awe-struck faces.

'That was amazing,' Debbie exclaimed.

Amy tossed her fag to the floor and put her arm around

Debbie. 'Stick with us, kid. There's more where that came from.'

'Can you help us?' Glory asked.

'Yes,' I replied. 'But I need to know more about how they recruited you.'

'There are always people lingering outside school,' Debbie replied. 'That's how it happened with Josh. I'd seen him talking to other kids and asked them who he was. They told me he gave them games and phones, and money. I thought he was a creep, but they said it wasn't like that. All you had to do was take a bag from one place to another, and that was it. I asked what was in the bags, but they said it was best not to know.'

Ghostly hands squeezed my heart. 'When was this?'

'Three months ago,' Debbie answered.

'It was the same for me,' Glory said. 'Only he was hanging around near the children's home, and none of the staff was bothered about what happened outside the building.'

'Do your parents know about this, Debbie?' I asked.

She shook her head. 'My mum and dad are too busy working to notice much. I'm fourteen, so they let me look after myself.'

'Okay.' I took Amy to the side. 'You talk to them while I speak to Becky.'

I left her to it and went to the kid.

'This is better than going to school,' Becky said.

I put my hands on her shoulders. 'Yeah, probably. How are you?'

She shrugged. 'I'm fine. Is this another of those things we don't tell my mum?'

'I guess so.' Of course, if Julia ever found out what I'd dragged her daughter into the last few days, she'd have a heart attack. 'We have to get you home now, but are you sure you're okay?'

'Of course,' she replied. 'I've seen worse on the telly.'

I thought of all the grown-up movies I'd watched as a teenager and worried even more about the kid. We returned to the others as Amy finished speaking to them.

'We've exchanged phone numbers,' she said. 'And I've given them yours.'

I nodded. 'Okay, we'll come up with something once I take Becky home.'

Becky grinned at me. 'Am I part of this gang?'

I touched her head. 'Yeah, a silent one. Now let's get going.'

We left the cinema together and went our separate ways. I watched them go and wondered what I'd let myself in for.

Then I stared at the kid and couldn't decide whether or not I'd lost my mind.

Chapter 18

Changes

My phone vibrating with a new text woke me early on Tuesday. Kronos gazed at me with wide eyes as I read the message.

John and I have had to dash to London. Important vote due in the HOC. Take a day off, and I'll speak to you later. Kate.

I crawled off the sofa as the dog licked my legs. 'Kronos!' I shoved him away to see Bruce sitting at the desk with his laptop.

'Morning, grumpy,' he said.

I shook my head, but it didn't kill the buzzing. 'What time is it?'

'Just after six,' he replied.

My yawn scared the mutt away. 'You got a client on the other side of the world?'

He turned to me, and I saw he was wearing his Batman dressing gown. 'Ginger and I had an idea about how to help the food bank when you were out jogging last night.'

I went to the kitchen, poured a glass of water, and returned to him. 'What idea?'

'What do you think about organising a local music event at the Raven with all proceeds going to the food bank?'

'It sounds great as long as I'm not the one organising it.'

'What are you doing with Kate today?'

'Actually, I have a day off. She and miserable John had to go to London for some mysterious vote in Parliament. Do you know anything about it?'

'Me? Why would I?' He got out of the chair. 'You having a day off is excellent because you can help us.'

'Who is helping us?' Ginger said as she walked in carrying fresh bagels, the aroma making my legs weak.

Bruce grabbed one from the box. 'Enola. She's got the day off work.'

Ginger looked at me with incredulous eyes. 'Off. You only started yesterday.'

I shrugged. 'Lucky, I guess. Tell me more about this charity event for the food bank.'

We sat around the table and spread butter over our bagels while Kronos stared at us and licked his lips. 'No,' Ginger told him. 'You know you can't eat wheat.'

'I've spoken to Ben at the Raven, and he said we could use it for free on Saturday. If we start early, sometime in the afternoon, we can get families in, switch to adults in the evening and finish at about eleven. I got up early to go through my contacts and email people. You can ask Kate to spread the word, Enola.'

I removed a bit of bagel from my teeth. 'I'm sure she'd rather talk to you, Bruce.'

Ginger laughed. 'Yeah, is this just a ploy so you'll get her on the dance floor?'

Bruce's cheeks turned into beetroots. 'Hey, we're only friends.'

Friends. After last night, were Amy and I mates again?

It certainly seemed like it, but the differences between us still existed. Or perhaps they were blurring on my side.

I hadn't slept well, but what about Becky? I'd got her home before Julia returned from work, and the kid had promised to keep everything secret, but it wasn't fair to ask her that. In a few days, she'd had three violent experiences and dealt with them with a surprising calmness that worried me. The incident with the gunman was bad enough, never mind adding the funfair and cinema events into the mix. She had to be repressing her feelings from her mother and me. Then there was what she'd told me about the school bullies.

I had to have a proper talk with her.

'So,' Ginger said, 'are you up for it?'

'What would you want me to do?' I answered. I needed a distraction, and helping the community was an excellent way to be distracted.

'Could you two go to the Raven and speak to Ben about the logistics?' Bruce asked.

'Logistics?'

He was warming up to the project. 'Yeah, see what parts of the venue we can use. For the afternoon slot, maybe we should ask some of the people who were at the centre on Sunday and make it a real community event.'

'That's a lot of organising to do in a few days, Bruce,' Ginger said.

'Why do you think I got up so early?'

I licked butter from my top lip. 'Aren't you worried we might get more of those protesters from the other day?'

'So what? Let them come. We can't allow others to stop us from doing something good. And anyway, those idiots are in the minority. More things bind us together than divide us, Enola.'

I pictured Paul Robinson in the old cinema, he and his Progressive Britain goons, causing trouble. Should I tell my friends about what happened? Did Ginger have a right to know I'd seen him again?

And what was I going to do about Becky? She'd only followed me to the Globe because of the example I'd set, of my casual, flippant attitude to danger. If she pursued risky behaviour now, what would she be like as she got older? Perhaps I had to cut our connections and see less of her? But at least with me around, I could protect her.

Couldn't I?

Or would my luck finally run out, and my actions would get her hurt?

'Are you in, then?' Bruce asked.

'Of course. Anything to help the food bank. Once I've showered and dressed, Ginger and I will take Kronos to the club.' I checked the clock on the wall. 'Do you know what time Ben gets there?'

He nodded. 'He said he'd be there for nine.'

'Should we tell the police?' Ginger asked.

Her question surprised me. 'What?'

'We should inform them about the event. They need to know in case those idiots return.'

'Yeah,' Bruce replied. 'Then Constable Davis can bring his American friend with him as protection. And don't you have Detective Inspector Parker's mobile number, Enola?'

'It's his work phone, for emergencies only.'

Should I notify Parker about the cinema? We had a way into the county lines operation, and I'd have to tell him about it, eventually. If it connected to Rook, I might finally have a way to get to him. Or her.

I'd tell Parker soon enough, but not now. I needed to see how it played out first, and it wasn't wise to inform the police about Amy's involvement. I didn't know where she was on their radar, but her many illegal activities must have alerted somebody in authority.

Ginger got up. 'Okay. I'll feed Kronos, and then we can coordinate our plans.'

I went to the shower, hoping the hot water would answer all my questions.

Chapter 19

Interlude

Kronos pulled on his lead. Ginger held him tight as we strolled towards the Raven. We had an hour to kill before the manager got to the club, so there was no rush to get there.

'Do you fancy coffee?' she said as we approached the café.

I pointed to the outside seats. 'You grab a table, and I'll get the drinks.'

A wave of comforting aromas enveloped me, transporting me to a world of warmth away from the chill. The smell of freshly brewed coffee infused the air, mingling with the subtle undertones of roasted nuts, chocolate, and caramel.

I closed my eyes and took a deep breath, savouring the rich, earthy fragrance that filled my nostrils. A heady scent awakened my senses and invigorated me. I ordered the drinks and waited, glancing through the window at Ginger and Kronos. I needed to talk to her about Robinson because there was no doubt he'd turn up again. And I had to know if there was some hidden reason for his re-emergence in

Ginger's life beyond his objectives with Progressive Britain.

The order arrived, and I joined her. Kronos gazed at the cups, and Ginger laughed.

'He stole Bruce's coffee once and was shitting bricks for the rest of the day.' She stroked the dog's face. 'He never learns his lesson, the poor mutt.'

'I know how he feels,' I said.

She sipped her drink. 'Something happened last night, didn't it? I could tell by the look on your face when you got back.'

'You were asleep.'

She shook her head. 'No, I was in my room and saw you come in. Did you get into trouble again?'

'Sort of. I bumped into those morons, Progressive Britain.' I warmed my hand on the cup. 'And Paul Robinson was with them.'

'Shit! What happened?'

'I sent them packing with their tails between their legs.' I peered into her eyes. 'Is he obsessed with you, Ginger?'

She sighed. 'God knows. All I know of him, which isn't a lot, are my mother's brief mentions of him. She never had a good word to say about him, but he was my father's friend when I was a baby. I wouldn't have known who he was if he hadn't said those horrible things about her the other day.'

There was something she wasn't telling me, but I didn't want to push it.

'How's your mum doing?'

She sighed. 'She's not doing well. It isn't easy to see her like this. She hardly recognises me anymore on my visits,' Ginger continued, blinking back tears. 'And the confusion and fear in her eyes when she does briefly know who I am... it's heartbreaking.'

Ginger took a shaky breath, composing herself. 'Her nurse says she spends most of her time lost in the past now. I just hope those memories bring her some peace, even if she's ceased to know the present.'

I touched her shoulder. 'I'm so sorry.' My heart ached for her pain and her mother's cruel illness. They were close once; I could only imagine how difficult witnessing this decline must be.

She smiled briefly before continuing, 'It's okay, Enola. I know you understand how hard it is to watch someone you love suffer.'

I nodded, thinking about my own experiences. 'Yeah, I do. It's tough.' And I thought about what Amy mentioned about watching somebody she loved suffer and die because of drugs. Should I get her to talk about it? Bottling up emotions was never good, even though I was an expert.

I imagined what it must have been like for Debbie and Glory, and who knew how many others, intimidated into working for the drug gang. I knew children were exposed to extreme levels of violence and trapped within the gang networks. If they didn't do what they said, there was always the threat of violence - a threat of violence towards them, towards their families. And once they were hooked, that's it, they're in. The exploiters have them in their back pocket.

I couldn't let that happen in my community. Rook might have been coming for me, but now I was coming for them.

'I've spoken about my dad, haven't I?' Ginger said.

'A little when we first met.'

'He died from cancer five years ago, just before my mum entered the care home. I struggled with everything, but Bruce was always there to help me. Meeting him at university was one of the best things to happen to me. And then later, I met you, of course.'

'And now look at us, like the Three Musketeers in that flat.'

'Will you find a new place now you have the job with Frost?'

I thought of the handgun at the bottom of my bag behind the sofa and pictured Kronos getting into it one night and pulling the weapon out.

'I should, really. It can't be good for you and Bruce having me there.'

She pondered my words. 'Well, the snoring is quite loud.'

I snorted coffee onto the ground and made the dog jump. 'Hey, it's not that bad.'

Ginger laughed. 'I'll record it next time and play it back to you.'

'That's not a bad idea. It would be better than most of that shitty music you play.'

'Wow, Ms Enola Gray, don't you be dissing my Elton John and Queen CDs. They got me through university, they did.'

'Christ, Ginger, that must have been some shit uni you went to.'

She shrugged. 'It was okay. That's where I discovered my alternative soul mates.'

'Is this the astrologist who took your virginity?'

Her lips shook with laughter. 'He didn't take it, Enola. I offered it up willingly, and it was well worth the wait.' She sighed. 'I wonder where he is now, with that mop of golden brown hair and a chest embezzled from the Greek Gods.' She laughed. 'Christ, I can't remember the last time I had a date.'

'Won't your tarot cards tell you where he is?'

Ginger narrowed her eyes at me. 'I know you're a non-believer, but there's no need to be sarky about it. You should respect other people's beliefs.'

'I do, mostly, unless they're pig-ignorant, bigoted ones.'

She nodded. 'Are we back to talking about Paul Robinson?'

'You realise he'll turn up again, don't you?'

'What did he say to you last night?'

What to tell her without revealing what actually happened?

'The usual hate speech. Are you sure there isn't more to him you're not telling me?'

She grunted like a jackal. 'Believe me, Enola, if anything, there's less to him. He's like the Frankenstein monster before they put the brain in, someone so forgettable not even his reflection recognises him, a man who slips in and out of rooms without leaving a trace. No one can be sure if he has human form or he's a shape-shifting ecto-plasm.' The bitterness in her voice confirmed she was keeping something from me about him. But I didn't get the chance to press it as she finished her coffee and stood. 'The manager should be there now.'

Kronos pulled her away, and I followed, hoping to see Robinson again to discover the truth about his connection to Ginger.

Even if I had to beat it out of him.

Chapter 20

The Raven

The door was open when we got to the Raven. It was the first time I'd visited the place during the day, but it still smelt of dried sweat and stale beer. And when I put my hand on the reception counter, I came away with a thick layer of dust on my fingers. I sneezed and tasted grime on my tongue simultaneously.

Without the rowdy energy of the night crowds, the place felt tired, almost mournful. The silent jukebox and darkened stage gave the place a desolate, abandoned aura despite the lingering smells of smoke and sweat. We went to the bar, where a burly man with tattoos covering his arms was wiping down glasses. He looked up as we approached.

'Can I help you ladies?' he asked, his voice gruff.

'We're looking to speak with the manager,' I replied.

He raised an eyebrow, sizing us up for a moment before nodding towards an office at the rear of the room. 'That's him,' he said. 'He's not the friendliest bloke, just so you know.'

We thanked him and approached the door, pushing it open. Inside was a small office cluttered with papers and empty beer bottles. A man with slicked-back hair and a scowl sat behind the desk.

'I told you, vultures, I'll pay you back next week.' He glared at Kronos. 'Bringing your attack dog won't help. I can't give you what I don't have.'

'We're Bruce's friends,' I said. 'Enola and Ginger.'

His grimace vanished, and he grinned as he got up and offered us his hand. 'Ah, sorry about that. I thought you were somebody else. I'm Ben.'

I shook his hand as I peered at the papers on his desk, seeing a familiar leaflet.

'Are you a member of Progressive Britain?'

He finished shaking Ginger's hand. 'Good God, no. Some bloke stuck them through the door this morning. My barman left them there, that's all. They'll be going in the bin soon enough.' He beamed at Kronos. 'Have you visited the Raven before?'

'Yeah,' Ginger replied. 'We've been to a few gigs here, including a few Bruce promoted.'

'Right, right. Now I think about it, I'm sure I've seen you here.' He pointed at Ginger. 'You're the psychic lady.' Then he turned to me. 'And Bruce says you're a whizz with computers.'

'Sure,' I said. 'It's kind of you to let us use the venue at such short notice.'

'Think nothing of it. I grew up here and will do anything to help the community. Shall we look around so you can plan what you want to do on the day?'

Ben led us out of the office, and we took the tour. Even though it was dark, seeing the venue in the daytime was strange. I let Ginger do most of the talking while I wandered alone, the memories flooding back as I went to the stage.

I remembered my first time there, fifteen and sneaking in to watch The Damned. It began a new world for me; the music was raw and intense, and the atmosphere was electric. I had never felt so alive. Seraphina, my friend and mentor at the children's home, had introduced me to the punk tunes released over thirty years before my birth, but when I'd asked her to take me to the concert, she'd refused.

'You're too young, Enola. You have to be eighteen to get in.'

Her refusal was another incentive for me to go to the gig. I'd plastered my face with makeup, including enough black eyeliner to block out the sun, but she only frowned at me.

'I look old enough.' I said.

'Yet you're not, Enola, that's the point. Give it a few more years. There's no need to rush your childhood away.'

But I'd never had a childhood; she should have realised that.

Amy blagged us to the front of the queue and charmed the bloke on the door. That night, I was a bundle of nerves; the music was loud, the lights dim, and the patrons wore leather jackets and heavy boots. But, even then, it was frozen in time, and I couldn't help but feel a sense of nostalgia for an era I'd never lived through.

I closed my eyes and was there again, the air thick with the scent of alcohol and sweat as the guitars and drums echoed through the club. The bass pounded in my chest, and the hairs on my neck stood on end. It was as if the music was a living thing, pulsing through the club's veins and in mine. It was gritty and raw with a hold on me, a power I couldn't resist.

It all returned to me, that night when I felt truly alive and free for the first time since my parents' deaths. Now, for a moment, I forgot about the world outside, the dangers and the challenges, and was lost in my past.

Then it changed, and I saw Debbie, Glory, and other children groomed, manipulated and exploited by Rook and his gang. My quest to find Rook had been driven by self-preservation, to locate him and shut down his operation before his thugs got to me. But that transformed overnight with the discovery in that old cinema of what was happening to kids in my community. I had to end Rook and the county lines drug gang to protect more people than just me, to halt the nightmare scaring me about Becky being sucked into that life.

But how far would I go to achieve that goal? Could I be as ruthless as Amy if necessary? I'd killed before, so why not again?

'We're finished, Enola. Are you ready to go?'

I opened my eyes back to the present, staring at Ginger and Kronos.

'Is everything sorted?'

She nodded. 'Yeah, Ben said we can do whatever we want. We'll delegate spots and times once we speak to Bruce and know who we've got for the event. But I need a pee first, and I can't do that here.'

My belly hurt as I laughed. 'Are you still traumatised after the last time?'

She scowled. 'You wouldn't be giggling if you'd seen a rat in the toilet.'

'It was dead, Ginger.'

'That's not the point, Enola.'

I continued laughing, and she scowled as we stepped outside.

Straight into Progressive Britain marching down the street.

Chapter 21

Eve of Destruction

About fifty of them moved slowly down the middle of the street, waving banners and placards. There was no police presence, but plenty of people watched the protesters.

'Shit!' Ginger said. 'We'll have to wait for them to leave before we can cross the road.' She looked at me. 'Unless you want to go around them?'

There was a chill in the air, but it was a beautiful day with the sun caressing my face. And I wouldn't let those idiots ruin it for me. Yet, when I glanced at their placards, my heart went cold, seeing a litany of things they hated: immigrants, refugees, asylum seekers, gay people, trans people, abortionists, atheists, single mothers, socialists, Marxists. They were anti-vax, climate change deniers who wanted *their* country back. I wasn't sure where it had been, but it didn't originate in their shrivelled minds.

The atmosphere was tense, with many folks looking apprehensive and uncomfortable. Those demonstrating were aggressive, and a few argued intensely with passers-by. Some tried to walk around the protest, giving the demonstrators a wide berth. I felt the tension and the sense of unease as people hurried to avoid the confrontation.

The protesters were a motley bunch, with a few wearing hoodies and caps, trying to conceal their faces and others who looked like regular people, dressed in casual clothes. There was a man in a crimson hat, shouting slogans into a megaphone, and others waving flags with the Progressive Britain logo. I studied it for the first time, seeing a red dragon wrapped around the letters PB.

Front and centre was Paul Robinson, screaming at a refugee woman with her baby outside the bakers. A volcano erupted inside my veins, a surge of lava replacing my blood. I noticed the mark on his forehead, the remnant of a dead rat kissing him. I put one foot on the road to confront him when Ginger pulled me back.

'What are you doing?'

I bit my top lip to soothe my throbbing heart, tasting blood and enjoying it.

'We can't let them get away with this.'

She released me. 'They're allowed to protest, no matter how stupid they are.'

'Sure, and I can tell them what a bunch of fucking morons they are.'

'There's more of them than you.' Kronos pulled at his lead and growled at the chanting mob. 'And that's not good odds.'

'Even Kronos knows what they are,' I said.

Ginger nodded. 'He's a clever dog, spotting ignorance from fifty feet away.'

She was right, but it didn't make me feel any better. I'd likely see Robinson again when he had fewer people around him.

'Can you believe this shit?' Bruce rushed over to us. 'Where are the police?'

'They're not causing any trouble,' Ginger said.

I grunted. 'That's debatable.' I scrutinised her face, recognising secrets hidden behind her eyes. 'What aren't you telling me, Ginger?'

'About what?'

I pointed at Robinson. 'About him.'

She sighed, and her cheeks deflated like a burst balloon. 'He's my uncle.'

Her words sucked the air from my lungs. 'What?'

Ginger grabbed my arm and dragged me into the doorway of a posh boutique, my attention caught by a pair of ruby shoes in the window.

'He's my mother's younger brother. They fell out years ago when I was a kid. You can probably guess what it was over.'

I watched Robinson rally his troops into screaming vile comments at the public. Bruce stood his ground, shouting back at them.

'Did he come to town to see you?'

She laughed. 'God, I hope not. I think he was shocked to see me in the centre.' Her grip on me increased. 'He doesn't know what happened to Mum, that she's in a care home.'

'Will you tell him?'

Ginger let go of me. 'Fuck, no. She wouldn't want him visiting her, and I don't either. He can stew in his own ignorance.'

The chanting increased as the wind got up. I hoped it would be strong enough to blow the banners and flags away, hoist them into the air like the tornado in *The Wizard of Oz*, and transport them to some desert island far from the rest of us.

Then Robinson stopped haranguing innocent bystanders and saw me. He came at me like a shark at a swimmer, wearing a T-shirt claiming "God Hates All Sinners."

'You're part of the problem,' he snarled, jabbing a finger at me. 'You and your kind are why the world is going to hell.'

'Our kind?' I asked.

He bared his teeth like a feral wolf. 'Yes, your kind, the invaders who want to replace the natural people of this country.'

Bruce sharpened his tongue. 'Not that it makes any difference, but I was born here, you stupid twat.' He glared at Robinson. 'And you're about as natural as a yoghurt.'

The tension around us increased. The torchless mob were all staring at us, joined by what was left of the public who hadn't shuffled away to safety. I put my fingers in my pocket, found my phone, and contemplated calling the police. Or at least texting DI Parker.

But it was pointless. It would be too late to make any difference, even if they came. It was a cold day, but the heat increased to a boiling point, especially inside my head. From the look on Bruce's face, I guess he felt the same. Ginger appeared calmness personified, while Kronos eyed Robinson as if he was the mutt's first meal of the morning.

I pointed at the mark on Robinson's forehead. 'What happened to you, Paul?'

He glanced between the others and then back at me. 'Don't worry; the truth will come out soon enough. After that, this place will be wiped clean, and the chosen ones will have the world to start over again without the mistakes of the past.'

I laughed. 'The chosen ones?'

His smile revealed sharpened teeth. 'Yes, all of us, those who have embraced the true destiny of this country.'

'Destiny?' I said. 'I think you and your friends are confused, Paul. All you have is a date with dentistry.'

'What?' he asked.

Ginger tried to stop me, but I was too quick, whipping my arm up and punching him in the mouth. His face exploded in a shower of red, and the gasps came from his followers and the public. He staggered into a man carrying a banner proclaiming we were all going to HELL. Robinson became entangled in the flag, wrapping his arms around it until the word HELL covered his snarling mug. Then, they both collapsed to the ground, with enough obscenities to make a stand-up comedian blush.

It would be wrong to say the rest of Progressive Britain turned ugly because they were pretty much that from the beginning, but their mood changed as they stepped towards us.

Then I heard the sirens.

For once, I was glad to see the police approaching.

Chapter 22

Season of the Witch

'The other kids think we're witches,' Amy said as we watched *The Conjuring* one night in her room. Half of the night shift staff in the children's home were either off sick or on holiday. And that meant we could basically do what we wanted.

I nodded. 'I know. Maybe they're right.'

Amy laughed at the screen as a ghost jumped out of a wall. 'Why would you say that?'

I kicked off my red shoes and admired the purple glittering on my fingernails.

'Think about it, Amy. Maybe those people murdered my parents to punish me.'

She shook her head. 'To punish you? Why?'

I shrugged. 'I read a book about reincarnation, you know, past lives. What if I did something terrible in one, and that's why my mum and dad were killed like that.'

Amy frowned. 'What did I tell you about listening to that spiritualist nonsense? Bad people do bad things, and sometimes there's no rhyme or reason why. Ghosts and spirits don't exist, Enola. You're too old to believe in that rubbish anymore.'

'You didn't say that when we had the Ouija board in the woods.'

She jumped off the bed and grabbed a can of cider, opening it with a loud swish. 'That was just us messing around.'

I shook my head. 'Not for me. I wanted to contact my mum and dad.'

Amy handed me a can. 'And did we?'

I opened the cider and took one long swig, enough for the sweet coldness to kiss my throat. 'No.'

'See, I told you. Just a load of nonsense.'

The booze warmed my insides as I pointed at the movie playing on the laptop.

'It's the season of the witch, Amy, and we're the main players.'

'Come on.' She grabbed my arm and dragged me towards the window.

I followed her out, and we climbed down the side of the house. Amy ran ahead as the wind whipped up my hair across my face. I thought about reincarnation, witches and superstition. What were the spooky things my parents said about the ghost tales of the town?

'It was rumoured a witch once lived here long ago in the woods, Enola,' my mother told me the Halloween before she died. 'People said an eerie glow could be seen in the trees on certain nights, and spine-chilling shrieks echoed from the tangled branches. There were whispered accounts of those brave or foolish enough to explore the woods being tormented by unseen forces. They called it the Witch Wood.'

Amy laughed when I mentioned the story to her.

'People are always saying stuff like that about this place.' She climbed up a tree and hung from a branch like a monkey, talking to me as she swung. 'The woods are haunted, or a dead girl walks amongst the trees, or it's where the witches come out at night. The wicked woman lives at the bottom of the river.'

'Wicked woman?'

She grinned. 'Yeah, the one who vanished. Like you will if you don't climb up here.'

'Stop messing around,' I said.

She jumped down and removed a small bottle of gin from her jacket. 'The only spirits here are these.' She waved the bottle at me. 'Do you want some?'

Of course I did.

We headed further into the darkness, months away from our fifteenth birthdays. We slipped into our favourite hideaway, deep amongst the bushes and shared the bottle between us. The surrounding trees creaked and groaned in the wind, spindly branches grasping at the night sky. I thought I glimpsed flickering lights dancing between their twisted limbs. Amy prattled on, oblivious, but unease crawled up my spine.

'Witches were real. The government put them on trial. I watched a documentary about it.'

Amy took a drink and shivered. 'The English countryside is full of places like this, where superstition once overwhelmed rational thought, and women, suddenly branded strange or outsiders, were ordered to be killed as witches. Once valued, their unique skills and knowledge became seen as dangerous threats. Baseless accusations flew; paranoia mounted. Too often, supposed witches faced gruesome fates at the hands of panicked mobs or prejudiced courts.'

'You saw the same documentary?'

She smiled. 'I did. Women and girls are always getting blamed for things they didn't do, Enola. We might as well kick against the pricks while we can.'

An owl hooted above us as I narrowed my eyes. 'Kick against the pricks?'

Amy laughed. 'My previous foster mother said it to me once. It means to resist incontestable facts or authority. I also heard it in a Johnny Cash song.'

I grabbed my ribs. 'Wow, Johnny Cash. So you've stopped listening to Adele and Beyoncé.'

She shrugged. 'It's better than all that old punk music you listen to.'

It might have been that night when I realised how much I loved her.

I reached into the bushes and pulled out some strange-looking mushrooms. 'We can keep these for later.'

Amy drank again before passing the bottle to me. 'It's not like they were actual Satanists or something. They were keeping old pagan traditions alive, being the village "wise woman" who people came to for advice. But then the stupid witch hunts started, and everything they did was considered evil. They were mostly poor or had mental health issues, the kind of people society treats like garbage. And then rumours spread, and paranoid idiots got all worked up over nothing. Those women were killed for no good reason. Just because they were different or didn't conform. It was so unfair and messed up.'

'People think we're evil and messed up,' I said.

She shook her head. 'That's mainly you.'

'I'm serious, Amy.'

She put the bottle against a tree. 'Yeah, okay. You mean the staff in the children's home.'

I nodded. 'Not all of them, but most. And it was the

same in the other homes I was in before this one. If you don't do what they say, then there's something wrong with you. It wasn't just me it happened to. I saw it happen with lots of other girls.'

Amy sighed. 'Me too.'

I grabbed the bottle and finished the dregs. 'So we can't go back. Right?'

She burped and then grinned. 'Damn fucking right.'

We were laughing when the coppers arrived in the woods.

Chapter 23

Don't Look Back in Anger

'We meet again, Ms Gray,' Detective Inspector Parker said as he wrote in his notebook. 'What's your version of events that happened here?'

Uniformed officers spoke to witnesses, including Bruce and Ginger, while a medic dealt with Robinson's broken jaw. Constable Davis was dispersing the Progressive Britain crowd and getting an earful of abuse for his troubles.

'He lunged at me, and I defended myself, Inspector. The same bloke attacked Ginger the other day at the community centre. Ask anybody here; they all saw it.'

Parker tutted. 'I have asked, and many claim you punched him without provocation.'

'Well, they would say that, wouldn't they? It's his organisation. Speak to the public, and I bet they say differently.'

He tapped his pen on the pad. 'Indeed, just as your friends did.' He glanced at the CCTV equipment in the street. 'What a shame those weren't working or nobody filmed the whole thing on their mobile phones.'

'Yes, what a shame.' I smiled at him. 'Anyway, isn't this a bit below your pay grade, dealing with low-level problems?'

Parker put the pen and notebook away. 'We were on our way somewhere else when we got the call to come here.' He nodded at Robinson, who continued to scowl at me. 'He might press charges.'

'Let him. I'm sure he and his organisation will be glad of the publicity.'

'He mentioned something strange about you.'

I waved at Robinson as a medic led him into an ambulance. 'I'm shocked.'

Parker stepped towards me and lowered his voice. 'It's no laughing matter, Enola. He claims you and Kate Frost are involved in criminal activity.'

I laughed so hard that my ribs hurt. 'What?'

'Shouldn't you be working with her today?' he asked.

I licked the dry blood from my lips. 'Day off. She and her PA had to go to Westminster for some emergency vote in Parliament.'

'There's no vote in the House of Commons today,' Parker said.

I narrowed my eyes. 'What? How do you know?'

'Because I watched the news, Enola, and there was no mention of that.'

'Well, Robinson is lying to you with another of his ludicrous conspiracy theories.'

He sighed and slumped his shoulders like he'd worked a twelve-hour day.

'Yeah, I guess so. Still, he spent ten minutes telling me how you and Frost are involved in the fifteen-minute city conspiracy.'

'The what?'

He frowned at me. 'Don't you read the news?'

'I'm too busy listening to true crime podcasts. You must know the ones I mean – where the coppers mucked up the investigation, and the wrong person was convicted for a crime they didn't commit.' His expression was unmoving, like a brick wall waiting for somebody to paint a smile on it. 'Like that young woman who vanished near the river years ago, and you lot could never find her. Were you a copper then?'

He ignored my question. 'Simply put, the fifteen-minute city principle suggests you should have your daily needs, work, food, healthcare, education, culture and leisure, within a fifteen-minute walk or bike ride from where you live.'

'That sounds great to me.'

'As it would to most,' Parker replied. 'But those on the lunatic fringe think differently. For them, it's an unprecedented assault on personal freedoms. Some online forums have claimed it's the first step towards an inevitable *Hunger Games* society where residents won't be allowed to leave their prescribed areas. They see it not as a route to a low-traffic, low-carbon future but as the beginning of a slippery slope to living in an open-air prison.'

I laughed. 'Yeah, who needs the convenience of walking to the shops, anyway? It's not like it would benefit our health, environment, or general well-being. Nope, let's keep fighting for the glorious freedom to waste our lives in traffic while destroying the planet.' I glanced at Robinson as he stepped out of an ambulance. 'And that's why you can't believe a word he says.'

'I don't know,' Parker said. 'They have a lot of money behind them.'

'Who? Progressive Britain? I thought they were only a few hundred nuts with nothing better to do.'

'Not according to the latest post on their website, where they claim to have received a large donation from an American billionaire.'

'You visited their website?'

'I spend a lot of time online, Enola. It's part of the job.'

I shook my head. 'Just when I thought the world couldn't get any worse.'

'So,' Parker said. 'If Robinson wanted to sue you, he'd have the money to do it.'

'Yeah, I'm living on my friend's sofa, and I'm two days into a job with an independent MP, of which I'm her second staff member. So, Robinson can take me for all I've got and get the handsome sum of fuck all.'

'There are rumours Frost is about to receive a hefty financial donation.'

'Rumours? From where?'

He grinned. 'We in the police hear everything, Enola. Didn't you know that?'

I did, which is why I considered telling him what happened at the Globe Cinema.

Then I thought better of it. 'As fascinating as this conversation is, Inspector Parker, I must be off. There's a charity music event that needs organising.'

'What event?'

I told him about it. 'Get yourself along for a sing-a-long, Parker,' I said as I went to Ginger and Bruce. 'I'm sure they'll play some Ed Sheeran for you.'

'Are you in trouble?' Ginger said.

I shrugged. 'Probably not.'

'We told the police Robinson came for you first,' Bruce said.

I patted him on the shoulder. 'I knew you would. Now,

where are we at for Saturday? Ben at the Raven gave us *carte blanche* with the venue.'

'That's great. I've got four bands lined up, and I just need to select their time slots. All we have to do is set up some community activities for the afternoon.'

My stomach rumbled. 'Okay, let's head to the café in the community centre for lunch and get the contact details for the people who were there on Sunday.' I put my arm around Ginger's shoulder. 'We've already got our first volunteer for the day.'

And maybe with everything that had happened to me recently, I'd let her use the tarot cards to read my future.

Chapter 24

Superstition

I sipped at my Coke. 'You never told me how you got into tarot cards, Ginger,' I said, wanting something to distract her from what she told me about Robinson. It was only a few months since the tragic death of her other uncle, Joe, and now she had this to contend with. Sometimes, I imagined having no family was a benefit until I realised it wasn't.

The café was quiet, a stark contrast to the bedlam we'd encountered with those protesters in the street. She smiled at me as Bruce fed Kronos bits of cake.

'It all started with my mom,' she explained. 'She was obsessed with English folklore and witchcraft traditions. When I was little, she would tell me stories about witches dancing around trees and wells at night. The idea of women gathering together under the moonlight to celebrate ancient rituals fascinated me.'

'I studied British folklore at university,' Bruce said.

I snatched a bit of cake from his hand before he could feed it to Kronos, and the mutt stared at me with sad, watery eyes.

'Didn't you do computer studies at uni?' I asked.

He nodded. 'Yeah, but you could combine it with something else in your first year.'

I had visions of him wearing a wizard hat like Gandalf from *Lord of the Rings*, sitting in front of a laptop and writing code to improve the world.

'What did you learn?' I said. 'Do you know where Merlin is buried?'

'The Armorican tradition places the tomb of Merlin in the forest of Broceliande, locked in a richly decorated cave, where he sleeps an eternal sleep. A thick fog veils him from passers-by, enclosed in a tower of air or a stone that turns on itself. But Merlin may be elsewhere, sealed in the trunk of the oldest tree, imprisoned for eternity.'

Ginger sighed. 'It's always about the men.'

'You believe differently?' I said.

She nodded, her eyes lighting up with memories. 'My mother believed that certain rituals, often labelled as witchcraft, were remnants of the old religious festivals and matrimonial rites of ancient groups. She saw them as a connection to our ancestral traditions and a way to tap into the mysteries of the universe.'

Her words intrigued me, and I remembered all my teenage conversations with Amy about witches. I leaned in closer, eager to hear more. 'So, how did this fascination with folklore lead you to tarot cards and astrology?'

Ginger smiled. 'Well, my mother used to tell me stories about how these women, with their torches and candles, would also read the stars and the tarot to gain insight into their lives and the world around them. It was all part of a holistic approach to understanding the mysteries of life and the interconnectedness of everything.'

'Sure,' I said while thinking of the link between her and Robinson.

'As I got older, Mum taught me about tarot and astrology. She had this amazing deck passed down in her family for generations. We would spend hours laying out the cards on the living room floor, fascinated by the images and symbols. She knew all about the zodiac signs and planets, too. She helped me make my first astrological chart when I turned fourteen.'

I remembered my fourteenth birthday. Amy and I climbed out of my bedroom window in the children's home and ended up looking at the stars on the hill. It was the first time I got drunk.

'You showed me those cards,' I said. 'You still have them at the flat, but don't use them for readings anymore.'

A wistful look overtook her face, and I knew she must be thinking about her mother in the residential home for her dementia.

'Yeah, they were getting frayed around the edges, and I didn't want them falling apart. They mean too much to me.' She paused for a moment, as if lost in thought. 'As a child, I was captivated by my mother's stories. I remember sitting with her in our garden, under the starry night sky, as she taught me about constellations and their significance. It felt like we were tapping into something ancient and powerful that transcended time and culture.'

She continued. 'I realised pretty early on that this wasn't just a hobby for my mom. She really believed in the tarot and astrology as a way to gain insight into life. When I had trouble in school or with friends, she always told me to consult the cards or my chart. More often than not, they offered me guidance and comfort.'

Her smile warmed my heart, and I was happy for her,

glad we had something to think about apart from what had happened outside. And of her uncle. I was also seeing a side to her I hadn't seen before.

'Can you put a spell on Paul Robinson and his motley crew?' Bruce said.

I assumed he was half joking, guessing he didn't know the truth about the angry man.

Ginger frowned. 'I'm not a witch.' Then she punched him in the arm. 'Though I would be proud to be one.' She smiled at me before dropping three sugars into her tea. 'A lot of my friends at university were using witchcraft for healing, both for the body and the mind. That's where I learned medieval witches had worshipped not a male Devil but a female goddess. This and other features of their worship suggested it had originated in Neolithic times, before the rise of patriarchy.'

Her words fascinated me. 'I read that the witch trials were a way of men controlling women.'

She agreed. 'To start with, let's consider how the concept of witchcraft and witches was intrinsically linked to women. If you delve deeper into early Christianity and the era before it, you notice that the negative connotations tied to witches diminish. It's important to remember that it wasn't until the beginning of the fourteenth century that witchcraft was firmly intertwined with heresy. These accusations merged into a potent suppression tool under the dominion of an almighty Church or a lethal yet frequently two-sided instrument of retribution wielded by ordinary individuals.'

'I didn't realise you knew so much about the subject,' Bruce said.

Ginger laughed. 'I'm a well-read woman, my friend.'

I slurped more of the Coke, enjoying the cold bubbles as

they slipped down my throat. 'When I was in the system, the boys in the care homes who hated me would, amongst other things, call me a witch. They didn't mean it as a compliment, but I took it as one.'

Kronos lifted his paws into my lap, and I fed him with sugar cubes.

'You put a spell on him the first time he met you,' Bruce said.

'He's a good judge of character,' Ginger added. 'That's how we knew straight away we'd be lifelong friends.'

'I thought you were just taking in another stray.'

She shook her head. 'I did that with Bruce.'

He shrugged. 'And look where that got you.'

We laughed together, three mates without a care in the world.

Then my phone pinged with a text. I checked who it was.

Amy wanted to meet me.

Maybe she needed her gun back.

Chapter 25

Closing Time

As I entered the pub, an overpowering smell of cider and fried food lingered over everything. I bought a soft drink, stroking the green-eyed cat slumped on the bar, letting it lick my fingers as Jim Morrison sang about breaking through to the other side.

'What's up with your hands?' the woman near me asked, giving me a look I could feel in my kidneys. She looked like she owned a collection of novelty dildos, figurines of dragons having sex, and who named her first child Pagan.

'I was in a fire,' I said.

She ignored the no-smoking sign and lit a cigarette. 'You should wear gloves to hide those scars.'

I removed the ice from my drink and rubbed it over my top lip. 'You should wear a mask to hide your face.'

Her cheeks flared like an exploding sun, snorting at me as a man with a slapped arse for a face joined her.

'Who's this, Brenda?'

Brenda puffed smoke at me. 'Some cheeky cow looking for a smack.'

500

I let the smoke sting my eyes and drew a sharp breath through my teeth. 'Your mouth is too big, just like your ears.'

She glared at me, but the bloke laughed like Basil Brush having an orgasm.

'She's fucking right, Brenda; you do have a big mouth.' He squeezed her waist. 'Which is just as well, eh?'

I glanced around the pub, discovering a veritable rogues' gallery of room-temperature IQs. How typical of Amy to want to meet in that place. I checked my phone, but there were no new messages since the last one she'd sent me, and I refused to reply to her again. After being apart for four years, we'd recently got reacquainted, yet she still loved to make me wait.

'Can't you take your booze, love?' Brenda said to me. 'That's because you're just a scrawny girl with ugly hands.'

I removed the straw from my drink. 'I've learned a lot about how memory works: once you lay down an experience into long-term memory, it's slightly edited each time you access it. You add things you've seen, conversations you've had, and a TV programme you saw. As a result, everything becomes mixed up, so over time, it's difficult to tell what's real and what you've added to it.'

'Eh?' Brenda said.

I sucked horrible-tasting lemonade from the straw. 'I was twelve the first time I blinded someone with a straw. Unlike this hard thing, it was the soft plastic type, so getting it right into the eyeball was challenging. Anyway, even though this was only a few years ago, I struggle to remember the precise details of whether he grabbed my arm and then tumbled backwards or if he fell and I left the straw sticking out of the socket.'

Her jaw dropped, exposing her elephant-like breath and nicotine-stained teeth. She flipped the cigarette into her drink as the bloke dragged her away. I returned the straw to my glass and pondered the impossibility of getting a decent soft drink in a pub.

Amy slipped into the newly vacated seat. 'Are you upsetting the locals again, Enola?'

The cat jumped off the bar when it saw her, and I knew how it felt.

'Did you pick this place just to upset me?'

'It's the closest place to the Globe unless you want to hang around outside in the cold.' She ordered a pint of Guinness. 'And I had to ensure you weren't followed by a ten-year-old kid again.'

I bent the straw in half, but it snapped back into shape.

'Becky's at home in bed.' I showed her the photo Julia sent me fifteen minutes ago.

'How cute,' Amy said. 'What's your relationship with the girl?'

Considering the age gap between Becky and me, it sounded strange to say we were friends, but we sort of were. 'She looks up to me.'

Amy drank half of her pint. 'Poor kid. I looked up to you and see where that led me.'

The laugh got stuck in my throat, so I nearly choked. 'You looked up to me? I think your memory is all twisted there, Amy. It was the other way round.'

She squeezed her eyes to resemble a constipated frog. 'No, Enola. You used me as an emotional crutch, shredding all your fears and woes and sucking the life from me. Then, when you'd had enough and were confident of surviving on your own, you buggered off to your safe life of working in the computer shop and taking your neighbour's dog for a walk.'

'That's not how it was, Amy, and you know it. You sunk

deeper into the criminal world, and I didn't want that life, so I had to get out. And that meant getting away from you.'

'If you say so, Enola.'

I slapped my hand on the bar. 'Wait. How did you learn about the shop and Kronos?'

She smiled. 'Kronos is the dog, right?'

'You know he is. Did you spy on me?'

She gripped her stomach and laughed. 'God, don't be so dramatic. My contacts stretch across the town, so when somebody tells me a young woman is jogging at night and beating up muggers and sex offenders, I guessed who it was. And then I got confirmation.'

'That wasn't what I did.'

'Oh, really? It wasn't you who hurt those blokes at the bridge, or the man in the abandoned shoe shop, or the couple near the river? I forget the rest, but I can get the details from my phone.'

I waved a hand at her. 'Just tell me why we're here.'

Before she could, a guy wearing a Batman T-shirt sidled up to us. 'Can I buy you lovely ladies a drink?'

Amy peered at his chest. 'You like Batman?'

He grinned. 'Sure. He has no powers, but he's the perfect superhero.'

She replied, as if she was talking to a baby in a pram. 'Batman at heart was always a superhero for the ultra-wealthy, as most of his battles are against those committing theft, bank robberies or property damage. However, Gotham's problems could be improved or even fixed with more progressive taxation of his real persona/alter ego, Bruce Wayne. And all his villains are people with mental health issues, hearing voices, dressing up in strange clothes, and struggling with the world. Then there are the female characters, wearing impractical skimpy costumes or fetish gear to satisfy an audience of teenage boys or middle-aged blokes who still think they're teenage boys. To some degree, he's the perfect metaphor for not just America's problems but the rampant capitalism filling its pockets whilst the planet burns, particularly with the key point about any version of Batman: the status quo is maintained, and nothing ever changes.'

His cheeks bulged, and I watched him struggle to speak. I jumped off the chair and dragged Amy out of the pub.

'Tell me why I'm here.'

She showed me her phone. 'Debbie got a message. A new drug intermediary is in town, and he wants to meet her in the Globe.' She glanced at the time on her mobile. 'In five minutes.'

I followed her down the street and into the cinema.

Maybe I'd finally get some answers about Rook.

Chapter 26

The Last of the Famous International Playboys

Debbie was in the same spot in the Globe as before, but alone this time.

'Where's Glory?' I said.

Debbie's hand shook as she sucked on an orange-flavoured vape. 'She couldn't sneak out of the children's home.' She puffed smoke above her head, and it drifted towards the ceiling, mixing with the dust highlighted by a thin silver beam of moonlight. 'But that's good. I didn't want her here for the new bloke.'

'Do you have his name?' Amy said.

Debbie nodded. 'Dave.'

I moved away from them, scanning the surroundings for anything out of place. The dead rat that had kissed Robinson's head still lay over a tattered cinema seat. It appeared like the only entry was the entrance we'd arrived through, but exits could be located at the rear or behind the screen. I left them talking and checked, finding a wall at the back of the screen before running up the steps to the end. There was a door there, but it was locked.

He'd have to enter as we had.

I returned to them. 'He won't come on his own.'

Amy nodded. 'I agree. Did you bring that gun?'

I glanced at Debbie. 'Of course not.'

'What will you do when he gets here?' Debbie asked.

Amy slumped into the seat next to the rat corpse. 'We'll have a pleasant chat and dissuade him and his boss from bothering any more kids.'

I stared at her and saw the thing that had sent me away from her four years ago.

'What if that doesn't work?' Debbie wondered.

My legs throbbed as I moved to the side to focus on the entrance.

'Don't worry,' Amy said. 'Enola and I are dab hands at dealing with scumbags.'

'Now, that's not nice to say, is it?'

I recognised the voice, looking up to see four men entering from the door I thought was locked at the back of the cinema. They marched down the steps as I grabbed Debbie and pulled her towards the screen. Amy didn't move or look at them.

'You pushed me into the river last year,' I said.

The big man put his hand on his chest. 'No, that was poor Kev. I'm Dave.' He glanced between us. 'You're Enola, setting our Debbie a bad example. Mr Rook won't like that.' He stood behind Amy, who still hadn't moved. 'This one, I don't know.'

'You tried to kill me,' I declared.

Dave stepped beyond the first set of seats, and this three mates followed, so they were all between Amy and me.

'No, that wasn't to kill you. It was a warning, that's all, one you haven't taken. Which is why I'm here now.'

I glanced at Debbie. 'You knew I'd be here?'

'Don't blame the girl,' he said. 'We've had people

watching you for a while. It's a shame, but your meddling means all three of you must disappear.'

'The police are coming,' I said.

He laughed. 'What?'

'I told the police when and where I'd be tonight. They'll be here in a few minutes.'

He shook his head. 'No, they won't.'

'You'll see,' I stated.

'Who did you call?'

I glanced at Amy, hoping she had a plan. 'A detective inspector.'

He grinned at me. 'The coppers are too busy to come here. Trust me, I know.'

'That's where I know you from,' Amy said.

Dave turned to her. 'What did you say?'

She wagged her finger at him. 'You're a disgraced ex-copper – David Star.' She smiled at him. 'My, how high you flew until you fell so far.'

'You know me?' he said.

'Yeah, I have associates who know your former companions. Bent coppers are ten-a-penny around here, but you stole drugs from crime scenes and then sold them on. Is that how you ended up exploiting young girls?'

He glared at her. 'Who the fuck are you?'

'Now, Dave,' she said. 'The crucial question is, who is Mr. Rook?'

He nodded to his thugs, who moved towards Debbie and me. 'Why do you want to know?'

Amy knocked the dead rat to the floor, so it landed at his feet. 'Because, Dave, I'm doing my civic duty, and it's important to clear drugs off our streets and to do that, we have to remove those who peddle such filth.'

'Yeah, right,' he said. 'You get rid of Rook, and somebody else will quickly step into his shoes.'

I pushed Debbie behind me as the goons stopped a few feet away. The closest one spoke.

'What are we waiting for, Dave?'

He turned from Amy. 'Don't you want some fun first? There are three of them and three of you.'

A fire raged in my head. 'Debbie's a child.'

He shrugged. 'And? You don't think these lads have had younger?'

'Who do you work for?' Amy asked.

He returned his focus to her as I prepared to face the others. 'You know you're all going to die, right?' Dave said. Amy stayed stony-faced. 'Nobody will find you. We have plenty of places to hide bodies.' He moved forward and leaned over her. 'Would it make you feel better to know who ordered this?'

'It might,' Amy said.

He placed his hands on her shoulders. 'Well, tough fucking luck.'

She sighed. 'You can tell your goons to move away from my friend now.'

'And why would I do that?' he replied.

Then I saw the moonlight shimmering on the gun she'd stuck in his gut.

'It's either that or you'll be pissing and shitting into a bag for the rest of your life, Dave.'

His groan sucked the air out of the room. 'Leave them alone, boys.'

The tall bloke turned to his leader and saw the seriousness of the situation.

'Fuck!'

Amy got up and pushed the pistol further into Dave, forcing him back.

'Indeed, it is a fuckable position we have ourselves in.' I dragged Debbie from the screen and nearer to the seats. 'Though not one you lads were looking forward to, right?'

'You're not going to shoot,' Dave said.

She smiled at him. 'Do you want to risk it?'

He said nothing, standing near her and seething.

'Let's go,' I said.

'I'll catch you up,' Amy said.

I could have argued with her. I could have stayed. But I peered into Debbie's eyes and knew I'd do neither.

I dragged the kid out and hoped she didn't hear the gunshots.

Chapter 27

A Change Is Gonna Come

I left the flat early on Wednesday before Ginger and Bruce got up, saying goodbye to Kronos as I went. It wasn't because of some desire to get to work, but because I'd had little sleep after taking Debbie home.

'What happens now?' she said as I took the county lines phone from her.

'You have my number?'

She nodded. 'Amy gave it to me.'

'Text me if you need anything. I doubt you'll hear from Dave or his colleagues again.'

I could see in her eyes that she wanted to ask me what had happened in the cinema after we left, but she didn't. I watched her go inside, and then I went home, tempted to call Amy, but I refused that temptation.

An aroma of coffee came from the café as I strode to the food bank, stimulating my senses. Then I turned the corner and walked straight into a bouquet of fresh bread and cakes from the bakery, and my stomach pleaded to me. I'd snuck out of the flat without the time to have breakfast and was paying for it.

I stopped to buy a coffee and cake and checked my phone. The drink warmed my mouth as I flicked through several websites, not expecting to find any news of bodies discovered in the Globe, but having to look, anyway.

Then I put the mobile down, nibbled on my blueberry muffin, and contemplated what to do about Amy. I knew what she'd done and didn't condemn her for it. Vengeance had driven my life for so long that when the opportunity came to make the people who'd killed my parents pay, I did.

It wasn't guilt or a moral wavering making me think about the events in the Globe, but more about me considering the possible consequences for Amy and me. Rook was still out there, and I didn't know who he was. And unless Dave was lying, he at least confirmed that Rook was a man. But what was my next move in uncovering his identity?

Plus, should I worry because Dave said they had people watching me?

I grabbed my phone and rechecked there were no messages from Kate Frost. Part of me hoped she was still in London so I could take the mobile I got from Debbie to somebody who might trace where it had come from. The first thing I did when getting back to the flat was check it, but there was only one contact on it, and I assumed it was Dave's.

However, I could call it.

I removed it from my jacket pocket and stared at the number. Would it ring somewhere and alert somebody to a corpse if I called it? Or perhaps Amy took it.

My heart jumped as my phone rang. I put the other one down and answered mine.

'You're up early,' Ginger said.

'Yeah, I couldn't sleep.'

'You got back late last night.'

'I didn't want to wake you or Bruce. So where are we at for Saturday?'

'It's all sorted,' she replied. 'Will you mention it to Frost? I heard she's on local radio today, so it would be great if she could give it a plug on there.'

'Sure, no problem. What are you doing now?'

She sighed. 'I'm off to the library for my final tarot session there.'

'Have they sacked you?'

'Sort of. I got a message from the head librarian last night that the council is closing it for good this weekend.'

'Shit. Why?'

'Seems they've run out of money. I'm guessing it will only be the first of many cutbacks.'

'Levelling up, eh?'

'Yeah, that's right. Bruce isn't happy about it, but few people will be when they find out. Anyway, I better let you go since I know you're keen to impress Ms Kate Frost, MP.'

She ended the call, and I finished my breakfast, wondering what other terrible things could happen to my community.

The food bank didn't officially open for clients until nine, but the manager let me in to get to Kate's office. She and Tate were already there when I arrived, both gazing at the computer.

'You're half an hour early, Enola,' Kate said.

'I'm keen to start work after yesterday.'

She closed the laptop. 'Yes, about that. I'm afraid I told you a little fib.'

'There was no emergency vote at the House of Commons?'

She shook her head. 'No, I'm sorry about that, but John

discovered somebody had hacked my mobile, so I couldn't tell you the truth.'

'Who'd hack your phone?'

She shrugged. 'It could be any number of individuals, organisations or countries. I've got a new one, which has undergone a rigorous security check.'

'Did you go to London?'

Tate spoke. 'If you're going to keep her on, you might as well tell her, Kate.'

'No, we didn't go to London. I would have brought you with us, but it was the last minute, and we couldn't risk losing the money.'

'Money?'

She nodded to Tate, and he reached under the desk and removed a case. He placed it near the computer and opened it. I leaned forward to look at a bag full of cash: dollars.

'An American friend of John's contacted him and offered me a financial donation: $100,000.'

I whistled loudly. 'Well done, but couldn't they have made a bank transfer?'

'The donor doesn't trust banks. The fees would have been enormous, and we want to put every penny into this community.'

I scrutinised her face, looking for something suspicious in her expression. Yet, I didn't find it, only seeing her honesty. I neglected to ask how the donor managed to get the money into the country.

'What will you do with it?'

'Have you heard about the library closure?' she said.

I nodded. 'A little while ago.'

Kate came around the other side of the desk. 'That's what we'll spend the money on; that and the food bank. It's the start of the regeneration of this community, Enola.'

I stared at the cash, feeling like I was in a criminal organisation. Yet even if I were, it wouldn't be the worst thing I'd done in the last twenty-four hours. It wasn't even close.

'That's fantastic, Kate. What will you do with the money now?'

She closed the case, picked it up, and handed it to me. 'You and John will take it to the bank while I complete all the legal paperwork. All political donations have to be registered. Are you happy with that?'

I pressed the case to my chest, as happy as I'd been in a long time.

Everything appeared to be going right for once.

Chapter 28

Money For Nothing

John drove us to the bank as I kept the case glued to me. The money must have loosened his vocal cords as he spoke to me more than ever.

'They know we're coming, so it shouldn't take long.'

'Who's your American friend?' I said.

He shocked me again by smiling. 'You've met him.'

He stopped at a red light for a group of school kids crossing the road with their teachers. I had a vision of a bunch of ten-year-olds pulling off a heist and taking the case from me.

'When did I meet him?'

'The other day at the community centre.'

I racked my brain for the memory. 'The bloke with Constable Davis?'

'Yes, Chris Blair. All three of us went to university together. Chris was there on a scholarship before returning home.'

'How did he accumulate his fortune?'

'From his parents. He inherited it.'

I imagined what kind of lifestyle that much money would bring, where you could give a hundred grand away like that. And I wondered what Blair was expecting for it.

Then somebody banged on the window, and I nearly jumped out of my skin. I twisted my head to see a kid grinning at me before a teacher dragged her away.

John laughed. 'Are you okay?'

My body told me to find a toilet, and I prayed there was one at the bank.

'Yeah, let's get this over with.'

He drove off as I crossed my legs, regretting having that coffee. It didn't take long to get there, and I hoped they'd have security waiting for us. John parked outside the front, and I jumped out of the car in anticipation, only to run into the last person I wanted to see.

A scowling, bandaged face screamed at me. 'You'll need all your money, Gray, when I sue you for this.' Robinson pointed at the scar on his head. 'This is going to ruin you.'

He stood between me and the door. 'Move out of the way, Paul.'

None of his Progressive Britain goons were with him, but he puffed out his chest.

'No, you can't bully me here.' He held up his hands, and everyone near us stopped and stared. 'Everybody will see you for what you are now.'

I spoke to John. 'Will you get rid of him?'

'You're the security expert,' he said.

Robinson fumed like a volcano, ready to explode, with steam coming out of his ears. He ranted at me, but I switched off, hearing The Stranglers play "No More Heroes" in my head. As I listened, I pictured myself lifting the case and smacking him in the face with it. Then I imagined the lid opening and all the crisp American money flying everywhere. If I didn't know they intended the cash for the community, it would have been worth it just to shut Robinson up.

'I know what you're up to, Gray.'

The hundred grand suddenly felt like I had a universe of stars in my arms.

'What?'

'You and that woman, Frost. I'm aware of your plans. You want to replace people like me, but it will never happen. We'll stop you any way we can. I promise you that.'

What if I kicked him in the balls? No, I'd definitely get arrested for that.

'What do you want from Ginger?'

His eyes lit up. 'Oh, you mean the psychic?' He spat the words at me. 'Has she told you who I am?'

'I know exactly who you are, Paul. You're the dogshit nobody cleans away, the chewing gum stuck to my shoe, and the turd that won't flush.'

The fire blazing inside his pupils turned his face crimson. 'And I know who you are, Enola Gray. I know exactly who you are.'

'Yeah? Who am I?'

He stuck his finger into my chest. 'You're the brat who got her parents killed, the girl who burnt down a school, the kid who punched a copper, the troublemaker who ended up in a juvenile centre.' His grin consumed his face. 'The whole world will soon know everything about you, Enola. I promise you that.'

'You're a creature of limited imagination, Paul.'

His eyes were a flaming red. 'Is that so? Then tell me how your boss, a woman with little experience and no political party behind her, could win the by-election in this community?'

'Probably because the voters were sick of the traditional parties. A bit like how I'm sick of your idiotic theories.'

He sneered at me. 'They're not theories, Gray. There's plenty of proof online of Frost's dodgy dealings with big foreign companies. She's a puppet for them, a delegate for the international socialist concept of so-called fifteen-minute cities and twenty-minute neighbourhoods. She's as crooked as you are.'

I sighed. 'Repetition of false teachings doesn't make them true.'

His cheeks flared red like supernovas. 'Corrupt bureaucrats want our entire existence boiled down to the duration of a quarter of an hour. It's a dystopian plan heralding a surveillance culture designed to imprison us. You'll have to apply for a permit to leave your zone. You'll be locked in your house; cameras will signal who can go out. And if your family lives in another neighbourhood, you'll need to ask permission to visit them. It's *The Hunger Games* coming true.'

I was close to clawing out my eyes. 'Paul, imagine walking into a room with very little light, just dim shadows skulking in the corners – that's what it's like inside your head.'

He pointed his shaky finger at me like a pistol. In my mind, I heard the gun from the night before and wondered what Amy would do in this situation.

Then he poked me in the ribs again. 'You wait, Gray. Progressive Britain will expose you and Frost for the traitors you are.'

His hot, fetid breath spread over my face, and I wanted to throw up. To puke all over his fucking bandages.

But he stepped out of the way and grinned at me.

'Come on,' John said as he led me into the building.

My heart pounded in my chest as I controlled my breathing. The place stank of lemon air freshener and was full of pensioners struggling to use their bank cards. A tall lady with American teeth said hello and took us into a private office. I put the case on the table, glancing at John as he spoke to the woman.

Was there a kernel of truth in Robinson's ramblings? Not the insane theory about the fifteen-minute cities but of the strange way Frost had acquired the cash?

And what was this with Tate, Davis and the American donor, Blair, being so pally?

The woman handed the cash to a colleague as if people came in daily with a hundred grand in dollars.

I watched the money go and knew there was something I was missing.

Chapter 29

Missing

Julia ran towards me as I entered the food bank, her cheeks apple red and streaming with tears. 'Is Becky with you, Enola?'

She stumbled, and I caught her before she fell. 'No. Isn't she at school?'

Julia trembled in my arms, her voice shaking as she spoke. 'I dropped her at the gates an hour ago, but a teacher just rang me to ask where she was. I thought she might have skipped school to come here. She's played truant before.'

I didn't know that. 'Have you called the police?'

She shook her head. 'No, because I assumed she'd be here.' She glanced at the clock on the wall. 'It's only nine-thirty. Is it too early to call the police?'

'No, do it now.'

She did as Kate Frost joined us. 'I told her Becky wasn't here, but she wanted to see you.'

'Right.' I removed my phone and rang Ginger. 'Becky's gone missing.'

'Shit,' she said.

I took a deep breath. 'It's probably nothing, what with

the kid always running off somewhere.' Which was likely my fault for setting her a bad example. 'To be safe, can you and Bruce look for her?'

'Of course, Enola. We'll do it now. Where are you?'

'At the food bank with Julia. She's on the phone with the police.'

I considered texting Detective Inspector Parker but thought letting his colleagues handle it was best.

'Okay,' Ginger said. 'We're leaving now. Keep in touch.'

She ended the call as Julia finished hers. Kate was speaking to Tate in the corner as Julia came to me. 'They're sending somebody over now.'

I put my hand on her shoulder. 'I'm sure she's okay, Julia. You know what she's like for getting up to mischief.'

She wiped a tear from her cheek. 'Yeah, I know, but....'

The whole weight of the world was on her face.

'But what?' I said.

'Well, I overheard her talking in her sleep last night, and it's got me worried now.'

'Talking in her sleep? When did that start?'

'A couple of days ago. I meant to speak to her about it, but I've been so busy.'

Becky was talking in her sleep? Was that because of what had happened to her the last few days? And was I responsible for that?

I gripped Julia's fingers. 'It's not your fault, Julia. You're doing all you can for her. She knows you're a wonderful mother, and she loves you.'

The tears came again as she pulled her hand away and rubbed at her face.

'But I should have done something after what I heard.'

'What did Becky say in her sleep?'

Darkness settled into the redness under her eyes. 'She

was rambling, but I could tell she was speaking to a man outside the school gates. So maybe that's who's taken her.'

A lightning bolt punctured my heart, and I nearly fell into the wall. Instead, I put my hand there to steady my trembling legs.

'There was a boke outside the school talking to her?'

'That's what I thought I heard. But she might have only dreamt it. She has a vivid imagination.'

Or it could be true. Dave Star said Rook had people watching me, meaning they knew about Becky and how close she was to me.

Fuck, fuck, fuck!

Did he take her to get back at me?

Of course he fucking did!

I grabbed Tate's car keys from the table. 'Stay here, Julia, and tell the police everything when they arrive, including about the man outside the gates.' I was sure they had CCTV at the school.

'Where are you going?' she said.

'I'll search for her.' I squeezed her arm. 'We'll find her, I promise.'

Rook wouldn't hurt her. This was all to get back at me.

That's what I hoped.

I ran from the food bank, knowing exactly where he would have taken Becky. Two sets of traffic lights and a stray dog in the road that I had to swerve around meant I arrived at the Globe Cinema later than I wanted. So I sprinted inside, through the foyer, and into screen seven. If Rook was going to take her anywhere, it had to be there since he knew that's where I'd return.

It looked the same as before, with the dead rat in the same place, its black eyes gazing at the empty screen.

Then I noticed the difference: the bloodstains on the carpet.

Fuck, what if they were fresh?

There were four sets close together. I knelt at one and touched the dark red, smelling burnt copper, but found dry blood. It was the same for the others, the results of Amy's actions with Steve and his thugs. It had to be.

I stood and ran between the rows of chairs, my lungs catching oxygen and turning it into a fire in my chest. The dust in the air appeared to twist and turn into something resembling fairies from a dream. I blotted everything out and searched between the seats.

'Becky!' I shouted, the only reply being my voice echoing off the walls.

My heart throbbed as I reached the top and stared at the door where Rook's goons had entered to take us by surprise. I took a deep breath and pushed it open. More bloodstains were on the floor, a drip pattern as if somebody had carried bodies away.

Amy. Who had she called to help her remove Steve and his mates? Her gang, probably.

It didn't matter, but I had to tell her about Becky.

Fuck! Maybe Becky was with Amy.

I nearly dropped my phone in a rush to call her.

'Yes, Enola, I'm fine. Thanks for asking.'

'Is Becky with you?'

'The kid? No, why would she be?'

'She's missing.'

Silence for twenty seconds.

'Shit, Enola. I'm sorry. What do you want me to do?'

The fire burning inside me finally exploded. 'Do what you always do, Amy.'

'What does that mean?'

'It means you do nothing unless it benefits you.'

'You think this is just fun for me, don't you, Enola?'

'No, I....' Fuck! I knew where the kid must be.

I ended the call without another word, sprinting down the stairs and out of the cinema.

Becky was at the funfair.

Chapter 30

Funfair

Ginger texted as I drove to the funfair.

We're in the woods, but there's no sign of her.

There were other texts from DI Parker, but I ignored them and focused on only one thing. I parked outside the main entrance, opposite where Becky and I had arrived the other day. If he had been watching me, I assumed Rook would have taken her into the building with the clown head where we'd encountered the drug addicts.

As I entered, a sense of dread washed over me. The place was desolate, with rusted carnival rides and dilapidated stalls scattered throughout. My footsteps resonated through the empty alleys, and the smell of mould and decay hung in the air.

I called out for Becky, but my voice only echoed back at me. As I moved further in, clouds covered the sun, so it resembled an eclipse, throwing shadows over everything. The wind brought the sound of rustling leaves from the nearby woods, my heavy breathing bursting from my lungs and reverberating off the cracked concrete path. As I looked around, I noticed the once-vibrant colours of the rides had faded into shades of grey and brown.

The dripping water vibrated through the empty stalls and booths as if the essence of the place was crying out in neglect. An eerie silence replaced the once-thriving atmosphere of children's laughter and carnival music, yet I heard the sounds of sobbing kids in my head. I blocked them out, knowing they were my memories returning to haunt me at the worst time.

I rushed forward, moving to the clown entrance ahead. My breathing was laboured when I got there, my legs throbbing as I stopped and put my hand on the clown's cheek. Cobwebs came away in my fingers as tiny spiders scuttled over my skin and onto my jacket. I left them and ran into the entrance, greeted by threatening shadows and deafening silence.

'Becky,' I shouted.

I paused, my head lost in a fog of my own making. All of this was my fault. I should have done something about Rook months ago, and Becky would be safe. Instead, I'd let her down just like I'd let everyone down.

Like I'd let my parents down.

Maybe Amy had been right, and my selfish behaviour had caused so much harm to many people.

My legs gave way, and I slumped, sitting in dirt and grime. The spiders crawled over my arms, and I remembered that nest in the wardrobe ten years ago. Instead of shivering like a coward, I should have jumped out and surprised those masked killers. It might have been enough to give my parents time to do something, to fight back. To do anything but die as I left them to. I was only a ten-year-old kid, but look at what Becky had done the last few days. She stood up to the gunman in the community centre. She wasn't scared of the junkies at the fair or the drug dealer at the Globe. If she could be that brave, why couldn't I have been when I needed to most?

I dug my fingers into the dirt and hung my head. The spiders crawled off me and disappeared into the gloom, and I wished I could follow them.

Then I heard Becky's voice.

'Enola.'

I jerked up, seeing her stride out of the shadows. My heart lifted until I saw the bloke behind her, his hands on her shoulders.

'Rook?' I asked.

Becky tried to run to me, but he pulled her back. I expected her to fight him or wriggle in his grasp, but she didn't. She was smiling.

'I'm not Rook,' he replied. 'Rook owes me.'

My legs shook as I stood, the dirt clinging to my fingers. 'Who are you?'

He stepped out of the shadows, his pale blue eyes matching Becky's, and I knew who he was.

'I'm William Cross.' The kid squeezed his hand.

'You're Becky's father?' He nodded. 'She told me you were dead.'

His scowl merged with the gloom lingering over his head. 'One of her mother's lies.'

'So where have you been all this time?'

'Where do you think?'

It was written in his smirk. 'Why were you in prison?'

'Because I kept my mouth shut, that's why. Rook was supposed to look after my family to provide enough money for my daughter. But he lied and betrayed me. And now I'm out, and he'll pay for that.'

'We're on the same side, William, but you shouldn't have taken her from school.'

'I didn't take her; she came voluntarily. And she's my kid. I can do whatever I want.'

'That's not how it works, William. Her mother is worried sick.'

He spat on the ground. 'Julia? She didn't visit me once. That was bad enough, and then I found out she told Becky I'd died. What sort of twisted mind does that to their kid?'

'Let her come to me, William.'

Becky lunged forward, but he dragged her back. 'No. I know what'll happen. They'll say I was a lousy father for dealing drugs, but I was only doing it to pay the bills for my family. They'll stop me from seeing her.'

'It would help you if you told the police who Rook is.'

He snorted. 'You must be fucking mad. Don't you know anything about Rook?'

'What do you mean?'

William shook his head. 'How do you think he's got away with it for so long?'

'Rook bribed the coppers?'

He spat and laughed simultaneously. 'Don't be fucking daft. Rook *is* a copper.'

My phone pinged with another message, and I wondered if it was from Detective Inspector Parker again.

'Do you know who he is?'

'I wish I did so I could wring his neck.'

'Okay, now let Becky go.'

I saw him waver, loosening his grip on her.

That's when somebody stuck a gun into the back of my head.

Chapter 31

Send in the Clowns

'I could have killed you so many times, Enola, and yet it will end for you inside a clown's mouth.'

That voice. I knew that voice.

Then he smacked me with the gun barrel at the base of my skull. Pain exploded through my head, making my eyes blur and thunder ring in my ears. I stumbled forward, catching my foot in the dirt and crashing face-first into the ground. My nose hit it, my chin, my lips parting to taste damp mud. I rolled onto my side and looked up at the bloke who'd fooled us all for such a long time.

'Davis?'

'That's Constable Davis to you, Gray.'

I inched backwards like a crab, hearing Becky's deep breathing behind me. 'You're Rook?'

He grinned and offered me a mock bow. 'At your service, Enola.'

I watched the spiders crawl over his shoes. 'You gave that cash to Frost, didn't you?'

He kept the gun pointed at me. 'I wanted to give something back to my community.'

'Your community? All you've done is exploit them, grooming and manipulating children before making money from the suffering and death of others.'

'Your perception is different to mine, Ms Gray. We'll have to agree to disagree.'

'Is the American a friend of yours?'

'Chris? He's the Yank equivalent of me, though he's taught me a lot about efficient distribution and how to move your money without attracting the attention of the authorities. Those in power are now too busy looking at cybercrime to worry about the traditional methods of moving cash around.'

'Does Frost know?'

'Does she know what?'

'Where the cash came from?'

He shrugged. 'I don't know her well, but I doubt she cares. You offer a lot of money with no strings attached to most people, and they won't care where it originated from. Especially politicians. It doesn't matter what party they come from; they're all happy to put a few bills into their back pockets as long as nobody knows about it.'

'You haven't told her about the strings, have you?'

'You're misjudging me, Enola. I only want the best for my community. Later on, when Kate gets settled at Westminster, John might whisper in her ear about certain things, and we'll see how it goes.'

'Tate's involved as well?'

Davis laughed. 'John's the brains behind the whole thing. Who better to manipulate the local drug trade than a police officer? Who better to get money in and out of the country than somebody with a connection at the ports? Who better to advance our long-term plans than the personal assistant to a young, inexperienced member of Parliament?'

I wiped the dirt from my hands. 'And you kill people for all that?'

He waved a finger at me. 'Now, don't get all self-right-eous on me, Enola. Four of my gang disappeared the other night, and I bet that was something to do with you.'

'I don't know what you're talking about.'

'You're lying, but it doesn't matter.'

'You owe me, Rook,' William Cross said behind me.

Davis kept the gun on me. 'Your own stupidity got you caught, Cross.'

'You were supposed to give my family money when I was inside. That was the deal.'

'There is no honour among thieves, Billy. Even some-body as dumb as you should know that.' I dug my fingers into the ground and inched forward, but he saw me. 'Don't get any stupid ideas, Gray.'

I stopped moving. 'So, what now, Davis?'

'It's simple, Enola. I arrived too late to stop Cross from killing you and his kid before turning the gun on himself.'

He raised his pistol towards Becky's father, and I pounced.

I threw the dirt into his face, so he jerked his arm up as he fired. The bullet whizzed past my cheek before I hit him in the guts. We went down together, rolling through the earth and thumping into a large wooden clown. The force disturbed a bunch of smaller clowns on the shelf above us, so they tumbled down, bouncing off my head and just missing my eye.

Davis punched me in the ribs, sending shockwaves through my lungs. I coughed and reached for the gun as he brought it to my face, firing again so the bullet grazed my skin. An inferno blazed through my face, but I took the pistol and wrenched it from him, throwing it into the shadows. He growled and grabbed my throat, squeezing hard. I tried to get my fingers into his chest, but the strength seeped out of me.

'Of all the scrawny no-marks I've dealt with as copper, you've been the most annoying, Gray. And that's why this will give me the most pleasure.'

I flailed my trembling hands at him, finding nothing but empty air. He dug his nails into my flesh and grinned at me.

Then a manic clown smashed into his skull.

It shattered into shards of porcelain, splattering over him and me. He fell off me, and I gasped for oxygen, sucking it into my lungs and jumping up. Davis rolled on the ground as blood streamed from his head. I looked for the pistol and found it in William Cross's hand. Becky was holding what remained of the clown figurine.

'Lower the gun, William,' I said.

'He has to pay,' Cross replied.

I rubbed at my throat and then spat into the dirt. 'And he will.'

Cross shook his head. 'No. He's a copper, and they all look after each other. Nothing will happen to him. I must make him answer for his actions.'

'What about Becky?' I asked.

'What about her?'

'I was ten when I saw intruders murder my parents,' I replied. 'That type of thing doesn't leave you, William. Not ever. Do you want that for your daughter?'

His fingers trembled.

I looked at Becky as she focused on her father.

'Do it!' Davis shouted. 'Shoot me and show your kid what a monster you are.'

I waited for the explosion, but it didn't come.

Cross handed me the gun and took Becky's hand.

Then I got my phone and called Inspector Parker.

Chapter 32

Opportunities

Julia hugged Becky as the police took Davis away.

Detective Inspector Jack Parker stood beside me, staring at his colleague as if he'd just watched aliens land at the funfair.

'Did he confess to you?' he said.

'Sort of. Hopefully, you'll find evidence of his criminal empire.'

'It won't be for lack of trying. And he implicated John Tate and Chris Blair?'

'He did, and Becky and her dad heard it all.' I glanced at William Cross. 'What'll happen to him?'

Parker rubbed at the back of his neck. 'Becky went with him willingly, but that's not the point. He shouldn't have taken her from school. I don't expect us to press charges unless Becky's mother is adamant about it, but I doubt social services and his probation officer will look too kindly on his actions.'

The kid waved at me. 'As long as it all works out for her.'

'Indeed. Now tell me about Kate Frost and a hundred grand in dollars.'

I shrugged. 'You better speak to her. I only know what little they told me this morning before landing me with the job of taking it to the bank. It was hardly some big secret.'

'Was it legal?'

'I don't know. You tell me.'

'You implied it was drug money.'

'It might be, but that doesn't mean Frost knew about it. You'll have to ask her.'

He shook his head. 'It won't be me. This is the NCA's case now.'

'Marvellous,' I said.

Parker smiled at me. 'I have more good news for you.' He showed me a video on his phone of Paul Robinson's arrest. 'This was just before I came here.'

'Why was he arrested?'

'The NCA had tracked his online movements for months, discovering several links to potential domestic terrorist threats. So he won't be bothering you again.'

It seemed like everything was finally looking up for me, apart from the fact I'd probably lost another job. Maybe I was under a bad spell where my employment was concerned.

'Enola!' Becky ran over and hugged me, followed by her mother.

Becky let go, and Julia held my hands. 'I can't thank you enough for returning her safely to me, Enola.'

She squeezed my fingers as the police took her estranged husband away.

'Think nothing of it, Julia.'

Becky grinned as Ginger and Bruce arrived, dragging Kronos behind them. Becky soon lost interest in me and ran to the dog.

'Are you okay?' Ginger asked.

'My throat's sore, but I'm fine.'

'Christ, Enola,' Bruce said. 'Davis was running the county lines drug operation?'

'Yeah, it seems so. Now it's up to the police to find the evidence.'

I didn't tell them about Tate and Frost and how I was likely unemployed again. Which meant I'd be staying longer on their sofa.

'That's great,' Ginger said. 'That's one more thing to celebrate on Saturday.'

We left the police to finish off and stepped out of the clown's head. As I got outside, my phone pinged with a message. I glanced at it as Becky chased Kronos around the funfair.

Well done. That makes us quits.

What do you mean?

That favour you owed me for the thing I gave you. It's done now. Until next time, Enola.

Becky grabbed my hand. 'Mum says there's a new funfair coming to town next week. Do you want to go?'

I ruffled Becky's hair. 'Sure, kid.'

Perhaps riding a rollercoaster would relax me.

I watched the spiders crawling from the clown's eyes as we left. Then I pictured Amy and me just a few years ago, dressing up as witches, wearing goth dresses and spraying our hair into magnificent spectacles. A faint smile pulled at my lips as I pictured us parading around the woods, hyped up on booze and rebellion, waving our wands at imagined ghosts.

And it hadn't even been Halloween.

Maybe my life had always been one long season of the witch.

BLADE
RUNNERS
An Enola Gray
Short Story
A. S. French

Chapter 1

Blade Runners

Y ou can't get lost if you don't belong anywhere.

That thought echoed in my mind as Amy and I snuck out of the children's home. The gutters overflowed with rain, sending knee-high splashes cascading off the pavement. Flashy drunks wearing shirts that sparkled like polished pistols had a blast carrying giggling girls across the treacherous puddles. The torrent pounded on my head, turning my once-tamed hair into a wild octopus. The streets glistened under the relentless downpour, reflecting the hazy glow of streetlights. The air was thick with the smell of wet concrete and the distant rumble of thunder.

As we raced through town, a puddle formed on the top of my shoe, as if I were the leader of a tiny water kingdom. Yet, amidst the chaos, we couldn't help but laugh at the ridiculousness of it all - kids playing in the rain like carefree children, teenagers running away, desperate to become adults.

Amy took me to the bridge over the river where, in the

chilled gloom, she handed me my present. 'Happy fifteenth birthday, Enola.'

The air was so cold it hurt my teeth as the moonlight bounced off the water and shimmered along the blade. 'A kitchen knife? Did you bring me here to gut a fish?'

She laughed. 'Well, you hog the TV watching all those episodes of *Restaurant Impossible*. You know all the other kids hate you for that.'

'What, they don't love me? Oh my god, can we all just take a moment to appreciate my incredibly fabulous life? Like seriously, I've achieved so much in my fifteen years on this planet. I mean, it's crystal clear to me I'll be the next superstar, right? Like, everyone will know my name and be dying to get a glimpse of me. I'm totally crushing it in life. I don't do anything, like at all. I used to bite my nails, but not anymore. Wow, I'm really just a tremendous success story, right? Who needs accomplishments when you have such an impressive lack of ambition? Am I right?'

Amy grinned. 'See, that's why you need a weapon for protection before anybody attacks you for your terrible sense of humour. So keep the blade, Enola. You'll thank me for it.'

We both had seen the devastation knives did, so I couldn't understand her reasoning for giving it to me. 'I'm not going to stab kids, Amy.' The wooden handle was chipped and rough against my skin. 'So throw it away.'

I offered it to her, but she didn't take it. 'It's not for dealing with kids, Enola. They're not the ones you have to worry about.'

'You couldn't have pinched me a better present?'

She shrugged. 'I nearly nicked you a Johnny Rotten t-shirt from the boutique on the high street. I know how much you love that terrible punk music.'

I pointed at Amy's head. 'You almost had a decent haircut, and look where that got you.'

She grabbed a sizeable chunk of her dark hair. 'I used that knife in your hand to achieve this modern design. It's another reason why you should treasure it.'

'You couldn't find a pair of scissors? Or a lawnmower?'

'You're only jealous.'

I waved the blade at her. 'Anyway, back to my musical tastes. Music from the 70s and 80s is much better than the shite you listen to. The melodies are forgettable, the lyrics are juvenile, and the performers look like they're auditioning for a circus. And let's not forget the auto-tune. They can't even warble in tune anymore. They need a computer to do it for them. Still, if I had to sing lyrics like "Baby, baby, oh" or "I like big butts and I cannot lie," I'd want to hide behind a screen too.'

Amy puffed out her cheeks. 'You're an old woman before your time.'

'You should have got me that shirt.'

She shook her head. 'I can just see you walking into the home as a punk, the safety pins, the ripped t-shirt and some spiky green hair.'

'I thought we weren't going back to the children's home?'

'We're not. That's why you need that knife if you're going to live on the streets.'

I pulled at the faded leather of my jacket and the holes in my top. 'Anyway, it's not about the look. It's about attitude. The rebellion. The refusal to conform to societal norms.' I glanced at the shimmering surface of the river. 'That's why we're here and never going back.' I grinned at her. 'You just need to be nicer from now on.'

Amy's eyes narrowed until they sparkled like emeralds on a Disney witch.

'It doesn't matter how nice I try, Enola; I always end up with my finger in somebody's eye or wiping a broken tooth from my shoulder.'

'You could have got me a spider. You know I want a pet tarantula.'

Amy laughed. 'Sure, and where will you keep it now we don't have a home to go to?' She pointed at my faded leather jacket. 'Haven't you got enough junk in there?'

I dug my fingers into my pockets, retrieving a toothbrush, a spoon, a worn paperback of *Frankenstein*, half a chocolate bar, and two pound coins. 'What more do I need than these things?'

Amy shook her head. 'Yeah, you have the whole world in your hands there.'

'That's because we live in a block universe, my friend.'

She scrunched up her face. 'What?'

'Okay, so back in the old days, people believed the universe was this four-dimensional stale meatloaf where nothing ever moved or changed. It was just this static thing, you know? Like my grandfather's glass eye. But our consciousness was the only thing that was like a wriggling maggot moving through this rancid meatloaf along the time axis. So, our thoughts and experiences were the only things bringing any flavour to this bland existence.'

Amy rubbed her chin. 'Gross, but I think I get it. It's kind of like how I thought living in our dingy house would be my dirty existence forever. The cigarette smoke perpetually staining the walls yellow and the distant smell of meth seeping through the vents were so permanent. But now Mom's in prison, I'm bouncing between children's homes, and nothing is static anymore. It's crazy how life can seem so permanently hopeless, but everything falls apart.'

I nodded. 'Exactly! And get this: in this giant mouldy meat cube, every wretched moment that ever happened or will happen was all festering simultaneously! It's like the past still reeked, the future already stank, and everything that ever existed was just one big garbage stew happening at once. Pretty nauseating to think about, right?'

'Woah, vomit-worthy, but I think I get it. Like how in my mind, I can vividly remember finding a syringe under the couch on my tenth birthday. And I can picture you and me boozing in some posh flat in the future. So it's like those moments are always coexisting in my twisted brain, even though they're years apart. Maybe I understand the nature of this cesspool better than I thought!'

'Ha, ha, yes, girl! You're fully grasping how much existence blows once you start swirling it around in your mind.'

'You're weird, Enola, you know that, right?'

'Is that why you ran off with me, Amy?'

She leaned against the wall, peering into my eyes, looking like she regretted our actions. 'It was this or having to watch *Gogglebox* again. This was the lesser of the two evils.'

I clutched my chest and laughed, a tremendous bellowing thing that burst from my lungs like dragon fire. My ribs throbbed as I bent over until it stopped. Then I looked up and stared into her eyes.

'Well, I can't argue with that.' I glanced into the shadows growing around us as a small boat sailed by, dumping something toxic in the water. It smelt of burnt rubber, and I squeezed my nose in a failed attempt to keep the stink out of my head. A rat ran over my foot, skittering towards the river's edge before Amy could skewer it with the blade.

Then, a large man slithered out of the darkness. 'Are you girls lost?'

He had a face made for the radio, with scars on both cheeks and eyes resembling burnt cigarettes. He had a lot of nose and even more chin, with an expression sculpted from a serial killer's heart. There was a skull tattoo on his neck, and he smelt of piss. His hair was a badly cut Beatles bowl sitting on his head, desperately trying to hide the pockmarks that scarred his mug. His ancestors would wonder why he had sunk so low in the criminal hierarchy. He approached with enough menace to terrify a Dalek, holding a knife like the one trembling in my hands.

'Such a lot of blades around town and so few brains,' I said.

His fingers were like fat maggots gripping the blade. 'I can keep you warm on this frosty night.'

'Bugger off, tosspot,' Amy added.

His eyes rolled as he thought about it, and I could tell from the exertion on his face that thinking would always be a problem for him. He growled through yellow teeth, waving the knife at her.

'I wasn't sure which of you to do first, but you just made the choice for me, skank.'

The wind cut across my cheeks. 'You remind me of a dog our neighbours used to have. Once loved by the family, visitors and strangers, who for some reason lost everything that made it lovable. All joy, all excitement, all fun, and friendliness. It would sit there miserably, making low, growling, discontented noises, wanting direct attention, then snapping at those who tried to help it. And it stank of shit as you do.'

He laughed like a volcano about to erupt and spat at my feet. 'Do you think you're brave with that knife, girl? I bet you don't even know what to do with it.'

I showed him the scars on my hands. 'I got these when I dragged my parents from a fire.' When the moonlight landed on my skin, the melted flesh looked like the Martian landscape. 'And I didn't realise they were already dead, even though I'd watched masked killers slit my mum's and dad's throats. It's funny what your brain tells you when dealing with stress.' I smiled at my friend. 'You wouldn't think two fifteen-year-olds would know what trauma is, but we do, don't we, Amy?'

She put her arm around my shoulder. 'Your blade doesn't scare us, mate. Somebody bigger and uglier than you attacked me with one five years ago. It was a big kitchen bread knife, and I grabbed it with my hands, trying to protect myself, screaming as it sliced my flesh.' She showed him her palms. 'My scars are nowhere near as bad as my friend's, but you can still see the marks.'

His eyes sparkled with a faint greenish hue, reminiscent of a bottle of expired salad dressing left in the back of the fridge for too long.

'I don't care,' he said. 'You'll do what I tell you, or I'll skin you both.'

Amy removed her arm from me. 'See, Enola. This is why you need the blade.'

He lunged at me, so I kicked him in the balls. His entire body convulsed, and his face crumpled like a botched batch of cookies. He attempted to reconstruct it slowly, as if trying to lift a grand piano with his mind. Then he hit the ground, bent out of shape like a toddler's drawing.

Amy laughed. 'Okay, perhaps I got you the wrong birthday gift.' The bloke rolled through the dirt, scarring the rats away. 'Though you could still use it on him and do the world a favour.'

I stepped towards him and raised my hand, catching my reflection in the blade.

And then I hurled it into the river.

I put my arm around Amy and giggled. 'Worst birthday present ever.'

We strode from the water, arm in arm.

'So,' she said. 'In this block universe of yours, will all this happen again?'

I laughed. 'Yeah, over and over again until you get me a decent gift.'

Amy grinned. 'Okay, next time, it's the spider.'

Enola Gray Mysteries

VOLUME 2

A. S. FRENCH

Thank You!

Thank you, dear reader for purchasing this book.

Many thanks to my wonderful wife for all her support and patience.

Extra special thanks to Karina Gallagher for being a dedicated reader of my work.

Cover designs by James, GoOnWrite.com

Mailing List & Free Books!

If you would like to join my mailing list and receive a free eBook then contact me at mail@andrewsfrench.com

About the Author

Andrew French lives amongst faded seaside glamour on the North East coast of England. He likes gin and cats but not together, new music and old movies, curry and ice cream. Slow bike rides and long walks to the pub are his usual exercise, as well as flicking through the pages of good books and the memoirs of bad people.

Find out more at www.andrewsfrench.com

Facebook: https://www.facebook.com/A-S-French-Author-150145625006018

Twitter: www.twitter.com/andrewfrench100

Instagram: www.instagram.com/andrewfrench100

And replies to all his email at mail@andrewsfrench.com

If you have the time, please leave a review at Amazon or Goodreads

Thank you!

Also by A. S. French

Crime Fiction and Thrillers

The Astrid Snow series

Don't Fear the Reaper

The Killing Moon

Lost in America

Gone to Texas

The Final Girl

Snowstorm: An Astrid Snow Collection

The Ophelia Red series

Ophelia Red

The Detective Jen Flowers series

The Hashtag Killer

Serial Killer

Night Killer

The Killer Inside Them

The Frank Walker series

Where The Bodies Are Buried

Bodies of Evidence

Crime Short Stories

Crime Stories: A Collection

Writing as Andrew S. French

Science Fiction

The Time Traveller's Murder

The Mercy Sleep

Bodies

Another Girl, Another Planet

The Thief of Time Trilogy

The Queens of Heaven

The Queens of Time

The Queens of Space

The Arcane Supernatural Thriller Series

The Arcane

The Arcane Identity

The Arcane Quest

The Arcane Ultimatum

The Ella Finn Fantasy Series

Ella and the Elementals

Ella and the Multiverse

Ella and the Monsters

Ella and the Dreamers

Supernatural Short Stories

Dead Souls

Dead Souls II

The Shadow

9 781914 308314